STARS AND BONES BOOK IV

Nightmares *in the* Ice

BEATRICE B. MORGAN

AUTHORS 4 AUTHORS PUBLISHING
Marysville, WA, USA

Published by Authors 4 Authors Publishing
1214 6th St
Marysville, WA 98270
www.authors4authorspublishing.com

E-book ISBN: 978-1-64477-185-3
Paperback ISBN: 978-1-64477-186-0
Audiobook ISBN: 978-1-64477-187-7

Edited by Rebecca Mikkelson
Line edited by Renee Frey
Copyedited and formatted by Brandi Spencer

Cover design ©2024 Practically Perfect Covers. All rights reserved.
Interior design and map by Brandi Spencer.

Authors 4 Authors branding is set in Bavire. Book title is set in Allura and Bilbo Swash Caps. Series title and other headers are set in Cinzel. All other text is set in Garamond.

STARS AND BONES BOOK IV

Nightmares
in the
Ice

BEATRICE B. MORGAN

AUTHORS 4 AUTHORS CONTENT RATING

This title has been rated 17+, appropriate for older teens and adults, and contains:

- Frequent brief implied sex
- Moderate language
- Intense violence

Please, keep the following in mind when using our rating system:

1. A content rating is not a measure of quality.

Great stories can be found for every audience. One book with many content warnings and another with none at all may be of equal depth and sophistication. Our ratings can work both ways: to avoid content or to find it.

2. Ratings are merely a tool.

For our young adult (YA) and children's titles, age ratings are generalized suggestions. For parents, our descriptive ratings can help you make informed decisions, but at the end of the day, only you know what kinds of content are appropriate for your individual child. This is why we provide details in addition to the general age rating.

For more information on our rating system, please, visit our Content Guide at: www.authors4authorspublishing.com/books/ratings

DEDICATION

To those who refused to let other people
tell them what or who they could be.

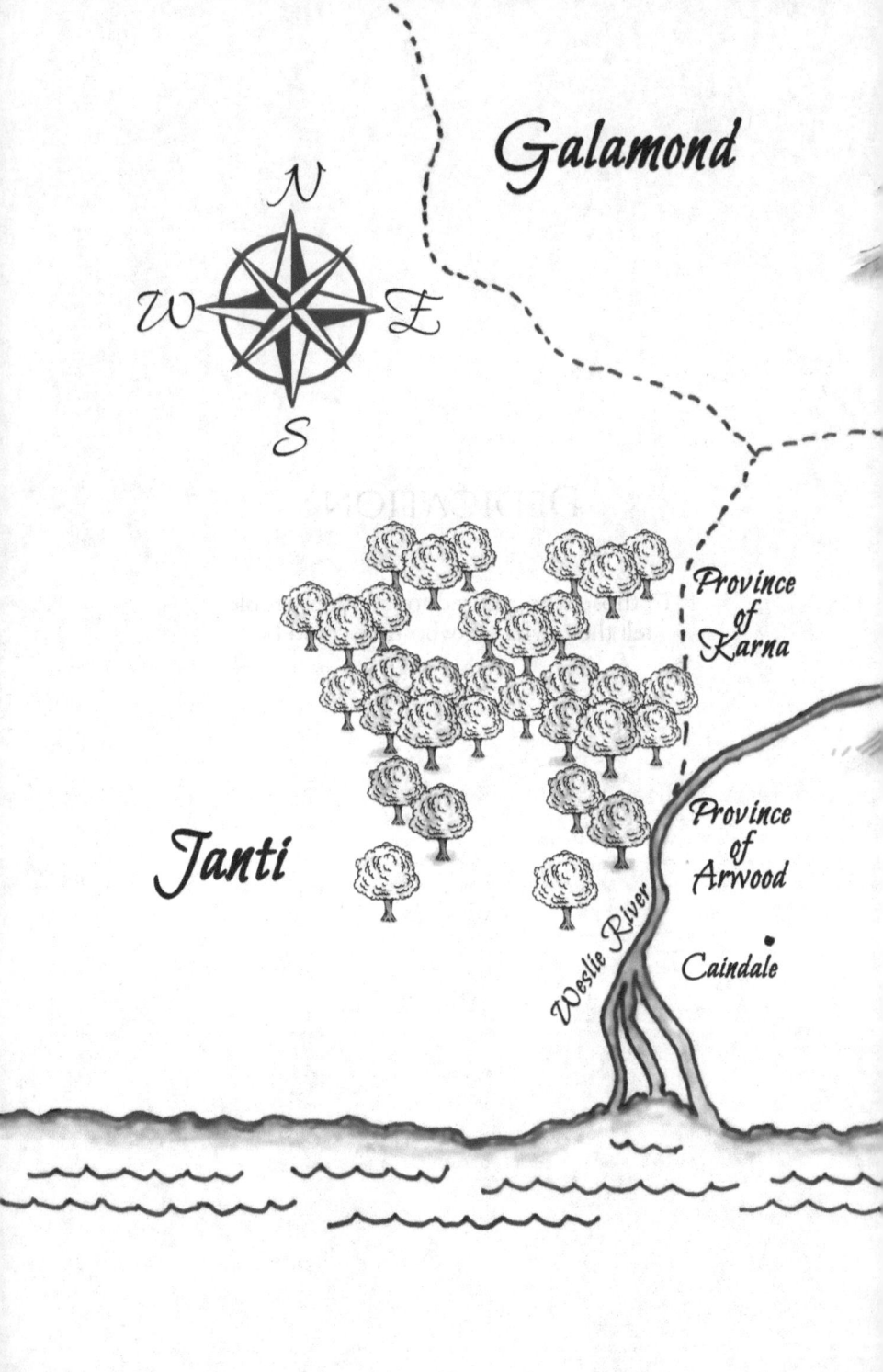

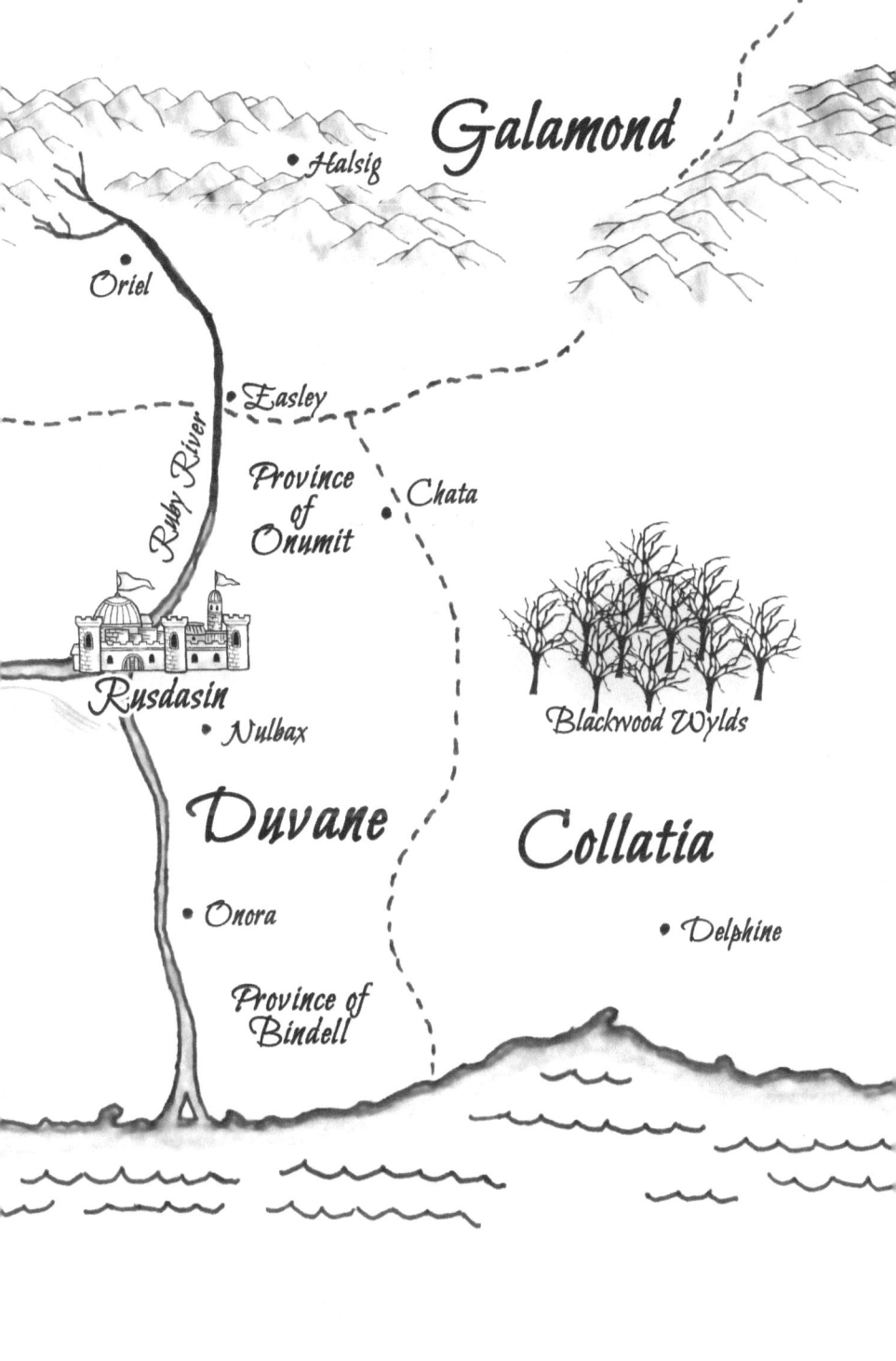

WORKS BY BEATRICE B. MORGAN

Stars and Bones:
Thief in the Castle
Mage in the Undercity
Dreams in the Snow
Nightmares in the Ice
Witch in the Wylds (2024)
Archmage in the Ruins (2024)

Hard as Stone:
Hard as Stone
Thick as Blood
Strong as Steel

TABLE OF CONTENTS

Chapter 1	1
Chapter 2	6
Chapter 3	12
Chapter 4	18
Chapter 5	24
Chapter 6	28
Chapter 7	32
Chapter 8	36
Chapter 9	40
Chapter 10	44
Chapter 11	49
Chapter 12	53
Chapter 13	57
Chapter 14	63
Chapter 15	67
Chapter 16	71
Chapter 17	76
Chapter 18	81
Chapter 19	86
Chapter 20	90
Chapter 21	95
Chapter 22	98
Chapter 23	104
Chapter 24	107
Chapter 25	113
Chapter 26	117
Chapter 27	120
Chapter 28	125
Chapter 29	130
Chapter 30	134
Chapter 31	139
Chapter 32	144
Chapter 33	149
Chapter 34	153
Chapter 35	157
Chapter 36	161
Chapter 37	166
Chapter 38	172

Chapter 39 178
Chapter 40 183
Chapter 41 187
Chapter 42 191
Chapter 43 198
Chapter 44 204
Chapter 45 211
Chapter 46 215
Chapter 47 221
Chapter 48 227
Chapter 49 232
Chapter 50 238
Chapter 51 245
Chapter 52 253
Chapter 53 261
Chapter 54 266
Chapter 55 271
Chapter 56 276
Chapter 57 280
Chapter 58 284
Chapter 59 289
Acknowledgments 296
About the Author 297

CHAPTER 1

Juniper Thimble hated the Marca and all it stood for—she always had. The very idea of locking mages away because of their magic seared her to the bone. The Order of the Knighthood called the Marca a school, but she knew it for what it was: a prison.

And she was its newest prisoner.

It was a dreary, cloudy late autumn morning. Juniper sat in an unadorned coach, watching the royal city of Rusdasin pass by. The incoming winter added a touch of frost to the air that infiltrated her lungs with every breath. The carriage jostled past a few bakeries, each wafting scents of cinnamon, ginger, and cloves. How many winters had she spent her extra coin on ginger snaps? That was a lifetime ago. That girl was a different person.

Yesterday, hundreds of people had lined the streets, wide-eyed and cheering, as Juniper and her friends—Squires Reid Sandpiper and Henry Julian—had ridden through the city. They had just returned from the quest that would grant Reid and Henry knighthood and save Prince Adrian Bradburn from enchanted poison. Today, normalcy returned. Shops opened their shutters and doors. People went about their daily business, ignoring Juniper's carriage.

Sir Isaac Pinul sat across from her in the coach. He had acted as the knight escort on the quest, and he acted as such for her now—because the Order decreed mages too dangerous to be left alone.

The quest had tanned his beige skin, lightened his sandy hair, and turned his usual fatherly expression grim. Isaac hadn't said a word since they had climbed into the coach. He had stirred her before dawn and rushed her out of Castle Bradburn with little fanfare. She hadn't even said goodbye to her friends.

At least the haste with which they had left and her grogginess hadn't allowed her to brood over the thoughts that had been tugging at her for the past several weeks—that she, Juniper Thimble, notorious thief and Undercity rat, was the lost heir of Collatia, Princess Isolde Balendin.

Too soon, the coach pulled through the thick iron gates of the Marca. Dread coiled in her gut and clawed at her chest.

The Marca was a fortress of dark gray stone, blocky corridors, narrow windows, iron spires, and overwhelmingly unwelcome. The battlements were not as wide or grand as Castle Bradburn, but well guarded by knights. Their silver armor dulled to gray in the dreary early morning light.

Seeing the Marca in person, Juniper's hatred for all it stood for twisted her dread into something hard and vicious.

"I would tell you it's not as bad as it looks," Isaac whispered.

"But it wouldn't make me feel any better," Juniper finished his thought.

He nodded. "I feared as much."

Isaac stepped out of the coach first and held his hand out for Juniper's. She took a deep breath, the last she would have outside the Marca for a while. She stepped out of the coach to meet her fate.

The front entrance was little more than a square of paving stones, scarred by centuries of carriages and hooves. Stone steps led to large unadorned oak doors. Carved into the stone above the door was an owl with its wings spread and a chain grasped in its claws—the seal of the Marca, the same emblem that decorated the knights' breastplates. Time and weather had left the owl and the stone around it pockmarked.

Isaac put his hand on her shoulder and gave her a calm nod of encouragement. She tried her best to ignore the owl on his breastplate.

She sighed. The courtyard smelled like wet stone and dead leaves. "I know. Best get it over with."

Isaac walked her into the Marca.

The oak doors opened with the same eerie silence as the gates, and they walked into a foyer as plainly decorated as the courtyard. The air felt stifled, hushed and full of trapped, muffled voices. It reminded Juniper of a library, the perpetual dust, the way the paper seemed to suck in all sound. A single magelight hovered near the ceiling, casting its pale yellow light over the foyer. It smelled strongly of sweet silver polish—unnatural magic, she had come to learn, the *safe* magic the Marca taught mages to use.

The Marca divided magic into three categories: unnatural, natural, and black. Unnatural magic involved a mage manipulating the magic within the air to perform little tricks and spells. Natural magic involved a mage using the raw magic within themselves either as a force of its own or to manipulate their element. The Marca frowned upon natural magic. The Order saw it as vile, as a breath away from black magic. Black magic was the worst, involving inhumane and deplorable spells and evil thoughts—or so they said. Juniper had never done black magic and had never sought to learn any more about it. Especially not after witnessing Nexon use black magic to break into the minds of her friends and use them like puppets to kill, or how he had used Ison to create those monstrosities from the blood and bones of innocents.

BEATRICE B. MORGAN

"Our first stop is the overseer's office," Isaac said, and he started into the Marca.

Juniper had no choice but to follow—though her mind played through a mad escape plan of bursting through the courtyard, using her ice magic to blast anyone out of her way, and running all the way to...somewhere else. She knew safe houses scattered through Rusdasin. Though her odds of making it out of the courtyard before being struck with Mage's Bane were low.

She'd heard rumors the knights patrolling the battlements had arrows tipped with it, ready to spear runaway mages. She'd rather not find out the hard way.

"The Marca has a decent library," Isaac told her in that softened voice of someone trying to find a silver lining.

"I will save my judgment for when I see it," she said.

"It does pale in comparison to the Royal Library."

She huffed. Despite her dread, she walked with her head high. She was Juniper Thimble, and she did not cower.

The same gray stone continued on the interior. Grim paintings and tapestries spotted the corridors, dulled with age. Magelights hovered near the ceiling in even intervals, illuminating the corridors in dreary light, leaving few shadows.

The overseer's office was overly neat and felt as unwelcoming as the exterior. Tall, narrow windows left three stripes of cloudy sunlight across the room, like bars. The rest sat in shadow. In front of the windows was a large oak desk, and behind it sat a woman silhouetted with the sunlight behind her. Juniper blinked, straining to see the woman. Someone shut the office door. The clack echoed through Juniper's chest.

"Ah, right on time." The overseer's voice was like creaking iron. She stood with willowy grace and glided around the desk, into Juniper's view. Age lined her face, particularly around her eyes and brow. Her charcoal hair was twisted into a tight bun, and her immaculate robes were dark, shimmery silk. She took in Juniper with clinical dislike, looking down her nose as if Juniper had interrupted something. The *tick-tick-tick* of the grandfather clock echoed off the stone walls.

Isaac stepped forward, his face unreadable, professional. "Juniper Thimble willingly comes to the Marca."

"Yes, of course," said the overseer. Disapproval hung on her words.

Juniper had no doubt the overseer thought King Bradburn's decision to acquit her foolish and unjust.

The overseer smiled, but it held no warmth. "Let me formally welcome you to the Marca, Miss Thimble. You may address me as Overseer Margret. As my title suggests, I oversee all that happens within the Marca. My word is law. Understand?"

Juniper wanted to tell the other woman the only rules she followed were her own, but she hadn't been in the Marca a day. Far too early to make enemies. So instead, she said, "Understood."

"This way, please," said the overseer.

Juniper followed her into an adjacent room lined with shelves holding hundreds of strange metal and glass instruments. Isaac waited in the office. The overseer stood at a podium and wrote Juniper's name across the top of a fresh piece of parchment.

"A few basics before you settle in," said the overseer. "Is Juniper Thimble your real name?"

"Yes," Juniper lied.

"Middle name?"

"I don't have one."

"Age?"

"Seventeen."

"Is that your natural hair color?"

"Yes."

"We'll call it brown," Overseer Margret muttered as she scribed it onto the paper.

Juniper would have called her hair auburn, but she didn't want to argue this early into her stay. She knew when to pick her fights.

"Your element?"

"Water."

"Your parents' names?"

"I don't know."

"Hometown?"

"Rusdasin."

The list continued. The overseer took her height and weight and studied the lines on her palm—then harrumphed a disapproving note. Juniper wanted to ask what she'd read on her palm, but decided she didn't want to know. Margret used a strange ring-shaped instrument that informed them she was not allergic to any of the metals the Marca commonly used.

Once documented, the overseer retrieved a set of plain purple robes and a blue sash from a closet. She thrust the bundle into Juniper's arms. The purple robes were the same as all Marca mages wore, and the blue sash identified her as a Water mage. Juniper ran her fingers over the material. Not soft, but not hard or starchy. She had worn worse.

"You will receive seven sets of robes," said the hag. "They will be ordered and delivered to your dormitory within the week."

Back in the overseer's office, Isaac waited patiently. He stood by the window, face impassive and stoic.

"The Marca has all a mage could ever need," said Overseer Margret in a dry, practiced tone. "The mess hall provides three meals a day. We have study rooms, courtyards, job assignments, research possibilities, and leisure activities. You will receive a job assignment once we have better knowledge of your talents and skills."

Juniper half listened as the overseer went over a long list of dos and don'ts. Obey the Order. Obey the knights. Obey the overseer.

Too many rules and too much obeying for Juniper's liking.

"Understand?" asked the overseer, her tone sharp.

"Yes, I understand." She had other words for the old hag, but she couldn't say them on her first day.

"Good." The overseer turned her attention to Isaac. "Thank you for bringing her to us, Sir Pinul. We will take care of our newest ward."

Juniper caught the tone—the overseer was dismissing Isaac. Juniper's stomach twisted back into knots.

"See that you do. King Bradburn will want updates on her status," said Isaac, his tone curt but laced with warning. He looked at Juniper. "I will see you soon, Juniper."

"I look forward to it," Juniper said, and she did. A friendly face among these drab stones would be something to look forward to.

Isaac nodded his farewell and left. The door closed behind him, and just like that, he left her in the Marca. Each of his retreating footsteps thudded against her insides, curling her dread tighter and tighter. Overseer Margret gazed down her nose at Juniper as if she knew it.

But Juniper could do this. She could play by the Marca's rules for a while. King Bradburn had promised to send her as an ambassador to Collatia, and she believed he would. Until then, she would survive.

She had no other choice.

CHAPTER 2

"Kind of him to see you through the transition," drawled the overseer. Without Isaac there, she didn't bother to lace her words with false pleasantness. She glared down at Juniper with the hate of ten scorned women. "Let me be clear, Juniper Thimble, you are here because the king has allowed it. You are here only because you slithered out of the Order's clutches. You deserve nothing short of Mage's Bane."

Juniper met the hag's cruel stare with her own.

"Knight Commander Fowler brought it to my attention that your friends are soon to be knights," Margret drawled. "Fowler can send his knights wherever he sees fit. Where your friends are sent, and how dangerous their missions are, depend on your behavior."

Juniper's fingers tightened on her new robes, thankfully out of sight underneath them. She fought hard to keep her face passive and unintimidated. Disbelief and disgust wormed within her dread—the overseer was *threatening* her.

"If you give him any reason, Fowler will make sure your friends do not return. Do I make myself clear?"

Juniper hadn't eaten breakfast that morning, but if she had, she might have emptied it then. Her hands trembled, but she forced herself to nod. "I understand."

"*Ma'am.* You will address me as ma'am or overseer."

Juniper swallowed her spite and said calmly, "Yes, ma'am."

"Good." The overseer smiled, vile and menacing and victorious—it reminded Juniper of the monstrous wechun. The comparison gave her a horrible feeling. "Now, follow me. I will show you to your dormitory."

Juniper followed the hag into the corridor, half listening as she drawled on about the importance of the Marca and its history. Juniper wanted to wrap her blue sash around the woman's throat and forever silence her, but she gripped her robes tight. She occupied her thoughts with painful and creative ways of ridding the world of Overseer Margret.

The hag led her through drab corridors; all the while, she went over rules, locations, and procedures. The older mages lived on the higher floors; the younger mages lived on the lower floors. All mages earned their keep, except the youngest mages. Juniper spotted mages sweeping and dusting—using magic, of course. It filled the air with the scent of silver polish, that strange, clean and slightly sweet metallic scent. It wasn't as pleasant as the floral scents of natural magic.

"Understand?" snapped Overseer Margret.

Juniper hadn't been listening, but she nodded and said, "Yes, ma'am."

It appeased the hag. She smiled, stretching the wrinkles on either side of her face. "You're learning fast. Keep it up, and you'll do just fine," she said, though Juniper doubted she meant it. "Your lessons start tomorrow. You will attend the basic classes that every mage must pass. They start at the first bell, first classroom."

"How will I know when that is?" Juniper added quickly, "—ma'am."

"The girls will explain it," the overseer said. "When you finish the basic lessons, you will attend specialized classes of your choosing. You will have every other morning off. The seventh day of the week is your free time."

Juniper nodded as she took all the information in. Too many bells.

And last, after what felt like a hundred corridors and a dozen staircases, they arrived on the fifth floor—the top floor. Through the narrow leaded glass windows, Juniper saw Rusdasin—the familiar rooftops, steeples, and puffs of chimney smoke. The windows gave off a subtle shimmer. Likely enchanted to keep mages from throwing themselves out of them.

The overseer stopped at a simple wooden door, one of several lining the corridor. She knocked once and opened it. The soft chatter on the other side died out at once.

"Girls," announced the overseer, "meet your new roommate, Juniper."

Juniper followed the hag into the dormitory. It was a simple hall lined with twelve living spaces. The few girls in the dorm looked as though they had been handed execution orders.

The overseer rattled through another set of rules: the dormitory was her home, treat it like one; keep her space clean and tidy; dirty clothes went into the hamper; clean clothes were to be folded and put away; wrinkles were not tolerated. While the overseer spoke, the girls in the dorm remained still as stone and silent. They looked about Juniper's age, give or take a year or two.

Juniper's new home, a fraction of the space she had occupied in Castle Bradburn, consisted of a bed with purple and beige blankets, a beat-up trunk, a nightstand, and a simple wooden dresser. The attached bathing room had four tubs, four toilets, and eight sinks. One wall held a row of twelve lockers, one for each girl. Each had a name etched into the front. Hers had already been added.

The hag left Juniper in the dorm. As the door closed behind her, Juniper let loose her breath—and her nerves.

She steeled herself. She had survived the Undercity, a wechun, the edge of the world. She could handle the Marca. She meandered to the small space that would be hers. The bedspread hadn't a wrinkle in it, until she plopped her new robes onto it. Wrinkles spread like lightning over the surface of the purple blanket.

"Hi," said a pretty girl with rich dark brown skin. Her long hair was braided back with silver beads and twisted into a knot between her shoulder blades. She wore a pale green dressing gown over her pajamas. "I'm beside you." She motioned to the space next to Juniper's. "I'm Abrielle."

"Juniper."

"Thimble, right?" Abrielle's eyes lit up.

"That's me."

"Oh, wow." Abrielle bit her bottom lip, trying to shove down her enthusiasm. "We thought they were joking when they said you were coming." Her eyes drifted down to the blue sash on Juniper's bed. "You're a Water mage?"

Juniper nodded.

Abrielle smiled and put her hand against her middle, though she wore no sash. "I am too. Though, I hear you're more practiced with ice. I've never been good with it. I'm better at the healing aspect."

"Healing? I didn't think Water mages were good at healing," Juniper said. From what she remembered, Fire mages excelled in healing. Fire and Water opposed each other and typically excelled at opposite things.

"Not usually," Abrielle said. "But there are exceptions."

A chime sounded from somewhere, a deep clatter of a thousand sounds at once—a bell. At Juniper's confusion, Abrielle offered a sympathetic grin.

"The bells refer to the time," Abrielle explained. "The first bell, what you just heard, means it's seven. The second bell rings at eight, and the third rings at half-past eight. Don't worry, you'll get the hang of it."

Juniper huffed. A clatter of laughter came from the bathing room.

"You'll adjust." Abrielle smiled, but it did not reach her eyes. After a moment, she let her smile fade. "We all went through the change from one life to another."

"How long have you been here?" Juniper asked.

"Since I was thirteen." Sorrow crept into her eyes. Old enough to remember her family. "I remember how horrible I felt when the overseer threw me into a dorm with eleven strange girls. I remember how alone I felt. We all do."

"Thank you," Juniper said, and she meant it. She appreciated Abrielle's kindness and sympathy.

"And if you forget something, don't be nervous to ask," Abrielle added.

BEATRICE B. MORGAN

The bathing room door opened, and a tall blonde girl with milky skin walked into the room. Her proud green eyes rolled over Juniper, sizing her up in a heartbeat. She wore only a towel around her body.

"That's Mabyl," said Abrielle. "She's a fire mage."

"I hear you talking about me," said Mabyl, her voice dry and bored. She strolled over with the grace of a dancer. "She explain the bell thing yet?"

"Yes," Abrielle said.

"Good." Mabyl leaned onto Juniper's footboard. "No one bothered to explain it to me, and I was late to everything the first day. Damn knights whipped me for it. Then the other mages explained it, like it was *so* easy to understand." Mabyl stuck her hand out to Juniper. "Welcome to hell, new kid."

"You make it sound so enticing." Juniper took the girl's hand. Mabyl's grip was surprisingly strong. "I don't understand why no one wants to come here."

Mabyl laughed, but Abrielle looked frantically toward the dormitory door, as if the overseer might have heard.

"You'll fit in just fine," Mabyl said. "Though, if what they say about you is true, you should definitely watch your back. Some of the other girls might not be so keen on being roomies."

"Why?" Abrielle added.

Juniper answered for her, "To keep the pecking order. The other kids won't like a new kid coming in with a reputation and threatening their hierarchy."

"Exactly," Mabyl added. "Is that Undercity logic?"

"It's street logic," Juniper said. "The courtiers do it too. They're just sly about it. More verbal backstabbing than actually backstabbing."

Mabyl grinned. "That settles it. You're sitting with us for breakfast."

Juniper wasn't given an alternative. Mabyl strolled to her bed across the room and dropped her towel onto the bed. Abrielle went into the bathing room, and Juniper pulled off her castle-gifted dress and quickly pulled on her robes. She kept her chemise on—she didn't want anyone asking about the brand on her back or her many scars. At least the Marca robes were comfortable. She tied her blue sash around her waist as Mabyl appeared in her peripheral. She wore robes of the same purple and a red sash.

"Abrielle will catch up," Mabyl said, stringing her arm through Juniper's. "We'll save her a seat. Oh, I can't wait to see everyone's face when Juniper Thimble strolls into the mess hall."

Juniper wouldn't admit it, but she couldn't either. Mabyl led her back through the corridors and down to the mess hall on the first floor. The clatter of hundreds of voices bounced off the stone, and something warm pushed through the cracks in Juniper's dread. As they neared the mess hall doors, Juniper

9

recognized it as anticipation. She wanted to see their shocked faces, not unlike when she sauntered into Maddox's keep after an impossible heist. The jealousy of the other thieves had been part of the incentive to succeed.

Knights lined the corridor outside the mess hall, impassive and stone-faced. Juniper felt their eyes as she passed, but she ignored them.

Juniper held her chin high and her shoulders straight as she walked into the mess hall. It was a large chamber filled with square tables and purple robes. She followed Mabyl through the tables and toward the line for food. The chatter gradually shifted into hasty murmurs and gasps, and Juniper let herself think it was because of her. A part of her loved it. Even the Marca mages had heard about Juniper Thimble.

Mabyl guided her through the line of bland food, and Juniper settled on porridge and tea. The two of them sat at a table occupied by two other mages. Mabyl introduced them as Plum and Seema.

"So, it's true?" asked Plum, a thin-faced girl with brown hair and a peachy complexion. "Juniper Thimble has come to live with the mages?"

Plum directed the question at Mabyl, not Juniper. Juniper tightened her hands around her spoon. She hated being talked about as though she weren't there.

"No, she's just taking a tour." Mabyl leisurely buttered her bread. "Seeing if she likes it well enough to move in."

Seema chuckled. Plum frowned at Juniper.

"What do you think so far, Thimble?" asked Seema, a girl with pale brown skin and short black hair.

"Could use a few more windows," Juniper said, and she meant it. "Not that magelights don't offer adequate lighting."

Mabyl snorted. "Didn't you know? Sunshine makes mages go crazy."

Abrielle appeared at Juniper's other side with a plate of fruit and porridge. "They've increased security since last night."

"I counted twenty knights on the way here," Seema whispered. "That's twice as many as usual."

"I guess we have you to thank for that." Plum glanced at Juniper.

"My sincerest apologies," Juniper mumbled.

"They think you're a threat," Mabyl added.

"I would too," Juniper added listlessly. The other girls blinked at her. "What? I know what all I've done, and most of the knights do too. I would be a bit hurt if they didn't think me worth the extra security."

Plum and Seema glanced at each other, skeptical.

Mabyl nudged Juniper and said, "Best not let them hear you talk like that. One thing these knights hate is a mage with attitude."

Juniper followed Mabyl's line of sight to the nearest knight. He stood against the wall with his arms crossed. The magelight flickered off his silver armor. His bland, bored expression looked over the heads of the mages, unfocused. His Mage's Bane sword hung at his side, the blue scabbard so dark it appeared black.

Juniper picked at her food while the other girls talked. They threw out names she didn't know, talked about their classes and teachers, and Juniper barely paid attention. She was listening to the mindless chatter of the mess hall. Her name echoed on those murmurs and whispers. She felt eyes needling her, watching every movement. When she glanced up from her porridge, a dozen pairs of eyes shifted suddenly away from her. Every direction she looked, it was the same.

Except for the knights. They did not hide their gaze. The knight against the back wall of the mess hall met her gaze, his eyes glassy and bored. Juniper held his gaze only for a heartbeat, then turned back to her porridge. Something about his glassy expression sent a chill down her spine.

Mabyl laughed, and Juniper smiled as though she had heard.

She could do this, she told herself. All she had to do was wait, be patient, and not draw attention to herself. Even with the knights' eyes prodding the back of her throat.

CHAPTER 3

An entire month in the Marca, and Juniper still hadn't heard from King Bradburn. The Marca hadn't been a total waste of time. She had learned a few new things. The basic class had been dull yet informative. Most of the basic rules and laws of magic she had learned either from Ison, on her own, or in those short weeks she had spent in Mason Hobbs's study. She enjoyed the practical magic classes the most, even though they were only twice a week and observed by no less than three knights armed with Mage's Bane. The classes of art, history, mathematics, and literature were dreadfully boring.

Isaac visited twice, bringing her a small bag of sweets each time. She hadn't intended to share, and as she made her way back to the dorm, she considered all the places she might hide a bag of sweets. She had tried to hide the bag in her robes, but Abrielle caught sight of it. The girl said nothing, but her eyes widened at the sight.

"Sir Pinul brought them for me," Juniper confessed.

"That was kind of him," Abrielle said. "My family doesn't visit. They live too far south, but they send me a package on my birthday."

Feeling a pang of sympathy, she offered Abrielle a chocolate. It did not go unnoticed.

"It must be nice to have someone bring you sweets," said Carol, the most irritating of the girls, to Plum as they walked into the bathing room. Carol shot a spiteful look in Juniper's direction.

Plum responded, but the door closed and Juniper didn't hear what she said. That was probably for the best.

Juniper inhaled and held it, counted, and released it slowly. A stupid technique, but useful for control of both her magic and her anger.

Four weeks of the other girls' bitterness had worn Juniper's patience thin. The vengeful part of her wanted to remind them who she was and what she had done, but each time her anger rose, she reminded herself that anything she did could harm Reid and Henry.

"Don't mind them." Abrielle glanced over her shoulder at the bathing room door. "They're jealous." She added in a whisper, "Plum's mom died the year she came to the Marca. She's got no other family, and no one visits her."

"They're just mad they're not getting special treatment," Mabyl said from where she reclined on her bed.

"I'm not getting special treatment," Juniper defended.

Mabyl cocked her head, eyebrow raised. "Oh, you're not, huh? You don't see the knights bringing anyone else sweets. Or when you walked into class a few minutes late and Professor Simon pretended not to notice."

Juniper had noticed that. She'd thought he was being kind to a new student.

"Sir Pinul is a friend of mine," Juniper said.

"Knights are not friends," Seema added from her bed.

Seema's dismissive, cold tone irked her. She didn't know Isaac, none of them did.

"When you go to the edge of the world together, you become friends," Juniper defended, and the dorm went silent.

All eyes turned toward her. Mabyl sat up.

"It's true, then?" Abrielle asked at last. She scooted to the edge of the bed. "The stories they say about the squires and you?"

Juniper held the room, even the girls who generally ignored her. An uneasy bubble expanded in her chest. Strange—she had never been one to shy away from bragging before. But the journey to the edge of the realm hadn't been some heist or another bank vault. These girls were not fellow thieves she could beat up without consequence.

"Yes," Juniper said. "Sir Pinul, and Squires Sandpiper, Julian, and Berwick were sent north. I encountered them north of the city. They needed my help, so I gave it."

Blank faces stared back at her.

Ison had gone too, but she left his name out. He'd spent most of his life at the Marca, and the girls would likely know him. Thinking of Ison squeezed Juniper's heart. She hadn't seen him or heard about him since they had returned. While the squires had returned to the castle as heroes, Ison had opted to remain an apostate.

"And you lived in the Undercity," Mabyl added eagerly. She sat up and folded her legs underneath her. "You worked for a guild down there."

A thrill spiked through the room at the mention of the Undercity, curiosity threaded with fear.

"I did," Juniper said.

Several of the girls abandoned their quiet conversations and gathered around Juniper's bed. They came for a story—a tradition of sorts within the dorm. Juniper had half listened to the other girls retell fairy tales and folk stories in the evenings, but she had never told one herself.

13

"Go on," Mabyl said.

Juniper spent the evening telling them about the Undercity—the guilds and thieves, assassins and courtesans, the black markets and dark dealings. When she mentioned the mages, a collective breath was taken.

"That's where some go," Abrielle whispered. "If they get out."

Juniper nodded. "I'm friends with several."

"They made it," Mabyl whispered, not looking entirely at Juniper.

Those words stuck with her as the magelights dimmed and the girls returned to their own beds. Mages sometimes escaped from the Marca. The mages still inside had no way of knowing their fate—and Juniper had given them a sliver of hope that those mages had indeed made it to freedom.

Mabyl looked infinitely relieved by the news. She looked like she had other questions, but she didn't dare ask in front of the others.

A few of the girls, Juniper had been warned, loved to tattle to the knights.

Another week passed. No word came from King Bradburn. Winter arrived with chilled winds, spitting snow and sleeting against the classroom windows. Juniper watched the snow swirl while the middle-aged instructor lectured about the importance of mathematics and all the nonsense formulas Juniper had halfheartedly scribbled down. She hadn't needed mathematics to survive, and she doubted she would need them in the future. She supposed the Marca taught math just to keep the mages preoccupied.

Isaac visited again, bringing her news. Reid and Henry had been knighted. Juniper felt her chest deflate; she hadn't been there. She hadn't seen Reid become a knight.

"It's not very exciting," Isaac said. "It's a small thing with little fanfare. It's a short ceremony of recitations and oaths. All stuffy traditions. But it means Reid will be busy these next few weeks. He wants to see you, but between the king and Fowler, he hasn't gotten but a few breaths for peace."

He had answered her unspoken question—why hadn't Reid come to see her? They hadn't had a chance to talk about *them*, not since that night in the cave. She knew how complicated a relationship between them would be—him a knight and her a mage—but she had hoped he would at least come to see her.

"He will come when he can," Isaac promised, though she didn't know how he could promise such a thing.

"Thank you for coming," Juniper said sincerely. Despite how the other mages stared and whispered, or how the knights watched her, she was glad Isaac had taken the time to see her. "Isaac, has the king—"

"His Majesty is working on it," Isaac replied, the same answer as the last time she had asked.

Juniper sat near the back of the classroom, chin resting on her hand, while a thick-voiced woman named Professor Kline scribbled the names and dates of Bradburn kings on the chalkboard. She recited each king's accomplishments and failures—Juniper quickly lost interest in the lecture.

Adrian could likely repeat the history of his family with ease and with more enthusiasm than any teacher.

Juniper inhaled slowly, filling her lungs, then released it just as slowly. No one in the classroom spoke. It looked as though most others had lost interest, save for the few who sat near the front, enthralled by the very essence of learning.

Weirdos.

Her attention drifted to the three windows that lined the classroom. The leaded glass arched near the top, and a vicious set of spikes had been carved into the stone. According to Mabyl, the windows were enchanted to muffle sound.

How much force would it take to smash through one of those windows?

Kline mumbled about princes and princesses, and Juniper's thoughts again drifted—against her will—to Isolde Balendin. The lost princess. Could Juniper possibly be that lost princess? It sounded so bizarre and utterly preposterous. Her, a princess.

"Juniper."

She jumped—

Kline was staring at her. As were most of her classmates.

"I assume you are daydreaming because you already know everything there is to know about the Bradburn line," snapped Kline.

Juniper sat up straight. "I'm sure there are bits I could brush up on."

The boy sitting beside her glanced at the knight standing by the classroom door. The knight usually stared out of the window, looking painfully bored, but now he was looking at Juniper.

"Then please, answer the question," said the teacher. "The victory of what battle gave Prince Roland Bradburn his father's favor, thus securing his path to the throne?"

15

Juniper had no clue. Thousands of battles scattered Duvane's history, and she couldn't name more than two. "You've got me," Juniper said, shrugging. "That's one of those bits I don't know."

"Not even a guess?" asked Kline, brows high.

"It would be a wrong guess," Juniper explained. "Why guess at something I know I don't know? It would be easier to admit my ignorance."

Kline inhaled and held it, glaring down at Juniper.

"It's not every day you hear someone admit to being an idiot," mumbled Carol from the other side of the room.

A few students chuckled, most of them seated around Carol.

"Then please, enlighten us with your knowledge," Juniper said to Carol.

Carol's lips pursed.

"Ah, it appears that you are as much of an idiot as me," Juniper said.

The knight shifted, and the mages took a collective breath. Juniper tensed. She'd seen the knights react to the silliest of crimes, from laughing too loud to walking too fast.

"It is the Battle of Onora," snapped the teacher. She motioned to the large map pinned to the wall. "Carol, please come to the map and show us all where Onora is."

Carol started to stand—she slipped on a thin, clear sheet of ice. Carol careened backward and plopped on her back with the grace of a dead bird.

Laughter erupted, and Juniper joined them. In the moment of chaos, she willed her ice away. Carol scrambled to her feet, her face bright red. She glared at Juniper, her eyes full of hatred and humiliation.

"I slipped on ice!" Carol spat.

A few mages shot nervous glances either at Juniper or the knight by the door.

Juniper kept her face cool. "Oh, yes, because I'm capable of making ice way over there," she said sarcastically.

"That sounds like a confession," one of Carol's friends said.

Juniper had something witty to say to Carol's friend, but a shadow appeared by her desk. The knight stood beside her, glaring down at her as if she stepped in something nasty and trekked it all through the Marca.

The laughter died.

No one said a word as the knight grabbed Juniper by the arm and yanked her out of her chair and into the corridor.

"What?" Juniper spat. "I'm being punished because she's uncoordinated?"

"Natural magic is forbidden," said the knight. The words sounded well practiced and learned.

16

The knight pulled her toward the stairs at the end of the corridor. She passed a few other students tending to the upkeep of the Marca's halls, but no one dared look in her direction. They continued their chores as if she weren't even there. The knight hauled her all the way to the first floor. He pulled her through an ominous corridor that ran beside the kitchen, through several sets of heavy wooden doors, and into a narrow corridor of bland stone and...cells. Her heart skipped a beat.

"Wait," Juniper pleaded, though she knew it would do no good.

The knight signaled to another. A cell door was opened, and the knight threw her inside. She landed on a packed dirt floor. Before she could voice her protest, the cell door slammed shut. She saw it as it closed—a rune carved half on the door and half on the stone wall, so when the door closed, the rune completed.

And then, silence and darkness.

Juniper heard nothing beyond her own breathing, her own heart hammering, and her scuffling against the dirt floor. She saw nothing. Her night sight helped a little—she could make out the square of the room, the door. It felt like a tomb—buried alive. Her hands started to shake, and her breaths came in shallow spurts.

They had thrown her into a quiet room. Mabyl had told her about them—rooms enchanted to be unnaturally dark and quiet, where they threw unruly mages.

As her panic settled, she felt something else. The rune worked against her magic, shoving it down, oppressing it. She reached down deep, but her magic refused to respond. It felt like being smothered with a heavy blanket in the summertime. The oppression pressed against her whole being, making it difficult to breathe.

Juniper slumped against the far wall and focused on her breathing. In and out. In and out. It was the only thing she could do until the knight came back for her.

Had it been worth it?

It didn't take long to answer her own question, not when she had the memory of Carol falling on her ass to keep her company.

Absolutely.

CHAPTER 4

Juniper didn't know how long she sat in the quiet room. Too long. She fell asleep several times but woke up gasping for breath each time. By the time the knights returned, her entire body shook from weakness, and her thoughts were clogged from poor sleep.

The door creaked open, the rune broke, and all at once, the oppression evaporated and magelight washed into the cell. A tremor worked its way through her arms and legs, and a shuddering gasp tumbled up her throat. A heady nausea surged from her gut. She lurched forward but only dry heaved.

It took a tortuous moment for the fit to pass.

"That should be a lesson for you," said the knight standing in the door, the same knight who had thrown her into the cell. His shadow stretched along the floor and the far wall. "Now get up."

The knight escorted her back to the dorm. In her shaken state, she blindly followed. The windows revealed a city shadowed by thick gray clouds. They passed the mess hall—clattering with the sounds of dinner—but the knight did not offer her food. Not that she felt like eating. Everyone had likely heard what happened, especially with Carol's big mouth.

Juniper had the dorm to herself and chose to spend it washing off the dust of the quiet room. With no one in the bathing room, she lifted tendrils of water from the tub, froze them into spears, shaped them into snowflakes, boiled them into steam—it felt good to use her magic. The floral scents of natural magic stood out in the Marca, but in the bathing room, it mixed with the scents of soaps and oils. No one would know, and no one could tattle on her to the knights.

After a well-deserved soak, Juniper magicked the water from her skin and hair. She returned to bed with a long rest on her mind.

If only sleep had felt the same.

Abrielle returned from dinner first. She sat on the edge of Juniper's bed and pulled several hidden rolls from within her sleeves. "The knights like to keep us long enough to miss a meal or two," she explained.

The rolls had gone cold, but Juniper sank her teeth into one anyway. She hadn't realized how hungry she'd become. "Thank you," she said with her mouth full. She took another greedy bite.

"I was thrown into the quiet rooms for sticking my tongue out at a boy. Stupid, I know. That other mage also got thrown in. They said we were instigating a fight."

"Were you?"

"I don't remember." Abrielle's kind eyes darkened, and she put a hand over her chest. "I do remember the quiet rooms. They're horrible. It's like you can't breathe."

The dormitory door opened, and several girls walked inside. At the sight of Juniper, alive and well, their conversation ended. Carol sauntered in behind them, nose high and proud. She and her friends took their chatter into the bathing room.

Mabyl sat next to Abrielle and dumped a handful of blueberries into Juniper's hand.

"Don't mind them," Mabyl said lowly. "Carol got told off for provoking you. Almost cried. Now eat those berries. Fresh from the greenhouse. One perk of this place is we get fresh fruit all year around."

Juniper had a thought to superheat the steam in the bathing room—but she didn't. She didn't feel like visiting the quiet rooms again so soon. Or ever. She still felt the ghost of the rune's smothering power, sucking her breath from her throat and shoving her magic out of her reach.

Besides, she didn't need magic to get revenge on someone. It just made it easier.

Juniper had the following morning off, and while the girls went down to breakfast in their respective packs, she vanished into the library. She needed peace and quiet more than food. The Marca's library took a corner tower and smelled like dust, metallic magic, and candle wax. The air had the same muffled sound as any other, as if people spoke into pillows. Juniper picked a book and found an alcove on the second floor. Dreary sunlight poured in from a tall, narrow window, reflecting off each dust mote. As she plopped onto the faded blue couch, those dust motes burst in every direction.

She took a deep breath of the silence, the peace, the lonesome atmosphere. Here, no one could whisper about her loud enough for her to hear or stare at the back of her head. The knights couldn't glare at her if they couldn't see her.

She opened the book, ready to lose herself for a few hours. She could use a break from the Marca—and she finally understood what Ison had meant when he said any book was an adventure if it took him out of the Marca.

She began to read—and lost herself in the lengthy story of a man venturing north to the city to find his fortune. He wouldn't, of course—he would stumble disaster along the way.

"I didn't see you at breakfast," came a girlish voice.

And the illusion of adventure shattered.

Seema sat on the other side of the couch, a textbook for Air mages in her arm.

"I wasn't hungry." Juniper returned to her book, though Seema's presence made it impossible to escape.

"I saw what you did to Carol," Seema whispered.

"I don't know what you're talking about."

"Don't worry, your secret is safe with me."

"I'm fairly certain everyone knows by now."

"Oh, they do," Seema said. The superior mask she wore around Carol slipped, and something much more human and agreeable poked through. "Sometimes, Carol needs to be taken down a few pegs. She can be…"

"A brown-nosing bitch?"

Seema laughed. "Yeah, that. It's a nice change to have someone with the gall to stand up to her. She's afraid of you, you know."

Juniper didn't trust Seema to tell her the truth. Seema was friends with Plum, and Plum was friends with Carol. For all she knew, this encounter might be another devious attempt to humiliate or tease her. She missed the days in the Undercity when she could just punch whomever she didn't like.

An uncomfortable silence fell.

"Is it true what they say?" Seema whispered. She scooted a little closer. "That you used to be an assassin in the Undercity?"

Juniper hesitated. She had been a thief first, but she had taken a few assassination contracts. Seema didn't need to know that, though.

So, Juniper twisted the truth and said, "Yes."

Seema's eyes widened with a mixture of surprise and fear. "How did that work? Did people just come and find you when they wanted someone dead?"

"I worked for a guild. The guild master managed any contract."

Seema hung on those words, and she waited for Juniper to elaborate. When she didn't, her awe dulled.

"And now the knights are bringing you gifts," Seema whispered. A tone of spite wormed through her words.

Juniper slammed her book closed and met Seema's gaze. "Sir Pinul is not just any knight, and he knows how much I detested coming here, and how much I would love to carve my way out."

Seema didn't say anything. Juniper pretended to return to her book.

A few long moments passed.

"Do you want to copy my notes?" Seema asked.

"For what?"

"The class you missed." Seema pulled a few sheets of paper from within the Air textbook. "We have a test next week."

Juniper looked at the notes; Seema had drawn an elaborate family tree of the Bradburn line.

"Why?" Juniper asked. She shifted her glare from the notes to Seema.

Seema looked sheepish. "Because you missed the class," she said plainly. She looked down at her notes and flattened a wrinkled corner. "I'm trying to be nice."

"And you've done a great job so far," Juniper mumbled.

"I'm sorry Carol's being…Carol. Just take my notes. Good luck on the test." Seema stood, left her notes, and marched out of the nook.

Juniper waited for Seema's footsteps to fade, then pulled the notes onto the open pages of her book. Seema had small, neat penmanship. Juniper trailed the branches of the tree from King Lendon at the top to Adrian at the bottom. Against her better judgment, she looked over the lineage. Then she set Seema's notes aside and returned to her book.

To Juniper's surprise, their next history class came with a test on the Bradburn line. She didn't do exceptionally well, but she did better than she would have. Maybe Seema wasn't as bad as her friends.

Juniper's classes continued to be dull. The basic class lectured too much about mindfulness and control, and the teacher's soft voice seemed to have been enchanted to induce drowsiness. Juniper was the oldest in the class; most were children. The older an apostate, the greater likelihood of them having taught themselves natural magic.

Her afternoon classes were better, though only slightly. The lectures on history, art, and mathematics grated on her patience. She enjoyed the magic lessons. They learned simple spells, like how to fling dust from bookshelves, move small objects, detect poison, clean rust, stitch wounds, and how to use basic runes.

Once a week, the mages divided into classes based on element, and Juniper looked forward to Water class. They learned how the element worked, what spells worked best, and how their magic might work with patience and practice.

They did not learn how to harness their raw magic; they learned to manipulate water via unnatural magic. It made moving even small amounts of water much harder. Juniper quickly understood why Ison hated unnatural magic so much—it made little sense.

Professor Klamm, the Water instructor, was an old man who kept his white hair braided down his back. He had scolded Juniper in her first lessons for moving water by natural magic. They had been charged with moving water from one bowl to another, and she had easily commanded the water through the air and into the second bowl.

"No, no, no. Use the magic essence," Klamm had said, flourishing his hands through the air. Perfect spheres of water lifted from the bowl. "Like this."

"Why?" Juniper had asked. "It's so much more complicated than just lifting the water itself."

"It's how we do things here," the Water teacher had snapped.

Abrielle had nudged Juniper, silently pleading.

Juniper's skill at natural magic would have surpassed them all, even the teacher. She wasn't nearly as skilled at unnatural magic, and it frustrated her.

"Think of it as if you're using an invisible scoop," Abrielle had whispered. She moved a handful of water without slipping a drop.

Juniper focused—she felt the thin layer of magic in the air, and following Abrielle's instructions, gathered that essence into a scoop. She had moved the water, a scoop at a time, and survived her first Water class.

Unnatural magic resisted her command, whereas her natural magic gave no resistance.

Professor Klamm called unnatural magic *safe magic*, and Juniper wanted to laugh. The Marca taught mages to be weak, passive, and powerless.

She told these thoughts to Mabyl while they took their turn cleaning the dishes from lunch rather than attending afternoon classes—dishes were a rotating chore, and everyone had their turn to be elbow deep in dirty, soapy water. While Juniper didn't enjoy the dishes, the kitchens allowed mild privacy for conversations.

Mabyl laughed. "That's because a mage who can use their magic is a threat." She added in a whisper, "Which is why mages are brought in young. The older an apostate is, the more likely they are to realize what the Marca is doing. They've taught themselves to use their magic, and they are a threat. Which is why everyone was amazed when you got in."

"Fowler wanted me dead," Juniper admitted. "Still does."

Mabyl let out a low whistle. "And you've still got your head? Someone high up must really like you."

Juniper shrugged. "I did save the prince's life. Several times, actually."

"That might have done it."

Carol walked into the kitchen, and their conversation ended. She, Juniper had learned, loved to tattle to the knights. According to Mabyl, Carol thought it got her extra favor. However, no one had favor with the overseer, because the overseer didn't have a soul capable of feeling things like sympathy or compassion.

The days ticked by. Juniper felt the knights watching her at all times. They waited for her to slip up, to break a rule or miss a bell. Every corridor, every class, every meal. Her only glimpses of privacy came when she tucked herself away in the library.

As a thief, Juniper had plenty of alone time when she studied her targets. As the royal protector, she'd had an entire chamber to herself. Living with twelve other girls was proving taxing.

The Marca had a decent library, and Juniper spent most of her evenings and free time reading. Sometimes, she, Mabyl, and Abrielle would talk. Juniper told them about the Undercity, about her days spent in the castle, and about the quest to the edge of the realm. Her stories lit up their eyes. The stories were new, something different than the drab gray walls and endless lectures and classes. Her stories offered them a piece of the world they were not allowed to be a part of— a feeling she understood well.

Adventure novels had done the same for her when she believed she would forever live in the Undercity.

Juniper learned about her new friends too. Abrielle's family owned a unicorn farm in the Karna Province. She worked in the Marca's small farm where they raised animals—those that produced items for potions or for meals. Mabyl's family lived in the Onumit Province and worked in her grandmother's candle shop. Both had lived in the Marca since they were children.

Mabyl and Abrielle had become friends, and they made the Marca bearable.

CHAPTER 5

During the next Water class, each mage was charged with boiling a bowl of water the tedious Marca way. Juniper focused on the magic essence and urged it to heat, which would then heat the water. She just about had it when—*crash*—the young mage next to her accidentally shattered his bowl.

A shard of ceramic sliced through Juniper's arm. She gasped, and as blood began to ooze through the cut, Abrielle grasped Juniper's arm. Blood squished through her fingers. Warmth wiggled through the wound and through her blood, staunching the bleeding and easing the stinging flesh.

Abrielle removed her bloodied hand. Juniper's wound no longer bled.

"Thank you," Juniper said.

Abrielle rinsed her hand in the bowl of water, turning it a shade of pink. "It's no problem. I don't get a lot of chances to practice."

Professor Klamm rushed over. He commanded the spilled water into another's bowl. He examined the boy first. The ceramic had spotted his hands with shallow cuts.

Juniper whispered to Abrielle, "Your magic felt different from the royal healer's."

"Most healers are fire mages,' Abrielle explained. "But I've always been drawn to the healing arts. I can clot wounds and detect things within a body that shouldn't be there. I've taken a few courses on healing, and I'd like to one day become a professional healer."

"You could," Juniper said.

Abrielle brightened.

"All right, neither of you are dying. Head up to the healer. She'll patch you up," snapped Klamm, as if the boy had done it on purpose.

Juniper returned to the dorm that evening while Abrielle went to work with the animals and Mabyl went to work at the Marca's smithy—she used her proficiency for heating things to keep metals and stones warm while the few runesmiths and metalsmiths worked. Juniper hadn't yet been assigned a job. Rather than stay in the dorm with girls who ignored her and stared, Juniper found an alcove in the library to read. A magelight hung from the ceiling, tinting the space in pale yellow light.

She lost herself in the romantic adventure and didn't sense anyone else until Mabyl plopped down on the other end of the sage couch. She smelled strongly of hot metal and mineral-laden smoke.

"You smell like the Undercity," Juniper said.

"I was eyeball-deep in stone and ugly men," Mabyl said without humor. "Basically the same, right?"

Juniper nodded. She marked her place and set the book aside. "There was one mercenary whose nose had been broken so many times, it had nearly flattened against his face."

Mabyl chuckled.

Where Abrielle was sweet and cautious, Mabyl was shameless and bold. Juniper liked that about her; she could ask Mabyl anything and get an honest, if not slightly crass, answer. Mabyl liked stories of the Undercity and its inhabitants—especially stories of the mages. When they found private moments in the hushed, hidden alcoves of the library, Mabyl whispered the names of mages who had escaped. Some Juniper knew, others she did not.

"What about Remi Laird?" Mabyl whispered. "She was short, plump, and had stick-straight brown hair."

"Doesn't sound familiar," Juniper whispered. She sorted through the mages she remembered, the faces she had no names for, and the many mages who worked in the stalls. She hadn't gone to mage stalls unless Josephine had vouched for them or Xavier had gone with her.

Mabyl's face fell.

"But there were a lot of mages I never met," Juniper quickly added.

"I'd like to see them again," Mabyl whispered, eyes looking at the book in her lap but focused on something else.

Without no one easily listening, Juniper whispered, "But…how did they get out?"

Mabyl leaned a little closer, making it look like they were snuggling rather than whispering. On the library's upper floors, where the alcoves were guarded by towering bookshelves, Juniper had glimpsed more than a few locked lips and wandering hands. Thankfully, the books muffled any sounds she would rather not hear.

"There's supposed to be a hidden tunnel underneath this place," Mabyl whispered so lowly, Juniper strained to hear. "According to the legend, the hardest part is finding the stupid thing. The second hardest part is figuring out where it leads. It's on the first floor somewhere, and a long time ago, it was some sort of secret escape tunnel."

The first floor was not a place to get caught looking for a way out. The first floor held the barracks for the knights, the kitchens, the laundry, and a number of places mages wouldn't normally wander into.

"I suppose there is some credibility to it," Juniper admitted, "considering all the mages who got out. Maybe it connects to the Undercity?"

Mabyl opened her mouth to say something else when the sound of armored footsteps approached. Panic flared in her eyes, and to cover up the sudden silence, Mabyl pressed her mouth against Juniper's.

The armored footsteps passed without slowing down.

And without a batting of an eye, their conversation resumed.

It was a trick Juniper had learned in her first week—when two mages were having a conversation that would be better left unheard by the knights or snitches, they locked lips. According to Mabyl, if a knight came to see why you were being so quiet and discovered your hand down another mage's robe, they tended not to ask too many questions.

Juniper and Mabyl had been in the library that day too. Juniper had been naming mages in the Undercity when armored footsteps approached. Mabyl cut off Juniper mid-word with a kiss and grabbed her breast—the knight had paused, then continued his vigil of the library. Juniper, however, had been more than a little surprised.

"If I walked in on two girls touching each other, I wouldn't say anything either," Mabyl had said, grinning. "Hell, I might watch."

Mabyl's stories of sensuality could rival Ison's, and she shamelessly shared them all. Juniper quickly stopped feeling bashful about asking her questions. She made a mental list of all the things she wanted to try—she imagined trying them with Reid, and it brought a pinch of darkness to her heart. She had spent so long thinking she couldn't have him, and thinking that she might have him once again tore that old wound anew.

Eleven weeks and one day into her stay at the Marca, Juniper was lying awake after lights out. Several of the girls had snuck into the boys' dorm down the hall, including Mabyl and Abrielle. Juniper had been invited. She'd thought about going, just to see what it was like, but then she thought of Reid. She declined the invitation.

Reid. Were they together? Had that night in the cave been the result of nearly dying? Being a knight gave him a higher status. He could have his pick of noblewomen. What chance did she have against a noblewoman?

And, according to the gossip from the Marca stalls, Adrian had woken. Juniper inhaled deeply. Somewhere, Nexon was moving. They had lost eleven weeks to the nonsense of the Marca, unless the others had left her behind to find a way to stop him.

That thought widened the pit in her stomach.

It did not help that today was her eighteenth birthday. She had spent plenty of birthdays alone or working, but she had hoped for *something*. A card, a gift, flowers. Something from her friends outside the Marca. Yet there had been nothing. Had they forgotten her? Had the Marca erased her existence?

What were the others doing? She'd never felt so isolated from the world. Not as a prisoner in the castle, not even as she stood on the edge of the mortal world.

CHAPTER 6

Crown Prince Adrian Bradburn wished he had played sick. He and his father sat alone in the meeting room—no one else had yet arrived. He hadn't done much in the past eleven weeks, not since coming out of his poison-induced coma. For the first three weeks, he had been too sick to do anything but lie in bed and sip broth. His strength had gradually returned, as had his appetite and his ability to stay awake longer than a few hours. Last week, he had been, well, fine; however, he pretended to feel worse so he could spend it with Roslyn.

And with those glorious, passionate days with her fresh in his mind, the council meeting felt especially dull.

He wished he had stayed in bed that morning, continuing his exploration of her. He had committed to learning every curve and freckle on her body.

Knight Commander Fowler entered the meeting room with all the huffiness of a grumpy old man, dampening Adrian's thoughts of Roslyn. The door hadn't yet met the frame when his father's advisors entered, Rourke Hendle, his son Ronald Hendle, and the newest advisor who hadn't yet held the title a week, Cecil Hurst. Cecil was a middle-aged woman, retired from the City Watch. The public had a high view of her, Adrian had heard.

Cecil opened her mouth to say her greetings, but her words were cut short by Fowler slamming his fist onto the table.

"It is an outrage," Fowler spat. "Letting that criminal live. She is a mar on the Order's reputation. I've received a dozen letters a day since you acquitted her, from lords and ladies victimized by her thieving or killing. She needs to be executed."

King Bradburn regarded Fowler indifferently, but his eyes were cold. "We have spoken on this matter, Knight Commander," he warned. "We will not discuss it further."

The air thickened, and Adrian held his expression impassive. He didn't care for Fowler or the way he questioned his father's decisions. He had been doing it more and more recently, particularly where Juniper was concerned.

The advisors sat. Cecil glared at Fowler, not bothering to hide her dislike. Seeing the others sitting, Fowler straightened his shoulders and took the seat across from King Bradburn.

BEATRICE B. MORGAN

"Your Majesty," started Ron Hendle, a young man no older than Adrian. "What the knight commander means is that he wishes to make an example out of her to all the apostates, thieves, and assassins. Letting her live makes the Order look weak-willed."

The king glared at Ron, who cleared his throat and had the good mind to look sheepish.

"Maybe," Ron continued, "rather than death, punishing her might give the people of Rusdasin the revenge they seek."

"The people of Rusdasin think highly of Juniper Thimble," King Bradburn retorted. He glanced at Adrian, wearing indifference. "Roslyn Derean has told anyone who will listen about how wonderful Juniper is and how her lifestyle was brought upon her by a series of misfortunes."

Adrian fought hard not to smile. Roslyn had been hard at work. When she hadn't been sitting at his bedside, she had gone into the city. The people had flocked to meet their future queen and eagerly listened to anything she had to say. Roslyn had spoken to as many people as possible, telling them how the ex-thief had risked her life to save her friends. Roslyn had spread the word to every inch of the city—Juniper Thimble had a heart of gold. It had done wonders to clear Juniper's reputation.

Though they hadn't spoken about it, Adrian knew his father was proud of Roslyn's tactics. According to his mother, Roslyn would fit in better at court than she had first believed.

"Many think of Juniper Thimble as a vigilante for the people, one who saved the prince even though everyone assumed her the killer," said the king. "The people will not be happy with her being punished."

Ron pursed his lips, argument on his face, but he remained silent.

"We could talk of something more pleasant," said Cecil, her voice harsh but soft, one used to yelling. "Wedding plans?"

Adrian met Ron's eyes over the table. Adrian had known Ron most of his life, and while he had always been the bookish, snobbish sort, the promotion to advisor had made him insufferably arrogant. The two had shared few words outside of meetings, and those words were short and professional. Adrian blinked and looked at Cecil instead.

Adrian put a hand over his heart. "I wouldn't dare make plans without Roslyn's approval."

"That is wise," added his father.

And the topic moved on to the latest news out of Delphine, royal city of Collatia. King Crespin Balendin had renounced his crown and claim to the throne, and his younger sister, Myrisha, would be queen. The talk drifted to what sort of the gift they should send to the new queen, and Adrian lost interest. His thoughts drifted to the raven-haired girl he had kissed good morning.

Marcy hauled the basket to one of the hundreds of closets in Castle Bradburn. Her footsteps were silent, just another good servant, plain and unremarkable. They no longer had to move around in pairs, not since the Demon Crisis, but it didn't stop her from being nervous. Whenever she started down an empty corridor, the hairs on the back of her neck stood straight.

Sometimes, she had the eeriest feeling of being watched.

No servants had gone missing since, but she didn't want to test her luck.

Marcy came to the closet and set her basket down to open the heavy door. She wedged the door open with a wooden block left just inside. With the door open, the torches in the corridor brightened the closet's shelves. She started to put away the clean linens.

A conversation was happening on the other side of the wall. She had overheard a great deal of conversations, but this one caught her ear.

"…we are too close. In the next few days," said a voice smooth as velvet but malicious as frostbite. "I just need to tie up a few loose ends."

"Do you think she's the one?" said a familiar gruff voice.

Marcy couldn't match a face or name to the voice, but she had heard it somewhere.

"I don't know, and I don't care to find out," said the first voice. "I want her gone. However you can get it done. Soon."

The final word felt like a nail scraping down her spine.

Marcy stacked the last of the linens on the shelves, picked up her basket, kicked the doorstop, and sidestepped as the door closed on its own. She started back to the laundry room with a calm face, as if she hadn't heard a thing.

She turned the corner and passed Knight Commander Fowler, his face twisted in disgust.

Recognition spiked in her chest. He had been one of the voices.

Their eyes met, and she at once lowered her gaze. She felt his hateful stare, but she continued on her way. Head down, mouth a flat line—just as she had been taught to do—despite how her insides squirmed, how her heart pounded, how blood rushed through her ears.

Someone was planning something bad for someone else, and that someone had told Fowler to get rid of her—whoever *her* was.

Knight Commander Fowler passed without a word.

Marcy straightened her shoulders. What did she have to worry about? It wasn't any of her business. Court nonsense and political backstabbing. She adjusted her grip on the empty basket and turned the corner—and nearly walked into Ron Hendle. Startled, she dropped the basket.

"Oh! I am dreadfully sorry, sir," Marcy said quickly. She bowed, though she didn't have to for advisors. Still, better to be respectful than rude.

Ron gave her a kind smile and picked up the basket. He handed it back to her. "No worries, miss. I wasn't minding my own feet. Too many thoughts."

Clutching the basket to her chest, Marcy stepped out of his way. Ron had always been a nice young man, smart and good with words. The older servants said he would make a fitting husband for a lucky girl someday.

In the moment of hesitation before he continued his way, she thought about telling him what she heard, but thought better of it. No one liked a meddlesome servant, and tattling would only get her into trouble. She had heard enough horror stories of meddlesome servants; they never met good ends.

So she hugged the basket and continued to the laundry.

CHAPTER 7

Ison Rolin stood by the window overlooking the canal. The murky water rushed below. Ison's reflection ghosted in the glass—a skinny boy with pale, ashy skin and curly brown hair. Behind his own reflection stood the others. They gathered around the library table, talking over a map held flat by golden sparrow bookends. Amery—a guild sister to Juniper—had been among those who escaped the Undercity's infiltration by the City Watch, and she had opened her manor to others. Ison and his small team of rebels had commandeered the library as their base of operations against Nexon.

According to Xavier, Amery had bought the house unfurnished. The mages had managed to bring almost every single book from the Undercity guild hall; those books packed Amery's library, filling every shelf, stacking in the corners, and filling up the few reading nooks.

Amery's library now smelled like old books and candle wax. It reminded him of the Marca with its towering bookshelves, ancient stonework, and subtle sound of whispers. Ison had spent the majority of the two months tucked between the shelves, reading by magelight and sleeping on a bedroll under the window.

The initial panic of their return had settled, and for the past week, Ison's attention had been drifting out the window. To the little town that had once been his home. Was it even still there? Did his parents remember him?

He had an older brother, Idel, who had written to him every week, then every month, and then eventually not at all. What had become of him? He would be...twenty-two. He might be married. Ison might be an uncle without knowing it. And he might never find out either.

Bois sighed, and Ison glanced over his shoulder.

Xavier, Bois, and Silas—an older earth mage from the Dual Fangs—stood around a map of Duvane and Collatia. A dozen other maps, some stolen, some from the Undercity, and some hand-drawn, were rolled up in a basket beside the table.

They had been planning and planning. If they were going to infiltrate Nexon's camp at Baxion, they needed a plan.

The first step—where the hell Baxion was—had been solved by Silas. He had been there once with a small group of apostates. It had been forty years ago, but he had a sharp memory. According to Silas, Baxion was a settlement in the far north of Collatia, not connected to any other village or town by road, and run exclusively by mages—namely Nexon's followers.

Silas wouldn't be making the journey east with them. He had lost his leg to Mage's Bane; he walked with a wooden prosthetic and a cane. It bothered him too much to walk very far. But Silas had offered invaluable help—they had several routes across the border and a general location. Each route would take time and plenty of supplies, which the mages staying at Amery's had been slowly gathering to avoid suspicion.

Ison hadn't asked how they were gathering supplies. A part of him didn't want to know.

How had his life tumbled into accepting thievery so easily?

Necessity, his mind answered. They had to be quiet about their operation. They did not want Nexon or his spies to catch wind of it. If Nexon knew mages planned to enter his camp, he would alert his followers. Their plan would be ruined before it started.

"I can't tell you what to expect once you get there," Silas said. His watery eyes ran along the lines he'd drawn on the map. Each went east of Rusdasin, then north, then east into Collatia. "Just stay north of the Wylds." He pointed to the dark splotch on the map near the middle of Collatia. "Gods only know what unholy beasts you'll meet if you stray too close. Even Nexon's followers keep their distance."

The Blackwood Wylds were the location of the final battle of the Iluvin War, where the archmages had rebelled against Nexon and defeated him. The expenditure of magic had tainted the earth, turning it into a nightmarish land.

"It won't be a fun adventure," Xavier said, his cold voice teeming with sarcasm. His blue-gray eyes scanned the routes, calculating. His eyes were in sharp contrast to his dark brown skin. Ison looked away before Xavier could catch him looking.

"Most adventures aren't adventures until they're over," said Silas, his voice a sigh of experience. He straightened, hand on his back and groan in his throat. "I've told you all I remember."

"You've helped more than we could have hoped for," Ison said.

Xavier's blue-gray eyes flashed from the map to Ison. He felt Xavier's stare tingle along his skin. Ison glanced at the map, pretending not to have noticed.

"We would have been wandering through the forest for weeks had it not been for your guidance," Bois said in her sweet, girlish voice. Her cloudy eyes weren't looking at the map; she was blind. She used her air magic to sense the world around her. Though she couldn't see the map like Ison could, her magic felt the lines of ink, the small indentation left behind.

"She's right," Xavier said, his voice dry. "And I'd rather not piss in the woods any more than I have to."

Ison snorted a laugh—that had been his biggest complaint from his journey to the edge of the realm. He had hated the feeling of vulnerability that came when one dropped their pants in the woods.

"That's it for today." Ison dismissed them.

Bois and Silas left, leaving Ison and Xavier in the library. As the door closed behind Bois, Ison felt the faint sizzle of her magic go with her.

Xavier flexed his shoulders and leaned into the table, palms flat against the edge of the map. He scanned the possible routes again. When Ison had told them of his mad plan to sneak into Nexon's camp and tear it apart from the inside, Xavier was the first to volunteer. He hadn't even hinted that he might not go or that he regretted his decision.

His steadfastness bothered Ison, but it also…made him feel something else, something he couldn't identify.

"There is a real chance we won't make it out," Ison reminded him.

"I'm aware."

"We might not even get to Baxion," Ison said, thinking of the problems in the forest, bandits and animals and the elements.

"I'm aware." Xavier looked up. His cool eyes met Ison's—a glimpse of the assassin underneath. "Are you trying to convince me to let you go off into the woods by yourself?"

"No, I…"

"You're not a fighter, Ison," Xavier said flatly. "You'll need someone to watch your back."

Ison didn't argue; he knew. He had done little fighting on the squires' quest. Juniper had done most of it. Ison had fought to protect himself from apostates, but the guilt of taking those lives still bothered him. Those apostates had tried to kill him, he continued to reason, and if he hadn't fought back, he and Reid would be dead.

Ison shut his eyes and rubbed his face. All the planning and brooding had kept him up at night. He kept going over all the things that might go wrong, all the ways he might get them all killed, and the persistent feeling of guilt kept kicking him in the chest.

When he opened his eyes, Xavier stood in front of him. Ison swallowed; he hadn't even heard him move—the deadly silence of a trained assassin.

And…it was just them. Ison felt it—that silence. Like he should say something. About *them*.

But the words wouldn't come.

"Would you rather me not go?" Xavier asked, subtle emphasis on *me*.

Ison blinked. "No, no, it's not that," he said.

Xavier's eyes flinched slightly.

"I..." Ison didn't even know how to start.

"You what?" Xavier asked, his voice strong.

Ison swallowed. "I don't know how this is supposed to work."

Xavier didn't waver.

"I'm afraid you'll expect things of me that I'm incapable of giving. I'm afraid I'll ruin everything."

Xavier remained steady. His blue-gray eyes betrayed no emotion. "I won't push you," Xavier said, his voice low. "I'm aware of how horrible relationships are. It's just something to be used against you." Xavier's eyes narrowed, the slightest betrayal of what churned underneath. "As much as I tried not to have feelings for anyone, for you, I have them. I can't shake them; I've tried. And I would rather the bandits, bears, and mosscats *not* kill you on your way to topple an ancient tyrant mage."

"I appreciate that," Ison said. "Given my lack of fighting skill, it will be nice to know you have my back."

Xavier offered a sly smile. He didn't wear his usual assortment of daggers and throwing knives and hadn't since he started sharpening his magic. As if sensing Ison's thoughts, he summoned a dagger of his energy magic—the shadowy grays and blacks woven tightly together, a blade cleaner than steel.

Ison eyed the dagger. "Yes, I will feel safer with you guarding my back."

He already did.

CHAPTER 8

Juniper returned to the dorm fresh from her morning bath to find the girls chittering with excitement. Their high-pitched squeals pinged the anxiety her bath had washed away.

"Did I miss something?" Juniper asked Abrielle, who sat cross-legged on her bed, twisting her thick hair into braids. Her hands moved remarkably fast.

"News from the city has reached us late yet again," Abrielle said with a romantic sigh. "Prince Adrian and Lady Derean announced their engagement. One of the pledges told us this morning."

Something warm albeit slippery blossomed in Juniper's chest and spread like lightning through her limbs. Roslyn and Adrian were engaged. They would be together forever. Lucky them.

Something ugly and cold clawed underneath the warmth.

"Can you imagine?" Abrielle's eyes were full of wonder. "A royal wedding!"

Juniper dressed in fresh robes and crossed the room to toss her dirty robes into the hamper. Juniper ignored the stares of the other girls; she held herself tall and proud. She returned to her bed and worked a comb through her hair. She couldn't dry it by magic with everyone around. They'd know, and someone would tattle.

These eleven weeks in the Marca had felt like a lifetime. She couldn't imagine what five years would do to a person, or ten, or twenty. She would surely go mad.

"You traveled with Lady Derean," Abrielle whispered. She sat on Juniper's bed.

Ida, the shy girl who slept on Juniper's other side, turned her head to listen.

"I did," Juniper said.

"How is she?" Abrielle asked.

"I can confirm that Roslyn is as amazing and beautiful and smart as everyone claims her to be," Juniper said. Abrielle's eyes widened. "She will be a good queen."

The girl on the other side of Ida muttered, "That's why she gets special treatment."

Juniper met the eyes of the girl—she had a common name, but Juniper couldn't remember it and didn't make an effort to—for a short second, fear replaced the girl's spite. Juniper held her stare, watching that fear churn.

Abrielle looked between them, her own fear rising.

"She knows Jun used to kill people for money, right?" whispered Mabyl to the girl beside her, loud enough for the entire dorm to hear.

The girl swallowed. Dark rumors of Juniper Thimble had circulated like fire; Mabyl had seen to that. She had taken to telling stories of Juniper's few assassinations, inflating them with danger and villainy.

The dorm fell silent. Juniper held in what she could have said, what she could have done. A part of her wanted to throw an ice arrow through the stupid girl's shoulder, but she didn't.

The old Juniper might have.

But now Juniper had Reid and Henry to think about. She didn't want to get them into trouble because she couldn't handle herself. She could hold her tongue and her magic. She could bottle up her spite, bitterness, and anger.

She could endure.

The days slugged on, and Juniper sat in Water class. The lesson centered on cleaning water. Juniper tried to pay attention, but her thoughts drifted outside the Marca, to the mysterious escape tunnel somewhere under her feet. Not that she would go looking for it—she loved the story behind it.

"Juniper?" snapped Professor Klamm.

Her attention returned. Klamm scowled, irritation twisting his aged features. Juniper didn't bother to look innocent. She'd been reprimanded for daydreaming by all her teachers, and she had long stopped feeling shame for it.

Klamm bristled at Juniper's indifferent stare. "Since you are inclined not to pay attention, please come to the front and demonstrate the proper way to clean water."

A few chuckles came from the other side of the room, where those who didn't care for her sat. Juniper strolled to the front of the class, to the fishbowl of dirty water on the teacher's desk. She flexed her hand over the water— hesitating solely to further irritate the teacher—and then brought a clear ribbon of water from the dirty bowl and deposited it into the second bowl.

She used unnatural magic—Mabyl and Abrielle had been tutoring her. They took turns tutoring her in the library—so much dust to practice on! She had gotten better at using unnatural magic, but it felt like seeing through one eye or writing with her left hand.

Klamm frowned. He bent over the second bowl and hovered his hand above the water, trying to find imperfection within her work. After several minutes, he straightened.

"Excellent work," he said through gritted teeth. "I supposed that trick came in handy when you were wandering through the woods."

"It did."

"You may sit," he said sharply.

Juniper returned to her seat with a smug grin. Abrielle's eyes were wide, but she wore a small smile.

They were divided into groups of four, each with a bowl of dirty water. They took turns trying to clean the water, but none could do it as quickly or efficiently as Juniper. As they worked, no more chuckles came from the other side of the class. Juniper was whispering guidance to a younger mage in her group—who was doing much better under her teaching than Klamm's—when a knock landed on the classroom door. The young mage jumped, and the fragile ribbon of clean water splashed back into the bowl.

"What is it?" Klamm stomped to the door and yanked it open.

A terrified young mage stood on the other side. He wore the sash denoting him as one of the overseer's helpers.

"Well? What's worth interrupting my class?"

"Sorry," he stuttered, "but there's a knight here to see Juniper. 'At once,' he said."

The silence in the classroom turned cold. Klamm glared at Juniper, as if she had personally kicked him in the shins and brought punishment to them all. No one laughed. Juniper's heart skipped a beat. She thought she had done well to evade the knights' notice.

"Go on, then," Klamm said to Juniper. "Your presence is required elsewhere."

Everyone watched Juniper walk across the classroom to the door. She resisted the urge to grab fistfuls of her robes. What would a knight want with her? She had followed all the rules!

Juniper held her head high as she walked into the corridor. She spotted the immaculate silver armor at once. The knight stood down the corridor with his back to her, looking through one of the narrow windows. The young mage gave her a worrisome look, then started in the opposite direction.

And she was alone with a knight.

She gathered her courage and felt for her magic. Not that it would do any good against Mage's Bane. She started toward the knight and stopped several steps from him. "You called for me, sir?"

The knight turned at her voice. His honey-brown eyes met hers, and the knot in her stomach unraveled.

"Reid?" she gasped.

CHAPTER 9

Juniper blinked several times. The wintry sunlight streaming through the window warmed his bronze skin and highlighted his short chestnut hair in shades of gold. The sunlight reflected off his silver armor, flickering across the owl and chain on his breastplate.

"Sir Sandpiper," he corrected. He took a controlled, graceful step toward her.

"Sir Sandpiper," she repeated.

The words felt like warm honey on her tongue. Reid had always wanted to be a knight, and now he was. She bowed her head and gripped the edges of an invisible skirt in a curtsy.

Straightening, she said, "Forgive me, Sir Sandpiper, but aren't guests supposed to wait in the receiving room?"

That had been one of the countless rules—no guests beyond the lobby. Lest they learn the dangerous secrets of the Marca, whatever the hell the hag thought those were.

Reid shrugged. "I might have pulled some strings."

She looked him up and down. He looked good in his new armor, though he had looked good in his old armor too. It accentuated his broad shoulders and chest, his muscular build and physical strength.

"It suits you," she said. "I daresay you looked dashing. Are you about to set off on some adventure and sweep an unsuspecting maiden off her feet?"

The corners of his lips twitched upward. "I was hoping for a princess," he whispered.

Her heart thudded hard against her ribs, and she felt the color drain from her face.

Reid's brows rose at her sudden silence.

"Or, I suppose maybe-princess," she whispered, less confident than before.

His expression softened, and he opened his arms. Juniper fell into his embrace. Though he wore armor, she had nowhere else she would rather be. She rested her forehead against the owl on his chest; the ridges of the emblem pressed into her skin. His arms settled around her, gentle but strong.

Reid stepped away and offered her his arm. "Come, walk with me."

She slid her arm through his, and he led her down the corridor.

"I'm sorry I missed the knighting ceremony," Juniper said. "Isaac told me about it."

"It's all right," Reid said. "It wasn't nearly as exciting as I imagined. I recited oaths and age-old vows of loyalty and honesty. There were no trumpets or doves or shouting fans."

"Did you expect there to be?"

"They were part of my childish dream of it," Reid admitted with a smile. That smile faded. "I've spent the time since going to meetings, getting fitted for this new armor, doing menial things around the city—ceremonial things, like greeting lords and public officials. I received my Mage's Bane sword this morning, completing the odious affair."

Reid put his free hand on the new blade at his side, a scabbard such a dark blue it appeared black, with a golden hilt and smooth pommel. It gave her a chill to be so close.

"I'm not supposed to tell anyone," Reid whispered. "But each Mage's Bane sword is folded with a drop of the knight's blood. It seals the sword to the knight and makes it hard to use the sword without the knight's permission. It is my sword, and when I die, I will be buried with it."

"I'd rather not talk about you being dead and buried." Juniper squeezed his hand.

"I apologize for missing your birthday," Reid whispered. "I intended to come by that evening, but Fowler had me visiting a lord on the other side of the city."

"You didn't miss anything. I read and then went to bed early," Juniper said dismissively.

"Did you read anything exciting?"

Juniper blinked at the odd question. "No, it was an adventure novel from the library. I've read it twice since I've been here."

Reid's brow furrowed. "Did you..." He chewed on his words. "Did you get my package?"

"What package?"

"The package I sent to you for your birthday," Reid said. His gaze darkened, and his words dipped into a calm, cold anger.

Her heart leaped. Reid had sent her something. Or he had tried. "It must have gotten lost. Thieves watch the mail. It would be easy to snatch a package from a doorstep or from a distracted courier's cart."

Reid's grumble made it clear he didn't think so.

"What was in it?"

"It was supposed to be a surprise." Reid sighed through his nose. "It was a book Roslyn picked out for you, and a box of chocolates."

"Sounds delightful."

Reid tugged her inside a curtained alcove. The heavy purple drapes offered privacy from anyone in the corridor. Reid set his hands on her shoulders. His molten eyes searched hers. "You're unhappy," he said.

"I'm fine," she said too quickly.

His stare narrowed as he looked her up and down. "You've lost weight."

Had she? It was hard to tell in the robes. "The food isn't very good."

"You're pale."

"There aren't a lot of windows."

He cupped her cheek and ran his thumb underneath her eye. "You look like you haven't slept in a week."

"The beds aren't very comfortable, and the girl next to me snores like a bear."

Reid did not relent his stare. She stared back at him for a long moment and then sighed. He had always been observant. She glanced into the corridor to make sure no one listened—Reid noticed.

"It's not that bad," she whispered. "I've made a few friends, but..."

"But what?"

"There are those who think I'm getting special treatment," she whispered so low, she didn't know if she'd actually spoken at all. "They think I should've been killed. They don't like me and don't bother to pretend otherwise. And the knights are always watching me, waiting for a reason to punish me, and..."

And she was unhappy.

Reid leaned in closer. "And...what? Juniper?"

She tried to swallow, but it felt like something had gotten stuck in her throat. "And...seeing you living your dream, achieving what you always wanted...and hearing about Adrian and Roslyn... It makes me happy beyond reason and furiously jealous."

Bitterness settled into the pitiful happiness Reid's visit had stirred. His dream had come at her expense. If she hadn't helped them on their quest, they might not have made it. If she ran now, they would be sent somewhere horrible and likely killed.

Reid started to say something, but she interrupted. She pressed her hand against his chest, over the owl and chain. "But *you* are happy. And that makes me happy. I'm glad you came." She tried to give him a smile, to show that she was happy, even if she wasn't. "I've been left to wonder about you."

Reid studied her face, his own masked. "I also came for another reason," he said, his tone professional and curt. He removed his hands from her shoulders and held them at his side, one resting on his pommel. "His Royal Highness, Prince Adrian, has requested your presence at the castle. I have come to escort you."

Because mages were not allowed outside the Marca without knight supervision. Despite that, Juniper's heart jumped at the thought of going outside, of doing something other than classes and cleaning and trying to ignore the snide comments all around her.

"Really?" she whispered.

"I've already spoken with Overseer Margret," Reid said. "She wasn't happy about it, but I told her she was free to query Prince Adrian about it. You have her permission and the rest of the day off."

Juniper had never heard such sweet words. She beamed—a smile both genuine and unmistakable. A smile reflected on Reid, though she didn't know it was one inspired by her own. "When do we leave?"

Reid turned on his heels, shoulders straight, chin high, and offered her his arm. "This very moment, my lady. The coach is waiting at the gates."

She slid her arm through his. "Lead the way, Sir Sandpiper."

They started down the corridor, and a sliver of happiness threaded through her bitterness. How long had it been since she'd felt happy?

CHAPTER 10

Juniper took her first breath of fresh air in months and relished it. The crisp air kissed her face, her throat, her magic. It smelled of melting snow and muddy slush, of spring. She held it until her lungs ached. Then she took another. Slivers of a pale blue sky came and went on the other side of the wispy gray clouds. The chaotic clattering of the city had never sounded so inviting.

Not just any coach awaited Juniper—a royal coach of green and gold waited by the gates. The royal seal—a curved double-headed ax—gleamed on the side.

Juniper wanted to look back at the Marca to see if anyone was watching. Word would spread quickly—Juniper Thimble had been escorted to a royal coach by a knight! But as she climbed into the plush interior of pine and buttoned velvet, she decided not to care. The coach pulled through the silent Marca gates, and she felt an elation she didn't know could exist. Relief, she realized.

Reid sat beside her, and on the ride to the castle, she told him about her new friends and her lessons. She left out her enemies and the spiteful stories. Better that he didn't worry.

The gates of Castle Bradburn appeared, and something in her chest loosened at the sight of the iron masterpiece. The castle loomed. Its battlements and towers had never been so welcoming. Strange, how the castle she had once considered a prison now gave her a sense of deep comfort.

"Reid," Juniper asked as they passed through the gates, "Have you heard anything from the king about sending us to Collatia?"

"I haven't," Reid answered. "I've not seen him since the ceremony. Adrian tells me he's been busier than usual. The City Watch isn't sure what to do with the Undercity now that they have it."

Juniper chuckled, though she didn't miss the change of subject. She thought about prodding him for more information but didn't. "What do you mean they don't know what to do with it? It's prime real estate!"

"No sunlight, barely any running water, and more bloodstains than a healer's table," Reid added.

"Have you been there?"

"I have. A few weeks ago." Reid shook his head. "It was a horrid place. Impossible dark, and everywhere I went, it felt like someone was watching. I can't believe you actually lived there."

"The magelights would have gone out when the mages left," Juniper said. She hadn't thought of that—magelights had given the Undercity a constant source of clean light and had been enchanted to reflect the daylight above ground. "And it wasn't all bad. It was lawless and dirty, but it had a certain charm." Unlike the Marca with its laws and rules and *obeying*.

"Compared to your current living arrangements?"

"Paradise," she said before she could stop herself.

Reid's brows furrowed.

"What? I could go where I wanted, wake up when I wanted, and if anyone glared at me, I'd punch them." She flushed as the truth came out. "I was in charge of myself, and I took care of myself. I...I was in control."

Reid brushed hair behind her ear. "I'll talk to the king when I can. He's working on it, but he's been meeting...opposition...within the Order. Fowler is upset that you slipped through the justice he thinks you deserve."

Juniper let out a harsh, bitter laugh. "Because he wants me dead."

"Fowler is devoted to the Order," Reid said, his words carefully chosen.

A beat of silence—the coach came to a stop by the front steps.

"Have you heard from Ison?" she whispered.

Reid shook his head.

The footman opened the door. Juniper said no more.

Reid exited the coach first and offered her his hand. She accepted, and Reid escorted her through the front doors and into the vestibule of familiar gray stone. She had missed the grand tapestries, grim portraits, ancient suits of armor, and the sounds of crackling torches and distant whispers. The castle smelled of torch smoke and linseed oil, and she took a deep breath of it. Reid led her into a wide corridor with matching tapestries of red and gold, both marvelous displays of Bradburn's double-sided ax.

Quick-footed silent servants bustled between corridors, carrying trays of tea, baskets of linen, rags and tins of polish, and feather dusters. Juniper took it all in, every sound and smell. If she closed her eyes, she could imagine herself as Adrian's royal protector once again, being escorted through the corridors by her dutiful guardian, Squire Sandpiper.

Reid paused in front of polished wooden doors. It took a moment for Juniper to realize where they had gone—Reid's chambers.

"Doesn't being a knight get you a grand suite somewhere?" Juniper asked.

"It does not," Reid said. "When we are in the city, unless we have family to stay with, we stay in the Order's boardrooms."

"Those sound..."

"Like tiny rooms with a narrow bed and no window?"

"…that would be a downgrade from your current situation." And an upgrade from hers.

Nodding, he opened the doors to his chambers.

Reid had lived in the castle most of his life. Before having his own chambers, he had lived with his uncle, Captain Sandpiper of the Royal Guard. Reid's chambers were simple and modestly decorated. The doors opened into a sitting room, which led into the bedroom, which had an adjoining closet and bathing room. His chambers smelled like him, like leather, armor polish, and that woodsy scent. The burning hearth banished the winter chill.

Juniper strolled into Reid's bedroom and collapsed onto his four-poster bed. Gods, it made her bed back at the Marca feel like stone.

"Making yourself at home?" Reid asked.

Juniper rolled onto her stomach and covered her face with his pillow. "It smells like you," she said, muffled by the pillow.

"What was that?"

She turned her head toward him. He stood at the bedside, looking at her. "I said it smells like you."

His expression softened. He hadn't expected that. He swallowed, then walked to the other side of the bedroom, to his empty armor stand. He unbuckled his sword belt and set it on his dresser. He then began to unbuckle and untie his silver armor. Juniper angled her body to see him better. He removed his armor and the padded clothes underneath it a piece at a time, methodically revealing the strong muscles hidden underneath—a body trained for combat—and placed his armor on the stand. He changed into a simple black shirt and gray trousers.

Finished, he turned. He caught her stare, and the faintest blush came to his cheeks. She rolled onto one side of the bed and patted the other. Reid joined her, reclining into the pillows. A sigh left his lips.

"Did Adrian really send for me?" Juniper asked. Her cheeks burned as she added, "Or did you just want me in your bed?"

"Adrian sent for you," Reid said. "He invited you to dinner. Dinner isn't for a while, and I would be lying if I said I hadn't thought about you in my bed."

Those words heated her insides into molten metal. A grin spread across her face, and her mild blush turned bright. "Whatever should we do while we wait?"

Reid turned his head toward her, his eyes questioning and filled with cautious desire. She tentatively touched her fingertips along his temple and traced a line across his brow, his nose, his lips. He kissed her fingers, and a feverish warmth zapped through her body, her blood—burning. She pulled her fingers away and replaced them with her lips; she kissed him deeply.

His hand messed in her hair, her robes. Their joining lacked the passion of that night in the cave, but she attributed it to her exhaustion and coiled sense of dread.

Afterward, Juniper relaxed in his arms. The warmth of his body soaked into hers. Her cheek rested against his bare chest, listening to the gentle thumping of his heart. One of his hands held hers, and the other played with her hair. The hearth bathed his body in golden light, gilding his hair and turning his eyes to liquid gold.

She should ask what he thought about *them*, what he thought *they* were, but she feared those prodding questions would ruin the peace she had found. She didn't want anything coming between them again. She wanted what they had, whatever it was.

Instead, she said, "I've been making a list." Her breath bounced off his chest and came back to her lips.

"A list?"

"Of things I want to try."

Reid adjusted to look at her.

"In the bedroom," she added. Her face warmed. "I've learned things in the Marca."

His brow furrowed. "You've learned things? Were these things learned firsthand?" His voice held more than a little jealousy.

"No," she said. "But mages talk, you know."

Reid searched her face. He didn't answer for a moment. His thumb ran along her hip bone. Then, he said with a slight smile, "You did prefer those smutty mage books."

Her blush deepened. "Reading and doing are very different things."

"Are they?"

"Yes," she said firmly. "Most of what I've learned has come from Mabyl. She is very open about her...trysts. I haven't... Not since that night with you."

Silence stretched between them. Reid held her gaze, his own unreadable. It made her stomach turn over and turn back again.

"Is that so?" he whispered. He traced his fingers around her face, brushing hair behind her ear.

She nodded, her face warming with every breath. "The list isn't very long."

"Is this list a secret?"

She whispered a few of those things into his ear.

Reid's hand twitched on her hip. "We'll have to check a few of those off," Reid said. He kissed her. "But it will have to be later. We don't want to keep His Highness waiting."

Nightmares in the Ice

Reluctantly, she agreed. They cleaned up in the bathing room because she'd rather not meet with Adrian while smelling feral.

CHAPTER 11

Juniper held Reid's arm as he led the way to one of the castle's many parlors. The floor-to-ceiling windows on the northern wall offered a marvelous view of the royal grounds. The trees wore the reddish tint of early spring, and the dirt had turned to mud from the melting winter. The hearth burned, filling the parlor with glorious heat and the comforting scent of woodsmoke and embers. Adrian and Roslyn were already seated at a table arranged in the center of the parlor. Their joined hands rested on the table between them; the ring on Roslyn's left hand caught the late afternoon sunlight. The future queen looked like a dream in red silk. Her black hair was twisted into a braided crown and held in place with pearl-tipped pins, and her olive skin had soaked in enough Rusdasin sunlight to give her a warm glow.

As Juniper and Reid approached, Roslyn's gaze drifted from Adrian. Her entire face brightened.

"Juniper!" Roslyn jumped from the table and threw her arms around Juniper. "Gods, it's good to see you again." Roslyn pulled back, holding her at arm's length. Her smile turned downward, and her brows came together. "You've lost weight. Are they not feeding you enough? I'm sure we can sneak snacks in somehow."

"It's the stress and piss-poor food options," Juniper said. From the corner of her eye, she saw Reid's frown deepen.

Adrian stood and put his hand on Roslyn's shoulder, gently nudged her out of the way, and embraced Juniper.

"It is good to see you again," Adrian said, though his voice lacked its usual luster.

They parted, and Juniper took a better look at the prince. She hadn't seen him since before she and Ison had fled the castle—it felt like ages. Adrian looked thinner, and his creamy skin had paled considerably. His tousled blond hair had grown out, and his hazel eyes beheld her with familiar quizzical friendliness. Adrian remained a handsome young man, one of the few whose external beauty mirrored the internal.

"You're looking well," Juniper said.

Adrian offered her a pale version of his charming smile. "I look better than I did a few weeks ago."

"And much better than when I first saw him," Roslyn added. "Now, sit down and eat something. Both of you need to put meat back on your bones."

Over dinner, they talked. Roslyn was adjusting to the city; she and Her Majesty, Queen Catherine, had been hard at work replacing the wardrobe Roslyn had left behind in Galamond. The royal seamstress was thrilled about it. Roslyn already had a ridiculous number of dresses in an array of ridiculous styles. The thick woolen tunic and fur-lined cloak she'd worn on the journey south wouldn't do for a queen, the seamstress had said.

Adrian had healed well, though his stomach remained finicky. While they ate roasted chicken and sautéed vegetables, Adrian ate plain rice, fruit, and herbal tea.

Juniper answered their questions about the Marca without revealing too much or implying her disdain. She couldn't complain with Roslyn and Adrian exuding such happiness. All the while, Reid remained quiet. He looked almost uncomfortable. Did he regret bringing her? Did he already regret what had happened in his bedroom?

Servants cleared the finished meal and brought a carafe of warm spiced wine. A strange tension silenced their conversation as the servant poured three glasses of steaming wine—Adrian continued to drink herbal tea. Juniper sipped her wine loudly. They weren't allowed much wine in the Marca, and she savored the warmth and spices on her tongue.

Roslyn cleared her throat and tipped her wine to Reid. "Now would be a good time," she said, eyes bright as stars.

Juniper glanced at Reid. He looked as though he'd swallowed something slimy. He drank a gulp of wine and set the glass on the table.

"Reid?" Juniper asked.

"I have news," Reid said, eyes on the wine glass. "Fowler has assigned me to Chata. There have been more uprisings between rebel apostates and Duvane's army."

Juniper's next breath evaporated. Chata. The city was on the northeastern border between Collatia and Duvane. She waited for the part where Reid would tell her how the king forbade Fowler from sending him so far away and to such a dangerous city, but Reid remained silent.

A rock hit the bottom of her stomach, broke through, and tumbled into her ankles.

Hadn't she followed all the rules? Why were they sending him to Chata? If he went, he might not return. He would be gone for months, maybe years, or forever. Something might happen to him, or something might happen to her. She might never see him again.

No. It wasn't fair. The king said he would send them to Collatia! He said he would get her out of the Marca. She and Reid were supposed to go to Collatia together.

Reid was leaving her. A sickening, twisting feeling worked its way up her ankles and into her arms. The cave, his bedroom—another lie. She tore her gaze away from Reid and looked instead into her wine. She could feel Adrian and Roslyn both looking at her, judging her reaction.

"Juniper," Reid started.

"How long?" she demanded.

Reid didn't answer. She pulled her gaze from the wine and forced herself to look at him. His honey-brown eyes held worry, fear, and something else.

He'd known about this.

"How long will you be gone?" she asked.

"Until I am assigned elsewhere or relieved from duty," he said grimly.

Her hands shook. Her gut trembled. She felt like throwing her glass across the parlor and shattering it into a million pieces. She felt like throwing it at Reid for leading her on.

She dared not look up at Adrian and Roslyn, not when they had each day to spend together. They wouldn't understand the pain she felt at Reid's words, his departure, the inevitable misery she would feel in his absence.

She hadn't gotten him back at all. It had been a mean game of fate.

"Jun," he started, his voice softer.

She couldn't fathom a response. Tears pushed against her eyes, from rage and sadness. She blinked, wetting her lashes. A sob threatened to shake her chest, and she fought it. Not here, not in front of her friends.

Why did the world insist on her misery?

Reid knelt beside her, silent without his armor. His Mage's Bane sword grazed the rug.

"Don't," she begged. *Don't make it worse.*

She would be left in the Marca without him, without the man she had exposed her magic for, the man she had gone to the end of the world with, the man she endured the Marca for, the man she was supposed to go Collatia with.

"Jun," Reid repeated, his tone softer still but nervous. "Look at me, please."

Her chest squeezed, but she forced her watery eyes to his. She fought hard to keep the tears from spilling.

"You know I can't take you with me," he said.

She squeezed her eyes shut to keep the tears inside. It didn't work. One slipped through and drew a warm line down her cheek.

"But..." His voice quivered. "I am allowed to take my wife."

It felt like a giant hand clasped around her lungs, forcing the air out and forbidding any from coming back in. She dared open her eyes. Reid held his closed fist out to her. He unfurled his fingers, and there, resting in his palm, was a beautiful moonstone and silver ring.

"Juniper," Reid breathed, his voice a whisper. He swallowed. The fingers of his hand holding the ring trembled. "Will you marry me?"

A heartbeat passed. His words sank in, his meaning.

Another tear slipped down her cheek, trailing behind the warm line of the first. She swallowed. A heavy silence settled around her, and her heart skipped several beats. She didn't know what to do. She reached for his hand, the one holding the ring, and folded both of hers around it. His hand trembled.

If she married Reid, a knight, she could leave the Marca.

"Is that a yes?" Reid asked.

"Of course it is," she said, her voice scratchy and wet.

Reid released a sigh of relief and slid the moonstone ring onto her finger. Sunlight slipped through the clouds and glinted off the silver, making the moonstone glow. Juniper wiped at her eyes with her sleeve. Roslyn and Adrian wore knowing smiles; they had known about Reid's plan. Juniper choked on her tears, trying to laugh it off. Roslyn squealed in delight.

"It was my mother's," Reid whispered. His grip on her hand tightened. "She gave it to me before she…"

"It's beautiful," Juniper said, stopping him from having to explain; she knew. His parents and brother had been murdered by apostates when he was a boy. The moonstone ring might have been one of the few things he had of his mother's.

"As are you," Reid whispered and kissed her.

"Do you feel better?" Roslyn asked, sipping her wine.

"Gods," Reid said, a laugh on his lips.

"Is this why you've been so nervous?" Juniper asked, gesturing to her hand. Reid nodded.

"I admit, I don't think I would have started with 'I'm leaving you,' but it seemed to work." Roslyn tipped her wine glass toward Juniper. In a loud whisper, she added, "I tried to coach him on what to say."

Reid blushed. Juniper reached for his hand and held it tight. *Wife.* The word thumped with a strange panic and dread she'd never felt before, but she drowned it with thoughts of freedom—she would be leaving the Marca.

Reid would take her with him. Even Chata, with its spats of chaos and bloodshed, had to be better than the Marca.

Still, the word rattled around, echoing. *Wife.*

CHAPTER 12

After dinner, Reid escorted Juniper back through the castle, meandering toward the coach waiting in the front garden. Her panic and dread had transformed into a lighter-than-air feeling tingling from her fingertips to her toes. Husband. *Her* husband. Reid, her *husband*.

And she would be leaving the Marca!

She held onto his hand, fingers laced tight. She would have to let go when he dropped her off at the Marca, but she comforted herself with knowing soon she would never have to let him go.

Juniper glanced down at her moonstone ring as Reid guided them around a corner—the light from the window glinted off the silver—when Reid paused. She looked up to see the young advisor standing before them, looking at them with the sly smile of a calculating courtier.

"Ron," said Reid in greeting.

"Good evening, Reid," said Ron. His eyes moved fast between the two of them.

As his eyes rolled over Juniper, a subtle dislike glowered within them. Juniper recognized it. It was the same glower of defiance when one wanted to fight back but either couldn't or wouldn't. Likely her deplorable presence in the castle had sullied his silk-lined day.

"I hear congratulations are in order," Ron said in a practiced pleasantness. "Your first assignment as a knight. To Chata, no less. Despite the danger, the country is beautiful up there."

"Thank you." Reid tilted his head forward.

Ron shifted his gaze toward Juniper again, and that subtle gleam of dislike became a bitter smile. "It is too bad that you must leave your friends behind."

She bristled at his tone. Disapproval of her dripped off every word.

"Some of them, yes," Reid said, his tone indifferent. "But not Juniper."

Ron's brows rose slightly.

Reid lifted their laced hands so that the moonstone caught the torchlight. Ron's eyes fixed on it, and his smile flattened into a straight line.

"She will be going with me," Reid added. "As my wife."

Ron didn't speak. His eyes focused on the moonstone ring. "Congratulations," he said. He cleared his throat, and a forced complacent smile stretched his thin lips. "Now, if you will excuse me, I've business to attend to."

Ron sidestepped them and marched through the corridor with the pace of an irritated noble. Reid and Juniper started the opposite way.

At the end of the corridor, Juniper whispered, "Well, he's not invited to the wedding."

"He hasn't been the same since the king appointed him advisor," Reid whispered back. "Ron and I have known each other for years, but it seems the power of his position has gone to his head."

She harrumphed. "Not everyone can be as humble as you, love."

Reid smiled, then pulled her into a quick kiss that turned into two, then three. "I'd love to check a few things off that list of yours," he whispered against her lips, "but if I don't have you back to the Marca before full dark, the Order will come looking for you."

She sighed. "I know."

As much as she didn't want to, she had to. Just for a few more nights, until she and Reid went to Chata together.

After stopping by Reid's chambers—so he could don his silver armor—they headed to the front garden. The same sage and gold coach stood waiting. Juniper settled into the buttoned velvet seat and released a heavy sigh as the coach began to move.

"We don't have to go straight to Chata," Reid said. "We could...deliver a message from the king to Delphine first, considering the newly crowned Queen Myrisha. Her coronation was a few days ago. King Bradburn sent scouts, but they have not yet returned."

Scouts—spies. Juniper let that word go and instead asked in a dramatic whisper, "You would defy the Order?"

"Not *defy* the Order," Reid said hesitantly. "But adding something to the mission as requested by His Majesty and unknown by the knight commander."

Juniper grinned. "Now you're thinking like me."

She couldn't tell if Reid liked that or not. He leaned back, looking infinitely more comfortable than he had earlier.

"Fowler is insistent that I go to Chata, of all places," Reid said. "New knights often tour the kingdom first, a sort of pilgrimage. It symbolizes that a knight holds the safety of all the kingdom. I was looking forward to it."

"I wouldn't mind touring the kingdom," Juniper said. She added bitterly, "Fowler seems to be doing his best to keep us apart and miserable. First the Marca and now Chata. He's determined to keep us on opposite ends of the kingdom." She scoffed. "He's also done all he can to keep us from going to Collatia. Do you think he is doing it because that's what the king wants?"

Reid shrugged. "I wouldn't be surprised. Fowler does not like having his authority questioned, even by the king."

If Juniper had her way, she would eliminate Fowler from the picture. He had caused her nothing but problems.

The ride to the Marca ended far too soon. The coach pulled through the Marca's gates and into the stone courtyard. Her good mood tumbled, and dread returned. The thick towers shadowed the courtyard from the fading twilight. The single magelight that hovered above the main doors barely illuminated the stone, giving everything a ghostly glow.

Just as welcoming as the rest of the Marca.

Reid stepped out of the coach first and offered her his hand. She stepped out and immediately felt a thousand pairs of eyes. She fought hard not to look up at the windows.

"I'm sure the Overseer won't be happy about this," Reid said. "Or Fowler, but the law is the law, and they can't argue against it. We will marry before I leave." He added softly, too low for the knights or the driver to hear, "You won't be trapped in here much longer. Think you can hold out?"

Thinking of the day when Reid would take her away from here, she didn't have to pretend to be happy. A smile came over her lips. "I suppose I can occupy my thoughts with wedding plans." She glanced down at the ring. Maybe it was her elation, but the ring seemed to glow even in the shadow.

Reid smiled, but she saw the glint of hesitation.

It punctured her elation.

"We could wait a while," she added. "You know, to make sure everything is in order."

Reid kissed her hand. "We wait only as long as we must. In order for you to go with me to Chata, you must be my wife, not my betrothed," he said. She hesitated a moment too long, and Reid added, "If you are unsure—"

"I'm sure," she added quickly.

Reid escorted Juniper into the Marca's dreary, muffled foyer and the thick scent of metallic unnatural magic. They walked together until they had to part ways, she to her dorm and he to the overseer's office.

"The next we see each other," Reid said, "will be our wedding day."

Juniper's chest fluttered, and a chill crept over her skin. They parted ways, and as she trudged to her dorm, she pictured herself in white and Reid in silver. High society weddings were often odious things of flowers and wine—she had snuck in to several to pick drunken pockets—but in her imagination, she and

Reid married privately in a quiet courtyard, and only their favorite people were invited.

The magelights glinted off the moonstone.

Juniper let herself into the dorm, and at once, a hush fell over the room. Many of the girls had chosen to spend their evening time elsewhere, leaving the dorm mostly empty. Juniper ignored the few girls and their piercing stares and walked into the bathing room. Upon seeing it empty, she released a breath of relief.

Not even a moment had passed when Abrielle tumbled through the door, eyes wide and slightly breathless. She searched Juniper for any sign of distress, and finding none, her panic dissolved into a cautious smile.

"We all heard you were taken away by a knight," Abrielle said. "But you look happy."

Juniper bit her lip and held up her left hand. Abrielle clapped her hands against her mouth. Juniper ran herself a bath and while she soaked, she told her friend the story. Abrielle giggled over the romance.

The next time Juniper saw Reid would be her wedding day—a shiver ran down her spine and into her toes at the thought. However, the feeling of having to leave Abrielle and Mabyl behind in this horrible place dampened those thoughts. If only she could take her new friends with her.

CHAPTER 13

Overseer Margret looked at Reid as if she had never seen him before—her black brows rose nearly to her hair, her lips slackened, and shock erased all other emotion from her eyes. Reid stood for a long, uncomfortable moment under her gaze. She held her quill poised over a letter, and the ink had dripped two angry splotches onto the paper.

"You *what*?" Margret asked.

"Juniper Thimble and I are to wed," Reid repeated. He held himself stoic and proud, like a knight. He was a knight, not a squire, and this woman did not hold power over him.

She inhaled, set her quill back in the holder, and shook her head. "I'm sorry, Sir Sandpiper. Surely, you see how horrible of an idea that is. I simply cannot allow it."

"The matter of allowance is not up for debate," Reid said firmly. "I am informing you. In two days' time, I will return for Juniper Thimble. As my wife, she will travel with me to Chata."

The overseer's lips pursed. She flattened her hands on her desk and stood. "Surely, as a knight, you understand how important the Marca's teachings are. Juniper Thimble is an apostate, and her magic reflects that. You want me to release an apostate capable and willing of black magic out into the world? And to Chata, no less, where the apostates run wild? It is a horrible idea. I suspect Juniper put this thought in your head for the sole purpose of escaping into Collatia to join some apostate commune."

Reid tightened his fist but quickly released it.

The overseer examined the ruined letter and threw it into the bin beside her desk. She met his gaze with one of arrogance, a woman used to leering over the heads of her wards. "Juniper Thimble's best interests are to stay at the Marca."

Reid disagreed. Juniper's best interests were anywhere but the Marca.

"Two days," Reid said. "And I will return for Juniper Thimble. Make sure she is ready to depart."

He left the overseer's office without being dismissed and marched through the Marca and back to the waiting coach. He climbed inside, and not until the coach pulled through the gates and onto the street did he allow himself to relax. He rested against the plush seats.

The nerve of the overseer—she did not hold power over the Order. Suggesting that Juniper had an ulterior motive, that she had planted the idea of marriage in his mind just to join the apostates—preposterous! The apostates causing problems near Chata were likely following Nexon's orders, and Juniper would never join him.

Reid released a long sigh, emptying his irritation and anger along with his lungs.

He had entertained the idea of sliding his mother's moonstone ring onto Juniper's finger since their first night tangled in each other. He'd thought about it even when she refused to look at him. Only when he believed her dead had the idea faded, and then—by the grace of the gods—she careened back into his life. When she had given herself to him in the cave, he couldn't stop thinking about it, about her, about them.

Seeing Adrian and Roslyn together had solidified the worry in his chest, and when he confessed to Roslyn, she wholeheartedly agreed. *Ask her*, she'd said. *You love each other, so the answer is simple.*

As he had ridden to the Marca to fetch her, doubt and fear wormed through his gut and riddled his resolve. Most of his life had centered on becoming a knight, serving the Order, and ridding the world of apostates. He hadn't given much thought to marriage, but he'd always assumed it would be to a noblewoman, a lord's daughter, or someone of societal standing. And...Juniper was the opposite of everything he'd imagined his wife to be.

"Marriage is one of the most serious decisions you will make in your lifetime," Aunt Glenda had once told him. She had been kneading dough, and flour covered her apron and her arms and spotted her face. "You will be opening your life to another. You'll be opening your heart and soul to your spouse. A marriage relies on absolute trust, unconditional love, and compromise."

His aunt had made it sound so dire. Reid had nearly talked himself out of it by the time he arrived at the Marca. Then he saw Juniper, her sunken cheeks and hollow eyes. She needed to get out of the Marca before it killed her, and he wanted to be the one to save her. Mages left the Marca in three ways: conscripted by the king, married to someone with power, or dead. History was littered with mages who had married lords and ladies and knights to escape the Marca. If he married her, he could save her.

The vibrancy and spirit that had returned to Juniper during the evening vanished when they returned to the Marca. Reid knew then. He would be the one to save her. It hurt to leave her, but he combated his dread by knowing she would not be there much longer.

In two days, he would return for her. They would wed. They would leave for Chata together.

And...*marriage.*

The word felt like a stone in his chest, but what else could he do? He couldn't leave Juniper in the Marca, and he couldn't take her with him any other way. The king had tried to conscript her into his service, but Fowler had denied his request at every turn. Fowler argued that she hadn't been in the Marca long enough to tame her wild apostate magic.

Reid released a sigh. He had given her the ring. He had made her a promise, and he would uphold it.

The coach returned to the castle. Night had fallen, leaving the sky streaked with inky clouds and the air humid with the incoming spring. Reid started into the castle and headed toward his uncle's chambers in the barracks. His uncle was the captain of the Royal Guard, and his aunt oversaw the castle servants. Even this late, the barracks buzzed with voices and the clatter of practice swords—the off-duty royal guard.

Standing in front of his uncle's door, his knees trembled more than when he'd proposed. He had known Juniper would likely be happy about the ring. His uncle and aunt would likely not.

Reid inhaled deeply, steadying himself. He knocked.

His uncle opened the door, dressed in a plain housecoat with the royal seal over the breast pocket. He shared Reid's bronze skin and chestnut hair, though where Reid's eyes were brown, his uncle's were green. The same green his father's eyes had been.

"Reid?" said his uncle. "It's late for a visit. Has something happened?"

"Yes, but it's not bad," Reid said.

His uncle examined him for lies. Seeing no obvious injury, he stepped aside.

Reid took careful steps into his uncle's home. His uncle and aunt occupied chambers roughly the same size as a modest townhouse. Reid scanned the first floor for his aunt; he didn't see her.

"Glenda is upstairs." His uncle shut the door quietly.

"I have news," Reid said.

"Chata." His uncle nodded, expression glum. "I heard it from Fowler. He thought it best if he told me himself, the mad fool. I told him it wasn't wise to throw a young knight into danger like that, and he told me to mind my station." His uncle sighed and tucked his hands into his housecoat. "He's slipping. He'll start making worse decisions until someone finally puts him out of his misery. He's turning senile."

"Yes, there's Chata," Reid said, treading lightly. "But there is something else I must tell you before someone else does."

His uncle blinked. It seemed as though no one else had heard the news. Only Adrian, Roslyn, and Ron Hendle knew—maybe the king if Adrian had said something.

"You look grave," said his uncle. "Like you bear bad news."

Reid chuckled nervously, and his uncle's brow furrowed.

"Who has bad news?" came Glenda's voice from the top of the stairs. She wore her flaxen hair tied behind her head. She wore a matching housecoat to her husband, only longer and trimmed with gold lace.

"No one," said Reid, at the same time his uncle said, "Reid does."

Glenda frowned. She started down the stairs. "Well, best tell us in the lounge so I've got something soft to collapse onto and your uncle has something soft to hit."

Reid did not like the sound of either of those but did not argue.

His aunt moved into the lounge first and sat on the chaise. Reid walked to the smoldering hearth. His uncle stood beside the chaise, arms crossed. Reid made sure to stand out of arm's reach of both of them.

"Well?" Glenda leaned back. "Let's hear this bad news of yours."

"It's not bad news," Reid said, earning him two frowns. He huffed a sigh of resignation. "I proposed to Juniper."

Silence. Blank stares.

"She said yes," he added.

"You proposed," his aunt said, drawing out the word. "Proposed...what?"

His uncle's lips had gone tight and pale.

"Marriage," Reid said quietly.

Neither of them moved, blinked, or seemed to breathe for a torturously long moment.

Finally, his aunt set her hand against her temple, sighed deeply, and shook her head. "Bala's breath," she muttered.

"You did *what*?" his uncle asked, his brows nearly to his hair.

"This is a mistake," said his aunt.

"The thief?" said his uncle.

Reid curled his hands into fists at his uncle's hateful tone.

"Can't you see what she's doing?" his uncle said, motioning to Reid. "She is using you as a means to get out of the Marca."

"She didn't ask me," Reid said. "I asked her."

"She's gotten into your mind," his aunt mumbled.

Reid held in what he wanted to say, to shout, to scream at them until they understood. He loved her, and she loved him. He had felt her magic, felt her in ways that he hadn't known he could feel anything.

Finally, his aunt dropped her hand. She looked wearily at Reid. "Are you sure about this?"

"Yes," Reid said without hesitation.

"Do you know what kind of a woman she is?" asked his aunt. "Do you think you've known her long enough to see her true character?"

"She's saved my life on several occasions, putting herself in danger to do so," Reid said. "I am sure."

His uncle looked like he had a thousand reasons why Reid shouldn't marry Juniper, as did his aunt, though neither spoke. Reid stood his ground, waiting for the opposition, ready to battle each reason.

Finally, his aunt stood. She straightened the wrinkles in her housecoat. "It will end badly," she said, meeting Reid's gaze. She spoke pleasantly, though disapproval dripped from each word. "But if this is what your heart is set on, I won't stop you."

Reid's uncle stood still as stone. His stoic gaze betrayed no emotion. "If someone would have told me the king's plan would end with this," said his uncle, "I would have laughed." Yet he did not laugh.

Reid fought the urge to swallow, to wring his hands, but he stood firm. He kept his expression neutral. Like a knight.

"But I cannot allow this," said his uncle. "I cannot grant you our blessing."

His aunt left the lounge without a glance at Reid.

Reid's stomach flip-flopped. "Uncle—"

"No," the captain interrupted. He wore an expression Reid had never seen before—he couldn't begin to decipher it. "I know you can't see it like I do. You are your father's son. He married a girl he barely knew, against everyone's wishes, left us all, and look where that got him."

Reid felt a stone hit the bottom of his stomach.

"Please, Reid, do not repeat your father's mistakes." His uncle left the lounge.

Reid stood for a long moment in front of the simmering hearth. His heart pounded yet skipped every other beat. This had not gone at all like he had hoped. He had expected them to be upset, even mad, but he hadn't anticipated them to deny his marriage.

And he didn't know what to think.

Reid let himself out of their chambers.

Nightmares in the Ice

He would need a drink before bed. Maybe two.

CHAPTER 14

Reid returned to his chambers to find a blond knight standing beside the door. He recognized the knight but couldn't think of his name. The knight beheld Reid blankly, his eyes dull and expressionless. The gaze gave Reid a strange feeling of exposure.

"Sir Sandpiper," said the knight, authority on every word. "Knight Commander Fowler has a task for you."

Reid straightened. "Of course."

"You are to go to the Marca at once," said the knight. His voice mirrored the dullness of his eyes. "They have contained a troublesome mage."

"And Fowler asked for me?" Reid set a hand on his Mage's Bane. The Marca had its own stock of knights for keeping the mages in line and handling the troublesome ones—why bother him?

"Consider this a test," said the knight. "Those were his words. I did not ask for details. Neither should you."

Reid curled his fists at the reprimand. He was no longer a squire; he was a knight, level with this man.

"Then I take my leave," Reid said bitterly.

Those drinks would have to wait a while longer.

Reid turned on his heel and marched toward the front gates. A stable boy fetched him a horse, and as Reid rode through the darkened city streets, dread coiled in his stomach. The feeling only worsened as he approached the Marca. The moon came out from behind the clouds, but not even the moonlight illuminated the dark stone.

A knight met Reid in the foyer, his face expressionless. The magelights had dulled for the night, leaving the corridors gloomy and unsettling. Most of the mages would be sleeping or in their dorms, and the dark, quiet halls gave Reid a horrible pitting feeling.

"Sir Sandpiper," said the knight, his tone flat. "This way."

Reid's feeling of unease worsened as the knight led him to the far side of the Marca's first floor, too close to the execution chamber for his liking. Visiting that horrible room had been one of the things he had done as a pledge for the Order—one of the ways to weed out the weak stomachs and poor constitutions from the strong-willed.

And to Reid's dismay, it was to the execution chamber the knight led him. The chamber was tucked into the back of the Marca, near the quiet rooms and warded cells. Mages were not allowed in the corridor—grimly named Execution Hall—and it was guarded by heavy doors and several knights. The execution room itself held a single iron door.

A knight stood on either side.

Reid's unease turned into nausea. A task for him. He set his hand on his pommel of his Mage's Bane. Fowler couldn't mean for him to kill a mage. Executions were carried out by older knights, not fresh knights like him.

But if this was his task... Reid steadied himself and hardened his will. He schooled his face into neutrality. A knight had a will of steel—he must have a will of steel.

A knight opened the iron door, its hinges silent as the gates. Reid held himself tall and followed the knight inside.

It was a circular room made of the same dark stone. A single magelight hung near the ceiling, casting an unforgiving white light upon the room. Blood stained the gray stone, and fresh blood ran along the grout toward the rusty drain.

Reid saw the room, the bloodstains, the stone-faced knights, but it was the mage in the center of the room that made his heart stutter and pause.

Juniper. Naked to the waist, her robes ripped and bloodied, her hands tied to the posts. Her auburn hair had fallen from its braid. Her breaths came raspy and shallow. They had whipped her. A knight stood behind her, the whip still in his hand, the tip bloodied.

Reid felt the floor shift beneath his feet. Rage burned through his bones. The calm demeanor of the knights churned his rage hotter still, until he thought it might turn his skin to ashes.

"What is the meaning of this?" Reid demanded.

"This mage attacked a knight," said the knight holding the whip, his voice dull and lifeless.

Reid met the knight's eyes. He wore the same faraway expression as the knight who had fetched him. All of them in the chamber looked the same.

Fowler had sent him on this task?

"This mage summoned the demons," said another knight. "She tried to kill the prince. She attacked a knight. She confessed to it all."

Reid balked at the claim, not hiding his anger any longer. "That is absurd! This mage is under the protection of King Bradburn. She will be released at once."

"We cannot let someone as dangerous as her live," said the knight closest to him. "The only punishment fitting is death. Mage's Bane. Knight Commander Fowler's orders."

"This is outrageous!" Reid motioned to the door. "Release her at once. The king will hear of this."

No one moved. No one indicated that he had even spoken.

"It is only fitting that you be the one to deliver the blow," said another knight. "It was you to whom she lied, endangered with her black magic, and tricked with her games."

Reid stared at the knight, disbelieving. Their logic didn't make sense! Juniper hadn't summoned demons or tried to kill Adrian—she hadn't done any of that! Yet these knights had dragged her to the execution chamber, beaten her, and then summoned him to end her. *Fowler* had summoned him to end her—with his virgin Mage's Bane sword.

He tightened his hand around the hilt.

Why hadn't she fought back? Why had she allowed this to happen? Juniper could have frozen them all, and she...would have been seen as an apostate. Had she fought back? Is that what had warranted such a vicious punishment?

Juniper's rasping breath hiccupped, and through her messed hair, one of her midnight blue eyes met his. Consciousness drifted in and out. A gentle, invisible tendril of icy magic caressed his cheek. She knew why he had come. To take her out of the Marca, but not as his wife. As a corpse.

That eye held no anger, only defeat. Shame. Guilt. Humiliation.

Reid swallowed. He had seen the way a mage died on the bane. They suffered for hours, screaming, crying, begging for death.

Juniper blinked slowly, and then her eyes closed.

And Reid knew what he would do, even as his resolve quivered, even as his stomach roiled, as every fiber screamed. He unsheathed his Mage's Bane.

The darkness of the blade glittered in the magelight, the feathered red like veins of blood against the dark blue steel. He took a step closer to Juniper. He could feel the bond between them, the complimenting of their beings. He had felt it since she had gifted him a sliver of her magic, but he hadn't known what it was. Then that night in the cave, when they had confessed—that tether had pulled taut. Since that night, he had felt the threads connecting her life with his own. It was the threatened absence of her life force, the absence of her, the loss of her that he feared. He needed her.

"Sir Sandpiper?" asked one of the knights.

Reid ignored him and stepped closer to Juniper. He readied his blade. Did he imagine the sigh of relief escaping her lips?

Why would they call on him to execute her? Why would they even accuse her of such things? The king himself had acquitted her!

Then, her words came back to him—*Fowler hates me.*

Fowler had argued for her death since their return.

Reid glanced again around the chamber. The knights held their glazed and unfocused eyes on Juniper. Wrong. In every possible way. Reid's resolve shook for a terrible minute, then steeled. He tightened his grip on his Mage's Bane.

The knights stood stone still, their faces matching expressions of emptiness, eyes dulled and mouths slightly slack. They looked...dead, yet still breathing.

Dead yet still breathing—could it be possible? The empty stares, glossy eyes, emotionlessness, flat voices—they were the tell-tale symptoms of a thrall. The thought hammered against his chest. Thralls. Here of all places? In the Order? These knights would have learned resistance to such black magic, and for them to have become thralls...

It would have taken powerful black magic.

Nexon was a powerful mage and knew black magic. He also wanted Juniper dead.

The implications caused Reid's heart to skip several beats. Nexon wanted Juniper dead, and Fowler had tried his hardest to have her executed—this execution openly disobeyed the king. And to give the task of her death to Reid... It was a punishment for him and for her.

Reid's heart tumbled into his ankles. Because this was what Nexon wanted, and Fowler had carried it out.

Nexon had infiltrated the Order.

CHAPTER 15

Reid made his decision within a heartbeat. He adjusted his footing and unsheathed his Mage's Bane in one swift motion. He slammed the blade into the knight closest to him, the one who led him here. His blade pierced the leather in the weak spot under the arm; Reid didn't have time to feel the skin break, the muscles tear, the bones snap—he ripped the blade free and swung it across the throat of the next knight.

The remaining knights drew their swords—their faces remained blank, not a hint of surprise or anger or determination.

Wrong. Wrong. Wrong.

The knights fought slow and sluggish, as if they weren't used to fighting—a tell-tale sign of enthrallment. Whoever controlled these knights did not know the finesse of swordplay. Reid knocked the third knight hard into the stone wall, enough for him not to get back up. His sword collided with the final knight's Mage's Bane. Reid's strength outmatched his, and he had him on the stone floor and bleeding within a few rapid heartbeats.

Reid took a shattering breath. The reek of fresh blood and death filled the chamber, hot and metallic and horrible. He had killed knights, his fellow knights.

And he had already broken one of his vows.

You had to, he told himself. They were possessed, the epitome of the magic the Order vowed to eradicate from the world. As a knight, it had been his duty to end them. Nexon had forced them to act; these knights had not done this on their own.

Yet it hurt.

A sword unsheathed from behind him. He turned, sword ready—the knight he had attacked first now stood, blood seeping from the wound under his arm. His body wobbled as if it might fall apart. His skin was ashen and bloodless, his eyes glazed and empty. The knight had died, but the puppet strings of enthrallment remained.

The thrall raised his Mage's Bane sword against Juniper.

Reid roared. He charged at the knight, but not before he brought the blade down in an ungraceful arc. Reid pummeled the knight, but the girlish gasp told him he hadn't been quick enough.

The knight slammed into the ground. Reid didn't have time to think or decide. He buried his blade in the knight's neck, nearly severing the head. He took a single breath and yanked the sword free.

Juniper's raspy breaths turned pained. Reid pulled a dagger from his side and sliced the ropes binding her hands. She collapsed to her knees. The whipping had shredded her back, but it could be healed. The Mage's Bane sword had sliced through her side. It hadn't struck anything vital, but the Bane had bit deep enough to enter her bloodstream.

"Reid…" Juniper gasped, her breath shallow.

Reid dropped to the ground and took her by the shoulders. Her skin felt like ice. "I'm right here."

Her unfocused gaze found his, then the dead knights. She blinked, smearing tears along her lashes. One fell down her cheek. "What have you done? They'll kill you. Why didn't you just kill me?"

"Because I refuse to live without you," he said, and her pain-stricken eyes grew wide.

She gasped, and her next breath shuddered.

"The Bane. We have to get out of here before word of this spreads. We'll go straight to the king. He will be furious about this. And you need a healer."

She didn't have the energy to argue. Reid yanked the Marca's banner from the wall and wrapped it loosely around Juniper's shoulders. Her shaky hands grasped the sides and pulled it over her breasts, letting the back fall away from her wounds. Reid helped her to her feet, and she leaned heavily on him. Her blood seeped through the purple fabric.

Reid opened the door to the execution chamber. The knights that should have been standing guard in the corridor were gone, leaving the corridor empty. Odd. Why would they have left? Unless they were Nexon's puppets too. Reid would worry about that later. He led Juniper into the empty corridor.

But where to go? The Marca had a healer, but how would they get there without causing a scene? At the end of Execution Hall, the corridor turned left and right. Left would take them into the heart of the Marca, and their appearance would cause chaos. Right would take them—

"The kitchens," Juniper gasped.

Reid turned right without hesitation. He steered them to a plain wooden door, and holding Juniper upright with one arm, he wedged the door open with his other. It led into one of the kitchens. This time of night, it was empty. The pots and pans had been cleaned and stacked on the wooden shelves. The scents of dinner lingered, underlined with lye soaps and magic.

By the sounds of it, not everything had been cleaned. Two or more people were in the next room, cleaning and talking in hushed voices.

Reid steered them both into the darkened kitchen and shut the door behind him.

Juniper nudged him, eyes on the door leading to the other room. She started to step toward it but fell against him.

"Jun," he started.

"Abrielle," she whispered. Her eyes locked on the door.

"Then let me," he said. He guided her to one of the counters, to give her something to lean against.

He pulled open the door. Three mages jumped at the intrusion, pausing in varying states of cleaning goblets—a tall blonde, a skinny girl with braids in her hair, and a dark-haired boy who held his soapy goblet as if he might throw it.

"We're still working," said the blonde, her tone dismissive and peeved. She took in his bloodied armor with fearful and suspicious eyes.

Reid asked, "Which one of you is Abrielle?"

The blonde took a step forward, partially in front of the other girl. Her frown smoothed into defiance. "I am. Why?"

"That's the knight that took Juniper," the other girl whispered.

These are the mages Juniper had mentioned—the friends she had made. The realization cleansed the suspicion from his face. "Juniper is in here, and she needs help."

Without another word, the blonde—Mabyl—pushed past him and into the other room, where Juniper leaned over the counter. She spat a curse. The girl with braids in her hair—Abrielle—followed. Mabyl latched onto Juniper's shoulders and pulled her off the counter. Abrielle took in the bloodied banner with wide, fearful eyes.

"What happened?" Mabyl demanded of Reid. She looked at his Mage's Bane, and at the blood on his armor.

"What has Juniper told you about Nexon?" Reid asked.

Mabyl's eyes widened, and her sneering mouth straightened.

Reid continued, "Nexon has infiltrated the Order. He tried to have her killed. One the knights nicked her."

"The Bane," whispered Abrielle.

"Can you do something?" the boy asked Abrielle.

"Let me see," Abrielle said to Juniper. Her face straightened; her fear dissolved into steady determination. She examined the whipping marks, then pulled the banner from Juniper's quivering grip to see the shallow wound where the Bane had nicked her. Juniper folded her arms loosely over her chest. Abrielle hovered her hand over the wound, and soft blue magic began to glow.

The boy appeared beside Mabyl, holding his purple robes. He wore simple trousers and an undershirt. "Here."

"I'm sure Juniper would thank you kindly," Mabyl said, accepting the robes.

"It's not gone far," Abrielle said, her words sluggish with concentration. "One good thing about the Bane is that it's incredibly slow. I should be able to pull it out."

Abrielle's magic pulled a string of Juniper's blood from the wound. Juniper winced, but Abrielle didn't flinch. She dropped the infected blood into one of the sinks. In the magelight, it appeared black.

"You say the Order is infiltrated by this evil mage?" Mabyl said to Reid.

He nodded. "I don't know how far it goes, but Nexon wanted Juniper dead. He used Fowler and the knights to attempt it. But to be so blatant about it... I think he is making a move. He didn't care if he showed his hand by killing her. He wants her out of the way."

"So he can do something else?" Mabyl asked, her brows coming together. She turned toward the boy. "Finn, you thinking what I'm thinking?"

He grinned wolfishly. "This might be what we've been waiting for."

"If the Order is crooked, I say it's time we get the hell out of here." Mabyl turned her fierce stare back to Reid. "You wouldn't mind a few escaping mages, would you?"

He raised his brows. "You know how to get out of here?"

"There are ways." Mabyl looked him up and down. "Though I'm not sure I trust you, knight."

"Juniper needs to get out of here," Reid said lowly. "We need to get out. It won't be long before Nexon sends someone else after us. Word of what happened will spread."

And being in a fortress of possibly corrupted knights sent a thread of fear through Reid's resolve. The Order, always steady and true, had cracked. And it had taken something of him with it.

Armored footsteps marched past the kitchen door. Reid dared not even breathe, and by Mabyl's wide eyes, she didn't either. The knights were headed to the execution room.

"They'll see the bodies," Reid whispered. "We're out of time."

Abrielle pulled another thread of infected blood out of Juniper, who let out a low, pained moan as it left her body.

A shout came from the corridor. Then armored footsteps started to run.

They had found the bodies.

CHAPTER 16

Reid clutched the hilt of his Mage's Bane but hesitated. Mabyl didn't. She flung herself through the kitchen door and into the corridor. Fire erupted from her hands, lashes of orange, red, and blue—raw magic, Reid realized with a start. The floral scent burst through the stale, metallic air. Tendrils of fire wrapped around the knight's ankles, tripping him, and Mabyl dragged him back down the corridor.

Finn followed next. At his command, stone hands reached from the walls and grabbed the second knight, pulling him back.

Reid readied to strike at the third knight, but recognized him as Sir Darvel, whose eyes had gone wide with shock.

"Reid?" Darvel said at once—he looked between Reid and the rebelling mages. "What is the meaning of this?"

"Order is no longer safe." Reid still clutched his Mage's Bane, but he made no motion to attack. Neither did Darvel.

Reid glanced at the knights the mages had subdued. Finn's stone hands grasped an unfamiliar knight with dull eyes and blank face. Mabyl's fire held a young pledge who looked utterly terrified.

"You had better start explaining," said Darvel, his tone low and dangerous.

"The Order has been infiltrated by an evil Iluvin mage." Reid motioned to the enthralled knight. "Look at him. See his face? Even as a mage holds him within killing range, he remains calm."

Darvel cautiously moved his gaze to the knight while shifting his blade to defend. Something passed over his face—realization.

"He is a thrall," Reid said. "As were the knights in the execution chamber. They wanted me to kill Juniper."

"Sir Gilun?" asked Darvel. The thrall did not respond to the name. Darvel glanced again at Reid, shock and understanding merging into dismay. "I don't believe it… Why did I not see it before?"

"I didn't at first," Reid admitted.

"But who?"

"Nexon," Reid said.

Darvel's brows rose. "That's impossible."

"It's not, though I wish it were," Reid said darkly. "I've encountered the monster of a man myself. He is the reason Penet Berwick did not return with us."

Darvel looked nearly sick but then schooled his emotions into the steadfast resolve of a knight. He looked at the pledge.

"I-I'm not a thrall," begged the pledge. "I promise, sirs, I'm no thrall."

"He's telling the truth," Reid said to Mabyl, who looked disappointed as she released him. She did not send away her flames. Instead, they curled around her like wings.

"What about this one?" Finn asked, wiggling the thrall.

"Once a thrall, there is no cure," Darvel said darkly, his words pained.

Finn hesitated; Mabyl did not. Two tendrils of flame grabbed the thrall's head and twisted it. A sickening crack sounded, and he slumped. Dead. Singed flesh and hair wafted from the body as Finn dropped him on the floor. Mabyl released her magic—a light sweat gathered on her forehead and neck. She stumbled a step back, breathless.

"Rappa give me strength," breathed the pledge, eyes on the dead knight.

Then, another knight appeared in the mouth of the corridor. His dull eyes and expressionless face marked him as a thrall.

"Sir Hogarth," Darvel said as calmly as possible.

"Fowler condemns them all to death," said Hogarth, his tone dry and empty. He came closer, unsheathing his Mage's Bane.

"Hogarth," Darvel said again, his tone full of warning.

"Fowler condemns them all to death," Hogarth repeated.

"Thrall," Darvel spat, his face twisted into anger.

Hogarth raised his blade against Darvel. "Fowler gives the order," he said.

Darvel looked as torn as Reid felt when the understanding came. Reid shifted his bloodied sword at Hogarth. Darvel swung his blade first.

The fight began and ended in a few swift motions. Hogarth's controller lacked the fighting skill to defeat Darvel. Hogarth fell onto the stone, dead. His armor clanked and rattled, and his Mage's Bane clattered against the stone.

A commotion sounded a few corridors away—the mumble of stone-muffled shouts, orders, and shuffling armor.

"That is the barracks," Darvel said. The commotion came closer, armored footsteps and unsheathing swords. "This will be difficult to explain."

"The Order is no longer safe," Reid said to Darvel and the pledge. "We have to get out of here and warn the king."

Finn grunted—the stone floor rose up and the walls curved in, blocking the door. "That'll buy some time." Finn doubled over, panting. "I've never moved that much before."

"You did great," Mabyl said.

"Where did you learn such magic?" Darvel spat. "Raw magic is not used within the Marca."

Finn shot Darvel a sly grin. "It's not used within classrooms. There's plenty of stone to practice on when no one is looking."

Darvel frowned.

"Now isn't the time," Reid said. "We need to get out of here."

"Are you suggesting we fight our way out?" Darvel asked, appalled.

"Not at all," Mabyl interrupted.

She summoned a ball of bright orange raw magic and threw it at the nearest magelight. It collided with a spark of lightning; then the magelight turned a violent red-orange. The magelight down the corridor turned the same color, and the one after it followed. One by one, the magelights turned red-orange. It bathed them all in the violent glow.

"What did you do?" Reid asked.

"I sent the signal," Mabyl said calmly. "Now everyone else will know something bad is happening. They will know to either fight for their lives or hide." At Darvel's scowl, she added, "Most will hide."

"And in the meantime, we get the hell out of here," said Finn.

"And you have a plan?" Darvel asked skeptically.

"We do." Mabyl set her hands on her hips. "You are free to stay here. Since your evil mage knows your face and name, he's likely thrown you under the cart like he has poor Reid here."

Darvel glanced at Reid.

"I am going with them," Reid said. He refused to leave Juniper in their care, even if she called them friends.

"Fine," Darvel spat. "Lead the way, mage."

Reid glanced at the pledge, who looked like he might empty his stomach.

"I'm not staying here," said the pledge.

Abrielle and Juniper came out of the kitchen, Juniper wearing Finn's robes and leaning heavily on Abrielle.

"I've managed to stop the bleeding," Abrielle said to Reid. "But she still needs a proper healer."

Reid offered to carry Juniper, and she gave no objections—he easily lifted her, and she slumped against his shoulder. Mabyl led them down the corridor, past the kitchen, toward the warded cells and quiet rooms. Reid had seen both on his tour. Warded cells prevented any magic within, and the quiet rooms were the same, only dark. Both were plain stone rooms with dirt floors, pits for troublesome mages.

Mabyl led them into the corridor of quiet rooms. The ceiling was low, and the stone was old, wider and thicker than the newer stones. This section would have been the first built, or else it had already been here when the Marca was built over the ruins, like Bradburn Castle. Mabyl, Finn, and Abrielle began a search of each quiet room, for what, Reid didn't ask. He couldn't turn his attention away from the girl in his arms and her pained breaths.

"What are you doing?" barked Darvel.

"Looking for the marker," said Mabyl. "I'm not sure what it looks like, so we're—"

"Found it!" said Abrielle. She stood in the doorway to the last quiet room. "I think, anyway."

Finn and Mabyl went to the last quiet room. "That's it," they said together.

Mabyl jumped down the step to the dirt floor, which looked sickeningly bloodstained. "Let's hope the rumors are true. I don't want to search every one of these rooms."

The pledge offered to hold the door, which Abrielle did not object. With the door open, the runes remained incomplete. Finn used his Earth magic to move the ancient dirt a little at a time, further and further down, until they reached stone. A rune was engraved onto the stone—one Reid didn't recognize. By the confusion on Darvel's face, neither did he. Mabyl put her hand against the rune; then the stone moved. It slid to the side, dissolving into the wall.

And there, where that stone had been, was an old wooden ladder that vanished into the darkness below.

The legendary escape tunnel. It was real.

"I'll be damned," muttered Darvel.

"Unfortunately," started Finn, "no knight knows about it, so we'll have to kill you."

"Let's wait until we're safely out before we start killing each other." Reid motioned to the ladder, where Mabyl had already started down.

"That rune," whispered Darvel. "It looks Iluvin."

Reid accepted the knowledge but decided to think about it later. He shifted Juniper in his arms and started down the ladder. He held one arm around her middle, the other carefully navigating the rungs. She held her arms around his neck as tight as she could. Mabyl held a fire at the bottom of the ladder, shining light upward.

The ladder led into an old tunnel, maybe a sewer. Reid didn't want to think about what was happening in the Marca or above ground, if Mabyl's signal had started a full rebellion or not, or how many people would die tonight. He thought about Juniper instead, and focused on her shallow breaths.

"If you knew this tunnel existed, why not escape sooner?" Reid asked Mabyl as the others made their way down the ladder.

The fire mage shrugged. "Because first, one would have to get into trouble enough to be thrown into the quiet rooms and lucky enough to be thrown into the right quiet room. Second, one would then have to dig through the hard-packed dirt with their fingernails because the rune suppresses magic. It's also pitch black. Only the truly desperate have tried."

Abrielle jumped the last rung to the ground, and the pledge started down. Darvel followed, then Finn, who used his earth magic to seal the tunnel from below.

They stood in the dark with Mabyl's fire as the only light.

"Where does this lead?" Reid asked.

"We think it ends up somewhere in the Undercity or a safe house," Mabyl said. "Anyone who has gone this way hasn't come back to give directions."

"We're relatively safe," said Darvel. He took a step closer to Reid. "Now is a good time for a deeper explanation. What the hell is going on?"

"I'll explain on the way," Reid said.

And he did. Mabyl and Abrielle led the way through the dark tunnel, and Reid told Darvel—and by extension, them all—about Nexon's plan to rise again to power. He told Darvel that he suspected Nexon had Fowler in his control. He left out only a few details, including the part of Juniper being Isolde Balendin. With every word, Reid felt his chest tighten. Nexon had made his move, and Reid had a horrible feeling he would soon make another.

CHAPTER 17

Reid carried Juniper down the dark passage, thoughts churning too fast for him to pin just one down. Mabyl's fire illuminated the rough-hewn walls. They did not bear the marks of a chisel—this tunnel had been built with magic.

Just like the lowest levels of the catacombs under the castle. It worried Reid, all the ancient magic architecture under the city. Who had built it? Why had the ancients built over it?

After a long walk, the tunnel led into the sewers.

"Oh, look!" Mabyl pointed to runes carved into the mouth of the tunnel.

"That's why no one has found it." Reid recognized the rune. Ison had used it to hide their camp during their quest.

Mabyl stepped out first, followed by Abrielle, who immediately coughed and covered her nose. "Oh, that is horrible!"

"It's a sewer," Mabyl deadpanned.

Reid stepped through the barrier, and the putrid smell of soured chamber pots and garbage ravaged his nostrils and surged down his throat. He coughed once. He inhaled it and forced himself to get used to it.

"At least we don't have to swim there." Mabyl nudged Abrielle.

Abrielle frowned at her friend, then looked at the murky sluice like she might vomit.

They continued through the sewer in silence. Reid glanced at Juniper. Her breaths were still shallow but not as rattling as they had been.

He had thrown his name to the ashes. He had forfeited his place in the Order with this betrayal. His title. His future. His uncle would be furious and disappointed—more so now than he already was. He would blame it on Juniper.

And without the Order, he didn't know what to think. Everything he knew, everything that he had worked for, was gone.

Everything but Juniper.

Abrielle slowed to walk beside Reid. She looked at Juniper, worry creasing her brow. "I was able to remove most of the Bane," she said. "But I had to remove blood with it, so she'll need rest and fluids to replenish the blood loss."

Reid nodded. He would make sure she got both of those.

They walked for a while longer. Mabyl led the way down this tunnel and then that one—it took Reid a while to realize there were tiny symbols carved into the stone. Symbols to guide escaping mages. They passed several ladders to the surface—Mabyl paused at each one, glanced up, then continued. Then, at last, Mabyl stopped at a rusty ladder that led to an iron trapdoor. A crude little house symbol was carved in the trapdoor.

"A safe house," Mabyl said.

Reid couldn't tell if she'd meant to say it out loud. Mabyl's vigor had faded, and she looked and sounded as exhausted as the rest of them.

Mabyl climbed the ladder first. She put her hand against the underside of the trapdoor, but it didn't give. "I can hear something on the other side. It's muffled," she said.

She knocked against the trapdoor. A heartbeat passed, and she knocked again. From where Reid stood at the bottom, he heard footsteps, and then something heavy slid across the other side of the trapdoor. Beside him, Darvel's hand tightened on his hilt. The pledge mirrored his action.

The trapdoor lifted. Candlelight flooded the opening. A bearded man stood above them, an ax in his hand. Behind him, a dark-haired woman held her empty hands in a way that Reid had seen Juniper do—readying magic. They eyed the strangers, and Reid had no doubt how it looked—bloodied knights and weary mages.

"We mean no harm," said Mabyl, panic threaded her words. "We seek shelter."

The man considered them, then lowered his ax. "Then get up here," he barked.

The man and woman stood on either side of the trapdoor as they climbed the ladder. Mabyl went first, then Abrielle, and then Reid started up with Juniper. They stood in a cellar that smelled of wax and soot. Crates and barrels lined the walls, and shelves held all manner of jars, sacks, and jugs. The only light came from the candles along the walls. When they had all climbed into the cellar, the man closed the trapdoor and pushed a crate back over it.

"We've never had knights come through before." The man eyed Reid and Darvel with grave suspicion—particularly the blood and Juniper's limp body. "What in Bala's name happened?"

"They helped us escape," said Abrielle.

"The Order has fallen," Reid added.

"We might have started a riot to cover our escape," Mabyl said. "Has anyone else come through yet?"

The man shook his head. "We've heard rumors from the street," he said. "Customers saying that something is happening at the Marca, but no definite word has come through."

"It's been relatively quiet for a riot." The woman crossed her arms. "Regardless, I suppose you all want a safe place to rest and a warm meal before you jump into the real world, huh?"

"That would be delightful, ma'am," said Abrielle.

"We do not want to be a bother," said Darvel.

The woman waved her hand aside. "Nonsense. This is what we do. My name is Moria, and this is my husband, Denis."

"I'm Mabyl."

"Abrielle."

"Sir Darvel."

"Lex," said the pledge.

"Reid." He nodded to the girl in his arms. "Juniper."

"And she needs rest," Abrielle added.

Moria nodded. "Follow me, then."

She led Reid around the shelves and through an archway he hadn't noticed at first. It led into a hall lined with curtained-off rooms. At a wave of her hand, magelights came to life in each of the rooms, shining with pale white light. She led Reid to the one at the end and held aside the curtain while he carried Juniper inside. The room held a narrow bedroll, a washing basin, and a small pile of patched blankets.

"Make yourself comfortable," Moria said.

Moria left to fetch fresh water, and Reid laid Juniper on the bedroll, on her side to not agitate her wounds. Her eyes fluttered but remained closed. He brushed sweaty hair away from her face. The others filtered into the other rooms, too exhausted to talk.

A safe house for mages. He had suspected them to be scattered around the city, and a part of him wanted to report this place to the Order at once. He could have taken Juniper straight to the castle. Her injuries would be proof of the Order's wrongdoings.

Underneath his rage, he felt gratitude. These people had helped them without question. Underneath the gratitude, he felt cold, slippery fear. For the Order, for Juniper, for what it all meant.

Abrielle appeared in the doorway. She didn't wait for Reid's permission to enter. She knelt beside Juniper and pulled the robes away from Juniper's back. This close, in this light, Reid saw the damage. The tears from the whip had started to scab over—Abrielle's doing. The Mage's Bane wound had healed considerably.

A soft blue glow hummed under Abrielle's hand, and the bright floral scent of natural magic whisked through the air. Reid leaned against the wall and watched. As Abrielle healed, Juniper's breathing calmed.

"I've never attempted to heal something this bad," Abrielle whispered. "I—I don't know if I can."

"Try," Reid said.

Abrielle bit her lip and continued. Sweat broke out across her face and neck, her eyes sharpened, and Reid felt the magic in the air—it seemed to pulse. Abrielle wasn't used to controlling her natural magic, and it left a residue in the air. As a squire, he had been trained to detect that residue. The Order claimed it as a tell-tale sign of an apostate.

Abrielle slowly worked her magic, and the angry tears became inflamed welts. The whip had torn the hardened skin of the brand, the jagged spiral Maddox Hawk had burned into Juniper's skin, claiming her as a thief of his keep—little remained of it, a few sparse scars among the freshly stitched-together skin.

After healing the raw flesh of Juniper's back, Abrielle began on the Mage's Bane wound. This close, Reid could see the black veins spreading from the wound, crawling underneath the skin as the Bane ate through the magic in her body. The Bane had already spread several inches across her skin. Normally, the Bane would slowly ink its way through the bloodstream, devouring the magic, and slowly kill the mage. The black veins would cover the mage, and their skin would pale to ghostly white. The Bane darkened the eyes last.

Reid had witnessed death by Bane only once, to his parents' murderers, and at the time, he had relished the sight. It had haunted him ever since.

"Hand me a cup or something," Abrielle said, her voice thick with concentration.

Reid scrounged through the cellar and found an old tin cup. He set it on the floor beside her. Abrielle pulled a thin ribbon of blackened blood from Juniper's side and guided it into the tin cup. The blood looked like tar, thick and feathered with red.

Mage's Bane.

Juniper flinched as Abrielle pulled another ribbon of blackened blood. And another. The black veins had retreated a small distance.

Then, Abrielle lowered her hands and slumped. "I can't do anymore right now."

"Then rest," Reid said. "You've done much already, and you have my gratitude."

Abrielle nodded. She stood—wobbly—and made her way out of the room and to her own. Reid bent and put his hand against Juniper's cheek. She felt cold. Every other breath hitched, though her breaths had deepened.

The Order said killing someone stricken by the Bane would be merciful. Listening to Juniper's painful whimpers, he understood. But he knew he could not kill Juniper. And that refusal had cost him the Order.

Reid pushed sweaty hair out of Juniper's face and tucked it behind her ear. Her eyes cracked open, and slivers of midnight blue found him. A heartbeat passed before she closed them again.

"I'm right here," he whispered.

"Reid?" Juniper breathed.

"You'll be all right," he promised.

"Reid," she breathed again, softer.

"Rest." He caressed her cheek. "We will talk when you feel better."

Her breathing calmed, her face relaxed, and sleep took her. Reid reclined against the wall, watching her, keeping his vigil. There was nothing else he could do now.

CHAPTER 18

Sir Henry Julian stared intently at the game board—mostly to make it look like he had a clever strategy for victory. Prince Adrian stared at it from the opposite side. After a period of time Henry felt appropriate to have made an intelligent calculation, he moved one of his pieces. Adrian hummed—Henry assumed he had some mad strategy of his own. Unless he was pretending too.

This time of night, most of the castle was sleeping. Henry had been in the city most of the day, greeting nobles and lords as Sir Julian, one of the newest knights in the Order. He loved the attention, but he hated the redundancy of it all. He'd never been a fan of the sniveling nobles. On the other hand, the fairer sex seemed attracted to the silver armor. He had kissed quite a few soft hands in the past two weeks.

"And, hmmm…" Adrian tapped a finger on his chin, then moved one of his pieces.

Henry caught the subtle change in the prince's eye, the barely-there doubt. "Interesting move."

"I hope so," Adrian said.

Their game continued. The off-duty Royal Guard and a handful of knights, squires, and pledges lingered in the common room of the barracks, filling the space with the rustle of male voices. Adrian had spent the day planning a wedding, and when he had suggested a game, Henry had obliged. It was an escape from duty for the both of them.

"Have you seen Reid lately?" Adrian asked.

"I haven't," said Henry. "Fowler has kept us both remarkably busy."

Adrian half laughed, one of those short one-huff laughs. Henry tore his eyes from the gameboard and looked at his prince. The charming mask had slipped slightly, and something bitter appeared in the cracks. There and gone, and the charming prince returned.

"Is something wrong, Your Highness?" Henry asked.

"Many things are wrong all the time, Sir Julian." A curt, professional answer. "There will always be things wrong. Fixing one thing often creates two more wrongs. It's a never-ending cycle."

Henry wondered if they would continue to play games when Adrian became king. He took one of Adrian's pieces. "I hope your problem-solving skills on the board do not reflect those in the throne room, or this kingdom is surely in trouble."

Adrian laughed, genuinely this time. "Luckily, it is not just the king making decisions. That is what the council and advisors are for."

"How is Ron coming along?" Henry asked. He had known Ron a long time, but since he took the role of advisor, Ron rarely spoke to him.

That flicker of something darker came over Adrian's face again. "He is a fine advisor."

A lie—Henry recognized it. Adrian did not like Ron as an advisor? With all the other listening ears in the barracks, Henry did not question Adrian further.

Footsteps resounded through the barracks—a common sound—and only when those thuds marched to their gameboard did Henry look up.

"Sir Julian?" asked one of the recent pledges. He was barely a man, still gangly and nervous, no older than fifteen.

"Yes?" Henry asked, maintaining the air of a knight. Superior but humble. Firm but pliable.

The pledge swallowed. He hadn't mastered the art of the stoic mask yet, and nervousness shredded through his eyes. "Knight Commander Fowler requests your presence, sir."

"Here in the castle or in Vanten Hall?"

"Here, sir."

Henry sighed. "My apologies, Your Highness."

"No apology is needed." Adrian stood. "We both have duties to attend to. Since you have claimed more pieces, we can say you won this round. Unless you'd rather call it a draw?"

"A victory is a victory." Henry smiled as he rose. "I would have won anyway."

Adrian chuckled. "I don't know about that. Until the rematch, Sir Julian."

"Your Highness." Henry nodded in farewell.

Henry followed the pledge into the corridor, and Adrian started the other way. Two royal guards fell into step on either side of him, and Adrian immediately engaged them in conversation too low for Henry to hear.

"You know," Henry said to the pledge, "the knight commander can sense fear."

The pledge nodded. "That explains things."

Henry chuckled. "When I first became a pledge, I thought about my grandmother whenever I needed to look serious. She died halfway through dinner when I was ten."

"That's awful," said the pledge.

"Yes, and the memory still terrifies me, but it got the job done." Henry schooled his face into the serious mask of the Order. "So, think of some horrible killjoy when you need to look serious."

"I'll keep that in mind, Sir Julian," said the pledge.

They came to the knight commander's door. Henry knocked.

"Enter," Fowler barked.

"That's not a good tone," Henry whispered. He let himself inside. The pledge remained in the corridor.

Fowler's office in Bradburn Castle was plain and drafty. The Marca's banner hung on one wall, the Order's banner hung on the other. A bookshelf held a few books, scrolls, and writing instruments. Fowler stood behind his desk. Without his silver armor, he looked like a shrunken old man. Of course, Henry reasoned, he was. His graying skin sagged, age spots dotted his hands, and his hair had long gone white. Despite his age, Fowler's eyes remained as sharp as virgin steel.

"Sir Julian," said Fowler in greeting.

"You wanted to see me, sir?" Henry held his shoulders straight, his chin high, his face expressionless—one flaw and the knight commander would tear it apart.

"Yes. Something has happened at the Marca," Fowler said lowly. "It is unclear what, but I have instructed the Order to keep it quiet for now. I need you to go there and check on things. Bring me a report from Overseer Margret. Discreetly."

Henry's gut twisted. He nodded. "Yes, sir."

Fowler dismissed him, and Henry went immediately to the stables outside the barracks. He rode to the Marca, keeping his pace unhurried. The Marca loomed like a fortress, dark and forbidding. The inside was just as unwelcoming and unnaturally quiet. He marched toward the overseer's office. The usual metallic smell was punctuated with floral scents—natural magic had been used, and recently. Had there been an uprising?

He knocked on the overseer's door. A grunt acknowledged his presence, and he let himself inside.

Overseer Margret sat at her desk, what appeared to be a letter resting atop it, along with an open ink bottle and a well-used pen. She looked up at Henry with the eyes of a hawk—hungry and alert.

"Knight Commander Fowler has sent me for a status report, ma'am," Henry said.

Overseer Margret scoffed. "Of course he has." She dipped the nib of her pen back into her black ink and continued writing. "We had a spat down by the kitchens, at least five knights are dead."

Henry's stomach squirmed—*five* dead knights—but he stood firm.

"A small uprising followed. No dead, several injuries," Overseer Margret said as she wrote, the ink splattering with a contained rage. "We haven't assessed the extent of the damages, but after a quick headcount, I believe we are...missing a few of our mages."

Our mages. Henry didn't like the way she said those words, as if the Marca owned them.

"How many?" Henry asked.

Overseer Margret's eyes snapped up to him. Her pen paused. Her vicious gaze tore through him, and he had the horrible feeling of having spoken out of turn.

"That is something I will discuss with the knight commander."

He bristled at the reprimand.

She finished the report with her flourish of a signature, folded it, and sealed it with blood red wax. She pressed the Marca's seal into the glop. "Here." She held the report out to him. "Take this to Fowler. Tell him a more detailed report will be available in the morning or early afternoon. You may leave."

Henry had a dozen things he wanted to tell this woman but held his tongue. A knight did not lash out at others for silly offenses. So he tucked the report away and marched out of the office without a goodbye—hopefully, he wouldn't have to see that horrible woman for a long time.

He felt the overwhelming urge to rip open the report and see exactly what it said, but she had sealed it. Fowler would know he'd looked, and he'd rather not provoke Fowler's wrath.

On the way back through the Marca, Henry saw knights searching in every room, cranny, behind tapestries, and in closets—looking for the missing mages? An uprising would have initiated a lockdown protocol.

Henry returned to the castle. He'd thought being a knight would involve more...chivalry and fighting. Instead, he felt like a glorified courier. A part of him wished to go with Reid to Chata. He wouldn't have to deal with the Marca or the Overseer or Fowler, and he would be able to fight and protect.

Henry found Fowler in the same location he'd left him in, glowering down at papers on his desk. He handed the old man the report and turned to leave.

"I have not dismissed you," Fowler said as he read the letter.

Henry silently cursed his stupid mistake and turned back. He stood patiently while Fowler read through the overseer's report. Several times, it seemed.

"Henry," Fowler said after a long moment. His old voice wobbled. "I fear the Order is coming into a dark time."

"Sir?" Henry swallowed that growing sense of unease he'd felt since the Marca.

Fowler met Henry's eyes. His own were watery. "I fear there are those in the Order who do not hold the Order's best interests at heart. I fear that they may have already betrayed their oaths, betrayed the Order."

Henry kept his face stoic and calm. Did he mean the rebellion?

"I fear… I fear that Sir Sandpiper may be among the traitors," Fowler said, his voice quiet, reflecting the same disbelief that Henry felt.

"No, sir, Reid would never—"

"I understand your reluctance," Fowler said. "I feel the same. But Margret has never lied to me before. I sent Sir Sandpiper to the Marca, and now he and several others are unaccounted for. Including several mages known to harbor ill-intent." In that moment, Fowler looked his age, old and wrinkled and time-worn. "I fear that Sir Sandpiper might not be acting on his own…volition."

Possessed, was what Fowler didn't say.

Henry felt the word in his chest, felt the implication hammer against his heart and threaten his knightly composure. Possessed—just like Penet had been. Could it be possible? Could Nexon have somehow commandeered Reid like he had Penet?

"Henry," Fowler continued, leaning onto his desk. "I fear I must ask something of you."

"Sir," Henry said, steeling himself against the worst. A knight must be prepared to face the worst, the harshest, the most dreadful. "If Reid has been turned against the Order, he will not pass by me or my blade."

Fowler looked relieved. "Thank you, Sir Julian. If you hear of him, or others who have cultivated…strange ideas…please, report to me."

"Yes, sir."

"You are dismissed."

Henry marched out of the knight commander's office and toward his rooms in the Order's boarding house. His stomach roiled, and his heart tumbled around his chest. Reid, possessed? It didn't seem possible. But he had thought the same of Penet. If it were true, Henry would save his friend. Even if it meant killing him.

CHAPTER 19

They spent the day resting, or so Juniper assumed. She couldn't focus enough to hear more than the mumblings of the others. It felt like her body had been torn into pieces and roughly sewn back together. When she dared to move, barbs in her blood clawed at her insides, bringing tears to her eyes.

The journey here—wherever here was—was blurry. She remembered dark stone, flickering light, and pain—shards of broken glass in her blood, scraping against muscle and bone, tearing and ripping.

And Reid. He had been there.

Consciousness came and went. She had blurry memories of Reid holding earthen cups of water and warm broth to her lips, and of Abrielle helping her to the tiny bathing room. In those few moments of lucidity, Reid told her how Abrielle had taken out her blood infected by Mage's Bane, and she needed to replenish it.

She didn't have the voice to ask him for something stronger than water, or the mind for humor.

"Juniper," Reid's soft voice came.

She opened her eyes. He knelt beside her with another earthen cup. He helped her into a sitting position and held the cup to her lips. She sipped warm herbal broth.

"Abrielle has reduced the Mage's Bane to a nonlethal amount," he whispered. "You'll be all right."

She paused between sips and managed to ask, "Did you know about that?"

"Know about what?"

"Mage's Bane being nonlethal," she clarified. She took another long sip. The herbs within the broth warmed her throat and coated her insides. "I thought even the tiniest dose would kill a mage."

Reid didn't answer immediately. "I've heard rumors that a small enough dose wouldn't kill, only incapacitate," Reid said. "But when the Order uses Mage's Bane, they do not aim to incapacitate."

Juniper had another question, but it drifted from her mind before she could voice it. Reid helped her back down to the bedroll. A blanket covered her shoulders, and darkness reclaimed her.

When Juniper woke next, Reid was gone. With each moment of consciousness, the sluggishness of sleep faded. Her back ached. Her fingers and toes were cold. She was in a small room with earthen walls. A magelight hovered near the ceiling, the soft, buttery shade of dawn. Voices drifted through the curtain, but she could not discern words.

Her memory blurred, but she knew they had left the Marca. Gods, what had happened?

She remembered being in the bathing room, telling Abrielle about her engagement to Reid. The other girls hadn't taken the news well. Carol had called Juniper a whore, and Juniper had hit her. Not with magic—Juniper had landed a solid right hook to Carol's jaw. The bitter girl had fallen to the floor and started to cry, like she'd never thought it possible that someone would hit her.

"Be glad that's all I did," Juniper had spat. "I've slit throats for less."

But then Carol had run off and told the overseer. Knights had come and escorted Juniper to the overseer's office—and the rest blurred. The knights attacked her, or so she thought. She remembered being stunned, and falling, and being in the execution chamber. She remembered the vicious sting of the whip against her skin, lashes like lightning against her back.

By the time Reid had appeared, she no longer cared. The pain had pulled her down, numbed her, made her wish for the release of death.

Juniper heaved a sigh of the stale air—underground by the mineral smell and musk.

She closed her eyes to find sleep again. Her entire body hurt. It felt like she'd been through a wringer and back again, like something vital had been forcefully squeezed out. Was that what Mage's Bane did? Her magic remained, but it had curled inward, protecting itself, healing, hiding deep within her.

"I've brought you something to eat," said Reid.

Juniper opened her eyes. She hadn't heard him enter. Reid sat down beside her and set a pewter plate on the floor. It held a small loaf of brown bread and a bunch of grapes.

"No broth?" Juniper asked, her voice sleepy.

"Abrielle thought it best if you tried solid food," Reid said.

Juniper adjusted her arms and pushed her weary self into a sitting position. Abrielle had healed her back in sessions, and though the freshly healed skin stretched painfully, she powered through it. Reid's hands hovered close by just in case she needed his help.

"You're getting stronger." Reid tore the brown bread in two and handed one chunk to her. "How do you feel?"

She took a small bite of the oven-warm bread and washed it down with water. "Like my body was ripped apart and sewn back together," she said, her voice raw.

"Mage's Bane," Reid said, staring at his bread. He met her eye. "Juniper, what happened?"

In her shaky breaths between bites, she told him about Carol and the overseer and the knights. "I'm sorry," she said, her voice weak. "I didn't mean to—"

"Nexon has infiltrated the Order," Reid said darkly, his words laced with hatred. "The knights who attacked you were thralls."

She choked on her water.

"The Order?" she whispered. Nexon had the Order. Her stomach somersaulted, and the bread turned to sand in her mouth. Nexon likely had Fowler too. That explained Fowler's incessant need to be rid of her. "Reid? Are you all right?"

"I'm fine."

She knew that tone. He was not fine.

"Not on the outside," she corrected. "On the inside."

He turned his gaze away at that.

"Reid?" she asked. "You killed members of the Order."

He tore his bread in two, refusing to meet her gaze. "I know."

He had killed knights to protect her. He had chosen her over the Order. There had been a moment when she thought he would choose the Order, and yet he hadn't. She knew how much becoming a knight meant to him. He'd always wanted to be a knight. Reid, with his honor and sense of duty and natural righteousness. His dream, his envisioned future—gone. Because of her.

"Nexon caused this." Reid's tone was hard and cold. "He turned those knights against us. He has turned the Order against itself."

"Reid?"

He met her gaze, questioning and worried. "I'll be fine," he corrected. And he didn't want to talk about it right now.

"I'm sorry," she said, and she meant it.

"You need to eat." He motioned to the bread she'd nibbled on. "When you're stronger, we'll talk."

She bit off a small chunk of bread.

They would talk when she had gathered her strength, when her magic had recovered, and after he had time to think about it all. He had to sort through his feelings, and she would give him the time he needed.

"Our next step is to warn the king of Nexon and the Order," Reid said. "News of your escape will have reached him by now."

And the Order would know that Reid betrayed them. Fowler would relish the chance to inform the king of her escape and Reid's desertion.

"We need to send word to the others," Juniper said.

Reid brought his eyes up to hers.

"Ison and the others," she clarified.

He nodded. "I don't know how to reach them. They might have heard about the rebellion and assumed."

"We did make a dramatic exit." Juniper offered him a little smile. "Although, it could have been a little flashier."

Reid returned her small smile, but it did not reach his eyes.

CHAPTER 20

Blythe watched the panic on the street from her rooftop vantage point. This time of morning should have brought a flurry of shoppers to the streets, but the smoke billowing from the west side of the Marca had put a stopper in normalcy. The Marca stalls were closed and shuttered, and five knights stood guard in front of the closed gates.

People lingered on the street, watching and waiting for news of the strange occurrence. The smoke had appeared in the night, black and angry. By dawn, it had calmed into puffy white-gray. No other fires had started. No bodies were hauled outside, at least not through the front doors. The panic spread as the sun rose, and a steady crowd of gossip-hungry onlookers meandered past the Marca, pointing and staring and whispering.

Blythe was about to give up and go do something else when a carriage stormed down the street and through the Marca gates. The crowd outside paused to watch, kept at bay by angry-looking knights.

Fowler—whatever his title was—marched up the front steps. Maddox said he'd been losing his touch for years and needed to be replaced. Blythe watched the old knight storm into the Marca, flanked by two knights. The doors closed, and the commotion ended.

A shadow appeared on the roof beside her.

Ven had spent the morning weaving through the crowd, listening to gossip. He was better at blending in than her. Amery said Blythe looked too much like a predator with her sharp, clever eyes, while Ven—in his cheap trousers, patched shirt, and lopsided grin—looked like any other street kid. By the way he jingled, he'd snagged a few coin purses.

Blythe and Ven were the youngest members of Maddox's guild, or what was left of it. They lived in Amery's manor now. Blythe would turn ten in a few months, and Ven would turn eleven in one. Blythe and Ven should have been enjoying the summer, playing ball or whatever children did, but neither had been granted a playful childhood.

"What news?" Blythe asked.

"It's all hush-hush down there." Ven lounged in the shadows beside her. "No one knows what happened. It could have been an uprising, an alchemical accident, or spellwork gone wrong. The knights aren't talking. All anyone knows is that the Marca is in lockdown, whatever that means. Fowler's pissed, though. He came storming in and barking orders like some rabid dog."

"Hmm," Blythe responded.

"I overheard a few of the pledges talking," Ven said, his tone dripping with gold.

Blythe stole her ink-black eyes from the Marca and glared at him.

He grinned. "They were there when it all happened, on the top floor, overseeing some group or whatever. All of a sudden, the magelights went red. The mages panicked and hid. A few stupid ones attacked the knights. They were talking about dead knights too."

"So, people did die," Blythe said casually.

"Sounds like it," Ven said. "But the Order doesn't want people to know."

"Because it exposes a moment when they were not in charge," Blythe said. She'd heard Maddox and Amery talking about it. Blythe had been practicing her scaling on the side of the house, and Amery's window had been open. The Order cared much for their sense of control, Maddox had said.

"And," Ven said, drawing out the silence after the word, "rumor has it that a few mages and knights are missing."

"Missing or dead?"

"Unaccounted for, they said. And there was some kind of attack in the lower levels. The pledges heard knights complaining about having to track down an earth mage to move a wall."

"Which is why Fowler is in a mood," Blythe added.

"And if they aren't in the Marca and they're not among the bodies..."

"They might have escaped." Blythe glanced again to the street, where the onlookers waited for crumbs of news. "Xavier said there are secret ways out of the Marca."

"I've heard."

When nothing more happened for a long minute, Blythe stood. "I'm bored. I'm going to see what Ison knows."

Ven stood with her.

"You stay and keep an eye on this mess," Blythe said.

He pouted, but when she vanished into the shadows, he did not follow. Blythe used the rooftops as a private road to Amery's. She jumped over the stone outer wall and launched up the wall to the library's balcony. Ison had been spending most of his time there.

Blythe slid through the cracked library window. Ison was sitting at a table piled with dusty old books, his head bent over, reading. She hated the smell of old books. Like must and mildew—carrying all the mages' books through the tunnel had been a different kind of hell. Xavier stood on the other side of the room, leaning on the archway of one of the alcoves, eyes looking elsewhere.

Blythe felt a spike of pride. Xavier hadn't even noticed—

"Sneaking up on research isn't very nice," Xavier said. He turned toward the window and his blue-gray eyes found Blythe immediately.

She sighed through her nose. "I thought I had you."

Xavier smiled—the vicious and clever smile of an assassin. "No one sneaks up on me. But don't discount yourself yet. Give it a few more years, and you might take me by surprise."

Blythe soaked in the compliment. Something warm bloomed in her chest at the thought of her, the least loved daughter of a crooked father, becoming better than the best assassin in the Undercity.

Ison glanced at Blythe with the surprised look of someone who hadn't heard her approach.

"I brought news," Blythe said. "From the Marca."

"What?" Ison asked, blinking. His brow furrowed. "What happened?"

Xavier didn't budge. His face remained impassive and bored, though his eyes were quick and clever.

"Only a possible alchemical explosion or spellwork gone wrong or a rebellion," she said. "No one knows what happened. The place has been smoking since last night."

Ison's eyes widened, and his mouth fell open. Xavier's brows rose, but his expression barely changed. She quickly reported all that she knew.

"Mages are missing," Ison repeated, blinking rapidly. "What of Jun?"

Blythe shrugged.

"They are looking for them," Xavier added.

"If they escaped..." Ison rubbed his face.

"What do you know?" asked Xavier.

"There are stories of escape tunnels under the Marca. They've been passed down from mage to mage, and only a few know where they are. They're extremely well hidden and dangerous to look for." Ison stood, hands flat on the table. His knees quivered. "It's possible that Jun escaped, if she was able to find someone who knew the location."

"Let's say she did, and she escaped," Xavier said. "Where would she have gone?"

"There were supposed to be safe houses on the other side," Ison said. "But I don't know where any of them are."

"But some of our new friends who have escaped the Marca might," Xavier said, nodding to the library door.

Ison hurried to the door. He tripped over a stack of books and started to fall—Xavier grabbed his arm and hauled him back to his feet.

Blythe followed them as they went through the house, asking every mage they crossed. It took several mages before they found one who'd escaped—a fire mage who worked in the kitchens. His magic had saved Amery untold coin in coal and firewood.

"Why do you want to know?" he asked, looking Ison up and down.

"Haven't you heard?" Xavier asked coolly. "An incident occurred at the Marca last night. A few mages have gone missing. The whole place is on lockdown."

The fire mage's brows rose, then he told them. The safe houses bore a symbol—he drew it in the flour on the counter—a crude drawing of a house.

"They're hard to find unless you know where to look," said the mage. "They're hidden in doorways and shutters a lot of times. Safe houses aren't on main roads or anywhere people loiter, like near parks or restaurants. Look for quiet establishments, quaint and unremarkable."

At the news of the Marca's missing mages, groups of search teams fanned out to search for safe houses and possible survivors. Ison and Xavier went to search, and Blythe tagged along. She was glad to finally have something to do.

Even with several search parties, it would take days to search Rusdasin, maybe weeks. Ison spoke little and failed to hide his nerves.

They crisscrossed through the alleys, checking small shops tucked away from the public eye. Ison found their first safe house—two mages had made it there. Neither were thrilled to see Ison and Xavier, but with a quick explanation, the mages relaxed.

Neither knew the fate of Juniper Thimble.

"I heard a knight came to see her last night," said one of the mages, looking to the other for confirmation.

He shrugged, adding, "I didn't hear anything of her coming back, though."

"No, she did," said the other. "She hit that bitch, Carol. A mean right hook from what I heard. The overseer came for her, and that's the last I heard."

Ison looked nearly sick.

The mages didn't provide much else in regards to information. They had been in the larder when the magelights turned red, the signal to run, fight, or hide. Lucky for them, there was an escape route through the larder.

Ison and Xavier searched for safe houses the rest of the morning and into the late afternoon, finding none. Blythe was about to quit and go back to Amery's for something to eat when Ison spotted the crude drawing of a house again, this time on a musty little candle shop. A closed sign hung in its cloudy front window.

Ison knocked on the back door.

No one answered. Ison knocked again, but still no answer.

Xavier nudged him aside and used his magic to slither underneath the door. "There's life inside," Xavier whispered. "Several bodies in the next room."

Ison knocked again, and again. Finally, hasty footsteps headed to the door. Steel swished— Blythe instinctively folded her fingers around the hilt of her dagger. Xavier's fingers twitched toward the hidden blade on his arm. The deadbolt on the door slid back, then another, and then a third. Blythe's skin prickled. She hated the sound of a lock snapping open.

The door swung open. A bearded man stood on the other side, ax over his shoulder.

"What?" he barked. "We're closed. Can't you read?"

Ison nodded to the safe house symbol in the doorframe. "We're looking for friends," he said. He summoned a ball of grayish wind between his palms, a show that he was a mage and meant the other mages no harm. That he, too, was an apostate.

The faint aroma of flowers sprang from the magic—a smell that permeated Amery's house. Blythe couldn't decide if she liked it or not.

"Ison?" came a girl's voice from within the house. A tall blonde girl appeared behind the man.

Ison blinked in surprise. "Mabyl?"

For a moment, no one spoke. Then the blonde girl laughed, a victorious and vicious sound.

CHAPTER 21

Juniper heard voices coming from upstairs, soft and urgent. She was lying on her bedroll, on her stomach. Reid slept on the floor beside her, his chest gently rising and falling. His scowl had smoothed in his sleep.

Guilt weighed heavy on her shoulders.

Because of her, Reid's dreams had been dashed against the stones. Shattered and burned and stomped on. He hadn't said it, but she saw the defeat in his eyes. Felt it in his words. She would not have held her death against him. He had a bright future ahead of him, of legend and chivalry. She didn't.

But he had chosen her. Over the Order. Over knighthood. Whenever the guilt became too much, she reminded herself of that. Reid chose her.

And she worried he hated her for it.

The pain in her back had lessened to a tolerable soreness. The Mage's Bane wound felt like any other knife wound. All thanks to Abrielle's healing magic.

Reid stirred. His eyes opened.

"Good morning," she whispered.

"Is it morning?"

"I don't think so."

Their little room had no windows. She had no way of telling the time of day. Her meals hadn't been consistent either. But she could feel her magic rejuvenating from the Bane. According to her magic, the night was on its way.

It had been a day since they had fled from the Marca. A single day had turned the world on its head.

Reid groaned and sat up. "How are you feeling?"

"Better." Horrible, but better.

Reid examined her back. They hadn't wrapped the wound. Abrielle said it would heal faster. So Juniper remained naked to the waist. She slept mostly on her stomach, so few had seen more than her thrashed back. Except for Reid and Abrielle—and the knights Reid had killed, and Mabyl and Finn in the kitchens. She didn't like how long the list was getting.

"It's healing well," Reid said. His fingers brushed the sensitive skin of her back, and gooseflesh rippled over her arms and down her sides. He flattened his hand against her back, warm and calloused.

Juniper searched his face for any sign of bitterness or anger, but he kept his expression stoic and guarded. Like always. Like those early days, when he had been the squire in her way, and she the thief in his.

His eyes met hers. Bleakness stared back at her.

She reached a wobbly hand out to him. He grasped it with his own, lacing their fingers.

"I'm sorry," she whispered.

Something soft flickered in his eyes. "It's not your fault."

"The knights tried to take the ring," she said, unconsciously wiggling the finger that wore the moonstone. "I wouldn't let them. I told them they'd have to take it off my dead body. I didn't think they would take me seriously."

Reid looked at the ring. "When I walked into that room and saw you there, I knew I couldn't do it. I couldn't kill you. Not for the Order. Not for anyone. I couldn't lose you. I didn't want to live without you. I don't want to." He looked up from the ring and to her. "I love you, Juniper."

She wanted to ask him why he wore guilt in his eyes.

"I love you," she said instead. And she did. But her voice came out weak.

Reid lifted her knuckles to his lips. "I believe Nexon intended us both to die last night. He wanted to torture me with your death, and then his thralls would have killed me to cover his tracks. Then Fowler could have told the king any story he wanted." He released a sigh, his breath warm against her hand. "It doesn't matter now. Fowler showed his true colors. Nexon revealed his connection to the Order."

"And now we can start planning our counterattack," Juniper said. "Against Fowler and Nexon."

Reid's lips twitched into a smile; then his scowl returned. "You are in no shape for that."

"We don't have a lot of time," Juniper argued. "Either Nexon assumed he could kill us easily, or he is done hiding behind the Order."

Reid nodded. "I've thought about that too."

Nexon wanted Juniper dead because she had interfered with his plans, and because of a one-thousand-year-old prophecy that claimed a princess would stop him from returning to power. Nexon thought her that princess, though she didn't know how much of it she believed.

A silence fell between them. Reid's gaze lingered on the moonstone ring.

"I suppose this means we are postponing the wedding," Juniper whispered. She'd tried for humor, but Reid did not smile.

"We have more important things to worry about right now." Reid's scowl deepened.

The silence between them stretched.

Before Carol ruined the evening, Juniper had allowed herself fanciful thoughts of a wedding night. She had imagined being carried over the threshold, a hundred candles, expensive wine, and a slow and passionate night with Reid. How silly those daydreams felt now.

After a long moment, Reid asked, "What are you thinking about?"

"You, to be honest."

Reid gave her a small, modest smile. His cheeks reddened as he said lowly, "Your back is still healing. You're in no shape for that either."

A warm blush turned her cheeks pink as she said, "Well, your back is fine, isn't it?"

His brows rose.

"We could check something off the list while we wait," she whispered.

Desire darkened his eyes. She pushed herself off the bedroll and onto her shaky limbs. His eyes shamelessly traced her exposed skin. Their lips met in a tender kiss. She pressed her hand against his chest, to push him onto his back, but a flurry of voices drifted from upstairs; among them came one she knew immediately.

She half fell in her scramble to stand, and Reid caught her.

"That's Ison," she gasped.

CHAPTER 22

After a visit to the small washroom in the cellar, which was nothing more than a few jugs of water and a copper basin, charcoal soap, and a few scratchy towels tucked behind a moth-eaten curtain, Juniper tugged on an oversized shirt and plain trousers. Reid found them in the supplies, and they had the musty smell of storage. Juniper didn't complain. She would rather wear musty clean clothes than dirty, bloodied clothes.

She tugged on her leather boots. Her foot fit perfectly into the sole—*hers*. They had been given to her during her stay at Bradburn Castle, and they had survived the Demon Crisis, her return and escape from the Undercity, and her journey to and from the edge of the realm. The boots had held up well, all things considered. The leather had nicks and scratches, and the buckles no longer gleamed. A bit of blood had speckled the left one. Whether it was hers or not, she didn't want to know.

Reid had removed his silver armor and wore the same gray shirt and black trousers as he had during her visit to the castle.

Juniper climbed the narrow wooden stairs to the first floor of the safe house; the stairs led to the false back of a cabinet. The voices came from the other side. Reid showed her the hidden panel that slid aside when the rune in the bottom corner was touched.

"Something about body heat and intent," Reid said. "It's not one of the runes I know."

His tone struck her—he neither disapproved nor approved of the rune, but his indifference came cold. The same cold indifference masked his face. Before Juniper could ask, the panel slid soundlessly aside. A stack of crates blocked her view of the speakers.

Juniper tiptoed around the crates. A dozen candles burned, flickering the cellar in shades of shadow and burnt orange. Ison, Xavier, and Blythe stood in the cellar, talking to Mabyl, Finn, and Abrielle. Blythe's dark eyes darted to Juniper at once. At the twitch of Blythe's head, Xavier noticed. He nudged Ison, who followed his eyes. His gray eyes widened, and a smile of relief spread over his face.

"Jun?" Ison started for her. She met him halfway, walking into his embrace. "You're alive."

98

"And slightly wounded," Juniper said with a wince as his arms started to tighten around her middle. "Particularly on my back."

Ison quickly released her and gave her a sheepish smile.

Mabyl tilted her head to Juniper. "Oh, look who's awake. Welcome to the party. You missed the punch."

Reid stepped out from behind the crates. He took in the room, marking each face. His gaze settled on Xavier. Recognition flared, and a steep dislike burned through his stoic mask.

"Oh, someone's not happy," Xavier said, his tone carefree.

Reid curled his fingers toward his palm and took a step toward Xavier, who twisted his body to face him. Juniper saw the vengeful intent—she *felt* it. She threw herself between the two and flattened her hand on Reid's chest, over his heart, and flattened her hand against Xavier's chest where he kept a hidden blade. Juniper met Reid's eye and silently implored him to stop—she didn't want to know which would win; she didn't care. Reid glared but halted. Juniper turned her glare on Xavier, whose blue-gray eyes glittered with dangerous amusement.

"Considering the last time Reid saw you, you killed a knight, hurt Adrian, and tried to hurt me, I'd say Reid owes you a hit," she said.

"Or two," added Reid.

Xavier eyed Reid. "I suppose I can't argue. Though, if you want to get revenge on me, you'd best take a number. There's a long line in front of you."

"Fighting among allies will not help anyone," Ison said.

Xavier met Ison's stare, and something silent passed between the two. Xavier's amusement faded, and the dangerous glint softened.

Reid's gaze darted between Ison and Xavier. His brows rose, and understanding smoothed his anger. His surprise quickly faded into neutrality. Juniper patted his chest, bringing Reid's attention back to her. He covered her hand with his own. She took it to be an unspoken promise not to cause a scene.

"All right, gather around," said Mabyl. "We've got an update for you. That knight and his buddy went to see what they could find out from the Order. The Order hasn't openly claimed that anything happened."

"You just let them walk out?" Reid brows rose. "A knight and a pledge who know your hideout?"

"We put runes on them and told them if they told anyone about the hideout, the runes would kill them," Mabyl said smugly. Reid started to object, and Mabyl added, "The runes are bogus, but we'll tell them about it when and if they return."

Juniper chuckled; Reid did not.

"They wanted to be useful," Abrielle added. "They're curious about what's become of the Order, and unlike us, they can walk in and ask."

"And," Mabyl continued, "Ison here tells us there's a house by the canal where the Undercity mages are living. It's the base of operations against Nexon. That's where we're headed. Tonight, if possible. We'll move under the cover of dark."

"Amery bought a lovely little manor," Xavier said to Juniper. "It's a bit crowded, but not bad. Better view than the old keep."

"The real question is what to do after that," Mabyl said.

"We have to inform the king of Fowler's true loyalties," Juniper said. "Fowler will have already fed him some lie of what happened, pinning me as the enemy."

"And the sooner we tell him, the better," Reid added.

"Oh, another thing," Xavier started, then tilted his head to Blythe.

Blythe took the hint and said, "The Order isn't looking for you. Rumor has it that mages have gone missing, but no one knows who or if it's even true. The Order isn't talking."

Juniper glanced at Reid. His suspicions mirrored her own.

"Fowler intended to kill us both, then," Juniper said.

"He didn't anticipate us getting out," Reid added.

"And if he publicly announces that I've escaped, the king would be suspicious," Juniper said. "He knows I wouldn't have run unless I had good reason."

"And he knows I would not have turned on the Order without purpose."

"Fowler will try to keep it as quiet for as long as he can." Juniper sighed through her nose. "Until he finds us and finishes the job."

"The Order has increased their presence around the castle," Blythe said. "And knights have been moving through the city."

"Because he knows we would go straight to the king," Reid said. "He'll be scouring the city for us, to eliminate us before we can tell the king the truth about Fowler."

Juniper huffed and crossed her arms. "Does that fool honestly think a few knights will keep me from getting into the castle?"

Reid frowned. "I take that to mean you're not planning on going through the front gates?"

Juniper laughed. "Front gates are for guests."

"Other mages escaped during the incident," Finn added.

"And maybe more," Ison said. "Search parties are looking for them as we speak."

"If they've got brains, they'll join our side." Mabyl crossed her arms.

Juniper hummed. "Our little army of apostates is growing."

"Not just apostates," Reid added. "You've got knights on your side."

"Until your friends come back to prove my assumptions wrong, we've got *a* knight." Mabyl pointed at Reid.

"We should consider combat training for the new mages," Juniper said.

"We've carved out a basement under Amery's house that's proven perfect for it," Xavier said.

"The older mages will likely know something of combat, or at least have a handle on raw magic," Mabyl said.

"Like you," Reid added.

Mabyl scowled. "Hey, my magic got us out of the Marca."

"I'm not complaining," Reid said through gritted teeth.

Juniper put her hand to her mouth and whispered loudly, "That's his pouting voice. It sounds like he's complaining, but he's not."

Reid frowned, and she winked at him.

"Getting back to the topic at hand…" Reid cleared his throat. "Nexon has exposed his connection to the Order. Fowler has exposed his true colors. I think it's safe to assume Nexon thought his plan through, and he had something else planned that did not hinge on his connection to the Order being a secret."

"Something big," Juniper added. "Something where keeping that a secret wouldn't matter."

"I think it's worth mentioning," started Ison, "that we have reports of strange activity in the Undercity. The Watch reported there being movement in the ruins underneath."

"The ruins that connect directly to the castle." Juniper blanched.

"And we found evidence of another Transformation circle in those ruins," Xavier added. By the way Ison did not flinch or pale, he knew. "Nexon had been making more of those monsters. Amery and I took one out during the Watch's invasion."

"But the Watch hasn't found anyone or anything," Ison said.

Juniper leaned onto a stack of heavy barrels. She took all the information in, thought it over. "Do you think Nexon is keeping his followers in those ruins?"

"I'm more worried he's keeping a horde of demons," Ison said.

Juniper's stomach flopped. She met Reid's suspicious stare.

"He's planning an assault on the castle?" Reid echoed her thoughts. "He wouldn't be so foolish."

"But he could get inside through the ruins," Juniper whispered. "And with unknown numbers of the Order enthralled to Nexon—"

"—the castle is vulnerable," Reid finished.

"As are all the people inside it," Juniper said. Like the king, Adrian, and Roslyn.

"Mason is there," Ison said. "He won't let Nexon in so easily."

"But what if he's overwhelmed with apostates and thralls armed with Mage's Bane?" Xavier asked.

"He's the court magician for a reason," Ison said proudly.

"We have to get to the king first and warn him," Juniper said, mostly to Reid. He nodded. "Before Nexon or Fowler. Tonight."

"Are you healed enough?" Mabyl asked.

"Yes," Juniper said firmly. She ignored Reid's disbelieving stare. "A small team will sneak into the castle to warn the king. I'll go."

"As will I," said Reid.

"How is your sneaking?" Xavier asked, brows high.

"If the Order is indeed keeping my desertion quiet, I should have no trouble moving through the castle," Reid said.

"And if Nexon's thralls corner you?" Mabyl asked.

"You fight," Juniper said. She met Reid's stare. "If Nexon has the balls to attack you right under the king's nose, then he is indeed making his move. And we will fight back."

A moment of doubt passed over Reid's stoic mask; then his resolve hardened. He nodded. "We fight."

"In that case…" Mabyl summoned a magelight of bright blue. She split it in two and tossed one to Juniper. The light landed in her hand and hovered just above her palm. Rather than heat, it gave off a feather-light sensation, like hair tickling her skin. "If your sneaky plans go to shit, turn the light red."

Juniper blinked. "And…how would one do that?"

"With your magic," Mabyl said, as if it were obvious.

Juniper concentrated on the magelight. She vaguely remembered red lights during their escape. She felt the magelight tether to her magic. The touch was light, almost nonexistent. She reached out to the light with her magic. The light shifted between shades of periwinkle and sapphire, then turned white, then sage, then periwinkle again. As her magelight shifted colors, so did the one in Mabyl's palm.

"How do I make it red?" Juniper asked. Her magic managed a shade of chartreuse.

"Hmm," Mabyl said. "Any color works, I guess. Less urgent than red, but effective."

Finn found two small glass jars in the cellar, one for each magelight. Juniper tucked one into the pocket of her trousers. Mabyl kept the other.

"We will be ready to strike if you need us," Xavier said. "Us and any pissed-off mages we find."

"Hopefully, we find more than a few," Mabyl muttered.

CHAPTER 23

Night fell quickly. Reid donned his mostly clean armor, and Juniper found a button-up man's vest in one of the many crates in the basement. It hung over her frame, but her back couldn't tolerate snug clothing. She would have to make do.

"How is your magic?" Reid whispered as he secured his vambraces.

"It's fine," she said.

He frowned.

"It's not perfect, but it's better than nothing."

The Mage's Bane had made her magic curl up and hide, and it had been slowly coming back. The night had helped. She could handle herself in a fight, at least.

Reid started to speak but stopped himself. She knew what he wanted to say—that she should stay. He also knew she would refuse.

Under the cover of night, Reid and Juniper headed north to Bradburn Castle while the others headed south to Amery's. Reid and Juniper traveled in silence. Juniper's magic responded to the night, to the dark, to the lingering chill in the air. Her magic was sluggish, drugged from the Bane. Crisscrossing dark alleys, sticking to the shadows, tiptoeing down empty side streets—she knew this. She had spent years perfecting her thieving skills. She had spent so many nights wandering Rusdasin. Sneaking through it now brought back a sense of purpose, a sense of power and freedom that she had sorely missed.

She led them to one of the many hidden entrances to the Undercity, a ladder in the back of a print shop. The bittersweet smell of ink and the crisp, dusty scent of paper clung to the air. The shop had closed for the night, leaving a vicious silence behind. Reid moved as quietly as he could, though his armor clinked more than she would have liked.

She uncovered the trapdoor under an old rug and yanked it open. A wooden ladder vanished into darkness. She went first, and at the bottom, opened the secret panel that led into Maddox's old office. It looked just as it had, only darker. The window that overlooked the street was entirely black—she had anticipated the darkness, but the utter silence brought a chill to her skin that went deeper than her bones.

As her eyes adjusted, she spotted the glow of candles in the distance. According to Xavier, the Watch had made their camp in the center of the

Undercity. Rather than take over one of the many homes, the Watch had erected a small tent city.

Reid climbed into the office. Unlike her, he couldn't see in the dark. He took a mage stone out of his pocket—Ison had given it to him before they left—and in response to Reid's touch, it began to glow pale green. Unlike magelight, which glowed in response to a mage's natural magic, a mage stone glowed when in contact with flesh. Juniper had only been half listening when Ison explained them. Something about the complicated rune engraved on the surface, and something about the type of stone affecting the color.

The glow of the mage stone only accentuated the shadows.

"This is Maddox's keep," Juniper whispered. Her voice sounded far too loud, even as a whisper.

"Is it now?" Reid glanced around the office.

"I'd love to give you a tour, but we're short on time. Maybe later?"

"Perhaps."

According to Xavier, only a handful of Watch stayed in the Undercity. They didn't have the extra hands to have a full presence at all times. The Watch stuck on Undercity duty had been given the dull task of going through every house, room, and armoire. It would seem they had not yet made it to Maddox's house. It looked as though everyone had just left, leaving books open, cups abandoned, and shoes by the door.

As Juniper made her way through the keep, guilt tugged at her heart. How many people had she gotten killed by selling out the Undercity? How many of her own keep had died?

She shoved those feelings down. She didn't have time to worry about it now.

Luckily, because so few of the Watch occupied the Undercity, sneaking through was not hard. Juniper and Reid walked side by side down the street. Without the magelights, the shadows were bigger and thicker and deeper. The homes were quiet and dark. Only their soft footsteps sounded. With the thick silence and endless darkness, the Undercity seemed bigger and more dangerous than it ever had.

Juniper led Reid into the tavern she and Ison had come up through, into the basement, and to the grate that led into the sewers that led into the ruins. She bent down and yanked the grate off. It felt strange but fitting to be returning to the castle this way.

"You think this will work?" Reid whispered.

"I don't see why it wouldn't," Juniper said. "We have to get to the king, or Adrian, or Roslyn, or even Mason, and expose Nexon and Fowler."

A beat passed. They stood on opposite sides of the grate, both looking into the darkness below. Reid's mage stone shaded them both in pale green light and exaggerated the worried expression on his face.

"I'm worried about how deep Nexon's infiltration of the Order goes," Reid said. "I'm worried about what the king has already heard."

"He wouldn't believe anything bad about you," Juniper said. "The king knows you. Adrian knows you. Your uncle knows you. They know you would never turn on the Order unless something happened. The king knows you are one of the finest knights to ever join the Order."

Reid let out a soft, almost inaudible exhale. She knew the sound, and she knew that had it not been for the dark, she would have seen his cheeks warm and his stoic mask slip.

And she meant every word.

Juniper jumped down first. Her feet hit solid, slightly curved stone. A heartbeat later, Reid joined her. He held his mage stone, and she had her night sight. Without a word, they started through the ancient sewer.

The sewers gave way to the ancient Iluvin ruins, as dark and creepy as Juniper remembered. Only this time, the air felt different. The air felt…fresh. As they walked through the corridors and chambers, her suspicions were confirmed. She spotted signs of life—recent campfires, bedrolls, and abandoned articles of clothing and pieces of dried meat and half-drunk tea.

Underneath it all, the air carried a mixture of silver polish and flowers. Mages had been staying in the ruins and had already left.

Juniper met Reid's worried stare. His nostrils flared.

They were running out of time. Juniper hurried through the ruins, Reid a step behind her. She didn't see anyone, but she had the worst feeling of being watched.

CHAPTER 24

On the walk back to Amery's, Ison fell into step beside Xavier. He hadn't done it on purpose. It happened naturally. He couldn't believe he had found Mabyl again—he had idolized her in the Marca. She had been the fiercest of the mages, unafraid of the thought of rebellion, and the one to whisper of the secret warning signal.

Ison didn't notice Blythe until she fell into step behind Xavier. She appeared without warning, without sound, and often without nary a hint—it unnerved Ison, but he knew how useful her skills of stealth were.

"Anything?" Xavier asked without glancing over his shoulder. How he detected Blythe's presence, Ison didn't know.

"Something," Blythe said.

Xavier had sent Blythe back to the Marca to spy. She was to report back with anything. She hadn't been gone very long, and Ison could only imagine the news.

"A knight ordered the pledges into the sanctum," Blythe reported. "There's some sort of gathering happening. The pledges didn't seem enthused, but they did as they were told."

"Like good little soldiers," Mabyl said, her tone singsong.

"They are gathering forces?" Ison asked. "Do you think Nexon or Fowler is planning something for the knights?"

"Unless he plans to march on the castle," Xavier added, his frown deepening. Xavier paused—the others followed. To Blythe, he asked, "When do you strike an opponent?"

Blythe hesitated a beat before whispering, "When you have the advantage."

"The Order will be scrambling," Ison said, understanding dawning. "They will be reeling from the rebellion."

"And any sneak attack will have an advantage," Xavier said. "I say we go over and see what this meeting is about."

Ison swallowed. The thought of sneaking into the Order's stronghold sent a wave of panic and fear through his limbs. Mabyl grinned at the idea—of course she would—and Blythe looked as impassive as Ison had ever seen her. Finn didn't look keen on the idea, but he kept his words to himself.

"And…we might find more allies among the Order," Xavier whispered, as though the word *allies* made him a bit sick.

"And we would be close by if Juniper needed us," Ison said, his voice strained. He looked between Xavier, Mabyl, Blythe, and Finn. He was outnumbered. Mad, the lot of them. "Okay. Let's see what the Order is up to."

The Knights of the Order traveled all over the kingdom, but their headquarters remained in Rusdasin. Vanten Hall was an ancient stone temple named after the first knight commander. It was a gloomy structure of iron spires and thin steeples. A stone wall surrounded the complex, topped with vicious iron spikes. Ison had never been close enough to get a good look, and he had never wanted to be.

Getting to Vanten Hall had been a chore in itself—City Watch patrolled the streets, on edge and alert. Not as many people had ventured into the market districts, and the usual chatter had dulled into whispers. The uncertainty churned the fear into something malicious. Everyone knew something had happened at the Marca, but not what. Knights patrolled too, but they wore the glassy expressions of thralls.

Ison and the others stood in a darkened alley across the street from Vanten Hall.

"It's a fortress," Ison complained. "How are we going to—"

The stone under his feet moved. The stones unraveled and reformed a wide staircase and led into a tunnel.

"No problem," said Finn.

They filed into the tunnel, and Finn both commanded the stone to close behind them and open in front of them. It didn't take long to reach the sewers and to find a channel that connected to Vanten Hall. Thanks to Finn's power over stone, they could walk beside the sluice rather than in it. Ison would have to thank him later, and he would inform the laundry staff at Amery's to do so as well.

Finn crafted a narrow entrance into the lower level of Vanten Hall. Torches were sparse, and the shadows were many. The lower levels were made of dark gray stone and blocky cellars and storerooms, mostly. Few servants were working, and sneaking past them was easy. Especially with Xavier's example.

He was in his element, Ison realized as they crept up a narrow servant's stairwell. This was what Xavier had been trained to do—sneak and slither through the shadows, silent as a ghost.

They reached the top of the servants' passage and entered a corridor only slightly better lit than the others. Vanten Hall reeked of silver polish and a strange scent that reminded Ison of burnt potions. Xavier wrinkled his nose at the smell, and Mabyl scowled.

"That smells like magic," Mabyl whispered. "Bad magic."

Abrielle raised a brow. "Bad magic smells like burnt hair?"

Xavier put a finger to his lips and glared at them all.

Ison couldn't get the smell out of his nose. It smelled...wrong. It churned his stomach and made him nauseous. It triggered a physical panic, a cold sweat, and a quiver in his gut. Everything about the strange smell was *wrong*.

This way, Xavier said with the silent wave of his hand. Ison crept after him, and the others followed. They paused at a corridor, and to Ison's dismay, armored footsteps were headed in their direction.

Xavier crept to the edge of the corridor. His shadowy magic slithered around the corner. If Ison hadn't known what to look for, he would not have seen the shadows move. Xavier held up his index finger—one knight.

"We can take him," Mabyl whispered into Ison's ear.

The knight came closer, then paused.

"Who is there?" asked the knight in a dry voice that sent the hairs on Ison's arms on end. "The Knight Commander has ordered all knights, squires, and pledges into the sanctum. It is not optional."

Ison met Xavier's eyes. The knight's voice held no emotion, no fluctuation.

Thrall? Xavier mouthed.

Ison shrugged. He had never had the pleasure of encountering a thrall, though he had read about them briefly.

It was another thing the Order didn't think mages needed to know about. Now he knew why.

"Knight Commander Fowler has ordered all—"

Xavier jumped into the corridor. His shadows surged forward, knocking the knight off his feet. Mabyl followed him, and Ison went with them.

The knight stood and reached for his Mage's Bane blade.

"Funny meeting you here," Mabyl said, her tone overly sweet.

Ison remained still as the knight's glazed eyes searched over their party. His face remained calm, almost asleep, and then—a dagger made of shadow tore through the knight's throat. A bubble of fire appeared around the knight, and it burned so bright and hot that Ison squeezed his eyes shut and turned aside. He felt the heat radiate, as if he stood within the fire.

"There," Mabyl whispered.

Ison blinked. Where the knight had stood, only ash remained. Not even the bones. Ison felt his knees tremble. Mabyl had incinerated him. And, by the sweat on her brow, it had taken a toll on her magic.

"Are you all right?" Ison whispered.

Mabyl scoffed, grinning.

"That was a thrall," Xavier whispered. "Did you see the look on his face?"

Ison nodded. He'd known it, even before it had registered that he knew. "Someone else was controlling him, just as Reid said."

"I'm willing to bet there are more of those around," Mabyl said. "Are you prepared to fight for your life?"

Ison bit his lower lip. *No.* "I'll be all right."

Xavier and Mabyl took the lead. Ison walked in the middle. Finn and Blythe walked behind. Blythe held twin daggers, ready for anything, and she reminded Ison terribly of Juniper. He couldn't decide if that was a good thing or a bad thing.

After the first enthralled knight, they encountered few people. It seemed the entire Order had retreated into the sanctum. With the direction of a kitchen girl, whom Mabyl then ordered to get out while she still could, they headed toward the center of Vanten Hall. On the advice of the kitchen girl, they did not go directly into the sanctum but instead climbed to the second floor—a veranda that overlooked the sanctum.

It looked like a temple. Small statues of the gods sat upon pedestals at the front. Rows of wooden benches angled down a center aisle. Hundreds of candles burned on the altars before the gods, a hundred more behind them, and torches lined the walls. The flames spat shadows back and forth, under the knights, under the benches, behind the pillars. The strange stench was stronger here than in the rest of the hall, so strong it stole Ison's first breath. On his second lungful, he caught the subtle scent of silver polish, only it was...wrong. Twisted. Putrid. festering and rotten.

Several dozen knights had gathered in the center. Most looked confused. Ison counted a dozen thralls from his angle, standing at doors with blank faces and glossed-over eyes.

"I wager the knights in the middle are not thralls," Xavier whispered.

Ison nodded. He didn't see a single blank face among them.

The grand set of doors on the far side of the sanctum opened, and several sets of feet marched inside. Ison leaned forward to see through the balusters— and his heart dropped. Three thralls escorted Isaac Pinul into the room. He did not look happy about it. They pushed him to stand with the others, and another familiar face appeared among them—Henry Julian said something to Isaac, who shook his head and mouthed, *Not now.*

"This is all of them in the Hall," said one of the thralls, his voice reedy and dry, as empty as his eyes.

"We shall begin," said another knight, older than the others, with gray-streaked brown hair and a matching beard. He stepped into the middle of the aisle, the fire flickering off his shined silver armor—the owl on his breastplate appeared to take flight. "Knight Commander Fowler decrees a change in the Order."

At those words, a subtle murmur went through the knights. Isaac frowned, as did several others. Henry spoke into the ear of a young boy, likely a pledge.

"The winds of change are upon us, and there is dark magic in Rusdasin. We must be prepared to stomp out this wave of black magic before it takes us all," said the older knight. "Who will be the first to step forward and receive the rune of protection?"

None of the gathered knights moved.

Then, a thrall grabbed one of the pledges and yanked him to where the older knight stood. They forced the pledge onto his knees, holding him down by the shoulders.

"This rune will protect you from black magic," said the older knight to the trembling pledge. "This rune will enlighten you."

The knight flattened his palm against the forehead of the pledge. The pledge struggled. A short one-note gasp escaped his throat, and then his struggling stopped. His body stilled and slackened.

The knights released the pledge. He stood, his face void of emotion, his eyes glossy and dull. His body moved as if on strings, jerky and ungraceful.

"Who will be next?" asked the older knight.

"Gods." Ison sucked in his breath. "They're going to turn them into thralls."

"Shit," Xavier spat.

"Can we take them all?" Mabyl asked, her tone unchanged and unhurried. "There's at least a dozen thralls, and we can't say for certain if those knights will fight for or against us."

"They see what's being done to them," Ison said, fists curling. "We can't just sit here and do nothing."

So he did something. He sent a tendril of air to Henry's cheek. Henry swatted at it like a fly, but Ison persisted. *Look at me,* he willed—and at last, as a second knight was being forced into thrall-hood, Henry looked up.

NIGHTMARES IN THE ICE

In a heartbeat, his eyes found Ison and the others. Henry's fear mixed with confusion, and then realization. Grinning, he nodded at Ison. He put his hand on the blade at his side.

"That is our cue," Xavier said. "Finn, make it dramatic."

Finn commanded the stone under their feet. The stone reshaped into a smoothed surface, and they slid down into the room, shadow-daggers, fireballs, and wind flashing through the air. At the same time, a fierce cry rang over the sanctum.

"Do not stand for this!" It was Isaac. "This is not what the Order decrees! This is black magic!"

Ison's feet hit the floor, and he whipped tendrils of air around him. Thralls unsheathed their Mage's Bane, and he felt a shiver of fear. Henry appeared beside him, Mage's Bane blade angled to protect him, rather than attack.

Swords unsheathed all around him, but as the thralls attacked, Ison didn't have the time to see who fought with them or against them. It took all his concentration to fight for himself. Xavier stayed close—shadow spears, whips, and daggers—and Ison heard blood hitting the stone, bodies falling, flesh tearing.

He didn't look. He wouldn't look. Not until the fight ended, when the smoke settled, when he no longer felt like his own life might join the fallen.

CHAPTER 25

When Juniper had slipped through the ruins the first time, they felt never-ending and utterly empty. She had feared never finding her way out. This time, it felt like things scurried just out of her night sight. The shadows themselves seemed thicker, like spilled ink. Knowing there had been people recently in the ruins intensified the feeling. Every few moments, she thought she heard footsteps on the other side of a doorway, or voices down dark corridors, or even the breath of a stranger waiting just around the corner.

Despite her uneasy feeling and apprehension, she kept a quick pace. She didn't have a set path. Nothing looked familiar or strange. It all looked the same, stony and ancient. Not once did Reid ask if she knew where they were going or if they were lost. Gradually, after several sets of narrow stairs, the Iluvin ruins gave way to the castle catacombs.

"I know where we are," Reid whispered.

Juniper stepped aside. "Lead the way, sir."

Reid didn't hesitate. He started through the catacombs, mage stone illuminating his path. "As a squire," Reid whispered, "I traversed these tunnels in preparation for emergency situations."

"Like after Bala's Ball?"

"Just like that."

After stairs, passageways, and more stairs, Reid led them to one of many secret entrances into the catacombs hidden behind paintings. He found the release lever on the far right side, pulled it, and with a series of mechanical clicks, the painting swung open into an empty chamber. The painting overlooked a seating area of delicate rosewood and beige velvet. The hearth was cold. The mage stone illuminated the large desk on the other side, nestled between two towering bookcases packed with books and scrolls. Several smaller desks were arranged in front of the larger desk. No windows let in the moonlight. The only light came from Reid's mage stone.

"Where are we?" Juniper whispered as Reid stepped into the lounge. "A classroom?"

"Yes," Reid said. A small, victorious smile crept over his lips, though the serious gleam did not leave his eyes. "This is where Adrian and I did our studies as children."

"Why do you sound so happy about it?"

"Because we're in the Royal Chambers."

And he had bypassed any security that might have prevented them from getting to the king or stopped them from alerting Fowler or Nexon first.

"And they say knights are all brawn," she teased, winking at him.

"Who says that?"

"I *never* said that about you," she whispered. "I knew you had brains the moment I saw you."

He looked like he wanted to argue, but they didn't have time. They dusted themselves off and stepped into the corridor. The sudden brightness stung her eyes. Torches bathed the stone walls of the Royal Chambers in yellow-orange, making the frowning portraits glower. The light flickered off the polished suits of armor that lined the corridors, suits from all eras of Duvane's past—shades of ash, iron, and pewter.

Reid started to turn down one corridor—the quickest route through—but she halted him. He glared.

She put a finger to her lips, waiting for a patrolling set of boots to walk far enough in the opposite direction, and then whispered, "We can sneak around the guards. Where is the king?"

"We're going to Adrian's chambers."

"We're not going to the king?"

Reid turned a bit sheepish. "Going straight to the king still makes me nervous. We'll be waking him up."

She nodded—she understood.

She knew how to get to Adrian's chambers, and if she remembered the patrols correctly, they had a small window where they would not be seen. She listened—the corridor was quiet—and crept around the corner. Reid followed, though not as quietly as she would have liked. Sneaking took longer, but they reached the corridor of Adrian's chambers without detection. Juniper stepped into the corridor with a feeling of elation—that quickly dissolved. Two royal guards stood opposite Adrian's closed chamber door, faces passive and bored.

Reid started into the corridor, pretense of stealth gone. Juniper sighed through her nose. She'd rather sneak around them, but they hadn't the time.

The first guard glanced at Reid, and then his bored expression melted into surprise. His slightly slouched posture straightened. Juniper recognized him—his warm brown skin and pale brown eyes—as one of Adrian's normal guards. "Reid?" asked the guard.

"Ian," Reid replied, nodding toward the guard. "Please, is Adrian in his chambers?"

"Yes," Ian replied.

"Reid, what's this about?" asked the other guard, a fair-skinned and red-haired young guard. He narrowed his eyes at Juniper. She didn't recognize him. He must have been added after she had fled.

"Jax, something is happening," Reid said lowly to the red-haired guard. "The royal family is in danger. Find my uncle, wake him, and tell him to meet me in the Sun Parlor at once. Alert no one else. Understand?"

Jax blinked, then straightened. "At once, sir." The young guard started down the corridor, as if he had just finished his shift and had a long nap on his mind—avoiding suspicion.

"Reid?" asked Ian.

"I don't have time for an explanation," Reid answered. Ian's unease only grew. "Stand guard. Be ready for anything. If you see anyone with a thrall's expression, do not hesitate to draw your weapon."

"Thrall...?" Ian straightened and put his hand on the hilt of his sword. He gave a curt nod to Reid, and at once, his face became the impassive mask of the Royal Guard.

Reid stepped into Adrian's chambers first, and Juniper followed. The sitting room was dark, save for three candles burning on the sideboard. Reid headed for the bedroom, and Juniper pressed her ear against the door—Ian hadn't moved, and no one came charging down the corridor at the sound of their voices.

Her heart pounded with the thrill of it all, sneaking and lying and coaxing—she loved that part of thieving. She loved solving the puzzle of *how*.

Reid knocked on Adrian's bedroom door as he opened it. A single candle burned on the mantle, shadowing much of the room. Adrian sat up as Reid entered, his dark blond hair messed with sleep, hazel eyes glossy, silken pajamas skewed.

"Reid?" Adrian asked sleepily. He blinked, his eyes settled on Juniper, and the sleep melted into worry. "What's wrong?"

"We need to see your father, at once," Reid said.

While Reid explained the situation, Adrian dressed and Juniper found something to stare at in the opposite direction. Adrian secured a thin sword belt around his waist, off which hung a short sword. Reid frowned.

"Don't give me that face." Adrian set his hand on the pommel of his blade. "Destry has been giving me lessons."

Adrian led them—including Ian the guard—up a floor and to a set of mahogany doors that looked like all the others in the Royal Chambers. The two guards noted them at once.

"Evening, gentlemen," Adrian said as he opened the door to his father's chambers. "The captain should be along shortly."

Juniper followed Reid into the king's chambers. Ian the guard remained outside with the others.

Adrian put a finger to his lips and whispered, "Wait here." He went through an arched mahogany door on the right.

Juniper had never been in the king's chambers. The sitting room was thrice what hers had been. The plush velvet seats had been well used. The massive hearth had been carved from pale gray marble, veined with black and gold. The royal seal had been elegantly carved into the marble, a masterpiece of history carved around it. Rosewood bookshelves lined one wall, packed with books, sparkling baubles, figurines, carvings, and scrolls. The whole space smelled like fine perfume, honeyed tea, and fresh air.

A pelt of white fur rested underneath the seating area, though she had never seen an animal quite like it. The fur had pale green stripes, almost a golden sheen. Juniper walked around to the head of the creature—deep green eyes stared into the fire. It had short, stubby pointed ears, a round snout, a black nose, and hundreds of silver whiskers.

"What is this?" Juniper whispered to Reid.

"A mosscat," he whispered.

She started to say something else, but movement came from the room Adrian had gone into. Male voices followed, two of them, hushed and quick. Juniper swallowed her words and glanced sideways at Reid. He wore the same apprehension she felt, though he hid it much better.

The door opened again. Adrian walked in first, followed by King Bentley Bradburn. He wore a fine dressing robe over his dark red pajamas. The royal seal had been embroidered over the right breast. He shared his son's dark blond hair and hazel eyes, and he looked healthier than the last time Juniper had seen him. He held himself like a man used to giving commands and having them followed, like a man who carried a kingdom on his shoulders.

King Bradburn looked at Reid then Juniper. "All right," he said, annoyance and disbelief in his words and his eyes. "I'm awake. Tell me this story of yours."

CHAPTER 26

Thud, thud, thud.

Roslyn Derean ignored the first knock, and the second. Her bedchamber was still far too dark to get up. The low-burning fire in the hearth was hidden behind a lark green screen, shading the room in comforting shades of emerald and pine. The sun hadn't even risen! Neither she nor Adrian had gotten much sleep the night before, and her body yearned for it. Roslyn hugged the pillow tighter, smothering her face into the silken threads. Oh, the Bradburns knew how to live!

Thud. Thud. Thud.

The knocker resorted to pounding. Distantly, she heard someone calling her name.

Roslyn sighed into the pillow. She pulled herself out of the soft, warm comforts of her overly large bed and trudged across the room to her dressing gown. She pulled it over her pajamas, pushed her feet into her boots, and started into the sitting room.

Thud. Thud. Thud.

"Yes, yes, I'm coming," Roslyn said, not bothering to hide her irritation at this midnight intrusion. "But please, do knock a little louder. I'm not sure the king heard you."

She reached for the deadbolt, then paused. She felt a subtle shift of the air, like when a bear noticed her presence, or that moment between lightning and the thunder—a tilted silence. Roslyn drew her hand away from the deadbolt. In that same moment, her awareness kicked in. Her instincts shook off the dregs of sleep.

Who would be calling on her this late?

The knock came again, a heavy hand on her door—*thud, thud, thud.*

No voice accompanied it, even after she had responded. If it were Adrian, he would have spoken. The guards would have responded.

"Who's there?" Roslyn called, reaching for the candlestick on the mantle. Solid iron, just as she had asked for. The servant had given her an odd look, but then Roslyn explained—a candlestick is the best weapon to hide in plain sight. She closed her fingers around the iron.

"Roslyn," answered a voice, calm and smooth and utterly dreadful—worse than any wolf's howl. It sent a prickle along the back of her neck.

Roslyn tiptoed back to the bedroom, her steps featherlight and silent. She closed her bedroom door—and the chamber door burst with a thunderous clatter. Splinters rained against the bedroom door, and the impact sent Roslyn stumbling back a step. She felt the heat seep through the seams in the door— accompanied by the stench of burning wood, singed drapes, and pungent smoke. Red and orange light flickered underneath the door.

A shadow appeared in front of her bedroom door, blocking the flames with two legs.

"Sorry, darling, but you're on the list," said the voice from before.

An ashy floral stench filled the air—magic.

Roslyn dashed toward the bed as the bedroom door burst apart, raining burning splinters across the bedroom. She jumped as the impact hit her, rolled across the bed, and grabbed the daggers she kept under the pillow. She rolled off the bed's other side and landed on her feet, daggers at the ready.

A figure stood in her bedroom doorway, a man with awkwardly shaved hair and a cruel grimace. Fire burned on his fingertips. "No hard feelings?" said the apostate, shrugging. "It's not me who wants you dead."

Roslyn hadn't anything witty to say to him. She had never faced down a mage, let alone one intent on setting her bedroom on fire.

Sneering, the apostate started to summon another fireball—and one of her daggers found a new home in his throat. The apostate grunted and gurgled. He lobbed the fireball at her, but it dropped onto the floor like a wet rag and dissolved.

Burning splinters spread fire across her bed, and flames raced up the canopy and charred the bedposts. Flames licked up the drapery and across the linens. Roslyn caught her breath and quickly adjusted her thinking. Bradburn Castle was no longer safe. It was a battlefield. She grabbed her yew bow from the dressing room and the dark leather quiver—an engagement gift from Adrian. She had ten arrows and two daggers. It would have to be enough.

She slung the quiver around her shoulder and ducked to avoid the smoke. As she passed, she yanked her dagger from the apostate's throat. The sitting room was ruined. The furniture had caught fire or been blasted by chunks of the chamber doors.

From the sounds of crashing and blasting and the overpowering stench of flowers, she hadn't been the only one attacked by an apostate. She nocked an arrow.

Roslyn tiptoed through her shattered chamber doors and—

"Little bitch," someone spat.

The very stones under her feet started to move.

Roslyn dove forward just as the stone jutted upward. She rolled back onto her feet—the tiniest inflection of the air nudged her cheek, and she twirled—she barely missed a spear of stone. The tip ripped through the back of her dressing gown. As she twirled, she aimed and released her arrow. It landed true—slightly off center through the throat.

The spear lodged into the wall behind her, several inches deep, and the apostate collapsed to the ground.

Roslyn pulled the bloodied arrow free. No third mage appeared, and she took a breath to assess. Her guards were dead, slumped against the wall, bludgeoned with stone.

Distant screams rattled the night air. Voices came from every direction, shouting orders and war cries. Blasts shook the air, and tremors shook the very stone.

Roslyn took the sword belt from the thinner of the guards and fastened it around her waist. She took the dagger hidden in the second's boot and tucked it into her own. A blast came from a floor below, shattering wood into splinters and ash. A scream soon followed.

Roslyn took off down the corridor, toward the nearest screams, bloodied arrow nocked.

CHAPTER 27

King Bradburn said little as Reid and Juniper told him what had happened in the Marca. He sat facing the dark hearth, elbows on his knees, fingers laced, knuckles against his mouth. Adrian sat opposite him, silent and pale. Reid hadn't told Juniper the extent of the story, of what the knights had done to her and what they wanted him to do. Juniper barely remembered those moments, and hearing the tale from Reid felt worse than her blurry memories.

At last, the story came to an end. For a long moment, no one spoke. Father and son looked remarkably similar; stoic and worried—thinking.

"Fowler sent word this morning," said the king. "He advised me not to trust you. He said you had turned your loyalties to the rogue mages." He turned his unreadable hazel eyes to Reid. "I did not write him back. I did not believe him. And, am I glad to know I made the right decision."

Juniper felt Reid sigh through his nose, a barely imperceptible sound.

The king stood. "We must act quickly. If Fowler has turned his loyalty so obviously, we are running out of valuable time. We must speak to Mason. At once."

The king returned to his bedroom and returned a few minutes later in simple and regal clothes and his handsome leather sword belt.

King Bradburn, Reid, Adrian, and Juniper started into the corridor. Juniper felt a shift of stone, a tremor, like a distant earthquake. It shuddered up her legs and into her chest and rattled her heart. She turned to mention it to Reid, but her words never made it to her mouth. A fiery crash exploded somewhere close, within the Royal Chambers. Another sounded from below, then another. Fire and stone and steel. Bradburn Castle trembled. The air turned ashy and hot.

The king unsheathed his steel, and Reid pulled his Mage's Bane free. Adrian blanched and stepped away from the door. Though he wore a sword and claimed to know how to use it, she saw the trepidation—he hadn't experienced real combat before.

Juniper readied her magic but did not summon daggers of ice. Not yet.

"What happened?" Adrian breathed.

"Magic," Juniper spat. She felt it in the air, thickening with every heartbeat.

"Nexon's mages," Reid seethed on the heels of her words. "He's attacking."

"A surprise attack in the middle of the night!" The king turned to his guards. "Sound the alarm. Prepare for an assault."

Juniper reached into her pocket and withdrew the jar of magelight. Her magic caressed the light, turning the white-blue flame to pine green.

A thudding boom sounded below them, shaking the stones and knocking a few baubles from the shelves. They clattered and crashed to the floor.

"Roslyn," Adrian gasped.

Footsteps thundered down the corridor—a royal guard careened around the corner and skidded to a halt before the king. "Your Majesty, mages are attacking. They've entered the Royal Chambers."

No sooner had the words left his mouth, then Queen Catherine Bradburn stumbled into the sitting room of the royal suite, her hair braided over her shoulder, her unpainted face fearful and bloodless. She searched the group standing just outside her chambers, and her eyes fell onto her husband.

"Guardsman," the king barked at one of the guards. "Escort the queen to safety. Use the king's hatch."

The guardsman nodded and started toward the queen. She started to speak, but the king held up his hand.

"Now is not the time, Catherine." He marched into the sitting room and kissed his wife on the cheek. He whispered something too low for the others to hear. "Go. I'll catch up."

Queen Bradburn curled her delicate hands into fists. The worry did not vanish from her fine features, but determination joined it.

"Make sure you do." She cast her eyes at Adrian; then she fled into the bedroom along with the guardsman.

Another crash shook the corridor, rattling the iron torch brackets. The burst and zap of fire followed.

"Adrian, go with your mother," said the king.

"No, I'll stay and fight," Adrian said. He grabbed the hilt of his short sword. "Roslyn—"

"Is a fighter," Juniper added.

Adrian cast a pitiful look at her, and she knew then why the king wanted him to go. Adrian was not a fighter.

Two mages came around the corner, each holding whips of fire. Juniper acted without thinking; she summoned twin whips of ice. She lashed out at them as they lashed out at her. Her whips cut through the fire with a sinister *hiss*. Her whips became arrows—they struck each mage through the heart. The whips of fire dissolved, and the mages collapsed.

Juniper's heart thudded. She had felt the heat of the fire against her face. A heartbeat later, and she would have gotten burned.

"Adrian, go," Reid said, a plea.

Adrian started to protest, but his words died on his tongue. He looked at the dead mages, his decision obvious, even to him.

"We will catch up," said the king.

"I will hold you to that," Adrian said, his voice soft and wavering. He cast a fearful glance at Reid, then Juniper, and followed his mother into the bedroom.

"To Mason," said the king. "With haste."

Juniper pulled her magic back. She hadn't the energy to spare. They started forward—guards and Reid first—with the sound of fighting all around them, crashing and bursts of fire and cracking stone and rushing wind. Juniper thought she could *feel* the crackling of ice and the sloshing of water. It gave off a different power, and it tugged and pushed against her own—a tide of magic.

In the next corridor, Reid swiftly ended a fight between an earth mage and an air mage and one royal guard—he rebounded magic onto the earth mage and ended the air mage with his Mage's Bane. The guard slumped against the wall, panting.

"There are more," gasped the guard. "I–I saw them."

"We will take care of them," Juniper said. "All of them."

They ran toward the end of the corridor. An earth mage and a water mage blocked their exit, each weaving magic around their fingers. Juniper lashed whips of ice at the water mage. The water mage lashed back. Juniper reacted—her whip divided into twin spears, one pierced the mage's heart, the other the throat.

The earth mage threw spiked rocks at her, one thwarted by her ice, the other by Reid's blade. The earth mage summoned a spike from the wall—an arrow pierced his throat. The spike crumbled to the floor. The earth mage fell, and Roslyn stood down the corridor, bow poised.

She made her way to them and pulled the arrow free of the dead mage. After examining the arrowhead, she tossed it aside and pulled another from her quiver. She smelled of singed hair, and the bottom half of her dressing robe had splotchy burns and several tears. She had a cut on her shoulder, but it didn't look deep.

"Hey," Roslyn said casually. "We've got a problem."

"We have a few problems," Juniper added.

"We're wasting time," shouted the king, and he motioned them forward.

They marched through the Royal Chambers. The mages had come up through the portrait room—they'd left the doors wide open. The royal guards posted within sight of the door were both dead. The guards posted outside the Royal Chambers were dead, and the doors had been blasted apart.

So much death. The air reeked of death, of blood and magic, of singed flesh and dust. A corridor away from the Royal Chambers, they stumbled upon three mages standing over dead guardsmen. Their smug faces churned Juniper's irritation into boiling rage. Before the mages noticed them, she sent an ice arrow through the throat of the first. The other two barely had time to react. Reid took the second with his Mage's Bane, and Ian the guard took the third. The mages joined the dead.

They fought their way through the castle, toward the court magician's chamber. The corridors were littered with dead Royal Guard, unlucky servants, and a few mages. Juniper, Reid, and the guards took care of any mage who dared attack. Reid rebounded magic onto several mages with his wards. Juniper remembered how it felt to have her magic rebounded, but she felt no sympathy for these murdering mages.

They shouldn't have picked the wrong side.

A blast shook the corridor, and a whirlwind of marigold flames surged toward them. The paintings curled in the heat, and their rosewood frames blackened. The heat radiated against Juniper's skin—the hot breath of a dragon. A figure appeared in the center of the whirlwind, hands outstretched, commanding the fire, laughing.

Juniper willed her ice into a wall. Where the fire slammed into the ice, steam erupted. The flames melted her ice, and she refroze it. The water quenched one flame, and three more took its place. Juniper pushed her ice toward the fire mage, and the fire mage pushed back.

And Juniper had used a lot of her wounded magic.

The flames surged, and she stumbled back a step.

"Juniper," warned Reid. He held his fist in front of his chest—ready to make a ward.

"On three?" Juniper asked, her voice quivering.

"One." Reid stepped closer—directly in front of the fire mage. "Two."

"Three," Juniper gasped.

She stepped aside, taking her ice with her, and Reid took her place. His shimmery ward spread from his hand, and the surge of fire slammed into it in a fiery blast. He pushed—the fire rebounded. The fire mage cried in pain and collapsed. Before her magic could come back, Ian plunged his blade into her heart.

Juniper gasped for her next breath. Her insides squeezed from magic depletion.

"Jun?" Reid asked.

"I'm all right," she said. "A little winded."

"Can you continue?" asked the king. "We're nearly there."

Juniper swallowed against her dry throat and nodded.

They continued toward the court magician's chambers. Reid offered Juniper a dagger from his belt, and she accepted it. She flipped the dagger and caught it by the hilt, holding it at a killing angle. With her magic flickering, she might need steel. She hated the feeling of vulnerability that came in her magic's absence. Once, not that long ago, steel had made her feel as powerful as her ice. She used to never leave home without at least three daggers on her person. That Juniper would be sorely disappointed in her future self for being unprepared.

Few mages blocked the way to Mason's chambers. The window at the end of the corridor glowed with flames. The entire castle seemed to be burning. Juniper saw specks of people standing in the Royal Grounds, safely out of harm's way. They were not mages; they wore the simple clothes of servants.

"Your Majesty," Reid asked. "Did you station any knights in the Royal Chambers?"

"Yes, two."

Juniper caught Reid's meaning immediately. She met his eye and blurted, "I didn't see anything when we came through. They were gone before the fighting started."

"As if they knew," Reid added.

"Bala's breath," the king said, each word a plea. "Are there any knights left in the order who are not under Nexon's control?"

"At least two that I know of," Juniper said, looking at Reid. "And a pledge who doesn't look old enough to shave."

"Let us pray there are more," Reid said.

Mason's chamber doors were unlocked. Sword at the ready, Reid opened the doors. He started forward but stumbled to a halt. It took Juniper less than a heartbeat to see why.

Three dead knights lay in a heap in the middle of the court magician's sitting room.

CHAPTER 28

"Search every room," commanded the king.

At once, his guards spread into the chambers. The king shut the doors behind them. He took a shimmering golden key from his pocket and locked the doors. Juniper felt the change; the key possessed magic, and some sort of ward had passed over the doors. The king said nothing about it. He slipped the key back into his pocket and pretended Juniper hadn't noticed.

Reid knelt beside the bodies. He wore a masked grief. Juniper had the worst feeling he had known the dead knights, likely by name.

"Dead," he confirmed. He held his hand over the bodies. "By magic. I see no obvious wounds, and there's a magical residue around them."

"So," Roslyn started. She hung her bow around her shoulder and set her hands on her hips. "Care to explain what's happening?"

"Fowler is in Nexon's pocket," Juniper added. "And we don't know how many knights have been turned into thralls."

"The Order is no longer safe." Reid stood, remorse cast over his features.

"Oh, and Nexon's mages are laying siege to the castle," Juniper added casually.

"Damn," muttered Roslyn. "How did they get in?"

"Through the catacombs," Juniper said.

The guards returned to the sitting room. "The court magician is not here," said the first.

"He's gone," the king muttered, thinking—thoughts churned behind his eyes faster than words could travel.

"He would have heard the fighting," Reid said. "These thralls likely attacked, and Mason took care of them and left."

"What now?" Juniper asked the king.

The king was looking at the dead knights. Weight pulled his shoulders down, the weight of a kingdom, the weight of a castle under siege, the weight of betrayal. King Bradburn inhaled, filling his chest, and met Juniper's eyes, then Reid's, then each of his guards. He held himself tall and steady.

"We escape with our lives," the king said. "Castles can be rebuilt, but only if there are survivors."

"But what about everyone else?" Juniper asked. "All the guards and servants?"

The king did not look happy about his answer. "I am aware. But if I am dead, then the enemy will have won. As long as the Bradburn line exists, as long as I am alive to lead, I can lead."

"How do we get out?" Juniper asked. "The catacombs? We could go through the Undercity and then into the city."

"There is an entrance not far from here," Reid added.

"But what are our chances of being waylaid by angry mages or thralls? If Nexon knows you know about the catacombs, and now he knows we're here, he might have stationed someone in the catacombs," said Roslyn.

"I'd rather fight my way out than wait here and get backed into a corner," Juniper said.

"But your magic is dwindling," Reid pointed out.

"I won't wait for them to come to me," Juniper argued. "And I don't need magic to protect myself." She wiggled the dagger at him. Of course, she didn't know how much fight she had left. Getting to the court magician's chambers had sapped her magic and agitated her healing wounds. Her back already ached, and the new skin throbbed.

"If the escape tunnels underneath the castle have been compromised," the king said, ending their discussion, "then we return to my chambers. The king's hatch does not connect with those tunnels."

Juniper wanted to argue that they should have just stayed there or escaped with the queen and Adrian—of course, they wouldn't have gotten to Roslyn.

"At least the way back should be relatively clear," Reid said.

Reid and Ian led them into the corridor. Smoke and magic stained the air, mixed with charred canvas and flesh. It sounded as though the initial onslaught had ended, or at least slowed. Fewer crashes shook the castle, and fewer screams rattled the air. Juniper rallied what remained of her magic, but she felt the squeezing—she neared depletion.

They made it to the intersection of four corridors when Juniper caught the first whiff—like decay, like death, like rancid breath. It prickled fear along her bones, and her magic reared in response. White-hot panic surged along her skin and turned ice-cold in the space between one heartbeat and the next.

Before she could warn the others, the beast lunged from the shadows. It was about the size of a dire wolf with patchy brown-black fur and thick leathery hide that stretched taut over lithe muscles. Its long snout held jagged teeth, and its feet ended in talons longer than the human finger—each talon glistened with fresh blood.

The beast set its black eyes on Juniper, and icy fear overtook her. She felt the sting of the scar that traced down her front and those that lined her torso.

Reid met the beast's lunge with his own, slamming his Mage's Bane into its jaw and slinging it aside like a doll. He nearly cleaved the monster in two. It landed awkwardly, and before it could regain its footing, Reid severed the head from the body.

A heartbeat, then another, and another, then the beast burst into black ash.

"He's made more of them," Juniper breathed, eyes on the pile of ash. More servants, more innocent lives.

Xavier had been right about Nexon using the ruins to create them.

A second growl, and then a third—two more beasts sauntered down the opposite corridor. Reid readied himself. Roslyn poised her daggers to kill. The guards arranged themselves around the king. The first beast, a matted blond fur and taut pale hide, curved toward Reid. The second followed at its flank. The beasts made a circle of the party, eyes hungry and cautious.

And Juniper felt it—a spike of magic in the air. A beat, and then a fist of stone rose from the floor underneath the blond beast. The fist rammed into the beast's chest, cracking bones. The beast let out a horrible, pained cry. A hot wind threw the beast to the side, and then a stone spike thrust through its middle.

The second beast lunged—a burst of smoky energy knocked the beast out of the air. Xavier appeared from the shadows, jumped onto the beast's back, and thrust a dagger of his dark energy magic through the neck. His magic expanded into a disc, severing the head from the body.

From the opposite corridor, Finn and Mabyl ran toward them.

"We got your distress signal," Finn said. "We have several groups, all entered at different locations."

"What's the situation?" Reid asked.

"Chaos," Xavier said, holding his energy dagger over his shoulder like real steel. "Knights fighting knights, mages fighting mages."

"I'd never thought I'd see the day when mages and knights fought together," Finn said.

"The knights are not all corrupted?" the king demanded.

Finn shook his head. "Not all of them."

If standing in the presence of the king of Duvane startled any of them, none showed it.

"So, what's the plan now?" asked Mabyl.

"Get out alive," Juniper said. "With as many survivors as possible."

"What did you say?" Xavier asked, his tone sweet. He put a hand to his ear. "Kill as many dirty mages and thralls as possible? Oh, don't you worry. Leave that to us. You get out of here. You look like you're about to pass out, and I don't feel like carrying you to safety, and Reid needs his sword arm."

"He is right," Reid said, though he glared at Xavier. "We need to get His Majesty to safety."

"You also need to survive this night," King Bradburn said sternly to Juniper.

Juniper caught his unspoken meaning and fought hard not to roll her eyes— the whole prophecy thing.

"Go," Xavier said.

"We can handle it from here," added Finn.

Even though it felt horribly like betrayal, Juniper went with Reid, Roslyn, and the king. To escape while the others fought with their lives. She spotted evidence of Finn's magic down the corridor, pieces of stone taken from the floor and from the walls. She spotted scorch marks. She spotted bodies, mages and knights and royal guards.

They trekked back through the Royal Chambers. The halls were quieter than they were before—until they reached the doors to the king's chamber. Two knights stood on either side, helmets drawn over their faces.

Juniper gripped her dagger, and Reid readied himself.

"Step aside," ordered the king.

Neither knight moved.

Armored footsteps came from behind. A third thrall came toward them, Mage's Bane held loosely.

"They no longer listen to you," Juniper said. "They listen to their master."

The first knight started forward, and Reid met the Mage's Bane with his own. The second knight took a step—a bronze-skinned man in a bloodied tunic emerged from the king's chambers, sword drawn. He thrust his sword at the knight and knocked him off balance. A heartbeat and a clank of steel—the thrall hit the floor, dead. A heartbeat after, Reid took the other thrall down.

The third knight received an ice arrow through the helmet, and Juniper's magic threatened to seize. She widened her stance to keep the others from noticing.

"Uncle?" Reid breathed. "You're injured."

Captain Sandpiper nodded. He put a hand against his middle. Blood had soaked into his tunic. "The bastards outnumbered me. One got a cheap shot."

"You've lost quite a bit of blood," Roslyn said.

Indeed, Captain Sandpiper's tunic had soaked in too much. He'd paled considerably. He needed a healer.

"Aunt?" Reid asked.

Captain Sandpiper shook his head. "I don't know. I was on my way here when the fighting started. Those…monsters attacked the barracks. One of my men made it to me before the fighting spread. This was a planned assault, Your Majesty. We were hit in the middle of the night, and in our weakest points. Thank the gods you summoned me when you did, Reid, or I might not have made it."

"The Royal Guard?" asked the king.

Captain Sandpiper didn't answer. "Queen Catherine and Adrian?"

"Both safe, if the gods are listening," said the king. He nodded toward his chamber door. "Right now, we escape and regroup."

"You're leaving so soon?"

That voice—it sent shivers down her bones and into her magic. Juniper spun, dagger ready to kill.

Ronald Hendle sauntered toward them as if the castle weren't on fire and under attack. Blood spotted his tunic, but he looked otherwise uninjured. He walked alone and carried no weapon. His nonchalance bothered Juniper—she did not step out of her fighting stance. Reid noticed and tightened the grip on his sword. Roslyn reached for one of her few remaining arrows.

"Ron?" asked the king. "You need to get to safety."

Ron looked over the party, sounds of fighting echoing behind him. He started forward, hands behind his back. His eyes settled on Juniper.

And everything stilled.

Ron's eyes were ice blue—Nexon's eyes.

CHAPTER 29

Juniper stared into Nexon's icy blue eyes, the same that had stolen Ison and Penet, full of ancient cruelty and arrogance. Rage boiled through her magic, and she had never felt such a drive to twist someone's neck.

"You," Juniper spat, gathering what little remained of her magic in her empty hand. A dagger of ice and a dagger of steel.

Ron's grin widened. "You look surprised. Are you surprised?"

Reid gasped. His grip turned white-knuckled. "No. You possessed Ron too?"

"No, I haven't possessed this boy," said a cold, ancient voice. No sliver of Ron's tenor remained, not like when Nexon had possessed Penet or Ison; their voices had mingled with his. "I took this body. Another foolish boy blinded by his lust for power, just as the fool before him. Although, this one is more attractive. Ulgan had his uses, but this body is much more suitable."

Ulgan… Juniper knew that name.

"Ulgan?" the king breathed.

The truth struck something cold in Juniper's chest. Ulgan, the king's advisor. Nexon had been the king's advisor for years—Nexon had been at the king's side, in plain sight, all this time. He had never been hiding from them at all.

Nexon's ice blue eyes widened. "You honestly didn't notice?" He laughed, a cold crackle. "Unfortunately, none of you will be leaving here. At least not alive."

Brown-black magic flared from Ron's body—Nexon's earth magic, his archmage magic. Dark tendrils formed into a single column and surged toward them—toward Juniper. She summoned what magic she had left into a shield. No sooner had her shield formed than Nexon's magic slammed into it, shattering it and slamming her into the opposite wall. The impact shoved the breath from her body. Pain erupted along the new skin of her back.

Her power faltered. She stumbled to her feet in time to see Reid slash through the column of brown-black magic with his Mage's Bane—the Bane repelled the magic. Nexon's magic—where the bane touched it—paled and withered. Nexon cringed; his magic retreated a few steps. He spat a word she didn't understand, and his magic flared, swallowing the entire corridor in darkness.

Juniper coughed and gasped for breath. She couldn't see. The magic submerged them. The dark radiated power that pushed on her bones and made her own magic tremble. Nexon meant to crush them.

Bright yellow light surged from the other end of the corridor.

The two magics collided with a terrible crash. The two powers fought for dominance above them, a whirlwind of magic. The sheer force of it shoved her and the others to the floor. A curse left her throat, but the storm of magic whisked the sound out of her mouth.

The yellow magic pushed Nexon's back. She felt it wash over them, softer and gentle, but thrumming with ancient power. Yellow magic solidified into a translucent barrier between them and Nexon. Dark tendrils beat against it, thudding like thunder. Nexon shouted—his voice was muffled by the magic shield.

"You need to go," came the calm voice of Mason Hobbs. He appeared through the bright yellow, his robes singed and torn. One hand reached toward the barrier, holding it in place. Determination hardened his eyes and deepened the wrinkles on his face. "Your friends have stemmed the tide of chaos, but Nexon's thralls and followers are numerous."

The thudding ebbed, then stopped. Nexon appeared on the other side of the yellow energy barrier, glaring at Mason.

"You," Mason said in distaste. "I should have known you would resort to such dark magic. Stealing bodies for your own."

"A trick I learned when my body was left for the wolves," Nexon sneered.

"Better than you deserved," Mason said.

Nexon frowned. "It would take a powerful mage to throw me back. You're the new Archmage of Energy, then. I thought those rumors were false."

"I tried my best to make them so," Mason said grimly. "Wouldn't want you walking in unannounced." Mason grunted, and his wall thickened.

Nexon was thrown backward, out of sight.

"Your Majesty, you need to go. Now."

"Mason—" the king started to argue.

Nexon's magic thrust against Mason's wall, hard enough to shatter the stones on either side. The sound reverberated through the corridor, shaking the entire castle.

"Now, Bentley!" Mason commanded.

Nexon's magic slammed into Mason's barrier again, hard enough to shake the floor. Reid grabbed Juniper's arm and pulled her into the king's chamber. She didn't have the strength to resist. They ran into the bedchamber and into a spacious closet of armor stands, each holding ceremonial armor. In the dark, they looked like people. The king maneuvered to the far side, to a mirror set into the stone wall. The same key that had locked the court magician's chambers unlocked the mirror, and it swung inward.

The sound of the battle in the corridor tore through Juniper, shaking her magic like a rag doll. She felt each collision of archmage magic—it pulsed through her, right into her core. By the unease that cracked through Reid's mask, he felt it too.

"We can't just leave him," she whispered.

"Mason is giving us a chance to escape without Nexon right behind us," said the king, his tone firm. "We will take the chance, and don't forget that Mason is an archmage. He and Nexon are evenly matched."

Reid gave her hand a reassuring squeeze, retrieved the mage stone from his pocket, and took the lead into the secret chamber. The others followed. The king came last, locking the door with his strange key.

The passage wound down a tightly spiraled staircase. Juniper trailed her fingers along the wall. Her legs wobbled and threatened to give out. The raw skin of her back throbbed and itched. Her magic threatened to seize. Her lungs burned from inhaling smoke. But she continued. She kept her eyes on Reid's broad shoulders.

The sound of battle lessened as they descended, but her guilt grew heavier.

As a thief, Juniper had used plenty of people, but leaving Mason behind twisted her stomach into knots and left a sour taste on her tongue. Knowing her friends had come to her rescue and might still be fighting made it worse. Knowing some of her friends might be dead because of it... She swallowed the urge to dry heave.

The spiraling stairs led to a narrow tunnel. The end vanished into darkness.

"It leads into the city," the king explained. The exhaustion of the day had finally wormed into his voice. His words were low and husky, spoken by a king who had just fled his castle. "Gods willing, Catherine and Adrian will be waiting on the other end."

They walked for a while in silence. The tunnel widened. Somewhere, rats scurried. She thought she heard the chittering and flapping of bats. No lights appeared—only Reid's pale green mage stone lit the tunnel.

"That key of yours," Juniper asked. "It's magic, isn't it?"

"It is," the king answered. "A gift from my father to me, passed down from his father. From king to king. It is a skeleton key. Unlocks or locks most things. Remarkably useful."

Unfathomably useful, she thought.

BEATRICE B. MORGAN

"I saw mages fighting mages," said Captain Sandpiper. He frowned at Juniper. "Was that your doing?"

"Our little army of thieves and apostates." Juniper's voice lacked enthusiasm.

Captain Sandpiper's glare lessened, but only a little.

"As much as I'd rather not admit it, that little army might have saved our lives," King Bradburn said.

But at what cost? Juniper feared the answer.

They fell back into silence. They walked on, and finally a pinprick of light appeared far, far ahead. It grew brighter with each step. The prick of light came from the city, from the moonlight and candles and torches, not from flickering flames of destruction. Relief spread through Juniper's bones, but she dared not let it infest her. Not until they were truly safe.

CHAPTER 30

The king's escape tunnel included five iron gates the king unlocked with his magical skeleton key, and then ended in an unremarkable square room. It looked like a cellar, and it smelled like the canals. By the sound of water rushing on the other side of the stone walls, they were close. As they filed into the room, Juniper rested against the wall and doubled over. Every step felt like her back was being torn open a little more.

"They're not here," Reid said.

It took Juniper a moment to remember who he was talking about. Adrian and the queen had gone through the hatch first. They should have been waiting for them.

"Where would they have gone?" the king asked, panic evident in his tone.

"Would they have been able to get through those gates?" Juniper asked.

"Catherine has a key," the king said. "But she would not have left this room without protection, unless…"

"Unless she had no other choice," Captain Sandpiper added grimly.

"We can't stay here," the king said. "I will not hide and cower any more than I already have tonight."

"Amery's," Juniper breathed.

The king frowned. "A friend of yours?"

"Our new base of operations," Juniper explained. "We need to regroup, rest, find healers. We'll get all three at Amery's."

Captain Sandpiper's scowl deepened. "We need to find Queen Catherine and Adrian."

King Bradburn held his unreadable stare on Juniper, considering. After a long moment, he said, "Lead the way."

"Your Majesty—" the captain started.

"We will send someone to find them," said the king. "Right now, you need a healer."

Captain Sandpiper's side no longer bled, but he had lost a great deal of blood. His bronze skin had turned a nasty shade of white. He looked like he wanted to argue with the king, but he conceded.

King Bradburn unlocked the final barrier, a plain wooden door with no visible lock.

Reid walked through first, Mage's Bane at the ready. "It's clear," he said, and the others followed him into the city.

Juniper took a deep breath of city air, tainted with the muck of the canal and laced with smoke. The door led onto a narrow walkway that ran alongside a smaller canal. Murky water rushed past, reflecting a shattered night sky. Judging by the moderate and slightly rundown homes on either side, the clotheslines strung between windows, and the lack of perfumed air, they had walked into a lower middle-class part of the city.

Juniper took the lead, following Xavier and Ison's directions to Amery's as best as she could remember them. She suspected she already knew the house. Amery had commented more than once on an adorable manor by a canal. Her least favorite client owned it. He hadn't any children, and his wife had died young, leaving him bitter. That manor, she knew how to find.

Juniper led the way through the winding alleys, keeping to the shadows. Even from the ground, the north glowed. She could have climbed to the rooftops and scouted the damage, but she didn't want to see the castle burning— she didn't know if she had the energy either.

Rusdasin was quiet. The markets had closed for the night, the people had tucked away, but it felt…off. Underneath the usual quiet, uncertainty and fear hummed. The people would see the castle burning. They would know something bad happened tonight. The city itself seemed to be holding its breath until the smoke cleared.

By the time they approached the manor, her legs felt like jelly and her stomach felt full of stones. She wanted nothing more than to collapse on something soft and sleep for a few days. The manor looked as quiet as those around it. It was an old street of old homes, each surrounded by stone walls and hedges. The manor itself was of moderate size and built of pale stone, dark wooden shutters, old-fashioned iron trimmings, and pointed dormers. The canal ran alongside it, the water whispering against the slimy stone. An outer wall of stone blocked her view of the garden, and an iron gate barred entrance through the front.

But…something seemed off about the gate. Parts of the gate seemed to shimmer on the edge of her direct sight. Magic.

"Wait here," Juniper said mostly to the king.

She approached with caution, ready to dive into the canal at the slightest provocation. A few steps from the gate, and she heard footsteps. Running. She started to turn, to run—but then Ison appeared through the gate.

"Jun!" he cried, throwing his arms around her. He pulled away and quickly looked her over. His clothes were clean, not spotted with ash or burns. He hadn't gone to the castle. "Gods, I feared the worst. "I've been waiting for you. What happened? Are you all right? Why are you alone?"

"I'm not," Juniper said.

Reid led the others out of the alley. Captain Sandpiper leaned heavily on his nephew. Ison looked them over. His gaze lingered on the king, but his surprise was short lived.

"Are you disappointed?" Reid asked at Ison's frown.

"No," Ison said quickly. "It's just... You're the first to come back."

Juniper bit her lip. Xavier had mentioned several teams. None had returned?

"But the night is still young," Reid added. "And my uncle needs a healer."

"At once," Ison said.

Ison turned around and walked straight through the seemingly closed gate—and vanished.

"An illusion and a ward," Reid breathed.

Juniper heard the disapproval in his tone. Apostate magic, the Marca would call it, because they did not teach their mages to combine magics. Juniper swallowed her surprise and walked through the illusion-ward and, at once, understood why it existed. The sound hit her first, dozens and dozens of voices murmuring and talking. The sounds of life filled the air, not unlike the Undercity. The loamy scent of fresh soil hit her second. While the yard of the manor had looked unkempt from the other side of the illusion-ward, from within, it was bursting with herbs, stalks, and potion ingredients.

Reid stepped through with his uncle, and then the king followed. The guards came last. Ian looked over the illusion with wide, curious eyes.

Ison led them up the front walk and through the grand front doors. A brass and crystal chandelier hung from the foyer's tall ceiling and sparkled with a dozen magelights. The dark paneling, pale tile floors, and narrow archways reminded Juniper of the old-money homes she had stolen into—complete with a sweeping staircase with curving balusters. The house whispered with activity, even this late. Too many voices filled the air to make out words, and footsteps sounded as constant as the canal outside.

"We were expecting casualties," Ison said. He led them down a first-floor corridor and into a room decorated with the bare necessities: cots, blankets, candles. "Lie down. I'll send for a healer."

Reid and Ian helped the captain onto a cot. His bronze skin had paled into a shade of ash. His eyes were closed.

The king sat on another cot. Juniper hadn't seen him get injured, but she'd been preoccupied with herself. She didn't dwell on it long. She sat down on another cot. The strain in her limbs pulled her down. Gods, she didn't know if she'd be able to get back up again.

A stranger appeared in the doorway. He wore the green sash of a healer. Without permission or greeting, he marched into the room and knelt beside the captain. Mint green magic glowed on his palms, healing the captain's wounds.

No one spoke.

Then the mage stood. "There, he won't die, but he should rest for the night."

"Can't you heal him completely?" Reid asked.

"Yes, but then I would be exhausted, and he won't be the only one injured tonight," snapped the mage.

Reid started to say something, paused, and frowned at the mage. "Wait, I know you."

The mage blinked at him. "You do? Am I supposed to know you?"

"You were in the castle the night of Bala's Ball, a healer with the Marca." Reid's brow furrowed.

The healer's stare remained indifferent. "Yes, I was there. Now I'm here—thanks to you, or so I'm told. I was able to slip out last night. But that doesn't matter right now. Who else is injured?"

The mage gazed at them all, and his eyes lingered on the king. Though the king objected, the healer tended to him. Reid sat on the cot beside Juniper, watching the mage work. Another long moment passed, during which Captain Sandpiper opened his eyes and joined his nephew in a skeptical glare of the healer.

"There." The healer stood. "I've mended your ribs, but they're still fragile. You'll be sore, but you'll live."

The king huffed his response.

The mage raised his brows at the king as if he were an unruly child.

The king sighed through his nose. "Thank you," he said, though he didn't sound very grateful.

"Forgive his rudeness," Juniper said, her voice dry and weak. "His kingdom just suffered a blow, as did his pride."

The king glared at Juniper, but he did not argue.

The healer tended to a few burns on Roslyn, during which she said very little. He saw to the worst of Juniper's back, healing the torn skin but leaving the pain. The healer left, and a younger mage brought in a tray of cookies and tea—courtesy of Josephine. Juniper gladly made herself a cup, though her hands shook. The herbs within the tea soothed her stretched magic.

"You should try to sleep," Reid whispered.

"As should you," she replied.

Neither moved.

Juniper stared into the dregs of her tea. "Tonight didn't go as I thought it would," she whispered.

"It went as I feared," Reid said, "only my worst fears included one of us not making it back." His eyes went to his uncle.

"I'm worried about Adrian," Juniper said, low enough to keep it from reaching Roslyn's ears.

Roslyn sat on her own cot, knees folded against her chest, staring into her own tea. By the look on her face, she worried the same.

"As do I," Reid said. "But there is little we can do if we can barely see straight. We need rest. We need to be ready for whatever comes with the dawn."

"You're right," she said.

She absently finished her tea, thoughts a tangled nightmare of her friends, dead or mangled because of her. She stared into the dregs of her tea for a long moment, and then Reid's calloused fingers came around hers. He took the teacup from her hands and set it on the tray. He stood, gently pushed her back onto the cot, and tossed one of the mismatched blankets over her. Reid reclined on the cot beside hers.

The blanket smelled of the Undercity, like minerals and magic and dank stone. It smelled familiar and strange, and that smell leaked into her uneasy dreams.

CHAPTER 31

Reid tossed and turned, but he could not find the peace of mind to rest. He kept thinking about the Order, about the knights who had been turned into thralls, about the knights who had turned against Nexon and Fowler. He kept thinking about his uncle, how pale he had been, how heavily he had leaned on Reid, how close he had been to death. He glanced over at the other cots. His uncle slept, as did Juniper.

Reid gave up resting and silently slipped into the corridor. The manor buzzed with activity, even this late—or early. Voices echoed off the walls, hushed and urgent. He made his way through the manor, and after several rooms and questions, he finally found a familiar face on the second floor.

"Ison?" Reid asked. The mage's name came out a little too commanding.

"You should be resting," Ison said flatly, his own exhaustion showing in the dark circles under his eyes and his drooping eyelids.

"I've tried," Reid said. "Where have those from the Order gone?"

"They're across the canal." Ison started toward the stairs. "Come on, I'll show you."

Ison led Reid through the kitchens and into a cellar carved from the ground by earth magic. At the far end, the cellar angled downward and led into a tunnel. Reid followed with caution. The canal rushed above their heads, filling the tunnel with a watery echo. Magelights hovered at wide intervals but provided enough light. At the other end, the tunnel angled upward and into a similar earth-magic crafted cellar. The clatter and clamor of armor and the din of voices sounded above them.

"Whose house—" Reid started to ask.

"Ours now," Ison finished. He led Reid up stone stairs and into the kitchen. He hesitated by the cellar's entrance. "Xavier said he commandeered it. I didn't ask for details."

Reid sighed—likely stolen.

"We can't afford to be picky right now," Ison told him. "We have knights and mages who are scared and angry. They need shelter and help. Amery doesn't have room for them all, so we had to expand. The knights were appalled at sharing a living space with mages, so when this house…became available, they moved in."

Reid hated the notion of it all, but Ison was right. They could not afford to be picky.

"I'd rather not go any further," Ison whispered. He looked sheepishly at the kitchen door. "There's too much Mage's Bane for my liking."

"It's fine." Reid started toward the door. "Thank you."

"I'll see you later, then," Ison said. He started back through the underground passage.

Reid let himself into the corridor.

The house looked to have been abandoned for a while—by the dusty, musty smell—or at least used infrequently. Most of the furniture remained under sheets. He followed the din of voices to the first-floor dining room. Candles had been lit in the ivory sconces, and several lined the long dining table. Knights gathered around the table, using the natural divide to argue over.

"...and we have resorted to the level of the apostates," said Sir Willard. "We are consorting with the very type of people we have sworn oaths to eradicate from this world."

"And these apostates are the only reason you aren't a mindless thrall," said Isaac, who stood on the opposite side of the table from Willard.

"Fowler must not know of the crimes committed in his name," said Sir Nolmat, who stood beside Willard. "We need to inform him that the Order—"

"Fowler is not to be trusted," said Isaac.

"So says you and a handful of apostates!" argued Willard.

"And now we are no better than common street scum, hiding in this hovel," said Sir Killian, a knight a few years older than Reid.

"You are welcome to go sniveling back to the knight commander." Henry looked at the other knight coolly. "Go tell him what we've done. Maybe he won't turn you into a thrall."

Reid felt a rush of relief at his friend's voice.

"This is an outrage! We—" started Willard.

Reid walked into the dining room, and the onlooking knights parted for him. Those at the heart of the argument paused their heated words at his appearance. Any other day, the shift in the room at his presence would have surprised him, but his utter exhaustion had left him incapable of feeling such things. Reid paused at the head of the table.

Less than twenty knights had gathered. *Less than twenty.* His heart weighed at the implication that everyone else in the order had been turned into a thrall or killed. He spotted Henry and Isaac. Lex, the pledge who had escaped the Marca, stood near the back wall. Sir Darvel stood beside the shuttered window. Each wore a grimace or scowl. He understood the feeling. The foundation of everything they knew and trusted had been shattered in a few short hours.

"Reid," said Isaac in greeting.

"I'm glad to see you all alive and well," Reid said, his voice flat.

"Not everyone is grateful to have been rescued," added Henry.

Reid met Willard's eyes. "Is this so, sir?" he asked calmly. "Would you rather have become a thrall for the enemy rather than be standing here, complaining about it?"

Willard held Reid's gaze. "Your uncle would be ashamed of what you've done."

Not even the knight's attempted insults pierced the stonewall of exhaustion. Reid said coolly, "My uncle is across the canal with His Majesty if you wish to speak with him about it."

Whispers resounded around the room.

"The king is here?" asked another knight.

"Yes," Reid answered. "He is aware of Fowler's betrayal."

"What do we do now?" asked Lex.

It took a beat for Reid to realize the room waited for his answer. "That is yet to be discussed. For the time being, we rest and heal. Then we calculate our counterattack before the enemy strikes us."

"You say 'the enemy,'" said Killian, his eyes pinned on Reid. "Who is this enemy?"

"Nexon," Reid said plainly. Whispers of disbelief fluttered through the room. "The ancient Archmage of Earth who has slowly been rising to power for the past several centuries. Fowler is loyal to him, not to the Order."

Willard laughed. "You mean to tell me that the knight commander is loyal to a mage? An apostate, by the sounds of it?"

"Yes," Reid said flatly.

Willard's grin faded. "I refuse to believe such a ridiculous statement."

"Then don't," Henry added in the same flat tone. "But the truth stands: the Order is no longer what it should be. We were almost made into thralls, if you remember. That is the sort of black magic we took oaths against. The way I see it, there's black magic in the Order. We are the Order. So now we stomp out the black magic in the Order."

Several others agreed with Henry.

"And who put the runt in charge?" asked an older knight behind Willard.

"No one," Henry added. "I simply spoke out first."

"Before we argue about who is in charge, we need to regroup," said Isaac. "We are scattered, and the enemy knows it. We need to be a force, just as we've always been, regardless of Fowler's leadership."

"Then we chose a council," said Willard.

"I second the notion," said Isaac.

"I third," said another.

A round of agreements sounded through the room, Reid's among them.

The gathered knights selected five to act as council—Isaac, Willard, Darvel, the two older knights, Tegard and Monlen. Their first order as council was to elect Reid as the liaison to the other house, simply named the Mage House. Witnessing the Order operate gave Reid a rush of pride. This was what the Order was—organized, trained, intelligent, and able to function despite being confused and sundered.

"I will inform His Majesty of these events," Reid said, nodding to the gathered council. "He will likely want to meet with you."

"That would be best," said Isaac. The other knights agreed.

As the dividing of the house began, Reid headed for the cellar. A few steps from the earthen passage, Henry called his name. Reid paused, and Henry jumped the steps into the cellar. Spots of blood had long dried and started to flake from his armor.

The two of them stood at the mouth of the passage, the rush of the canal echoing upward like distant voices. Henry looked older—he was no longer the scrawny pledge who cared more for making people laugh than learning how to hold a shield. Reid and Henry had been pledges together, they had trained together, they had become brothers in arms. Henry had always had an easy smile, but he did not smile now.

"It's good to see you alive," Henry said.

"As it is to see you," said Reid.

Henry half laughed, and a glimpse of his humor returned. It quickly vanished. "Is all this really happening? Are we rebels now?"

"We are."

"Damn," Henry muttered. "Never thought we'd see the day, huh?"

"I admit, it's a shift that I'm not used to." Reid put his hand on Henry's shoulder. "But you are right about the Order. We will root out the black magic that has infiltrated the ranks. We will take back the Order and make it whole again."

"That is a lot easier said than done," Henry said. "But at least I can hit something rather than fight about it in words." He pretended to gag. "I hate all these politics."

"A necessary evil."

Henry groaned. "Reid, you should know, Fowler said he feared you'd been possessed."

"Me?"

Henry nodded. "I know, it sounds ridiculous, but he seemed genuinely worried. I've never seen the old man so..." Henry fumbled for the words, and his hands mirrored the search, fingers wiggling through the air as if he might find them. "...emotional."

"Fowler?" Reid's brows rose. "Are we talking about the same person?"

Henry half laughed. "I know, it sounds mad. But he got this watery look when he talked about you possibly being possessed. He seemed...genuine. And I think, if we can, we should try to see if he has really turned against the Order or if he's being forced into the position. It might be some clever ruse by Nexon to make us think that Fowler is against us when he really isn't."

"I'll keep that in mind," Reid said. "Henry, I'm heading back to the Mage House. Try to keep these old men in line."

"I'll try my best," Henry said with a scoff. "Tell Juniper I said hello."

With a shared nod of farewell, Reid started into the passage and Henry returned to the knights' house. The water in the canal hissed above Reid's head, hushing the sound of his footsteps. With every step, the pit in his stomach widened. It gripped his heart and his mind—too much had changed too fast. The world had been ripped out from underneath him and so many others this night, and he felt it reverberate in his chest.

Things were changing, and he had no choice but to ride or crumble.

CHAPTER 32

Juniper did not sleep well. Her depleted well of magic had granted her a few hours of rest, but the pain in her back kept her from sleeping deeply or for very long. The fight had stretched the raw skin, and it ached and throbbed like a fresh wound, radiating along every nerve. She lay on her cot until dawn began to glow.

She carefully stood—mindful of her back. Captain Sandpiper and King Bradburn still slept. One of the royal guards remained awake; the other slept. The lone guard looked at Juniper, his gaze listless and tired.

Reid and Roslyn had both already left.

Juniper let herself into the corridor and into a cacophony of sound—the nighttime chatter had risen into a daytime buzz, voices and footsteps and doors and things she couldn't readily identify. She found a communal bathing room down the hall. A sign on the door read GIRLS—BOYS GO UPSTAIRS. She let herself in. Medium-sized washing basins lined one wall, clean towels and basic toiletries lined the shelves, and the single toilet had been curtained off; a few chamber pots had been added.

She said nothing to the few other girls, and they said nothing to her. They looked as exhausted as she felt.

Juniper started toward a washing basin, but she didn't make it there. A few steps into the bathing room, and someone called her name. Juniper turned. A young female mage stood in the doorway. Under Juniper's glare, she seemed to shrink.

"Josephine wants to see you in the library," she said, her voice soft and timid. "At once, she said."

Juniper sighed and followed the young mage upstairs to the library.

Xavier, Ison, Josephine, and Mabyl stood around a table on which they had spread a map. Blythe stood by the window, staring down at the courtyard.

"Jun," said Xavier without looking up from the map.

Ison's attention snapped up to Juniper, and he offered her an exhausted smile. "Glad to see you're awake. It's been a long night."

"What news?" Juniper joined them at the table.

"The siege of the castle did not go unnoticed," Josephine said. "Panic has spread through the city. Nexon's mages are making their way through the streets,

144

along with thralls, making his rule known. His followers are calling this the dawn of the next Imperium."

"The next?" Juniper managed to ask.

"It is what Nexon called his previous rule," Josephine said darkly. "When magic ruled."

"Nexon claims the king is dead," Ison said.

"Several altercations have already occurred between Nexon's mages and those who don't agree with the change in leadership," Josephine said. "We have people among them, showing the people that there are those willing to fight back. Whispers of a resistance have already spread."

"Nexon's attack on the castle triggered another rebellion in the Marca," Mabyl said, pointing to the map of Rusdasin. Her finger rested on the Marca. "Full-on rebellion. According to the mages who escaped, knights started attacking everyone. Not all the knights, mind you. The fight took out the southern tower."

A red slash had been drawn through the Marca's southern tower.

"We have other teams in the city looking for survivors," added Ison. "We've recruited several mages from the Marca and a handful of knights from the Order. The mages are here, and the knights are across the canal. All of our teams from the castle returned. We lost a few, but most made it back alive."

"Alive, not unscathed," Mabyl added. "Our healers are working themselves to depletion."

"And we are running out of room," Xavier said. "Amery can only house so many, and the knights seem to take up more space than normal people."

"If we take any more houses along the canal, people will start to notice." Ison ran his finger along the map. "We need to remain hidden, and runes can only hide so much."

Juniper nodded, taking it all in. So much had happened. The world had shifted in the night, and she hadn't yet regained her footing.

"And you might want to know," Ison started, "Roslyn left before dawn with one of our search parties. She wanted to help find Adrian and the queen. She said there are a few safe houses they might have gone to."

The idea that Adrian and Roslyn were out in the city somewhere sank Juniper's heart and lifted it at the same time—Roslyn was a force of nature.

"Our scouts are bringing information from all over the city," Josephine added. "Thanks to my mages and Maddox's scheming, we've accumulated a network of spies."

"Maddox?" Juniper blinked.

"He's here somewhere," Xavier said dismissively.

"Our other plan remains the same," Ison told her. "Xavier, Mabyl, and I will infiltrate Nexon's settlement at Baxion, but with Rusdasin in the mess that it's in, we won't even make it to the edge of the city without being ambushed."

"Do you think it still exists? How do we know it wasn't a ploy to get us to look outside Rusdasin while Nexon amassed his army under our noses?" Juniper asked.

"Our friends in the Dual Fangs confirmed it. Some of them have been there," said Ison.

"Which means we haven't seen the extent of his army," said Josephine. "The bulk of the horde is likely still in Baxion, or on the way here."

Juniper groaned and dropped her head into her hands.

"We wanted your thoughts," Ison said.

"Why me?" she whined.

"Because you're in the middle of it, like it or not," Josephine said.

Juniper groaned—her head hurt too much to think.

She looked over the map, over the streets, buildings, and canals. She knew Rusdasin well, and even without the names, she followed the hand-drawn streets as if she were walking along them. She traced her common escape routes from the City Watch, and—

And the idea formed.

"You say we're running out of room up here?" Juniper asked.

She looked up from the map and met Xavier's eyes. A glint of understanding, and his lips quirked upward.

"We've got a whole city under our feet," Juniper said. "And we know it can hold a lot."

"It has a manageable number of entries," Xavier added.

"It's easily defensible," Josephine added.

"And compromised," said Ison, frowning at them all. "The City Watch took it, remember?"

Juniper shrugged. "So? We'll just have to take it back."

"Oh, yeah, no big deal," Ison muttered, looking bleary-eyed at the map.

"Besides," added Juniper. "We know the Undercity. The Watch doesn't."

Xavier grinned, and Ison sighed in defeat.

Juniper meandered back to her cot, ducking and swerving to avoid knocking into anyone. Xavier was right—they did not have any more room. They needed the Undercity back.

Another healer tended to King Bradburn while one of the guards watched. Reid and Captain Sandpiper—who looked remarkably better this morning—stood by the window. With their bronzed skin, chestnut hair, and scowls, they looked identical.

"Have you seen Roslyn?" Reid asked her.

"She went to find Adrian," she said.

Reid frowned, and his uncle mirrored the expression.

"She went with a search party," Juniper clarified. "They've been searching the city for survivors and brought them all here."

"And you think we're safe here?" asked King Bradburn, listless eyes on the ceiling.

"Considering we're surrounded by mages, assassins, and knights, yes," Juniper said firmly, and she meant it. "I have friends here, Your Majesty. They might be questionable, but they want Nexon gone as much as we do."

"And you think we can trust them?"

Juniper hesitated to answer. "Trust is a strong word. I'd rather say we can rely on each other for the time being."

The king half laughed, the sound full of disbelief. Juniper had never seen the king look so haggard. His royal command had left him, and he looked ten years older. Sensing her gaze, the king's hazel eyes fell from the ceiling to her. His frown deepened.

She clicked her tongue at the king and said, "That expression makes you look like an old man."

The captain's brows furrowed with dislike. Reid shot her a warning glare, but she ignored him.

The king's frown twitched. A mixture of irritation and exasperation flashed across his face. It was a small flash of his former intensity, a fraction of the gaze she had first seen in the dungeons all those months ago. That night, his gaze had made her knees weak, but now she held it with her own. A challenge.

And he met that challenge. His slumped shoulders straightened. His fingers twitched into fists. "I've just lost my castle," King Bradburn said grimly. The air thickened. "My kingdom is in danger from an ancient mage. My people believe me dead. I don't know how many of my guards and servants are alive. The fate of my wife and my son remains unknown." He motioned to Juniper and added, "And I was saved by criminals and apostates."

"And a knight." Juniper nodded to Reid.

The king huffed. "The matter still exists. My kingdom has fallen."

"Well, I can't fix any of those things immediately," she said.

She reached under her cot for the vest she'd worn the day before and stuck her hand into the deep inside pocket. Captain Sandpiper took a step toward her, hand on his hilt. Reid threw his arm between his uncle and Juniper. He blinked at his nephew, then stepped back. He did not release his sword.

Juniper said to the king, "But I do have something that might make you feel better."

The king closed his eyes and released a long, careful sigh. "Unless it's a jug of mead or strong wine, I'm in no mood to—"

Juniper pulled her hand out of her pocket—the king went silent. She held his crown in her hand.

CHAPTER 33

The crown gleamed. The morning light sparkled off the rubies, diamonds, pearls, and gold. The king's solemn expression slipped, and he gawked. Gooseflesh erupted over Juniper's arms at his breathlessness, the utter surprise.

"I told you I'd get out with it," Juniper said.

The king's lips parted, he blinked, and then he laughed.

Just like that, the tension dissolved.

"It was just sitting there, in your closet, like you wanted it to be stolen." She turned the crown over in her hand, catching the light. "That's where it is most of the time, isn't it? When you aren't trying to lure thieves."

"It's true," the king said.

Juniper handed the king his crown, but he did not place it upon his head.

"You're a scoundrel," the king said, though his tone was light. "But you kept your word. That's admirable."

"Reid's wearing off on me." Juniper winked at Reid.

He stared at the crown, astonished. "I didn't see you take it."

"No one did," Juniper said. "That defeats the purpose of the surprise." She looked back to the king. "I will help you regain your throne, but since it's a bit harder to steal, we'll just have to take the whole castle with it."

"And how will you do that?" King Bradburn stole his eyes from the crown and pinned them on her.

"We start here," Juniper said. "With our ragtag team of apostates, knights, thieves, and assassins. We build our resistance. We take back the Undercity, then take back Rusdasin from the bottom up. We strike back and string Nexon's body on the front gates."

Reid's brows rose. The king blinked at her.

"You want to take back the Undercity?" Reid asked.

"You think a ragtag team will stand against an army of apostates wielding black magic?" Captain Sandpiper asked. "Not to mention those beasts."

"It's better than lying down and taking it," Juniper said.

"And we have the support of the Galamond forces," said a familiar voice from the doorway.

Adrian strolled into the room. Dust and dirt spotted his tunic, but he looked otherwise unhurt—albeit exhausted.

Juniper's next breath evaporated.

"Adrian," gasped the king.

The king started to rise, but Adrian held up his hand to stop him. Adrian plopped onto the cot beside his father and let out a grievous sigh.

"Mother is fine. She's with Roslyn," said Adrian. "Roslyn has guaranteed us her father's support, whether he knows it or not. Those were her words, not mine. She also said King Nesdin will send soldiers if she asks."

King Bradburn let out a low chuckle. "Even with Galamond as an ally, we don't know the extent of our enemy's numbers. Or how many of those beasts Nexon has created." His voice quivered slightly over *those beasts* because more of those beasts meant more of his people had been slaughtered and transformed.

"Do you think you could get us a few of those dire wolves, Jun?" Adrian asked, grinning. Roslyn must have told him about that.

Juniper shrugged. "I don't think they really listen to me."

"There is Collatia," Reid added. "The archmages are the ones who defeated Nexon last time, and we'll need them if we want to defeat him again."

"The archmage in the Collatian court is the best lead we've got," Juniper said. "He might know where the others are."

The king nodded. "And Myrisha might listen to you," he said softly.

Her stomach flipped and flopped.

"You want to send a thief as a diplomat?" Captain Sandpiper looked as though he'd swallowed something rotten.

No one spoke, and the captain's confusion grew. He looked from the king to Juniper to Reid.

"Uncle," Reid started. "I neglected to mention something. I didn't think it was an important detail at the time, but Juniper is Myrisha Balendin's cousin."

Captain Sandpiper glared at his nephew. "What in Bala's name are you talking about?"

The king motioned for the captain's attention. "Before his death, Sebastian sent Sir Pinul to my doorstep, holding his infant daughter. Sebastian asked me to keep her safe should the unthinkable happen to him. I sent the infant to live with the couple who run the greenhouses. They had lost an infant a few days prior."

The king nodded to Juniper. Captain Sandpiper looked like he might vomit—a mirror of what she felt.

Averting her eyes from the captain, she added, "And then Collatian rebels found her, but she thought them to be knights from the Marca, and she ran from them and found bandits instead. Those bandits stole her and sold her in the Undercity."

"To Maddox Hawk," added Reid. "Who trained her to be a thief."

Captain Sandpiper gawked. He half fell onto his cot, looking at Juniper as though he had never really seen her.

"Her real name is Isolde," Adrian added playfully. "Isolde Balendin."

Juniper clutched fistfuls of her dirty shirt.

"And she is the rightful queen of Collatia," said the captain. Juniper's stomach fell into her ankles at the words. "Don't you think sending her might come across as a threat to the current monarchy?"

"I don't want to be queen of anything," Juniper said quickly. "And I will tell them so. My objective is to gain an alliance against Nexon, nothing more."

The king gave her a fatherly grin. "You're becoming quite the young woman." He adjusted himself on the bed, lifting himself to better recline. "When I first met you in that dungeon, I never would have thought we'd be having this conversation. Yet here we are."

"I'm sure stranger things have happened," she muttered.

The king nodded. "Be that as it may, I refuse to leave Rusdasin in this mess. This is my city. These are my people. I will not turn by back on Rusdasin in its time of need."

"We're not in a state to travel." Reid looked pointedly at Juniper. "We're injured and scattered."

"And Josephine tells me Nexon's followers are patrolling the streets," Juniper said grimly.

"Then it is settled," said King Bradburn. "First, we take care of Rusdasin. Then we will worry about Collatia. For right now, we rest, we heal, then we plan."

King Bradburn closed his eyes, ending the discussion.

Juniper and Reid returned to the corridor. They paused outside the door. She turned to speak—she felt like she should say something. Reid's silver armor no longer gleamed. It had several nicks and scratches and smudges of soot and blood. Dark circles hung under his eyes, and underneath his fatigue was an emptiness.

Reid met her gaze, then looked elsewhere. "I should go and inform the knights of our plans."

She blinked and looked at the far window. The city looked almost normal, aside from the smoke lingering in the sky. "I should tell Ison and the others that the king agrees with the plan."

They stood for a moment, then another.

"Reid," she started. "Do you think your uncle will hate me a little less now that he knows?"

"I can't say that he hated you to begin with."

"I detect doubt in your tone."

Reid smirked, but it lacked his usual mirth.

Juniper frowned. "Are you just sparing my feelings?"

"He knows how I feel about you," Reid said softer. "I told him and my aunt about our engagement before all of this."

Her heart thumped. In all the madness, she hadn't had time to think about their engagement. The moonstone ring remained on her finger. She only took it off to wash. Juniper tore her eyes off her ring. Reid's gaze drifted out the window, to the streets.

There hadn't been word of his aunt. From what they had heard, the barracks had been hit hard by the apostates. There was a very real possibility that Reid's aunt had not made it out of the castle. Juniper wanted to tell him that they would find her, that it would be all right, but she couldn't bring herself to stoke the sliver of hope. Instead, she said nothing. She curled her fingers around Reid's.

"Juniper! There you are," came a pleasant tone from behind them. Abrielle stood with her hands on her hips. She wore simple trousers and a tunic instead of her Marca robes. "I've been looking for you. How is your back?"

"It's fine," Juniper said.

"Did someone else take a look?"

"Yes, that prissy mage," Juniper lied. "I forgot his name."

Reid frowned at her. He knew that prissy mage hadn't done more than stop the bleeding.

Abrielle frowned; she didn't believe her. "Come on, you can't go around injured."

"Fine," Juniper conceded.

Abrielle and Juniper started one way, and Reid started the other. Finding an empty room was impossible, and Abrielle ended up taking her to the library. Ison was asleep on a bedroll under the window, and Xavier was leaning over a table piled with maps and notes. He didn't say anything as Abrielle led them into a nook created by towers of books.

Juniper took off her loose men's shirt and held it against her chest as Abrielle's gentle magic eased the soreness of her skin, loosened the tightness, and soothed the sensitive flesh.

In every other healing session, Juniper had been too out of it to pay attention. Now, she felt the prickling of magic against her skin, in her blood. She felt the itching sensation of her skin slowly stitching itself back together. She imagined them stitching the city back together the same way, a little at a time.

They could do it. They could fix this. She just didn't know how.

CHAPTER 34

After her healing session with Abrielle, Juniper returned to the first-floor bathing room to wash. She then pulled on the simple robes that Abrielle offered.

"I feel remarkably better," Juniper admitted.

"You smell remarkably better too." Abrielle grinned.

They returned to the corridor just as the front doors of the house opened. A small commotion followed—several haggard strangers entered the house.

"What's that?"

"A team's returned." Abrielle's quick eyes took in the scene. "It looks like they've brought a few survivors."

Juniper climbed the side of the staircase to see over the crowd. The team had brought back five people, all wearing the brown and beige uniforms of Bradburn's servants, dusted with ash and dirt. Juniper scanned the five new faces, but she saw none she knew. Glenda had not returned with them.

Her heart fell, even as relief washed over the frightened servants. She knew she felt a fraction of the dread Reid felt. While she didn't care for Glenda, she cared for Reid; his grief extended to her.

The servants were led into the house for healing and a warm meal. Roslyn stepped through the front doors and closed them behind her. Her jacket and trousers were dusty and covered in tears and minor burns. Her raven hair was tightly braided. The singed part of her hair had been cut away, and sweat glued her new feathery bangs to her forehead and temples.

Roslyn spotted Juniper and marched to the stairs. "It's madness out there," Roslyn said, a bit breathless. "It'd rather face a bear than a horde of crazy mages."

"You could use a healer," Juniper said, pointing to a particularly harsh burn on Roslyn's hand.

"I'm fine," Roslyn protested.

Juniper clicked her tongue. "I can only imagine what the queen would say to that."

Roslyn rolled her eyes, but she allowed Abrielle to lead her to the healers.

Juniper meandered away from the commotion. She'd never been in a house so packed with people, and she craved the loneliness that came from a rooftop, where she could watch it all with a bird's view. She went upstairs—the second floor was mildly less chaotic than the first—and found a small dark hall. It held two doors, neither of which gave off the commotion of life. A single window at the end of the hall allowed in dreary sunlight. Juniper hesitated at the edge of the sunlight's reach, within the safety and familiarity of the shadows. Without all the people and commotion, the second floor was colder. Wind whistled through the dormers and the eaves.

She bent forward, hands above her knees, and took a breath of the brief illusion of loneliness.

She didn't see the shadow as much as felt it—the calm approach, the gentle shift of loneliness to something darker.

She opened her eyes. Dark boots, scuffed and worn, stood across from her. She steeled herself and met the gaze of Maddox Hawk. Despite the situation, he wore a fine suit of charcoal and plum. His dark hair was clean and tied behind his head in a short tail. His dark eyes glittered at her with sinister amusement.

The last time Juniper had seen Maddox, he'd been murderous—she had betrayed him, the guild, and the entire Undercity—and he had been ready to rip her throat out for it.

"Good to see you unhurt," Maddox said, his tone light.

"I'd like to say the same to you," Juniper said, mimicking his tone.

"You didn't think Amery would leave me down there, did you?" Maddox stepped closer.

Juniper held her tongue. She hadn't been thinking of Maddox when she told Amery her plans. She had been thinking about Amery.

Maddox smiled—cold and unforgiving. "I admit, the new guild hall is nicer. It has a better view."

"I can't argue with that," Juniper said lowly.

Maddox's gaze sharpened. "I can see why you'd want to leave me. Your knight is quite the young man. Strong, handsome, and tied to the royal family. He's quite the catch."

Juniper bristled at Maddox's emphasis on *he's*—implying that Juniper was not the catch.

"I'm still rearranging my new office, but I have a few jobs for you. To repay what you've cost me."

"I no longer wear your brand," Juniper said.

Maddox's brows rose in mock surprise, but his eyes did not mirror the emotion.

"Nexon's thralls whipped my back to ribbons and tore through the brand," Juniper said as if she spoke of fair weather. "The healer stitched my back together with new skin."

154

"Is that so? Don't worry, that can be changed, as can all of this," he whispered. "What price do you think Nexon would pay to know the location of his enemies? I'm sure it would be fitting of a king's treasury."

Her skin turned hot and cold at the same time. Maddox's grin turned a shade mad.

"You wouldn't," she whispered back. "I thought you like the new guild hall?"

"I do, but I'm a vengeful bastard," he hissed—the same words she'd said about him once. Maddox leaned in closer, pinning her against the wall. "I also hear you're engaged. Would you like some pointers for your wedding night?"

She bristled. "Pointers would have been helpful several months ago. I'd rather not soil my experience with something so *minor*."

Maddox's grin widened. "Care to find out?"

"Amery and I can compare notes later."

Footsteps sounded in the hall. Maddox glanced to the side, and Juniper took the chance to duck under his arm. She hurried into the hall and back into the chaos of the first floor. She neared her room when the door opened—King Bradburn and Captain Sandpiper stepped into the hall. Adrian and Roslyn walked a step behind, their fingers laced.

"You're just in time," said King Bradburn. "I've arranged a strategy meeting in the library. It's time to think about our next move. No time to dally."

Juniper followed King Bradburn and Captain Sandpiper up to the library. Reid appeared from an adjoining corridor, Henry beside him. At the sight of Henry, Juniper felt a relief spread through her limbs. He had survived, and he looked unhurt.

"Sir Julian," said King Bradburn.

"Your Majesty," Henry said, nodding his head to his king.

They continued to the library, where they met Xavier, Amery, Bois, and—to Juniper's surprise—Maddox. Juniper met her guild master's eye while she purposefully joined King Bradburn's side of the room. Reid stood beside her, his hand brushing hers.

Maddox smirked. Juniper could almost hear him saying, *Remember who you belong to. I bought you. I put a roof over your head and food on your table, and taught you how to defend yourself. You owe me.*

Josephine waved her hand, and a rolled map flew from the shelves and unrolled itself over the table. It was a hand-drawn map of the Undercity.

"We are running out of room," started King Bradburn. "Juniper suggested we relocate to the Undercity. I believe the plan has credence."

"I agree," Josephine said.

"How many of the Watch are typically there?" King Bradburn studied the map.

"Few," Maddox answered. "Rumor has it that there are fewer since the siege on the castle."

"The easiest way in is through the tunnel under the house that leads to my old keep," said Josephine, pointing to the tunnel's location on the map.

"What if the Watch isn't happy to see us?" asked Xavier.

"I will speak to them first," said King Bradburn. "If diplomacy does not work, we will have no choice but to use steel."

"In the meantime," Josephine added, "I have people in the streets helping those they can. The Watch and the Royal Guard have made their stance against Nexon known, and the streets are not a friendly place. Skirmishes happen on every corner. Business and industry are faltering. People have fled the city in fear. The city and its remaining people need to know that the resistance is more than just rumors."

"After we reclaim the Undercity," Maddox said. "Fighting back will be easier."

"I agree," said the king. "First, the Undercity. Then, Rusdasin."

CHAPTER 35

Juniper and Xavier led a small group through the escape tunnel under Amery's house. Juniper had only heard of the tunnel from Xavier, and after a few steps in, she hated it. She hated the cramped quarters, low lighting, and musty smell of wet dirt, sweat, and stone. The tunnel angled steadily down, then evened out and stretched into darkness.

Several mage stones and magelights illuminated the path ahead in shades of pale green, blue, and gray.

Finally, the tunnel angled upward. Xavier took the lead. He opened the false panel that led through a wardrobe and into a room of Josephine's keep. Juniper climbed out behind him. With Xavier's mage stone glowing, her night sight did not reach as far, and the darkness seemed so much more pronounced.

The silence of the Undercity grated on her ears for only a moment—Reid and Henry followed them into the keep, their armor clinking and their footsteps thunderous. They both wore the stoic mask of a knight, and each held the hilt of their Mage's Bane.

Xavier crept through the keep first, Juniper on his heels and the others a step behind. He led them through the front door and onto the dark street. Without the magelights, it was nearly black, save for a torch bobbing in and out of view down the street: a lone watchman patrolling.

Juniper made her way to the street and planted her feet. Xavier stood a step behind. Reid stood beside her.

It felt strange to stand in the middle of the street, waiting for the watchman to notice them. Every instinct told her to run, hide, vanish into the darkness. Xavier mirrored her agitation, only he did not hide it as well—his fingers twitched, and he subtly swayed, an assassin ready to bolt.

The watchman approached, his expression bored and unfocused until he spotted them. His entire gait changed. His eyes sharpened, his shoulders straightened, and he drew the blade from his side.

"Halt," commanded the watchman. He quickly looked between them. "You are violating the law and trespassing on—"

"Stand down," came the king's booming voice from behind Juniper.

The watchman's gaze settled on the king, and recognition widened his eyes. The king stepped forward, a mage stone of bright yellow in his hand, and paused

157

a step in front of Juniper—to display he was in charge, but close enough to be easily defended should the watchman attack. The color drained from the watchman's face.

"Stand down," repeated the king. "We are here at my command, soldier."

"Your Majesty?" asked the watchman. He blinked several times. "I— I...forgive me, but they said you were dead."

"Who said such things?"

"Our men on the surface."

"Well, as you can see, I am very much alive," King Bradburn said. "Put away your weapon. I, King Bentley Bradburn, am commandeering this area known as the Undercity until further notice."

The watchman hesitated.

Reid stepped forward. "Are you ignoring a direct order from your king, soldier?"

Juniper took a step forward, brandishing daggers of pretty blue ice. "Have your loyalties shifted? Perhaps to a certain someone who laid siege to the castle and now claims to be in charge?"

Xavier twirled his shadow daggers.

The watchman blanched. "No, no, I remain loyal!"

"Then put your weapon away," barked Captain Sandpiper. He and Josephine had joined them on the street.

The watchman fumbled but slid his blade back into the scabbard.

Reid released a breath of relief. Juniper spied a quick glance over her shoulder. Reid was looking at the darkened row of stone townhouses opposite Josephine's. In the flickering torchlight and glow of mage stones, each window was a pool of darkness.

The watchman escorted their party to the center of the Undercity, to what had been part of the old market and what was now the tent city the Watch had erected. Crates and barrels made a crude perimeter, and a hundred candles doused the space in flickering shades of light and dark. Behind the tent city, the crude fountain continued to gush excess water from above, where the Ruby River and Weslie River met. The rush of water through the pipes filled the air with a continuous roar.

They made a strange procession—apostates, rebel knights, thieves, and assassins, being escorted by a confused watchman. They approached, and the small conversations between the other watchmen ended abruptly.

Josephine snapped her fingers, and the old magelights around the market began to glow, dimly at first but gaining brightness with every moment. Once more, mirrored daylight filled the Undercity. With a wave of her hand, every candle snuffed out. Thin trails of smoke filtered toward the ceiling.

The few watchmen—Juniper counted sixteen—looked at their king with a mixture of respect and surprise.

"Gentleman," started King Bradburn. "The situation above is dire. I would not be here otherwise. I have been pushed from my home by a mage who seeks only destruction and power. We have numbers, and we need space to gather ourselves for the coming battles. I am taking the Undercity for this purpose. Because of the secretive nature of this, I am ordering all of you to remain in the Undercity. I am conscripting each of you into my service."

No one among the Watch argued. Several stood straighter—to be promoted from common City Watch and into service to the king? An honorable promotion, indeed.

An older watchman stepped forward. He wore decorations on his pauldrons. "Your Majesty," he said, bowing his head. "It is good to see you alive."

"Are you in charge of this post?" asked King Bradburn, each word that of a commander.

"Yes. Lieutenant Seymour at your service, sir."

"What news have you heard from the surface?"

"That there was an attack on the castle," answered Seymour. "And a subsequent rebellion at the Marca. Rumors suggested that you had fallen, and our men reported the surface was in a state of chaos. A mage has taken control. Some are calling it the next Imperium."

"Yet you remained down here?" asked the king.

"We were twice in number," answered Seymour. "We could not all abandon our duty down here, sir."

The king nodded. Juniper thought it sounded a lot like an excuse for why they hadn't rushed topside to assist the fighting.

"I will not lie, the surface is in a state of chaos," answered King Bradburn. At this, a murmur of unease traveled through the Watch. "And we are what stands in the way of total devastation. We are assuming the Undercity as our fortress."

"We, sir?" asked Seymour. He looked at those gathered around the king.

"Yes." The king glanced behind him, at those who stood with him. "We are but a fraction of the rebels. We consist of apostates, knights, thieves, and soldiers, but we seek the same: to reclaim Rusdasin from the enemy. Will you and your men join us?"

Juniper thought it silly to ask, considering he had just conscripted them into service.

However, Lieutenant Seymour did not hesitate. He closed his fist and set it over his heart. "We are at your command, Your Majesty. Men?"

Each of the Watch mirrored the Lieutenant's motion, fist over the heart, and just like that, they had taken the Undercity back. Juniper had expected it to be a lot harder and bloodier, but she did not complain.

Xavier whispered to Juniper, "Welcome back."

CHAPTER 36

Over a barrel festooned with a forgotten game of cards, King Bradburn, Josephine, Maddox, and Lieutenant Seymour discussed how to divide the Undercity—Juniper hadn't the care to stay and listen, so she slipped away from the crowd and started toward the quiet and familiar streets.

The magelights glowed only above the market. The rest of the Undercity remained dark. Juniper didn't mind; she had her night sight. As she left the light, her eyes adjusted, revealing the darkened world in shades of dark blue and gray. She needed time to herself, to think—she hadn't had much time in the last several days to think, save for the small moment Maddox had ruined.

She ran a hand through her hair, and the cool metal of her ring grazed her scalp. She held her hand in front of her. Even in the dark, the moonstone seemed to glow.

Marriage. She hadn't thought about that much either. She was no longer trapped in the Marca, and Reid was no longer going to Chata—they didn't have to get married. A darker thought sprang forward, one she had previously shoved aside—if she hadn't been trapped in the Marca, would Reid have proposed? Had he only proposed because he thought he had to?

She saw the glow first, then heard his footsteps.

"Juniper," came Reid's voice. His armor clinked as he jogged to catch up with her. "Where are you going?"

"Nowhere," she answered. "I wanted to take a walk. All the stuffy politics are getting old."

"I am inclined to agree."

A beat passed.

"Reid..." she started.

"Yes?"

"I..." She didn't know where to start.

Reid reached for her hand, folded his warm fingers around hers, and tugged her to a stop. For a moment, he held her gaze, the mage stone glowing in his other hand. It turned his brown eyes into dark green pools. "Something is bothering you," he said.

She clutched his hand. "I'm tired. So much has happened, and there's still so much to do."

"Is that all?"

Hardly. She didn't know who she was—Juniper or Isolde. She didn't know how to be anyone else. Nexon wanted her dead. They had lost the castle. King Bradburn was starting to rely on her, and the responsibility tasted like poison.

She brought her left hand up to their joined hands, cupping his hand between both of hers. The moonstone glittered in the light of the mage stone.

"Do you still want to get married?" she whispered. "Now that we don't have to."

A beat passed, then another. She tore her eyes off the moonstone and met his. His gaze had gone unreadable. She hated and loved it.

"We don't have to," he said. "But my offer still stands. I want you in my life, Juniper. That has not changed."

Juniper swallowed against the lump in her throat. Reid hadn't said he still wanted to *marry* her. He wanted her *in his life*. She wanted several people in her life, including Roslyn and Ison and Abrielle—she did not feel the same way about them as she felt about Reid.

"We have time," Reid said. "We can wait as long as we like."

"And we don't have to spend our honeymoon traveling to Chata," she said, though her words came out flat. She had a thought to give him back his ring until he was certain he wanted her more than *in his life*. Or maybe that was how marriage worked.

A small smile tugged at the corners of his lips. She couldn't tell if it reached his eyes. "That is very true," he said.

Juniper continued her walk with Reid. Without realizing it, her feet took her to Maddox's keep. The stone townhouse looked so strange and forbidding in the mage stone's glow. Even standing at the gate, she felt like an intruder. The keep had been home, and she had betrayed it and those within it.

Reid stood beside her, steady as stone.

"I don't know if Maddox is mad at me or not," Juniper said.

"He didn't seem mad."

"He couldn't very well strangle me in a crowded house," she said darkly. "And he is good at hiding his anger."

"Maddox is a smart man," Reid said. "He likely understands what you did, or he thinks he has gotten a better deal because of it. Amery's house is nicer than this. And Maddox is working side by side with the king."

"That's strange by itself," she muttered.

And Maddox had already contemplated betrayal.

With no pressing matters, Juniper let herself through the gate. Reid followed. The front door was closed—as she had left it when they passed through on their way to the castle. Even that felt ages ago. She let herself into the darkened keep. It smelled the same, only mustier and danker.

She had turned her back on Maddox. She had sold him and the Undercity out. She had betrayed him. She no longer wore his brand.

This keep wasn't home.

"I spent so long thinking I would die down here," she whispered as she made her way through the foyer cautiously, as if someone might be lurking in the shadows. "I lived with thieves and murderers and considered myself the best among them—the worst of the worst. I spent so long thinking I belonged down here, that I was incapable of living topside with normal people."

She started up the stairs, running her fingers along the smooth banister. Reid followed a step behind. Her feet took her to the top floor and to her closed bedroom door. The utter silence of the keep unnerved her. Even in the dead of night, the keep had never been this quiet.

"Now what do you think?" Reid asked.

"I'm thinking how this place isn't home anymore," she whispered. "It hasn't been for a while."

She let herself into her old room. It looked the same as the day she'd left. Amery had straightened up and taken a few of her things. Both beds had been made. She had left Juniper's things—that had been part of their deal. They did not touch each other's things without permission. Not that Juniper had anything worth taking. Mostly clothes and books.

Reid meandered into the room, his mage stone illuminating the plain walls, the few shelves, the clothing left in the hamper. Seeing him here, of all places, felt...strange—her new life walking into her old life.

Her new life. When she imagined home, she thought of Reid.

She had never associated home with a person before, and the notion made her nervous. People had proven to be fickle and capable of lies.

With Reid's attention on the room, she glanced down to the moonstone. When she agreed to marriage, she had seen it as a way out of the Marca—the lesser of two prisons. She loved Reid, but the thought of being a wife tied her stomach in knots. Nothing made her feel as uneasy.

In all her childish daydreams and wishful thinking, Juniper had never imagined having a husband. Lovers, yes, but a husband? No. She never thought she would have the time for one, and in those dark corners of her mind, she never believed herself worthy of a decent husband. There were too many good girls topside, too many girls with skills in the kitchen and for homemaking.

Whenever Juniper envisioned her future, she assumed she would be a thief until someone stabbed her in the back, or she slipped up on a job, or she retired and became a mentor. She'd never given serious thought to having a husband or a family or living outside of the Undercity life.

Mrs. Sandpiper. Lady Sandpiper. She didn't know how to feel or think about a future she had never imagined.

Reid meandered to her bookshelf and held the stone closer to the spines. "These are mostly adventure and romance," he mused.

"I admire a healthy dose of both," she said. "Adventure and romance are two things I thought I wouldn't have in my life, and I made up for the lack in books."

The admission warmed her cheeks. Thankfully, Reid's attention didn't move from the bookshelf. He ran his finger along the spines and chose a particularly well-read novel.

"*Dark Thunderheads.* You've read this one several times," he said.

She blushed. "It's one of my favorites. I bought that book with the money from my first job. Maddox laughed at me when I brought it back. Not a mean laugh. He said there were worse things I could have bought. Then he told me about a print shop he held stock in that would give me a discount."

"Did you accept the discount?" Reid asked with a knight's disapproval. He glanced at her over his shoulder.

"Of course I did," Juniper said, aghast that he would think otherwise. She put her hand over her heart in mock shock. "I could buy two books for the price of one!"

Chuckling, Reid pulled the book from the shelf. "What's it about?"

"A bastard girl who inherits the king's magic, naming her as his rightful successor. She runs away, and the royal children each send someone to kill her so they might inherit the magic and become the next ruler. She falls in love with the bounty hunter, who then gets betrayed, and they have to save the kingdom together," Juniper said. She had the sudden urge to read the book again.

Reid opened the book to a random page. His brows rose considerably. "I thought this was an adventure novel?"

She laughed. "Did you find the smutty forest scene?"

He cleared his throat and replaced the book on the shelf.

"A healthy dose of romance," she said. "They also explore the kingdom while evading assassins and mercenaries. The sense of adventure kept me going while living between cavern walls."

Reid examined several other books. "Most of these are about the ocean."

"I've never seen it," Juniper said. She folded her arms across her chest. "The idea of leaving dry land and setting sail where no king holds power, where there are no rules besides those set by the crew, where I could go anywhere I wanted, when I wanted…" She released a dreamy sigh. "I know, piracy is much more glamorous on paper than in real life."

"I'm sure it is," Reid said. "I've never met a real pirate, but I've heard they reek of sweat and seawater."

"I can't imagine why."

Reid closed the space between them. "Do you want to see it? The ocean?" Juniper drew her eyes to his. She felt the promise in his words and saw it in the molten gold of his eyes.

"Yes," she whispered.

"Then you shall see it," he whispered. He tilted her chin upward and kissed her tenderly.

"Reid?" she said against his lips.

"Hmm?"

"Want to cross something off the list before someone comes looking for us?"

He kissed her again. "What do you have in mind?"

She bit her lip as she reached for the buckles at his sides. Getting a man out of armor reminded her of the dresses women wore—buckles and clasps and laces, and a maze to get in and out of. Without his armor, she felt the warmth of his skin through his clothes, the taut muscles of his arms and legs and chest.

Juniper pushed Reid toward her bed and then onto his back. She climbed on to the bed, straddling his hips. She had wanted to try this for a while, even before Mabyl had mentioned it. Reid did not object; he held onto her hips as they crossed the first item off her list.

CHAPTER 37

Reid had never thought a woman could capture his attention like Juniper did. Her skin against his set a fire in his blood, one he never knew existed. How could he have thought he would be better off without her?

None of that mattered now. Those dark days were behind him. He had her, and he would never let her go.

Juniper lay against his chest, her cheek against his heart. The mage stone rested on the bedside table, and without a touch to activate the rune, it had gone dark, leaving the room in darkness. With Juniper so close, the darkness felt featherlight.

"That was fun," she said, her hot breath against his chest.

Reid wrapped a lock of her hair around his finger. "You'll just have to practice to get better."

She giggled, her breath warm against his skin.

They lay a while in her bed, in the dark, with their breathing as the only sound, when light flared outside, banishing the dark.

Reid's heart thumped in panic, and then—

"The magelights," Juniper said, her tone groggy. She sat up and put her hand against his chest, as if she had sensed his panic.

The light grew steadily brighter until it mimicked the cloudy daylight above.

Juniper pulled herself off him, much to his reluctance, and they freshened up in the now-bright bathing room.

Reid followed Juniper down through the keep and to the street. He blinked at the difference. The tent city no longer glowed ominously, and the magelights glowed as bright as natural daylight. It appeared, in a strange way, as if the sunlight seeped through the cavernous ceiling and into the Undercity.

They returned to the City Watch's outpost to find teams heading in every direction. The king, Maddox, and Josephine stood around a map of the Undercity. Captain Sandpiper stood beside the king, and his gaze narrowed at Reid as he and Juniper approached.

"Where have you been?" his uncle asked. His gaze drifted over Juniper, and dislike darkened his eyes.

"Getting a better feel for this place," Reid said before Juniper could say something sarcastic.

Maddox's dark eyes glanced at Reid. He had the distinct feeling of being exposed, like Maddox knew exactly what he had been doing, with whom, and where. Maddox's gaze returned to the map, but the feeling of exposure remained. Captain Sandpiper's frown deepened. "We've arranged teams to perform a sweep of the Undercity," he told Reid. "A preliminary precaution, but also a way to perfect the few maps we have."

They had divided the Undercity into sectors—one for Josephine and her mages; one for King Bradburn and his men; and one for Maddox and those loyal to him. The middle of the Undercity, previously the market, had been renamed the Commons—neutral territory and meeting space.

Juniper took the news with a straight face, staring at the map of the Undercity with cool eyes. If the dividing of her previous home bothered her, she didn't show it. Of course, like she had mentioned before, the Undercity was no longer her home.

But the castle was still his home, as was Rusdasin, and Reid would fight to the death to protect it.

"Reid," started King Bradburn. "I am tasking you with finding an appropriate place for my family to stay." He motioned to the sector that would be his. "Somewhere in here, a central location would be preferable."

Reid nodded, accepting the assignment, though it struck a chord in his chest—he wanted Reid to find him a new home?

"It's not a glamorous job," King Bradburn said. "Adrian is going with you, and I would prefer him not to wander the Undercity alone."

King Bradburn looked knowingly at Juniper.

"We'll keep him safe," Juniper said, in a tone that implied the opposite.

"Reid will keep him safe," interjected Maddox. He looked pointedly at King Bradburn. Something silent passed between them, and Juniper bristled beside him.

Reid did not like the idea of Maddox and King Bradburn sharing thoughts. The men were as different as they could be. Maddox turned his calm stare to Juniper, and Reid fought the urge to curl his fingers to a fist—Maddox looked at Juniper with possession.

"I want you to help the former Undercity residents into new housing," Maddox said, motioning to the sector that belonged to him—it included his keep. "You know your way around, and most of them will listen to you. If not, you know what to do."

Juniper sighed dramatically. "Yes, yes, keep the peace."

"Exactly," Maddox said. "Please and thank you. And, also…if you get the chance, I want you to go topside and see if you can track down Tomas Uhls."

"What use is a fence going to be?" Juniper asked.

"He's also a decent enchanter and smith," Maddox said. "If he's still alive, he would prove useful."

"We could use a smith," agreed King Bradburn. To Juniper he said, "But do not put yourself in excess trouble."

Juniper's face melted into one of smooth arrogance. Reid recognized it. She had no intention of staying out of trouble.

Reid's heart skipped a beat—if the prophecy was right, and Juniper really was the returning princess, then she was instrumental in defeating Nexon— Nexon had every reason to seek Juniper's death.

"I'll see if I can track him down," Juniper said, setting her hands on her hips. "Without throwing myself into trouble."

Juniper squeezed Reid's hand and gave him a wolfish grin. Then, she vanished through the crowd. Reid watched her auburn head until he could no longer see her.

"She'll be fine," Maddox assured him. "She's the best thief in the Undercity. She knows how to take care of herself."

Reid held Maddox's dark gaze. He didn't like how Maddox appeared both relaxed and alert, like a man with daggers up his sleeves and in his boots. Which, Reid reasoned, were both likely. He still thought he owned Juniper, and it burned under Reid's skin. This man had bought children like bags of flour.

Anything Reid had to say to the man was cut short when Adrian appeared at Reid's side. Maddox used the distraction to vanish.

"Shall we meander through our new home and see which property snags the eye?" Adrian hummed and wiggled his eyebrows.

"You're awfully cheery about it," Reid said.

They started away from the Commons and into King Bradburn's sector.

"It's not every day one sees the beginning of a revolution and the emergence of a resistance," Adrian said, tucking his hands into his trouser pockets. He'd patted off most of the dirt from the fine threads, but some remained. "And it's not every day one goes house shopping."

Reid tried to soak in some of Adrian's optimism, but it didn't work. It never did.

They meandered through the stone streets of King Bradburn's sector. The residences looked much the same, gray or reddish stone with accents of different types of wood. Some resembled townhouses, like Maddox's keep, while others were a series of shacks stacked haphazardly upon one another. Reid spotted several townhouses that reached the ceiling—pillars, he realized, that maintained the Undercity's stability.

Whoever had built this place knew what they were doing.

After a few laps of the houses near the center of the sector, Adrian selected a townhouse built into a pillar that rose to the ceiling. Like most of the other residences, it had been hastily evacuated—upturned wooden stools, emptied cabinets, earthen jugs still full of water, forgotten shoes and clothes. Like Maddox's keep, it had running water. The water did not flow as smoothly as it did in the castle; it spurted and splattered into the washing basin. The whole place smelled overwhelmingly like burnt bread, though Reid suspected it had something to do with the abandoned bakery next door.

Reid examined every room, looking for lurking threats and trying to find out what the house had been previously used for. He did not want his king and prince staying in an old brothel. However, he concluded that this townhouse had been used for living, not pleasure-selling.

Adrian climbed all the way to the top floor. An uneven wooden table held the remains of an abandoned gambling den—copper pieces, rings, slivers of gemstones, bone dice, and playing cards had been skewed in a hurry. It had four windows, one on each side of the house, and overlooked the Undercity. Adrian sauntered to the window that faced the Commons.

"Yes, I think this will suit my father's need to see everything," Adrian said. "I also like a nice view. What do you think, Reid?"

"It doesn't have bloodstains, at least." Reid had spotted several of those on the way here, as well as on his previous tour.

A beat passed, but Reid didn't notice. He was looking at a tarnished bracelet under the table. Adrian appeared in front of him, worry on his face.

"What's bothering you, Reid?" Adrian asked.

"Too many things."

"All right, let's start at the top of the list." Adrian folded his hands behind his back and puffed out his chest. He looked much like his father.

Reid sighed. He didn't want to talk about it.

"There's the fact that we were kicked out of our home," Adrian started. "Our lives were nearly lost. All my favorite shirts, gone. Then there is the fact that Fowler betrayed us and has tainted the Order with black magic. You have been handed a severe blow, I imagine. And now we are reclaiming the Undercity, of all places, as our base of operations. Have I missed anything?"

Reid grunted in response. How could Adrian be so casual about all of this?

"Oh!" Adrian snapped his fingers. "And you're recently engaged."

Reid released a sigh—he hadn't meant to. Adrian pounced on it.

"Wait," Adrian said, brows furrowed. "Out of all of those horrible things I mentioned, the one that bothers you the most is your engagement?"

Reid didn't argue, and Adrian gaped at him, dumbfounded.

He didn't know how to explain it. His agitation at the subject and the confrontation must have shown, for Adrian continued, "I thought you were certain about Juniper?"

"I am," Reid said at once.

Adrian's brows rose. "And yet you are also uncertain?"

Reid sighed through his nose. "I don't know. It's just…Juniper is not the wife I imagined. She's… She's not…"

"She's not the ideal woman as set forth by our society," Adrian said dryly.

Reid shrugged his agreement.

"Those were my mother's words when I told her about Roslyn. She thought I'd lost it. She suggested that Roslyn had bewitched me, and her affection for me and mine for her was a ruse in an attempt to grab the throne." Adrian laughed and tucked his hands into his pockets. "And now they are friends."

Reid paced from window to window. He spotted people meandering through the streets. Mostly knights—Henry and Isaac had been put in charge of helping the knights filter into the Undercity. They would be staying in the king's sector.

"I told my uncle and aunt before all of this." Reid felt Adrian's gaze, but he couldn't meet his friend's eye. "They were not happy. They did not give me their blessing. They suggested that Juniper was using me to get out of the Marca, and that she would run for the apostate camps in Collatia at the first chance."

"Captain Sandpiper has been glaring more lately," Adrian said. *At Juniper* was what he didn't add.

"My uncle said I was making the same mistake as my father," Reid confessed.

"And what mistake is that?"

"My uncle believes my father rushed into marriage. He also said I would end up like my father if I continued on this road," Reid said lowly. His uncle's words felt like a jab, but they also felt true—Reid didn't know which felt worse.

Adrian appeared beside him, but he didn't speak.

"I always thought I'd marry some noblewoman or a lord's daughter," Reid said. "And Juniper…is just what your mother said. She is the opposite of everything I thought a wife should be, everything my aunt and uncle think she should be."

At the mention of his aunt, his heart squeezed. She still had not been found, and none of the servants could tell them anything about her. Reid did not want to admit it, or even think about it, but he would likely never see his aunt again.

"But Juniper loves you," Adrian said, "which, in my opinion, is the more relevant qualification."

Reid nodded.

"Would you rather marry Juniper and be happy, or marry some noblewoman and pretend to be happy?" Adrian added darkly, "There are plenty of people who marry for looks, and I refused from an early age to be among those fools. I'd rather be a fool in love."

And Reid agreed. He loved Juniper. No, she was not the ideal woman of society, but was that what he wanted? He didn't know.

"And…" Adrian said in a charming tone, "she *is* a princess."

Reid half laughed. "As far as Isaac believes," he countered. He didn't know if he believed the tale or not.

Adrian meandered to the window. "Oh, there's Father. Let's go show him which house we picked."

"We?" Reid asked, starting after Adrian. "You picked it."

"*I* picked it if he hates it; *we* picked it if he likes it," Adrian said, jogging down the stone steps, a laugh in his tone.

CHAPTER 38

Juniper sauntered down a shadowed alley, hood up, gait drunken. It had taken a few clever questions and threats, but she found where the Undercity scum had hidden themselves. They had relocated to the west side of the topside slums. The tight quarters, narrow alleys, and stacked housing provide a maze for the new black-market stalls, hired swords, and brothels. The air seethed with whispers and smelled of cheap ale and body stink.

Maddox hadn't outright blamed her, but he'd implied it. He wanted her to find Tomas Uhls, but he also wanted her to see what she had done to the Undercity. She spotted a few faces she recognized, mostly vendors and fences. The guilt over her betrayal had come and gone, and it had faded into an old wound, but seeing the Undercity reduced to this, it returned sharp and hot.

She didn't know how far the rumors of the Undercity's fall being her fault had gone. She kept her face shadowed and her eyes downcast—not completely hidden, because that would look suspicious.

She asked a few unfamiliar shopkeepers about Uhls in a voice deeper than her own and flashed a dagger she'd lifted from one of the City Watch before coming topside.

It all led her to a dump of a house—a pile of shacks stacked five high with blankets for curtains and unsteady, drunken laughter spilling onto the street. Somewhere nearby, someone plucked an out-of-tune lute.

Just like home.

Only, not *home* anymore.

Juniper meandered inside the house. The lighting was low, and curtains hushed the natural light. Sweet-smelling elixirs perfumed with hallucinogens and painkillers scented the first three floors, alongside the inebriated chatter and groggy laughter. Juniper meandered through the smoke clouds and gambling tables. Dark dealings tended to be on the top floor.

She found Tomas Uhls tucked into one of the rooms on the fourth floor, his dirty blond hair tied back, his skin shined with sweat, and wearing a green-and-gold tunic far too extravagant for his business. His bodyguard—a mountain of a man—stood by the door and looked her up and down as she entered.

"You lost?" Tomas Uhls said in a tired, slimy voice. He leaned back in his chair and pretended to examine an oversized ruby ring on his finger.

"Not anymore," Juniper said in her own voice. "I've been looking all over for you, Tomas."

Uhls arched a brow at her. Then, realization dawned and stretched his lips into a villainous grin—a salesman's grin. He nodded to his bodyguard, who closed the door.

Gods, it was warm in this place. Juniper felt sweat beading on her neck, sucking her cloak to her skin. She ignored it.

"So, you're not dead after all," Uhls said, his words curved in an educated lilt. "And you've got the nerve to slink back to my doorstep?"

"Maddox sent me to find you," Juniper said plainly. She needed to get out of this room—she was feeling dizzy from the heat. It marred her thoughts and blurred her words.

"Did he now? What does Maddox want?"

"He didn't specify," Juniper lied. She locked her knees to keep standing. Her palms were slick, and sweat beaded along her hairline. "He wants to talk to you."

"And he expects me to know where and when?"

"I suppose he did," Juniper said.

Uhls looked at her hard, his sharp eyes taking in things she didn't intend to give away—or pretending to, she could never tell. Right now, with sweat trailing down her spine, she didn't care.

"I have other business to tend to," Juniper said. She turned to leave.

"Leaving so soon?" Uhls chimed.

The bodyguard grabbed her shoulder, and at the same time she saw it—a rune, carved half on the wall and half on the door, so when the door shut, the rune completed. Just like the Marca's nasty tricks. She didn't know the rune, but the sweat dripping down her neck, the blurry thoughts, the dizziness—Uhls's doing. She reached down into her magic, but it quivered in response. The rune was disrupting her magic.

"I delivered the message," Juniper spat. "We have nothing further to discuss."

"Oh, I think we do." Uhls stood and took a piece of paper from his makeshift desk. He unfurled it with a swish of his wrist.

It was a wanted poster. She recognized the harshly drawn face as her own. A seal marked the bottom of the poster, an old-fashioned dagger with a fat blade and a cage-hilt. The words on the page came in and out of focus; she couldn't read it.

"Is that supposed to mean something?" Juniper growled.

"A messenger passed them out this morning," said Uhls. He turned the page around and read, "By order of the Imperium, the grand magister offers a reward of ten thousand gold for the thief known as Juniper Thimble. Anyone caught harboring Thimble will be executed. Anyone caught withholding information that could otherwise lead to her capture will be executed. Anyone caught interfering with the law of the Imperium will be executed."

Juniper scoffed. Nexon had resorted to putting a bounty on her head?

Uhls rolled up the wanted poster and tucked it away. "The message said the new king would pay twice as much gold if you were brought in alive, but dead works too."

Juniper laughed, though it lacked confidence. "I'd love to see you try."

The bodyguard grabbed her by the arms. Juniper reflexively summoned her magic and—flurries appeared and quickly withered. She tried again, but her quivering magic sank further away from her command.

The bodyguard's fist slammed into her stomach, knocking the breath from her throat and the thoughts from her mind. She crumpled forward. His other hand grabbed her cloak and pulled her upright.

"Secure her hands," said Uhls. "Don't want her trying anything until I get my gold."

"Want her dead?" asked the bodyguard.

"No, not yet," Uhls said. "Let them deal with it."

The bodyguard heaved Juniper's limp body onto his shoulder. The door opened—she felt the immediate difference. The shackles around her magic shattered, and her magic began to claw its way back to her.

Uhls led the way through the townhouse, and she heard several whoops as they navigated the gambling den. She didn't see much of it from her dangling angle.

"Oh, looks like you caught a good one," came a familiar singsong voice, perfumed with honey. From under her hood, Juniper saw wisps of blonde hair and a red dress.

"Not as good as you, darling," Uhls purred.

"Careful, I'm susceptible to flattery," chimed the girl.

With every moment, Juniper's mind cleared. She knew that voice, and her panic subsided with each word the girl said.

They were on the first floor, then outside the front door. The cooler air leeched the unnatural heat from her skin and clothes. It nudged her magic, nursed it, coaxed it.

"Are you sure you can't stay a while?" whined the girl.

"I've got business, darling," said Uhls, a bit peeved.

"Are you sure?" came the girl's voice.

A flash of red and blonde—the bodyguard grunted and stumbled. Juniper seized the chance. Tendrils of ice grabbed his ankles and yanked his feet from underneath him. As he fell, Juniper jumped. As she jumped, a dagger of ice sliced through the ropes binding her wrists. She landed on her feet, albeit wobbly.

"You bitch!" Uhls growled, face twisted into an ugly grimace.

Helena Thimble stood over the bodyguard with a dirty bottle in her hand like a sword—she had cracked it into the bodyguard's skull. Her blonde hair was done up in a messy bun. Dirt and ash spotted her fair skin. Her red dress had been torn in several places, leaving the sleeves uneven and the hem in tatters.

Uhls drew a blade, but before the steel left the scabbard, Juniper shot a blade of ice through his throat.

Helena tossed the bottle. It shattered against the cobblestones. She looked Juniper up and down, then let out a low whistle. "You've looked better, sister."

"As have you," Juniper said. "The dirt doesn't go with your skin tone."

Helena smirked. Her eyes flashed over Juniper's shoulder. "We should go." She grabbed Juniper's hand. "We're already drawing attention."

Indeed, curious faces looked out of alleys and windows, and a strange silence had fallen over the street. Uhls's blood slowly made its way across the damp cobblestones.

Helena pulled Juniper through a mostly empty side street. They crisscrossed alleys and narrow streets, crossed a canal, slipped through the backroom of one building and out the other side, and finally came to a small rose-colored house that had seen better days. A faded and broken sign by the door suggested it had once been a flower shop.

Helena pulled her inside. The main room had been made into a homey little cottage. A quilt hung over the front window, mismatched pillows and blankets formed a nest of a bed, and a mismatched tea set rested on a blanket-draped crate. By the looks of it, several people lived here.

"I don't think the other girls are here right now," Helena said.

"You live here?"

"It's not bad," Helena said. Her tone indicated otherwise. As a popular courtesan, Helena had gotten used to the best the Undercity had to offer.

"What happened?"

Helena's eyes darkened. "Mages came into the shop. Darleen told them to leave, and they killed her." She wrapped her arms around herself. "The girls and I…uh, relocated here."

Darleen had run the lingerie shop where Helena had worked as both sales consultant and courtesan.

"We took the Undercity back," Juniper said.

Helena's finely plucked brows rose. "You did what?"

Sitting opposite each other on silken pillows, Juniper explained the situation to Helena. Her sister remained silent through most of it, tapping her chipped nails on the hardwood floor. Helena told her how mages had stormed through the streets, using blank-faced knights like hound dogs, declaring a new age of magic, and anyone who objected did not survive.

Despite the setting and the circumstance, Juniper was glad to have found Helena. She'd worried for her sister.

Helena let out a graceful sigh. "And Maddox thought Uhls would be useful? The man's scum, inside and out."

Juniper shrugged. She'd accepted that Uhls had been a ruse. It didn't matter. Uhls was dead. "You still dabble in poisons?"

Helena winked. "I've got one that's only reactive if you inhale another. I'm quite proud of it."

"We could use you," Juniper said. She glanced around the house. "And, you know, you could live in the Undercity without worrying about power-hungry mages and enthralled knights busting down your door."

"Especially now that I've been seen with the city's most wanted," Helena said, grinning.

"Flatterer," Juniper said, pretending to blush.

Helena's grin faded. "Seriously, Jun, those mages are out for your blood. This magister, or whatever he's calling himself, is looking for you."

"And you, by extension." Juniper inhaled deeply and let it go quickly. "I guess you have no choice but to hide in the Undercity with the rest of the decent people."

Helena grimaced at the putrid pink walls of the cottage. "Can't be much worse than this. When do we leave?"

Juniper walked Helena to the nearest Undercity entrance. Juniper went first so that the guards waiting at the bottom wouldn't attack. After a quick introduction, they let Helena through.

"I'll catch up," Juniper said, and started back toward the surface.

"Wait, where are you going?" Helena called.

"I want to check something," Juniper said and hoisted herself through the trapdoor before Helena or the guards could dissuade her.

She climbed to the roof of the nearest building and took a deep breath of the frigid city air. Her little spat with Uhls had caused a stir—the chatter of panic flitted through the streets. Juniper had often fantasized about being the most wanted in the city again, but it didn't feel as victorious as she thought.

Juniper jumped to the next rooftop, away from the black market. She kept her eyes on the streets. Mages patrolled, laughing like they owned the city. She supposed, in a strange way, they did. Temporarily. The resistance would take it back.

Thralls patrolled too. Blank-faced knights stood guard on street corners and stalked behind mages. After several city blocks, Juniper realized—all thralls were knights. Did that mean something? Were knights somehow more susceptible to being a thrall? Were regular soldiers not good enough? Maybe something in their mysterious training made them better thralls.

She would ask Reid or Isaac when she got the chance. Or Henry since they were on the same side now.

A shriek a street away grabbed her attention. Juniper rushed to the next rooftop and crouched at the edge just in time to see a girl fall—a rope of raw magic grabbed her ankles. Three mages stalked toward the fallen girl.

"Let me go!" cried the girl. "I—I don't know anything!"

The mage whose magic bound the girl's legs laughed—Juniper's stomach turned over with rage. She would recognize that bitter-bitch laugh anywhere. Carol.

Carol's magic flipped the girl onto her back. Juniper knew her too. Ida, the quiet girl who had slept a bed away from Juniper.

"You say you don't know anything," Carol sneered, "but I think you know some things."

"I—I don't!"

Carol lifted the girl into the air. Ida let out a fearful shriek.

"We'll teach you a thing or two about disrespect," snapped the mage to Carol's left in the voice of one not used to power.

Juniper followed along the rooftops as Carol and her cronies took Ida into a small warehouse. Ida's shrieks echoed off the stony walls. Juniper landed on the warehouse's slanted roof, and she quickly and selfishly formed a plan, not at all fueled by her desire for revenge.

CHAPTER 39

Henry stood against the wall of the tavern as Captain Sandpiper and King Bradburn told the knights of their new assignment: to patrol the Undercity alongside the mages. Henry didn't mind the assignment, but the others of the Order did not take the news as easily.

"You want us to patrol with apostates?" asked one of the knights.

"Half of them came from the Marca," argued Isaac.

"The other half have never been," argued the first knight. "And they likely know black magic."

"As do the knights who tried to turn you into a thrall," said another knight.

"Enough," said King Bradburn, and the room fell into silence. He continued in a calm, commanding voice, "Either you accept these conditions, or you don't eat. This is war. Hard choices must be made. There are not enough of you to patrol the entire Undercity. We will all work to keep this place safe, and we will all pull our weight. Is that clear?"

No one argued with the king.

Captain Sandpiper and King Bradburn led the knights out of the old building they had claimed as their new headquarters and marched toward the Commons. Patrol teams would consist of at least one mage and one knight. It would keep the power balanced regardless of who or what they encountered. Henry didn't mind teaming up with a mage—he knew how beneficial having magic on his side of a fight could be, and he would feel considerably better about wandering the Undercity with someone who could shoot fire or ice from their fingertips.

As the knights approached the center of the Commons, the mages approached from the other side. They walked behind Josephine.

The mages halted on one side of the gushing fountain. The knights stopped on the other. And the standoff began—Henry felt the tension rise. The bittersweet metallic and floral scents of magic wafted from the mages, the very smell knights were trained to associate with apostates. Henry's panic rose in reflex, and he fought against it.

"Ah, our escorts are here," said one of the mages in the front, a tall blonde with sharp eyes. "Here to slap our hands if we breathe too loudly?"

"Here to brainwash us into your own thrall?" asked another of the knights.

"This is not why we're here," said Lex, a pledge, but his voice lacked volume of confidence. "We are to form patrols."

"You don't know mages like we do," snapped one of the older knights.

"And you don't know magic like we do," said the tall blonde bitterly. "Care to see some of it tested out?"

"Try it," growled the knight, hand tightening on his Mage's Bane.

The blonde and the knight stepped toward each other. Henry felt the subtle shift into chaos, and his feet acted on their own—and then he was standing between the knight and the mage. Henry put his hand over the knight's, preventing him from drawing his blade. The knight glared at Henry, and Henry glared back.

"This is not the time for violence," Henry said, each word careful.

He looked at the mages. The blonde mage had halted, her brow quirked. Tiny flames danced across her fingertips. The mages behind her held their hands up in defensive positions, prepared to throw fire and ice and stone.

"Lower your swords and your magic," Henry said.

The knight scowled. "But these mages—"

"—are here for the same reason you are," Henry snapped. The surge of his own voice surprised him, and as all eyes turned to him, mages and knights alike, that surprise dwindled into something stronger and warmer. It propelled him forward. "Fowler is no longer our leader. He has defied the very Order he claimed to serve. He has broken his vows, but you have not." Henry turned to see the knights, squires, and pledges better, and by doing so, turned his back on the mages. "You took an oath to stop black magic, to prevent magic from being misused. These mages may be apostates, but so are we. We are all rebels now, and we have a common enemy. That enemy is not each other."

"Henry is correct," said Sir Darvel. He joined him in the middle. "If we continue bickering, we sliver our chances of survival."

A murmur began through the Order, and Henry could hardly believe it. He felt a presence at his shoulder, but it took a moment to realize it was King Bradburn.

"Let us begin," said the king.

The knights and mages began to mingle. Under the supervision of Josephine and King Bradburn, they paired off in twos. The patrols headed to their designated location or route, and Henry could hardly believe it had happened without a spat.

The king set his hand on Henry's shoulder.

"Those were fine words, Henry," said King Bradburn.

Henry's face flushed, though his dark cheeks hid it well. "Thank you, Your Majesty."

"Tell me, where do you see the Order going from here?"

Henry blinked in surprise. He hadn't been ready for such a question. And to be asked by the king himself—he scrambled for an answer. "Rebuilding," Henry said.

The king's brows rose.

"The Order has a purpose, a good purpose. That purpose has been twisted into something evil, but that doesn't mean we can't straighten it out and return to that true purpose."

"That will take time," said the king.

"Most things do," Henry said. His father had said those words often, to curb Henry's impatience as a child.

The king said his farewell and started speaking lowly with Captain Sandpiper. Henry followed the other knights and greeted his patrolling partner, a blonde mage with pale eyes and a faraway look. She smiled a kind greeting at him.

"I heard what you said," she said, her voice sweet and feminine. "The others listened too. I think you're right about all of it."

"Thank you." Henry looked her up and down. She was pretty in a doll-like way, with petite features and soft edges. Her pale eyes strayed just over his shoulder, unfocused. Magic radiated around her, though Henry did not sense a threat within it. "My name is Sir Henry Julian."

"You are a knight," she said.

"Yes."

"I've heard about you," she said with a coy smile.

He flashed his lopsided grin. "Only bad things, I'm sure."

Her expression didn't change. Odd. Girls tended to swoon or flutter their eyes when he smiled.

"Ison said you were trustworthy."

His grin faded, and he took another look at her. "You know him?"

"Ison and I are friends." She held out her delicate hand. "My name is Bois."

He took her hand. Her grip mirrored her voice and her magic, soft and gentle, as threatening as a kitten.

They started toward the eastern edge of the Undercity, to the hole to the surface they were to guard. It felt like standing watch in the castle, only less…scenic.

"It's not so bad down here," Bois said as they walked between two squat buildings with dark windows.

Henry wanted to argue. He did not like the Undercity. He had the constant feeling of being watched. "Have you spent time down here?"

"Yes," Bois nodded. "I lived down here before Juniper told the Watch about us. Then I lived with Amery topside. Now I'm back."

"Ah, you are one of the Undercity mages," Henry said as if it solved something. It didn't. He had categorized the mages into Undercity mages and Marca mages. In his mind, the Undercity mages were more dangerous and probably better to have in a fight than a Marca mage.

"I hear they are arranging combat training for mages," Bois said. "I thought about going."

"Have you not learned combat on your own?"

"Did you learn combat on your own?" Bois tilted her head at him, but she didn't look directly at him. Her gaze remained far away.

No, he hadn't. He felt sheepish then. "I thought being in the Undercity would have presented the opportunity for combat and raw magic practice or something."

She giggled. "Is that what you think mages do all day when they're not in the Marca? Cultivate their magic to kill and fight?"

"I...uh..." Henry closed his mouth before he said something stupid.

"Mages live just like anyone else," Bois said kindly. "We read, take walks, and socialize. I even played a game of dice now and then, but eventually the dealer says I'm cheating."

"Do you cheat?"

"Sometimes."

"I didn't take you as a gambler."

"I like games of chance and skill mixed together so that there's always a chance you'll lose and a chance you'll win," she said.

They came to their appointed position, a hole carved into the stone with a heavy wooden ladder leading up into darkness. Henry stood on one side and Bois stood on the other.

"Do you find it strange, Sir Julian, that the bad people are now living topside while the good people are hiding in the Undercity?"

"It is a bit strange," Henry conceded. "Though it won't be permanent."

"No?"

"We will defeat Nexon and take back what is ours," Henry said firmly. "Or die trying."

"You are sure of that?"

"I am," Henry said. "Nexon stole a friend of mine, turned him against his friends, and he died because of it. Nexon will pay for that. My friend will not have died for nothing."

Henry tightened his fist around his Mage's Bane. He daydreamed of thrusting a blade through Nexon's chest for what he did to Penet.

"You want to avenge your friend," Bois said. "That is understandable."

"Not just my friend," Henry said. "Nexon has hurt a lot of people. He needs to answer for all that he's done, all the people he has murdered for the sake of his own power."

Bois didn't say anything for a long moment.

"Why?" Henry asked.

"Oh, I just wanted to make sure you were here because you wanted to be, not because your king demanded it," she said simply. "Your heart and your head are in this to win, not just one or the other."

Henry blinked. "Oh."

"And you can remove your hand from your sword," Bois said. "I'm not going to do anything, and no one is coming through. I'll know far in advance."

Henry started. He indeed gripped his sword, but Bois was facing the other direction. "How…"

"I'm blind," Bois said. "But I use my magic to see the world around me, and I can see things in greater detail than you, Sir Julian. I can see the seams of the stones, the faint inflections on the human face when one lies, and the ripped stitch in your tunic."

Henry gawked; Bois was right about the stitch. He'd ripped it that morning.

"Magic can do that?" Henry whispered.

"It can."

The strange sensation he had felt when he first met Bois—that had been her magic mapping him out. But…the stitch on his tunic was *under* his armor. He chuckled and added, "What else are you looking at under there?"

Bois did not blush. She merely smiled.

Henry laughed. Maybe patrolling with Bois wouldn't be too bad.

CHAPTER 40

Juniper made her way into the warehouse through a loose panel on the ceiling. She dropped into a loft that smelled strongly of mildew and rotting wood. The sunlight filtered in above her, illuminating the aging barrels, crates, chests, and a million dust motes.

Voices drifted up from the main floor. Carol's cronies laughed and teased, and Ida whined. Juniper crept to the edge of the loft and peered into the warehouse floor. Crates, crates, and more crates—some as large as shacks and some as narrow as coffins. Barrels were stacked in every available nook and cranny. Windows high on the first floor allowed in a pitiful amount of sunlight and left puddles of shadows.

It would do perfectly—Juniper was going to enjoy this.

Carol's cronies tossed Ida into a pile of moldy straw. She fell with a yelp. Carol stood over her, and her cronies fanned around her. Carol wore an arrogant smirk that made Juniper's sense of revenge turn white-hot.

"I don't know anything," Ida cried. She rolled onto her back. By how she held her left arm, she'd been hurt.

"Strange, but I don't believe you," said Carol in a voice that grated on Juniper's ears.

"I swear!"

Juniper threw a ball of ice behind a large stack of crates. It smacked against one crate and landed on the stone floor with a hefty crack. Carol's next words ended before she spoke, and all three of them looked toward the sound.

Carol huffed. "Go see what that was," she snapped to the mage on her left. "Likely a squatter. Teach them a lesson about spying."

Juniper rolled her eyes as one of the mages started toward the *mysterious* sound. Too easy.

Carol turned her attention back to Ida. "My friends told me that you were on the street. You would have seen her. Everyone saw her."

"I—I didn't," Ida said, her voice shaking. "I heard the commotion, and I stayed away."

Juniper eased down from the loft, silent as a shadow, and made her way over the towering crates as the mage made his way toward the sound. The mage paused, and Juniper tossed a tiny ball of ice into a nook made of crates. The mage jumped, but he started toward the sound like any good goon—as he entered the nook, Juniper gathered her magic.

"What's this?" asked the mage. He knelt by the pieces of ice.

Before anyone could answer that question, Juniper wrapped tendrils of ice around the mage. A swift and precise blow to the neck, and he fell unconscious. She gently lowered him to the floor.

"My friends told me they saw you watching," Carol said.

"Your friends are mistaken," Ida snapped.

A smack echoed off the walls, followed by Ida's yelp.

"You won't talk about my friends that way," Carol growled. "Now, tell me where she went."

"I—I don't know."

"I think you know."

"I don't!"

Juniper climbed back to the top of the stack of crates. Carol glared down on Ida, but the other mage was looking to where the other had vanished and not returned. Juniper tossed another ball of ice. It clunked against the crates and rattled to a stop between them.

Carol groaned. She nudged the other mage. "Go see what's taking so long."

The mage, to her credit, hesitated. She knew something was wrong, but she listened to Carol and started to where the ice had clattered.

"Where are you?" the mage whispered. She gathered whips of air around her—Juniper could just see the distortion in the air; she had seen Ison use the same type of magic.

Juniper sent a ghostly whip of her blue magic and flicked the mage's ear. The mage gasped and spun, and upon seeing the space behind her empty, paused. Her eyes darted back and forth. She took a step forward and peered around the dark narrow gap between crates.

Tendrils of clear blue ice magic rushed out of the shadows to greet her, smothered in dust and cobwebs. The mage started to scream, but a tendril of magic closed around her mouth. Another wrapped around her middle, and a third around her knees. The tendrils yanked her through the gap and out of sight.

"What happened?" snapped Carol.

From Juniper's shadowed vantage point, she saw Carol's wide eyes scan the shadows. Carol and Ida were both looking toward where the other mage had vanished, where her scream had been nothing more than a brief gasp and swish of fabric. Whereas Carol wore surprise and fear, Ida wore surprise and relief.

BEATRICE B. MORGAN

"Looks like you and your friends aren't so high and mighty after all," Ida taunted.

Carol summoned a whip of her reddish magic and lashed it across Ida's face. She let out a yelp of pain, and blood beaded on her split lip.

"I'm not leaving until you tell me the truth," Carol snapped. "Where is she?"

"I haven't seen her, I'm not lying!"

"And I still don't believe you," Carol said.

"Why?" snapped Ida. She pressed her hand against her lip. "Because you're worried about bringing back bad news to dear old Margret?"

Carol let out a very unladylike growl that might have been a laugh.

Juniper crept a little closer. Margret? Carol was gathering information for the overseer? Interesting.

"I was told that you were seen with Juniper Thimble," Carol said proudly.

"You were lied to," said Ida. "I've been hiding just like everyone else."

"You fled the Marca."

"I saw my chance, and I left," said Ida. "I didn't want to join Margret's little team of enforcers."

Carol straightened her shoulders.

Juniper crept to the edge of the wall of crates and jumped. She landed on the floor behind Carol with a dramatic swish of dust—in the gloomy sunlight, it looked like ash. Carol spun, eyes wide, and Ida looked like she wanted to laugh.

"Did I hear my name?" Juniper asked, her voice sweet.

Carol gawked.

And the thrill of the surprise flared like fire through Juniper's blood. Oh, this was what she loved! The sheer surprise of having duped someone.

"Did I hear that right?" Juniper crooned. She put her hand behind her ear. "Dear old Margret is looking for me?"

Carol's reddish magic surged toward Juniper. She brought up a shield of clear blue ice without moving—Carol's magic crashed against it, smashing like rotten fruit.

"You've been practicing the bad magic," Juniper teased.

Carol sneered. Juniper thickened her ice shield, crisscrossing veins of deep blue ice among the clear. Carol's eyes widened, and in her moment of hesitation, tendrils of blue ice surged around the edges of the shield and rose around Juniper like great dragon wings—she relished the panic that mixed with Carol's rage.

"But you've got a long way to go," Juniper said.

Her ice wings came down on Carol. In the moment before the crash, Carol's rage vanished, and she wore nothing but fear. Her lips parted to scream, but the

185

impact of ice tore the sound from her throat. Juniper's ice shoved Carol off her feet and threw her over Ida's head. Carol crashed into a stack of crates and fell to the floor. A weak groan escaped her throat.

Juniper hadn't thrown her hard enough to kill her, though she had severely wanted to. She sauntered past where Ida was staggering to shaky feet and stood over Carol. "Since you're in the mood for questions," Juniper purred, "you are going to answer a few of mine."

"Yeah, right," Carol croaked.

Juniper sent a needle of ice through Carol's side, in a nonlethal part. Carol let out a squeal of a scream.

"What does Margret want?"

"She's looking for you," Carol said, her voice strained.

"Me?" Juniper asked in mock innocent surprise. She would be happy if she never saw that old hag again. "Why ever would she be looking for me?"

"I don't know," Carol gasped. She clutched at her side. Her breaths and the position of her hand implied a broken or bruised rib.

Juniper felt a slight pitting of guilt, then reminded herself of the quiet room, of being whipped. Her guilt vanished.

"'Scour,' she said," came Ida's strained voice from behind Juniper. "The master demanded it."

Juniper's next thought scattered at those words—*the master*. She felt the subtle shift of the air a heartbeat too late.

CHAPTER 41

Juniper started to turn—a stone fist slammed into her shoulder, and another struck her side. She fell forward. The stone floor shifted under her feet, shattering what balance remained. She hit the floor hard. The impact knocked the breath from her throat. As Juniper sucked in another, magic slithered around her shoulders and legs. Strange, prickly magic clawed toward her throat.

Her triumph warped into a sharp, angry, bitter panic—trick, trick, trick!

She fought against the magic gripping her shoulders. Her own wiggled underneath it, saving her skin from the prickly feeling. The magic squeezed and flipped her onto her back, slamming her into the ground.

Carol staggered to her feet, clutching her side.

"You fell for the trap, just like Margret said you would," Carol said. "Because you just have to show off and be the hero, don't you?"

Ida's magic held firm around Juniper's shoulders, squeezing. The fear and panic had left her features, and she wore calm indifference. Underneath it, she wore triumph.

Juniper gasped for her next breath and managed to say, "I followed you in here to kick your ass, not to save hers."

Carol half laughed.

"We have her," Ida said, her voice flat, but not in the same way as the thralls—it came out bored. "Send the signal."

Juniper tried to speak, but the magic around her tightened. The breath squeezed out of her throat in a dry gasp.

Carol gathered a ball of reddish magic and cast it through the hole in the ceiling. The ball exploded into red sparks. Juniper felt it more than she saw it—magic spreading through the air, bright and obvious.

Movement came from the other side of the crates—the other two mages were waking up. The first stumbled around a crate, rubbing his head. A heartbeat later, the second mage came from the same side, looking unhappy and tired. The two shared a confused look.

"Let's go," Carol commanded.

Ida's magic tightened and lifted her into the air. The toes of her boots brushed the ground. Juniper did not struggle as much as she could have. They marched through the warehouse doors and into the late afternoon. Juniper felt the dimming of her magic in the daylight, of having left the shadows.

Red sparks still hovered and slowly rained over the warehouse. It had gone high enough that any mage or thrall within ten blocks would have seen it.

"Margret will be so happy to see you." Carol grinned over her shoulder at Juniper.

They started north, toward the Marca. Halfway down the block, another group of mages came from a side street. Two thralls stalked behind them.

And Juniper's window of escape was rapidly closing.

She sucked in what breath she could manage with Ida's magic squeezing her chest and commanded the muddy slush under Ida's feet to thicken and harden into ice. Her feet slid, her balance fractured, and her magical control with it. In Ida's moment of hesitation, Juniper gathered her magic—clear blue ice feathered with raw magic exploded around her. Juniper's magic shredded through Ida's. The force threw Ida back, and without her magic holding her, Juniper fell to the ground.

She landed and rolled, and as she bounced back onto her feet, she sent another surge of ice and dirty slush. It knocked Carol and her two cronies off their feet.

Juniper had a moment to decide—fight or run? Five mages and two thralls were running toward her. Three mages and one thrall came from another street. Carol and her cronies were staggering back to their feet.

Juniper had no doubt she could take on them all, but she had already flirted with disaster enough today. Her back throbbed from the fight. And, she *had* promised not to take unnecessary risks. A few mages she could handle, but untold numbers? She didn't know how many had seen the signal and were on their way to her location. Each thrall came with Mage's Bane too.

She darted into the nearest alley and ran. She crisscrossed alleys, jumped over walls, climbed up drainpipes, and ran herself breathless. She paused in an alley several blocks away, pressed her back against the brick of the house, and caught her breath. No one pursued.

The Marca mages, or the Enforcers, as Ida had called them, might have freedom, but they did not know Rusdasin like she did.

As Juniper's breathing calmed, her injuries made themselves known. Bruises throbbed along her back and shoulders where she'd been slammed into the warehouse floor, and something in her left knee pinched. Nothing a half-decent healer couldn't fix. She had limped back to the Undercity with much worse injuries.

BEATRICE B. MORGAN

She started south. Two blocks brought her to the Ruby River. The wide river rushed by, lapping the stone bank and brushing against the small boats docked along it. Shops and restaurants lined either side, and a few people had braved to leave their homes. Despite the chaos, seasoned meat and buttered bread wafted through the air, mixing with the dank river.

Juniper walked along the wooden dock, dropped to the boat level, and made her way to the wide bridge. Underneath the bridge, a hatch led into the sewers, and a trapdoor led into the Undercity.

The guards jumped as she slid down the ladder, as if they had been talking and not paying attention to their posts. One knight and one mage, both were strangers to her.

"On your guard, gentlemen," Juniper said. "You're lucky it was me and not the captain."

She patted the knight on the arm as she slipped past them and into the Undercity. Compared to that morning, the Undercity looked remarkably lively. Chatter once again filled the air. All the magelights had returned, and their light again mimicked the later afternoon daylight above.

She meandered toward the old market. The migration from topside had ended, and people were settling in. Several stewpots had been set up, steaming and boiling and filling the air with watered-down herbs.

"There you are," came Ison's voice. He appeared at Juniper's side. "You made it back all right?"

She half laughed. "Of course I did."

Ison tilted his head to the side. "I heard you ran into trouble."

"Nothing more than usual."

Ison frowned.

"I'll tell you about it," Juniper said. "But after you fill me in on what I've missed."

Ison and Juniper made a lap around the outer edge of the Commons—what used to be the market—and he told her how he had been busy getting the mages settled into their sector.

"I haven't seen much of anyone else," Ison said. "I assume they've been busy. Everyone is nervous about all that's happened. First Nexon takes control of their city, and now they're hiding in the Undercity. No one knows what to think about this Imperium."

Juniper quickly told Ison what had happened topside.

"Margret is looking for you?" Ison asked, brows furrowed. "Because *the master* demanded it?"

"Which proves that Margret is helping Nexon," Juniper said with a sigh. "To be honest, I'm not surprised. She hated me from the start."

"Not only has Nexon put a bounty on your head, but his followers are scouring the city for you," Ison said. Worry added lines to his young face. "These Enforcers."

"They don't stand a chance."

"That's not the point," Ison said, bringing them to a halt. "Jun, topside is lawless. Magic isn't bound by the Order like it was before. It's dangerous for you to be wandering around with a price on your head."

"It's not like I'm wandering down the street," Juniper said. "And I'll remind you, I've had a price on my head for the better part of seven years. I'm careful. I know when to play with risk and when to back away."

Ison sighed through his nose. He didn't believe her. Had he always been so fussy?

"Fine," Ison said. "Do you know where you're going to be staying?"

"Hmm?"

"You're more than welcome to bunk with the mages," Ison said, motioning to Josephine's sector. "I'm sure Maddox wouldn't mind you in his sector, and King Bradburn would probably do the same."

Juniper considered it. Maddox's keep no longer felt like home, and she didn't want to stay with mages—it reminded her too much of the Marca. That left King Bradburn's sector, even if it was filled with knights and guards.

No sector felt like where she belonged.

And then she thought of Reid.

"I'll find something," Juniper said. "I'm sure there's plenty of hovels to crash in. Or I'll make Reid share."

"Let me know if you change your mind," Ison said. "I'm at Josephine's keep."

Juniper waved off his concern and started toward King Bradburn's sector. The very notion that she might not have a place to sleep gave her a horrible sense of unease. She'd never felt anything like it—an unfathomable uncertainty.

CHAPTER 42

Juniper didn't immediately go to King Bradburn's sector. She wandered through Maddox's—to report Uhls's death—but she didn't see him. She didn't look very hard either. Juniper would bet gold he already knew about Uhls. He had a strange sense about things like that.

She wound her way into King Bradburn's sector. The knights, City Watch, Royal Guard, and castle servants had made their homes here. They were working to clean and organize, to make the cavern feel like a home. She caught several casting weary glances toward Maddox's neighboring sector. She could only imagine how the knights and guards felt to be living within a stone's throw of known criminals.

She spotted several empty and dark homes within the king's sector, but she didn't stop to claim any. Instead, she returned to the Commons and found a healer. A healer's hut had been set up, almost in the exact place it had been before. The healer said nothing about her bruises or the achy skin of her back. A few minutes of awkward silence and tingly magic, and she left the healer's table feeling better. She found a rooftop on the edge of the Commons to sit on. She watched the odd mixture of mages, knights, and criminals below. Nobles and servants and commoners mixed in among them. All corners of Rusdasin appeared to be present.

And it was starting to feel normal.

Juniper brought her legs up and rested her chin on her knees. Margret and Fowler were working with Nexon. Margret had likely been recruiting mages into Nexon's clutches for years—like Carol and Ida. Fowler had been collecting mages from all over the kingdom—Nexon had a selection of followers. And with the Order tightening the noose on mages, the mages were more likely to turn on the Order and join Nexon.

Nexon had set the perfect trap.

She heaved a sigh. She'd always hated the Marca.

The magelights slowly turned from the pale gray of late afternoon to the gloom of early evening. By the murkiness, it was raining. Cooking pots all over the Commons sizzled with stews and soups. Water mages brought clean drinking water from the fountain. Strangers dared share space and food.

Boots marched on the street to her left, several pairs. Curious, she crawled to the edge. King Bradburn and a small entourage marched toward the Commons. She spotted Reid, and in less than a heartbeat, his eyes met hers. He motioned for her to come down, and she obliged.

Reid lagged a step behind to walk beside her. Captain Sandpiper scowled at her, but he continued to march beside the king, hand on his pommel.

Juniper did her best to ignore him. To Reid, she asked, "What's happening?"

"The king is meeting with the others." Reid reached for her hand and laced their fingers together. "You should be there."

Reid tugged on her hand, and they followed the king's party to a large tavern in the Commons. The tables had been arranged in a circle—Kind Bradburn sat at one end, flanked by Captain Sandpiper and Adrian. Three royal guards stood behind them, eyes on the crowd. Two of them had been guarding the king's chambers the night they escaped. The other had been guarding Adrian's. Juniper stood to the side of the king, beside Reid.

"Where's Roslyn?" Juniper whispered to Reid.

"She and Her Majesty stayed at the house," Reid whispered back.

The door to the tavern opened, and Josephine walked inside with the grace of a queen. She sat at the table, flanked by Ison and Mabyl. Finn, Bois, and Nera stood close behind.

"Settling in?" Josephine asked King Bradburn.

"As much as we are able," he replied.

"If there is anything we can do to make your stay more comfortable, don't hesitate to ask," Josephine said, her tone genuine.

King Bradburn nodded to her.

The door of the tavern opened again, and Maddox Hawk sauntered inside. He wore black and gray and an assortment of daggers, including two tucked into his leather boots. His dark eyes glittered as he took in the room—as if they had gathered for him. Amery and Xavier flanked him. Blythe and three others followed—Juniper knew their faces but not their names. Each had come with a plethora of steel, hidden and not.

The air in the tavern thickened. King Bradburn's fingers started to clench into a fist, but he stopped himself. He quickly regained his kingly composure.

Because Maddox had entered with obviously armed thugs—he had made a subtle threat for dominance. Juniper stepped a little to the side, to be within the king's peripheral. A reminder. She was on his side, not Maddox's, and she equaled at least a dozen of his thugs. Adrian glanced at her, a knowing look on his face.

"Greetings," Maddox said, sitting down at the other side of the table. Amery and Xavier sat on either side of him.

Over a dinner of stew and fresh biscuits, King Bradburn, Josephine, and Maddox discussed the next step in their resistance to the Imperium. It was the strangest meeting Juniper had ever heard of—a crime lord, a king, and an apostate. Everyone in the Undercity respected at least one of them, which made the three of them the perfect leaders for the resistance.

"I have arranged patrols and guards," reported Captain Sandpiper. "Every entry will be guarded at all times by at least one mage and one knight."

"We still need supplies," Josephine said. "Blankets, food. We have our stores, but it is not enough for the added bodies. We will quickly run out of the essentials. We have a few days of food, but that estimate changes with every refugee we take in."

"Then we take what we need," Maddox added simply.

"Steal?" asked King Bradburn.

"We don't have much of a choice," Maddox added. "We have no gold, and even if we did, buying a hundred blankets and barrels of ale would draw suspicion. I will see to the acquisition of supplies."

Neither King Bradburn nor Josephine argued. King Bradburn's stoic face betrayed nothing of his thoughts. He likely understood their desperation.

"And we'd be stealing from the people who stole your throne," Amery added sweetly.

This did not change the king's expression.

"I can spare a few mages if you need added protection against the magic threats topside," Josephine added.

Maddox nodded to her. "I might take you up on that offer."

"We need to discuss our protection and the arming of the resistance," said King Bradburn. He looked at Josephine. "How comes the mages' training?"

"We have a small space carved out, safely tucked out of the way," Josephine reported. "Our mages will be learning to harness their magic by this time tomorrow."

The king turned his attention to Reid. His eyes briefly flitted over Juniper. "How goes the combat training?"

"We have a space, and most are willing to learn. Even a few mages have requested to learn swordplay, and the knights have obliged," Reid reported. "Sir Pinul and Sir Darvel are there now. However, we lack steel and armor."

"We will add that to our list of needed supplies," said Maddox. He whispered something to Xavier.

Juniper held her eyes on Maddox. Not once did he look in her direction. Once, she would have been terrified of his indifference. Now, it irritated her. Was he mad she'd returned? Or was he mad about Uhls's death?

The talk shifted into procedures and regulations—rules for the Undercity. Juniper almost laughed. She reminded herself that the Undercity had changed. The people here—especially the Marca mages—were used to rules. The rules remained simple: no fighting, no stealing from each other, no obscenities in the street, among others.

Juniper's attention drifted. She caught Adrian's eye—he had often complained of sitting through his father's odious meetings.

Finally, the meeting ended, and the strange council adjourned. Maddox left first, followed by Josephine, and lastly, King Bradburn. Juniper walked behind him, beside Reid. They paused in the street as the processions started toward their prospective sectors.

"I never thought I'd sit through a meeting like that," Reid said.

"That was by far the most interesting meeting I've ever attended," said Adrian, coming to stand on Reid's other side. Adrian wore a bright grin. "How often do rebels plan to overthrow a tyrant?"

"Juniper," came Maddox's call. He strolled toward her, hands in his pocket, dark eyes pinned on her. His small army of thieves and assassins had vanished— from sight. She knew Maddox better than to think he'd dismissed them. They lingered elsewhere, waiting.

Reid stepped closer to her, and his hand tightened on his hilt.

King Bradburn approached her other side and said, "A moment, please."

Josephine appeared beside Maddox. The three of them formed a wall, effectively blocking Juniper from a casual escape. Cornered. Instinctively, she tensed.

To Maddox, she said, "Let me guess, you need me gathering supplies."

"No," answered the king. "Nexon has put a target on you. His followers are looking for you. It is far too dangerous for you to be wandering...topside."

The word came out clunky on the king's tongue.

Juniper frowned, argument at the ready, but Josephine said, "Ison told me what happened."

"What happened?" Reid said, scowling.

Juniper sighed through her nose. "Nothing happened."

Reid's frown deepened. He didn't believe her.

"Nexon has tasked his followers with scouring the city for Juniper Thimble," Josephine added. She glared down her nose at Juniper, daring her to deny it.

The king and Maddox observed, Josephine had already told them.

Juniper pursed her lips. "I'll be fine."

"I agree," Reid said, crossing his arms. "If Nexon has his people actively looking for you, you don't need to go topside unless absolutely necessary."

She glared at him, and he glared right back.

"I have plenty of able bodies," Maddox said. "No need for *you* to get your hands dirty."

His tone pricked against her mind—she met his dark eyes. They glittered with secrets. Did he know about Isolde?

"He's right," Josephine said.

"Reid can help you settle in," Maddox said. His eyebrows rose, and Juniper knew in that moment he knew or suspected everything. He knew exactly who Reid was, and what he was to Juniper.

She looked around at them all—she was outnumbered.

"Fine," she spat.

And just like that, the confrontation ended. She walked with Reid toward King Bradburn's sector. It buzzed with activity, not unlike the castle. He led her through the winding streets and to one of the pillars of the Undercity. Two guards stood at the door.

"The king is staying here for the time being," Reid said. "As are my uncle and I."

Juniper heard the inflection in his voice—his uncle and him, without his aunt.

"You are more than welcome to stay here with us," Reid said. He started inside.

She hesitated. She could stay in the king's house, or she could find her own place. There were plenty of quiet little hovels scattered around. She would have a hovel to herself, whereas if she stayed here...she would have Reid.

She followed Reid into the king's house.

The pillars scattered the Undercity, holding up the ceilings at structural points. She didn't know if they were natural or carved. The houses within the pillars were carved, and until now, she had never been in one. The walls were thick reddish gray stone, veined with black and white. The walls and doorways were slightly curved, like bubbles in the stone, and the stairs spiraled up the center of the pillar.

The first floor held the kitchen, washing, and dinning. The second floor had been converted into sleeping quarters for the guard, including Reid and Captain Sandpiper. The third had been taken by Adrian, Roslyn, the king, and the queen. The top floor was a meeting room—barrels and crates held uneven planks between them, on which was a hand-drawn map of the Undercity.

"It's cozy," Juniper said as she took a lap of the top floor. Windows looked over every side, giving the king a splendid view of his new domain.

Reid led her onto the second floor and into the room he had taken as his own. It was about the size of her old room at Maddox's keep. Old linens had been pulled over the wooden bedframe and fresh water rested in the water jug by the basin. It smelled a bit musty.

"It's not glamorous," Reid said. He glanced at the small circular window.

"But it's a bed and a window," Juniper said. "That's more than some have."

A beat passed. Juniper glanced out the window and found the Commons. The magelights had gone dark and smoky. Her magic agreed—full dark would soon be upon them.

"Does the king's command upset you?"

"You mean the one where he forbade me from leaving the Undercity?" Juniper asked, a bit bitterly.

Reid frowned. "Nexon wants you dead, and there are plenty of people desperate enough to try their hand at getting the bounty on your head. We can't give Nexon any more opportunity that he already has."

"And I know you're right," Juniper said with a heavy sigh. "I'm not made of glass, Reid. I can take care of myself. I've spent my life fighting; I don't see how anything has changed."

"Everything has changed." Reid reached for her hand and held it between them, stealing her attention away from the window. She met his molten honey eyes—he wore that look that turned her bones to liquid metal. "Nexon is afraid of you. He thinks you are the one meant to stop him, and he will do anything to get rid of you."

She groaned. "I'm not…"

Reid stepped closer. "You're not what?"

She had meant to say, *I'm not special.* "I don't know how much I believe this prophecy nonsense. What if Isaac is mistaken about me? What if I'm not who he thinks I am? And even if, by some cruel grace of the gods, I am Isolde, that doesn't mean there's not some other princess hiding somewhere. And…even if I am the one, what the hell am I supposed to do against Nexon?"

"It doesn't matter that you don't think you're important," Reid said, his voice low and warm. "Nexon does, and he will do whatever he can to get his hands on you. Please, Juniper, stay here. For us. For me."

"I suppose," she started, "for you, I could lounge around the Undercity for a while. I have been thinking of taking a vacation."

Reid offered her a small smile of relief. He kissed her cheek. "There is plenty of work to do. You could teach the mages combat magic or how to wield a dagger. I will be teaching others swordplay."

Juniper groaned at the very idea of teaching. She felt as though she was still learning. She finally understood Ison's dismay when she had asked him to teach her.

"Before that, I could use a bath and a long nap." Juniper patted Reid on the chest and headed into the washing room on the first floor. She could still smell the musty warehouse on her clothes.

CHAPTER 43

The bathing room had no windows—for good reason—and so Juniper cast her own magelight to the ceiling. It was one of the few useful things she'd learned in the Marca. Her light shone blue-white, a bit too harsh for her liking, but she hadn't learned how to change the color. The room wasn't anything special—its washing basin and shelves had been carved from the same reddish gray stone as the walls, ceiling, and floors.

She turned the heavy knob on the faucet, and water gurgled through the old pipes and splattered into the stone basin. Her magelight fractured along the surface, and the water itself looked like ink. Thankfully, the king had chosen a house with plumbing. She would take slow plumbing over no plumbing any day. After the basin had filled, she heated it with her magic.

She magicked the grime and sweat and dirt from her skin and hair. Then she relaxed against the smoothed stone, letting the water soak the strain from her muscles and her mind.

She crafted a snowflake the size of her hand in the steamy air, intricate and delicate. She crafted the ice slowly, stealing steam from the air as it filtered up, filling the air with its gentle crackling. The Mage's Bane had finally worn off, and she no longer felt the squeezing of her magic when she used it. But she felt the change. She felt it every time she saw a knight or a dark blue scabbard—hot panic and frozen dread. Her magic trembled when she stood too close to a knight or his sword, even Reid's. Her magic remembered the pain, the looming death as it ate through her blood.

The snowflake had grown twice the size of her hand. She let it fall into the warm bath, where it immediately dissolved.

Gods, she hadn't realized how exhausted she was. Voices chattered all around her, inside the house and outside, but she hadn't the energy to eavesdrop.

When the water had started to cool, she got out. She magicked the water from her skin and hair, washed what she could from her clothes, and entered the main room as Captain Sandpiper and Reid entered the house.

"You look exhausted," Reid said. He looked her up and down. "Though cleaner."

"I am both of those things," she said.

Reid motioned her toward the stairs, and she headed up to Reid's room. She neared the curtain-door when Captain Sandpiper growled, "You will be sleeping in your own room."

"Uncle—" Reid started.

"You are not married yet," Captain Sandpiper snapped. He stepped around Juniper and marched to the end of the hall, to the room on the other side of his own, and pulled the curtain aside. He focused his glare on Juniper. "You will sleep in here."

Juniper frowned. The captain would be in the room between Reid's and hers. She sighed—she was too tired to argue about it. She dragged herself through the curtain he held open. The captain let the curtain fall and marched away. He and Reid spoke lowly, but Juniper didn't have the mind to listen.

She sat on the edge of the creaky wooden bed. Someone had dressed it in mismatched blue and beige linens. Like Reid's room, hers came with a jug of water, a small barrel for a table, and a circular window. Juniper pulled off her boots and her outer clothes and clawed underneath the blanket.

The murky magelight had darkened into the midnight hues. The chatter of the Undercity lessened but did not diminish entirely; it never did.

Juniper slept terribly. Her dreams came and went, each more ridiculous than the last. In one dream, Juniper wrapped herself in nothing more than a thin blanket in hopes to surprise Reid, but she found his uncle waiting in Reid's room instead. He told her Reid had moved to the top floor of Maddox's house, and that he didn't need Juniper anymore because he already had grandchildren.

When she woke, the dream of Captain Sandpiper was the one she remembered. She knew she shouldn't let a stupid dream bother her, but she could still hear his voice, *I don't need you anymore. I already have grandchildren.*

She rubbed the sleep from her eyes and sat up. The magelight glowed pale blue, the beginnings of dawn. Juniper pulled herself from bed and pushed through a few simple stretches and exercises. As the magelight brightened, sounds of life came from the king's house. Captain Sandpiper woke and marched into the hall. He paused, and Juniper imagined him glaring at her curtain and debating whether or not to see if she had slept in her room or snuck into Reid's in the night.

Footsteps sounded on the stairs. Captain Sandpiper spoke lowly, his cadence dry. Reid's warmer voice replied, "I'll catch up, Uncle."

"Don't be late," said his uncle, the frown clear in his words.

A lone pair of boots marched to her curtain, and Reid stepped inside. He wore his silver armor. His Mage's Bane hung at his side.

"Oh, you're awake," Reid said. "Uncle and I are heading to the training facilities."

She had the urge to ask him if he had any children he'd like to mention, but instead she said, "If you and your uncle are training them, they'll be perfect little soldiers in no time."

"You are welcome to come along," Reid said, though his words implied otherwise.

She half laughed. "I'm sure your uncle would mind. I'll see you later."

Reid hesitated, and she knew she'd suspected right. His uncle did not like her, and his animosity had only grown.

"We'll return to the house for lunch," Reid said. He pressed a kiss of farewell to her forehead.

Juniper listened to his armored steps as he marched down the hall and down the stairs. She lingered for a moment longer, then wandered down to the kitchens for something to eat. She slid past the curtain without a sound and—Adrian nearly jumped out of his skin. He stood on the other side of the kitchen table, a piece of bread between his teeth. Seeing her, his panic diminished, and he laughed.

Ian the royal guard leaned against the far wall. He had jumped at Adrian's surprise, pulling his sword several inches out of the scabbard. As Adrian relaxed, so did Ian. He slid his sword back and resumed his lean against the wall.

"Someone's not supposed to be in here," Juniper teased.

"Neither is someone else," he said, wiggling the bread at her. "I thought you were the cook. She's already chided me once about being in here. I take it you slept through breakfast too?"

Juniper shrugged and cut her own piece of bread from the loaf. It was stale—yesterday's.

"I thought everyone had left," Adrian explained, mouth full. He swallowed. "Father has gone to meet with the knights, Mother and Roslyn have gone to oversee the fledgling market, and Reid and Captain Sandpiper have gone to train the resistance." He heaved a dramatic sigh.

"It looks like it's just you and me," Juniper said. She took a large bite of bread.

"And Ian," added Adrian. "He's become much more serious in the past few days, though I can't blame him." Adrian looked over his shoulder at Ian, whose face remained stoic. Adrian sighed and looked back to Juniper. "What do you say to a game of cards?"

"That sounds more fun than my plan of sitting and brooding," she said.

Juniper and Adrian went to the top floor—Ian dutifully followed. They rolled up the Undercity map and used the makeshift table for their games. Adrian had found a rather risqué set of playing cards—the face cards showed naked men and women—under the mattress in the room he'd claimed as his own.

As they played, she realized just how much she had missed Adrian's company. He radiated happiness like sunlight. He had made her time trapped in Bradburn Castle tolerable, and it seemed he would assume the same role in the Undercity. He made the morning go by much faster than her brooding.

"And you win this round," Adrian said with a sigh, dropping the rest of his cards onto the table. He wouldn't have won—his hand was horrible. "That makes the score three to five."

She dropped her cards too. "It's my poker face," she said, winking. "You wear your emotions too obviously."

"Is that a bad thing?"

"Not at all," she said, and she meant it. "It's part of who you are. We can't all be good at the same things. That's boring."

Adrian took in those words. He nodded. He reclined in his chair—it let out a squeal of protest, but it held. His hazel eyes glanced to the ceiling, and the calm, pleasant mask slipped—only for a moment, and then it returned. He settled his gaze on Juniper.

"Are you all right?" Juniper asked.

Adrian blinked. "All things considered? I suppose."

She tilted her head. "And otherwise?"

Adrian held her gaze a heartbeat—and within that heartbeat, his happy mask parted, revealing a whirlwind of emotions underneath.

"You can talk to me," Juniper said. "You've offered me your ear plenty, it's only fair I do the same."

Adrian leaned onto the table, whirlwind pulling the sunlight from around him. "It doesn't feel like anything has been the same since I woke up," he said in a quiet, fearful voice. "I sometimes wonder if I woke up in a different world, or if I even woke up at all."

"Why?" she asked softly.

"Roslyn is here, and she and my mother are getting along," Adrian said. "I... A part of me knew that Roslyn and I wouldn't be able to be together, and yet we are. Reid is a knight. You were in the Marca. And then the siege happened, Fowler is a turncoat, and we're living in the Undercity." He rubbed his face and groaned. "I fear that I'll wake up at any moment and realize it has all been a dream."

"I wish it were," Juniper said without thinking.

Adrian's brows rose brows. "You do?"

She started; she hadn't thought her statement through. Adrian leaned forward, curious eyes boring into hers.

"I…" She didn't know how to word it. "I don't regret all of it. I just wish I had more time to process it. Everything happened so quickly. A part of me wishes I were back at the castle, playing a lady and not worrying about evil mages trying to kill me or take over the realm or raise armies."

"Ah," Adrian said, nodding. "Then we share a similar thought. When I…fell asleep, nothing was horrible. I mean, for me. You and Reid were at each other's throats, but I thought you'd work it out in the end. And you did. When I woke up, the very air felt…threatening, darker. Something had changed. I felt it. I didn't know what or when or how, and it scared me. It's better now that I know what and how and when."

"You know," Juniper started, "had you not gotten sick, Reid and I might not have made up."

"Is that so? Is there a story that goes along with it?"

She blushed, and Adrian's smile widened. "We had to work together to save you, and…well, things happened. Strange how traveling to the edge of the realm can bring people together. Look at Reid and Ison."

Adrian put his hand up, laughing. "Save the steamy details for Roslyn."

She grinned wickedly. "She already knows."

Adrian laughed harder.

They sat in calm silence. Chatter from the Undercity slipped through the window, and it sounded like someone somewhere was singing.

"Can I ask you a question?" Juniper asked.

"Of course."

"Is this what being a prince is like? Being locked in houses and treated like glass?" She glanced at Ian.

Adrian's smile faded. "I admit, most of the time it is. My father is allowed to do as he pleases—with an armed escort, mind you—but I am made to stay inside where it is safe. My mother and Roslyn have gone too, but like my father says, the kingdom doesn't rest on their shoulders."

"In a way, the kingdom does rest on Roslyn," Juniper added, wiggling her eyebrows. "You know, heirs don't grow on trees."

Adrian smiled. "I suppose it does, though my father would likely say something like, '*There are more women for such things*,'" Adrian mimicked his father's commanding tone. "He is a great man and a great father, but sometimes he sees only the big picture. He forgets that the pawns of his rule are people too."

"Not to mention Roslyn could throw a spear through a man's heart while blindfolded," Juniper deadpanned.

Adrian nodded. "My father doesn't think I could hold my own, not like Roslyn or Reid or himself."

"Why aren't they teaching you how to wield a sword?"

"Destry tried." Adrian laughed, but it came out bitter. "What if I were to get into a real fight? I might get bruised or worse, lose a finger. What kind of a king would I be with only nine fingers?"

"I could teach you," Juniper said plainly. "Up here or out in some empty room."

Adrian's brows rose and his humor faded. "Really?"

She nodded. "Everyone needs the opportunity to learn how to defend themselves. And it's fun. You might never get into a real fight, but this way, you have something else to do other than sit here and gamble with stones and buttons."

Adrian's face lit up. "All right, lead the way."

CHAPTER 44

Juniper searched the townhouse and found sticks. Not the best, but it would do for a basic lesson. She and Adrian—and Ian, reluctantly—moved the makeshift table aside to give them more room. She went over footwork, grip, and blocking. Adrian had been taught a few basics by Sir Destry, and going over them did not take very long.

Adrian did not lack skill—he lacked confidence. He had been raised in comfort with other people to fight for him. He had never developed the mindset of a fighter—but Juniper didn't tell him that. He had natural grace that would be a boon in a fight, and she was a bit jealous.

The swordplay lesson wasn't just for Adrian. Juniper needed something to do other than sit and dwell on her uselessness and captivity. And, though she wouldn't admit it out loud, she had been relying on her magic too much.

They fake-fought until one of the servants called them down for lunch. At the sudden realization that they had been up there so long, they both laughed. They went down to the first floor's dining room, where mismatched chairs had been arranged around a long table. It looked oddly like the Undercity, but also regal somehow. The servants had done a marvelous job of turning the Undercity house into a place fit for a king.

Granted, there had been several luxurious brothels to choose from. Juniper tried her best not to think about where the furniture had been found or what might have happened on it.

Adrian and Juniper were already seated when the others returned, dust clinging to their boots and sweat on their brows. Reid and his uncle looked exhausted. The king looked as though he had spent an hour arguing, and the queen looked disgusted. Roslyn alone looked like she had enjoyed herself. Adrian had told Juniper how much the Undercity fascinated Roslyn and horrified his mother.

Reid dropped into the chair beside Juniper.

"How did it go?" Juniper asked.

"The facilities are acceptable," Reid said in a monotone. "We found old blades with mostly dulled edges, and the few smiths we have are working to smelt the unusable metals into armor for the recruits. A few of the mages offered to help. They are better at smithing than I realized. They can heat and cool metal far faster than a regular flame, and shape it with better skill."

Juniper sipped her tea. "You sound peeved about it."

Reid glanced at her, his brow creased and his eyes annoyed.

"And you looked peeved too."

He frowned. He glanced across the table to where his uncle, the king, and an older royal guard were talking. Roslyn, Her Majesty, and Adrian were in another conversation. Reid whispered to Juniper, "I find it strange to be relying on magic when I've spent most of my life fighting it."

"Magic can be useful," Juniper said. "Not just with the smiths. Water mages are constantly pulling clean drinking water from the fountain. Air mages are growing plants and herbs. Earth mages are shaping better homes. Magic isn't just about blasting our enemies into smithereens or...whatever else people do with magic that's bad."

Reid wore an unreadable expression. "Like breaking into the minds of others and controlling them?"

Her heart skipped a beat. Like Nexon had done to Ison, Penet, and his thralls. "Yes," she whispered. "Like that."

Reid sighed. "Josephine has offered to teach the mages and anyone else who wants to learn mental resistance."

"I think it's a good idea," Juniper said.

Reid's brows rose. "You do?"

"That way, even if someone knows how to break into someone's mind, they won't be able to because everyone will be able to block the intrusion." Juniper put her hand to her heart in mock modesty. "Not everyone can be as naturally good at mental defense as me and you."

His lips twitched upward. "I suppose that's true."

"Think of it like...teaching someone to defend themselves with a sword, only they're defending against magic with magic."

Thoughts churned behind Reid's eyes. She felt the difference in those thoughts and the thoughts he had when they first met. He had been adamantly against all magic, even skeptical of healing magic. And now, Reid Sandpiper, devout knight, was considering the uses of magic. She could hardly believe it.

"Our enemy will come at us from every angle possible," Reid whispered. "With steel and magic. We cannot allow our...morals to stand in the way of defending ourselves from the worst."

His eyes and his tone suggested otherwise. Juniper didn't think there was much morality in hating magic, but she kept that to herself.

After lunch, Juniper thought she would show Adrian a few clever disarming maneuvers, but the king decided Adrian should go with him instead—to an afternoon meeting with the knight council. Reid and his uncle returned to training. Roslyn and the queen readied to leave as well—Juniper started upstairs to find something to occupy her time when Roslyn called her name.

"Come with us," Roslyn said.

Queen Catherine looked skeptical. She held herself like a queen, hands folded delicately over her stomach, shoulders straight, chin forward. Even in simple trousers, plain tunic, and worn cloak, she looked horribly out of place.

"To do what?" Juniper asked.

"There is a shipment of goods coming in," Roslyn said. "We were going to make sure Maddox doesn't skim off the top."

"That does sound like him," Juniper said.

"Want to come and look intimidating?" Roslyn asked. "He might think twice before skimming if he knows you're watching him."

Juniper sighed dramatically.

"Oh, stop it," snapped the queen. "You'll otherwise be sulking around here, and sulking leads to early wrinkles."

"You might want to tell that to the captain," Juniper muttered.

Roslyn laughed, and to Juniper's surprise, the queen's lips twitched upward.

Juniper gave in and followed them into the Commons and to a large tent made of smaller tents pitched closely together. They had arranged it like a warehouse. Piles of goods had been stacked for sorting—blankets; bags of rice, flour, and sugar; candles and silverware; swords, daggers, and pieces of armor; paper and ink; books, clothes, and everything a household might need.

Maddox's thugs stood at both ends of the warehouse, watching. Juniper recognized both of them, and they her.

"The stores are building well," said the queen as she looked over a tower of mismatched fabric—clothes and linens thrown together.

"Did you expect otherwise, Your Majesty?" came Maddox's slick tone. He glided from around the tower of fabric. His dark eyes wandered up and down the queen, and to Juniper's surprise, the queen didn't so much as flinch. She met Maddox's glare with one of her own.

"I had no doubt, Maddox," she said. "I am only surprised that you have accumulated so much in such a short amount of time and displayed it rather than hoarding it for yourself."

Maddox chuckled. "You think so little of me? I'm ashamed." He didn't sound ashamed. "And my scouts found something that I tucked away just for you."

Juniper and Roslyn shared a quick glance; the royal guards stepped closer to the queen. Juniper readied her magic.

Queen Bradburn laughed, sweet and bitter all at once. "I am sure it is a set of silken pajamas."

"Better." Maddox vanished around the tower of fabric, and the queen followed. Roslyn followed a step behind—with a hand on the dagger tucked under her shirt.

Maddox led them to the far side of the warehouse, where guards and thieves worked together to sort the steel and armor. The useless items went into the smelting pile, while the rest was further sorted by function and size. Maddox retrieved a handsome yew bow from its resting place beside a crate—held away from the rest. Maddox held it out to the queen.

Juniper almost laughed. Had Maddox lost it?

But the queen did not laugh. She lifted the gifted bow from Maddox's hands and turned it over, trailing her fingertips along the bowstring, along the grain of the bow. She plucked at the bowstring.

"Freshly strung," Maddox said. "Just this morning. Take it out back. See how she does."

He set a quiver of arrows on the table. The queen fixed her eyes on it, as if she expected a trick, some double cross. Juniper felt the same—Maddox wouldn't give something for free. He sauntered back through the warehouse, leaving them to wonder.

Maybe the looming Imperium had changed him—though Juniper highly doubted it.

The queen glanced at Juniper, then Roslyn, then one of the guards. No one objected, and the queen lifted the quiver over her shoulder and headed outside. Crates formed a makeshift range. The queen pulled an arrow from the quiver and nocked it.

"With a bow," Roslyn started, "it's important to—"

The queen released the arrow. It struck the crate with a thud, right in the center.

Roslyn's brows rose nearly to her hair, and whatever advice she'd been about to give died in her throat. Juniper mirrored her surprise.

The queen glanced over her shoulder. "You were saying, Roslyn, dear?" The queen smiled. "I told you I knew my way around a bow."

"I thought you were joking," Roslyn said, dumbfounded.

The queen's smile widened, a smile full of charm and wit. Without the makeup and heavy jewels, her natural beauty shone—the same beauty her son had inherited.

They returned to the king's house for afternoon tea, and the queen told Juniper and Roslyn about her younger years. She had grown up in the northeastern farms and spent her childhood in the forest. She had learned archery alongside her brother. She had gone on hunting trips as often as she had gone shopping with her mother.

"When I met Bentley, I saw a life of glamour and ease," she admitted, her voice soft. "I thought my future would be filled with parties and brunches and pretty dresses. It has been, for the most part, but I didn't realize I would be giving up everything else to get it." She looked up from her tea and to Roslyn. "That is why I didn't want Adrian to marry you. I thought you saw the same, and that you would hate it."

"Do you hate it?" Roslyn asked.

"No," said the queen. "I don't regret marrying Bentley. I love him. Though, I sometimes wish he had an older brother to be king and we could leave all these decisions to him."

Juniper held her teacup to her lips. She had never seen this side of the queen. Without her painted mask and jewels and heavy skirts, she was human. She radiated the same warmth and light as Adrian, the kind that bolstered those around her. The queen looked up from her tea and met Juniper's stare. Even now, the queen's stare unnerved her.

"Is that why you were so mean to me?" Juniper asked.

The queen laughed—a lady's pretty chime. "No, I knew exactly who and what you were. I disagreed with Bentley's plan and did my best to talk him out of it. He didn't listen to me. I thought him mad for inviting a criminal into our home, to spend time with our son. I...didn't know you very well, and I made no attempt to change that. I apologize. Adrian and Roslyn have told me much about you. Far more than enough to change my mind."

"You had every right to think so lowly of me," Juniper said. "But I accept your apology."

"And we are all in this resistance together," said the queen. "We haven't the time or spare energy to fight among ourselves. And, I didn't realize who you *really* were. A Balendin, I mean. By what I've been told, you didn't either."

Juniper flushed. "I didn't."

She didn't like that everyone else knew about Isolde Balendin. She felt...exposed. She didn't know if she wanted to believe the story or not, and everyone else talking about it as if it were real unsettled her stomach and twisted her guts into knots.

Dinner at the king's house was quiet—everyone was exhausted. Reid retired early. After taking her turn in the washing room, Juniper headed to the front door. The house was crowded with guards and servants. Too crowded for her tastes. She had the tavern and an ale in mind, but as she approached the door, the guards on either side barred her path.

"What are you doing?" Juniper demanded.

"By the order of His Majesty, you are to remain here," said one of the guards.

Juniper frowned. She opened her mouth to argue that she had left the house earlier, but then she realized—she had left with the queen and her guards. She had been under guard.

"This is ridiculous," Juniper snapped. "Let me out. I'm just taking a walk."

The guards did not move. They didn't even flinch. "You must remain here," one said.

She glared at him. Neither guard balked under her glare. Blood pounding in her ears, Juniper stormed upstairs with as much dignity she could muster. She tiptoed past the bedrooms and the murmurs within and slipped to the top floor—it was empty and had the best view. The candles had been put out, leaving it in shadow. Juniper paused in the familiar dark. It soaked into her growing panic and unease, soothing it, cooling it.

She took a deep breath of the musty Undercity air. The king had ordered his guards to keep her inside. He didn't trust her.

She paced between the southern window and the northern window. The nerve of the king! Locking her in here like some bird in a cage. Through the southern window, the Commons glowed with magelight and midnight activity. Through the northern window, she saw to the edge of the Undercity—a dark reddish-gray blur. She should have gone with her own hovel on the edge of the Undercity.

Her thoughts drifted to the edge of the Undercity, where pockets had been carved right into the stone walls, some reachable only by rope ladders and narrow stone steps. She'd always thought them cozy and private.

And then her thoughts drifted below the edge, into the ruins below. The Iluvin ruins.

NIGHTMARES IN THE ICE

Her curiosity and defiance twined too quickly for her common sense to catch up, and before logic could ruin it, she climbed out of the window, jumped onto the roof of the next house, and took a thief's path toward the northern outskirts.

No one—not kings, guards, or jailers—could keep Juniper Thimble in a cage.

CHAPTER 45

Ison drank the first cup of tea without tasting it. Nera poured him a second without asking if he wanted one.

"You look like you need it," Nera said. Pity eased into her pleasant smile. "Are you doing all right?"

"Yeah." Ison clutched the teacup a little tighter. "I've been busy, that's all."

A burst of laughter came from the second floor—a normal sound in Josephine's keep. The mages were settling, though uncertainty lingered. Many still felt lost and displaced. Josephine had suggested the youngest mages move into the keep with her while the older mages divide themselves into the houses around it. Ison and Nera remained at Josephine's. Nera oversaw the kitchen and helped with the younger mages, while Ison oversaw the potion-making. The workshop was in the keep, and it would be far too much work to move it somewhere else. Besides, the keep made him feel safe.

Nera looked over the stewpot as the concoction within boiled, and Ison sat at the small table pressed against the kitchen wall. He glanced into the potion workroom—a door connected it to the kitchen—where he had several potions simmering overnight. They would be done soon.

"You're overworking yourself," Nera said.

"I'm working myself enough," Ison countered. "There's too much to do to rest. The mages need training and someone to tell them that being an apostate isn't a death sentence."

Nera hummed a note, neither disapproving nor approving.

Silence slithered in, and Ison welcomed it. There had been so little of it. Strange, how he had craved the commotion and chaos of Josephine's keep because he feared silence, and now he sought it.

Second cup of tea gone, Ison checked on his potions. Nera brought him a bowl of porridge and took the rest into the dining room. He ate while he worked—bottling finished potions, transitioning others, and beginning a new batch. The clatter and commotion drifted from the dining room, children laughing and talking too loudly. It felt like the Marca, but also not. It was a freer version, where children weren't scolded for being too loud or chewing with their mouths open or not eating fast enough.

He hauled the finished potions to Josephine's stall in the market. The initial panic of being back in the Undercity had receded into a dull unease. While he didn't feel endangered walking to the markets alone, he still felt eyes on his back and steered away from the shadows lurking between the stalls and stones. The market felt different than it had before, yet it was still the Undercity.

Potions delivered, Ison started toward the mages' training grounds. Mages capable of fighting had been drafted to patrol with the knights or fortify the Undercity. Others had volunteered to teach those who couldn't. Luckily, Ison had been exempt from patrol and teaching; no one else had the potion-making experience or knowledge.

Earth mages had carved the training grounds underneath Josephine's sector. Ison headed down the sloped entrance and into the domed chamber. Magelights glittered along the ceiling, shading the space in daylight. The mages filtered around him, heading for their groups—Josephine had separated the mages based on element and skill level. Water mages gathered around bowls of water; fire mages gathered around candles; earth mages gathered around piles of stones; and air mages gathered around nothing. Already, the chamber reeked of the thick floral scents of natural and raw magic.

"Look who found his way down." Mabyl appeared beside him. She nudged him. "I admit, I almost miss the knights on the edge of my vision. It added a bit of risk and kept me on my toes."

"I'm not sure we can spare any knights, but I'll let the council know they're missed," Ison said, meaning he would tell Henry or Reid, and they would inform the council. Ison wouldn't walk into the knights' headquarters even if they claimed to be on the same side. "How are things going?"

"Freakishly well." Mabyl crossed her arms. "Everyone wants to learn, and I've never seen some of these kids so attentive. I can feel my own magic getting stronger." She summoned a bright yellow flame in her palm.

"You had a bit more practice," Ison reminded her.

Mabyl tossed him a knowing smirk.

How many evenings had they spent in the library, talking about the forbidden natural magic? Mabyl had been the first to actually try it, and Ison remembered being terrified of the flame in her hand, because he knew they would all be caught and thrown into the quiet rooms or worse.

"But getting these kids to understand they might have to use their magic in combat isn't as easy." Mabyl doused her flame. "We tried a few duels, but they panicked. It's a good start. I mean, we've come this far in a few days. Just think where we'll be in a few weeks or months. Nexon won't stand a chance."

Ison felt a stiff panic at the mage's name. Even now.

212

More mages entered, and the chamber quickly filled with splashes of water, bursts of flame, flying stones, and gushing wind. Ison strolled through the chamber, observing. Mabyl kept pace with him, curling a flame around her fingers.

"Mabyl," Ison asked when they had circled back to the entrance. He scanned the arena one last time. "Do we not have any energy mages?"

"No." Mabyl frowned. She doused her flame in a curled fist. "The only one in our dorm was Carol, and she's on the other side."

"What about Gert?" Ison remembered the energy mage; he was a few years older than Ison and had magic like jade.

Mabyl shrugged. "He got conscripted a few months after you left, and gods only know where he ended up."

Ison sighed. He had seen firsthand how useful energy magic was—Xavier could form his magic into keys, weapons, or anything he desired. The Marca had never had more than a few energy mages at a time, and they always left—either conscripted or married or sent somewhere by the Order.

"I heard some interesting gossip this morning," Mabyl started, "from your boyfriend."

Ison bristled—he didn't know which to tackle first, the gossip or the boyfriend.

Mabyl's eyes glittered, soaking in his reaction. Her grin widened and turned wicked. "So, it's true?" she whispered. "You're settling down?"

"I won't call it settling down." Ison's face warmed. "We're not... I mean... I don't think... We haven't talked about it."

He and Xavier hadn't mentioned whatever the hell they had—it suited Ison. They hadn't the time, and Ison got a sickening feeling at the idea of a *relationship*.

"He's cute," Mabyl said. "In a dangerous and dark sort of way. If you two ever need a third to spice up a night, let me know."

Ison half laughed. He didn't know if Xavier was the type for that—any talk of physical romance had been short and vague.

"I'll keep that in mind," he said. "What about the gossip you heard? Or was that the gossip?"

"No." Mabyl stepped closer and whispered, "Xavier let it slip that one of our mutual friends is long-lost royalty."

Thankfully, Xavier had implied the secrecy of it too.

Ison nodded, confirming Mabyl's suspicions, and her eyes grew wider than he'd ever seen them.

"For real?" she whispered. "I thought he was shitting me."

"He's not," Ison whispered. "But it's complicated."

"It was complicated before," Mabyl said, laughing. "And here she is living in the gutter with the rest of us."

"As is King Bradburn," Ison said.

Ison spotted Abrielle among the water mages. He was glad she had made it out. Ison had worked with her in the Marca stables. Hopefully, she passed on her knowledge of healing to the younger mages. They would need all the healers they could find.

The chamber radiated with magic—more magic than he had ever felt. The classrooms at the Marca had but a sliver of it. Ison reached out to it—it listened without objection—and a dull silver figure formed in his palm. He made the figure walk around his palm. It was a basic illusion, nothing more than a trick on the eyes. He'd never been good at illusions, but the magic in the air was almost overwhelming. Unnatural magic had never come so easy.

"Feeling forlorn about your lover?" Mabyl asked, looking at the figure.

Ison blinked; he had made the figure in Xavier's lithe image. He hadn't meant to. "Can you feel that?" he asked. "All the magic in the air?"

Mabyl nodded. "It's a little intense."

"The Marca commanded their mages to use only unnatural magic, but natural magic is what makes unnatural magic," Ison said. Why had he never put the thoughts together before? His stomach pitted as the truth surfaced. "With such a stunted supply of unnatural magic, we didn't learn much more than illusions and party tricks. Fowler, and by extension, Nexon, made sure mages didn't know how to use their magic."

"And they made sure that the only way a mage could learn would be to go to Nexon," Mabyl added darkly.

Ison dropped his hand and let the little figure evaporate. "Bastards."

"The lot of them," Mabyl agreed.

CHAPTER 46

Juniper ghosted through the Undercity. She felt like her old self, before Isolde, before Reid—she felt like Juniper Thimble again, not some strange amalgamation of Juniper and Isolde. The tavern leading into the ruins had opened for business again, and getting through unnoticed wouldn't be easy—not with Maddox's thugs watching it.

Instead, she glided through the dark toward the northern outskirts of King Bradburn's sector. Most had chosen homes closer to the Commons and the king, leaving the streets to the north vacant and dark. The magelights didn't glow as bright. They emitted a hushed midnight shade of silver, barely more than cloudy moonlight. It didn't bother Juniper. She didn't need them to see.

She dropped onto the slanted roof of a two-story building. She lowered herself as a patrol rounded the corner—the knight was a stranger, but she knew the mage from Josephine's, though she couldn't think of his name. Their conversation was hushed but pleasant.

She waited for them to pass, ears perked, eyes alert for twitching shadows, body fluid and ready to move—a whisper slithered from the alley beside her, cold as frostbite yet warm as summer breeze. Gooseflesh erupted over Juniper's skin. She held her breath, but no more whispers came.

The patrol passed, and Juniper crept down the sloped roof, toward the darkened alley.

She sent her magic over the edge of the roof first. She detected no people, no animals, no threatening presence. She detected...something, but she couldn't tell what.

She peeked over the edge.

There, in the corner of the alley, tucked underneath mismatched curtains of crimson and plum, was a carved figure of a cloaked woman. The figure rested on a small barrel draped with a black cloth. Several candles lined the barrel, half of which still burned. Their flames were small, the light dim and nearly nonexistent. If anything, the candles seemed to make the alley darker.

Juniper dropped into the alley. She had found a shrine to Bera, goddess of shadow. Her makeshift shrines dotted the Undercity in dark corners and dead-end alleys. Juniper tried to stay away from the temples, even the makeshift ones. They all felt like tombs, watching and weighing every fiber of her existence to some ridiculous standard. But Bera's shrine did not give off that feeling—it felt welcoming but abrasive at the same time.

No more whispers came.

A year ago, Juniper would have laughed at herself, but after her experience with Blugo, she'd recanted her thoughts on the gods.

"What?" Juniper whispered to the empty air.

No one answered.

"Unless you have a way into the ruins, I'm busy," Juniper said to the shrine.

Still, no one answered.

Juniper turned to leave, feeling foolish, when a cold breeze brushed against her cheek. She jumped and turned—a shadow slid down the alley. Her heart gave a hard thump, and Juniper dashed after it. She skidded out of the alley as the shadow slithered down another—she chased the shadow through the alleys, across empty streets, always almost out of sight.

She bolted out of the alley after the shadow and then slid to a halt—she had reached the northern outskirts. Juniper glanced up and down the street, but the shadow was gone.

Juniper set her hands on her hips, feeling foolish.

She glanced up and down the empty houses at the edge of the Undercity, the puddles of shadow between them and within their empty windows.

A laugh sounded, a very human, very manly laugh.

Thinking it was a patrol, Juniper hurried to the closest alley. She ducked into the shadows and waited for the footsteps to pass. When no footsteps came, she peeked out of the alley. If they weren't patrolling, what were they doing? Juniper crept out of the alley and toward where she'd heard the laughter. A few streets over, she spotted two guards standing outside a rundown house.

The house had been built into the northern wall, among dozens just like it.

Ison had told her about the house on the edge of the Undercity, the one that led into the Iluvin ruins. He hadn't been able to tell her exactly where it was, and she had forgotten about it.

Bera had solved the problem of how to get into the Iluvin ruins. Juniper wanted to laugh and curse at the goddess.

She ghosted over the rooftops, closer to the little house. With only two guards—a young pledge and a nervous-looking mage—it presented minimal trouble. She knew how to deal with guards.

Crouching on a rooftop across from the house, she threw a pebble down the alley. It clattered, drawing the attention of both the knight and the mage. The knight stepped away first, hand on his Mage's Bane. The mage focused on the knight and the alley, assuming the threat came from the dark. The mage stepped into the street, eyes on the knight's retreating back, pine-colored magic ribboning around his fingers. Another pebble toss, and the mage inched away from the abandoned house.

It took only a moment for Juniper to slip inside undetected, and another to find the backroom with the woven rug. She pushed it aside to reveal the dark passage—the stone angled sharply down and vanished into darkness. She started into the passage. A few blinks, and her eyes adjusted to the dark.

The passage had the uneven walls of hasty earth magic. It led down into an ancient, circular chamber that reeked of dank air, lingering decay, and mildew. Five archways led off the main chamber, each carved with Iluvin runes. One of the doorways had been blocked by earth magic—the wall of stone that had been erected after Xavier and Amery found the transformation circle.

Juniper chose a hall on the opposite side of the chamber and started walking. The only sounds were her breathing and her footsteps, as light as they were. The walls seemed to soak in all other sound, and the hallways gave the eeriest feeling of being buried alive. She didn't hear or feel any sign of Nexon's followers. Of course, now that they had the castle, they had no need to hide in the ruins.

Juniper wandered through corridors and chambers and ran her fingers over the ancient whorls, the worn runes, and the drawings. She hadn't had the chance to explore. Every time she had entered the ruins, she had been in a hurry or anticipating something awful. But now, she had all the time in the world. Or, at least until someone realized she was gone.

She walked through identical chambers, corridors that curved and doubled back on themselves, and after a while, she detected a pattern. The ruins were set up in a circular fashion—certain chambers served as hubs off which four corridors branched. Along those four corridors were smaller chambers that looked to have once been apartments or housing. The arrangement of each house was nearly identical—stone benches by the door, stone slabs like bunk beds, and hanging iron pots that might have once held plants or magelights.

A corridor wrapped around each section, connecting them together. Juniper navigated four of these sections before she came to something different—a wider corridor with smaller one-room apartments. Most had molted blankets on the floor or decayed hay or packed dirt.

They looked like—Juniper's heart tumbled into her stomach—cells. They reminded her of the royal dungeons, the tiny cell she had been thrown into.

She found several corridors of cells, too many for her liking. She'd stumbled into a dungeon. Hundreds of prisoners could have been kept down here, and they would have been so far underground, no one above could have heard them scream. Was this what the Iluvin ruins had been all this time? The ancient dungeon of whoever had lived here before the Bradburns?

She stepped into one of the cells. The iron door had been ripped from its hinges. Even in the dark, she spotted scorch marks on the stone walls.

What had happened here? It would have taken a great fire to have left those scorch marks, but how could they be so isolated to one wall? Juniper checked the next cell—no scorch marks.

Juniper fought a shiver of unease. She hated dungeons.

She continued to explore, further and further within, until she came to the end—a solid wall of uncarved stone. She walked along the wall and found the beginning of an archway, partially carved from the surrounding stone. Juniper ran her fingers along the final strokes of magic against the stone. Had construction ended when the Great War began? Or before?

Juniper turned back and wandered down another corridor, then another, and another still. She went up and down stairs, through archways. She wandered until she came to something different—a huge room that looked like a common area. Benches circled the middle, and most had collapsed. Ancient carvings spanned the arched ceiling.

Juniper slowly navigated the room, eyes on the ceiling. The old carvings had faded with time, but without weather and human hands, remained mostly intact.

The carvings depicted what she thought was a layout of the ruins, only with people holding swords, whips, and what looked like discs. She followed the carvings with her eyes—while minding her feet—and what she saw near the center of the ceiling stole her breath.

It was a dragon. Curved horns, spiked tail, and talons—a *dragon*. Each scale had been carved with masterful detailing. Juniper couldn't take her eyes off it. It looked like the dragons that guarded the gates to the garden of the gods, only different—a different species?

Iluvin words circled the dragon, the letters angular and curved.

The carvings illustrated people walking away from the dragon, each holding a disc. Smaller dragons spotted the ceiling, and… Juniper gasped as the realization hit her—the people were not carrying discs. They were carrying eggs. Dragon eggs.

The dragons, the cells, the eggs…these ruins had not been for people. They were an ancient breeding ground for dragons.

Her knees felt weak, and she conceded to sitting on one of the only remaining stone benches. The entire ceiling depicted these breeding grounds. People bringing dragon eggs, hatching those eggs, and caring for the dragons like livestock.

A thousand years ago, this place had been crawling with dragons.

And now they hardly existed.

The mural did not explain what had happened to the dragons. Maybe the dragons were why Bradburn had invaded the city and destroyed the castle. He destroyed the dragons too.

Juniper slumped forward. She wanted to know what the ancient Iluvin people did with those dragons. The drawings did not depict them as monsters. If anything, they seemed to be revered. As far as she knew, Iluvin held dragons in high regard.

She sighed. She'd love an army of dragons to take into battle against Nexon.

A sound caught her attention—a footstep, then a swish of fabric against stone.

Juniper sucked in her breath and cast a magic net around her—like Bois did. Juniper hadn't practiced the art of it in a while, and though she couldn't see the world as defined as Bois, she could sense the big and obvious, like people. Her magic didn't find anyone.

The silence of the ruins pressed in once more, but she did not trust it.

She crept toward the corridor where she thought the sound had come from. Halfway down the corridor, she heard the scuttle of fabric. A few steps later, her magic net detected movement.

Two bodies, human, stood at the end of the intersection of another corridor. Her wild imagination pictured two ancient Iluvin dragon masters, skeletal and vengeful, lingering here after all these years with a hidden stock of undead dragons—but she shoved that thought aside.

It was far more likely that someone had wandered into the ruins looking for her.

The two were speaking softly, barely audible.

They knew she was there—why else whisper so? Unless they did not want her to know they were there.

Anyone looking for her would have spoken, not run from her. She crept closer, silent as a shadow, until she could see the two strangers with her night sight. A boy and a girl, around her own age, stood at the end. They were looking down the corridor, toward her, but in the pitch-blackness, they couldn't see her. Their widened pupils darted over the shadows.

The girl had a rune painted on her cheek. The boy had the same rune painted on his temple. Neither looked friendly, but neither looked outwardly dangerous either.

Refugees or enemies?

"I see you," Juniper whispered.

NIGHTMARES IN THE ICE

Both the boy and the girl jumped. Air surged down the corridor, and Juniper summoned a shield of ice. Air slammed into the shield—knocking the breath from her throat. As the next blast of air rushed toward her, she bent her ice like an arrow. Her ice sliced through the air, and invisible spears crashed into the stone on either side of her, loosening dust and dirt from the seams.

"Get her!" hissed the girl. "We'll be heroes! The master will be thrilled."

Juniper's sympathy vanished. She had wandered into Nexon's territory, it seemed. Unfortunately for these mages, they had wandered into Juniper's territory.

Couldn't have that.

From her ice shield, two fists of clear blue ice formed.

The boy summoned a flame to his hand, and as its red-orange light spilled into the darkness, Juniper pushed her ice forward. Twin fists of ice surged from the dark, and she relished the sight—the ice emerging from the darkness, the widening of the eyes, the beginning of the inhale of surprise, the impact to the chest—both mages tumbled backward. The boy's flame went out, and their shouts of protest ended as they crashed against the floor.

Silence returned.

Juniper lowered her ice shield.

Flame erupted on the other side—the flash of light stole Juniper's vision. At the same time, the girl jumped to her feet. Something hard slammed into Juniper's chest and threw her backward. Juniper cast her magic net around her—she found the two mages staggering to their feet, the flame the boy carried, and the stone hammers the girl twirled around.

One of those hammers flew toward Juniper. She dodged and sent an arrow of ice toward the girl's throat. The girl blocked the first arrow, but the second arrow found its home in her chest. The girl gasped and fell backward.

Her stone hammer clattered to the ground. The boy lashed out with his flames, lobbing fireballs at Juniper. She cast a shield of ice over the corridor. The fireballs hissed against the ice, but this time, her ice was stronger. As it melted, she refroze the droplets and shot them at the mage. His fire couldn't block all of them. Ice struck his shoulder, his thigh, and his side. In his moment of distraction, Juniper aimed another at his face. He dodged—his attention moved to the ice—and a dagger of ice landed in his throat. His fire died, and the ruins again fell into darkness.

Juniper stood there, regaining her breath and her night sight.

Nexon's mages had found her, which meant either they were wandering around the ruins, or she had wandered closer to the castle than she thought.

And a stupid, reckless plan formed on top of her previous plan.

220

CHAPTER 47

Juniper followed the direction she thought the mages had come from. She had come from one direction, and if they had been in the dragon ruins, she would have heard or seen them. It didn't give her much, but with a little wandering, she found it—a ladder leading up to a trapdoor. The ladder was new, untreated oak, as was the trapdoor.

She started up, one rung at a time, listening. She didn't hear anything on the other side. A tendril of ice slithered through the seams and gently pushed the trapdoor up. No one raised an alarm; no dagger or stone fist came flying through—Juniper pushed the trapdoor open further.

It opened into the castle catacombs. Water rushed in the distance—the sewers. Underneath the rushing of water, she heard the cadence of voices. The nearest torch glowed several corridors away, and its ghostly flickering left her in darkness. Juniper pulled herself through the trapdoor. She crept through the thickest shadows, keeping a space between her and the voices. She'd rather not cause a riot.

Someone had been down here to light torches, but only along certain passages. She kept to the dark, slinking through empty corridors, up spiraling stairs, and at last came to what she was looking for—the back of a painting, a secret way into the castle.

A logical voice in her head that sounded suspiciously like Reid told her to turn around and leave while she could, while the way back was clear and safe. But another voice, her own, dared her to go further in. See what she could find.

Her own voice won.

With her night sight, she found the secret door's lever easily. Before pulling it, she pressed her ear against the back of the painting. She heard only silence.

She gently pulled the lever. The painting swung open, and Juniper stepped into Bradburn Castle. The room looked to have been a parlor, but she couldn't tell for certain—the furniture had been charred and smashed, piles of books lay half burned, and one of the bookshelves had been toppled. It smelled like burnt wood and paper and, underneath it, magic.

Juniper readied her own. Gods only knew what she would find.

She crept across the room and to the plain wooden door—plain wood, not the mahogany doors of the Royal Chambers or polished wood of the upper floors. The toppled and burned furniture looked to have once been plain wood. It all suggested she had entered the lower chambers of the castle.

She let herself into the corridor. Voices murmured from somewhere, the sound soft and echoing, as if the castle itself was whispering secrets. The corridor went left and right; Juniper chose left and started to stalk. Her ice churned underneath her skin, ready and waiting to strike.

The lower levels of Bradburn Castle lacked the glamour of the upper floors. Whereas the upper floors held countless paintings, suits of armor, and decorative furniture, the lower levels were sparsely decorated. The plain stone walls held old-fashioned iron torch brackets, thicker and heavier than those above. The only suits of armor she saw were broken or dented or missing pieces. She passed a small alcove full of paintings in need of a new frame, and another stuffed with broken furniture and crates of dishes.

Juniper caught a whiff of lye and lemongrass, and that confirmed her suspicions—she'd entered the servant's chambers, or whatever they were called. She recognized the lemongrass and lye from how her freshly laundered clothes and linens had smelled.

She followed the smell of clean laundry. The splatting and splashing of the washing replaced the soft din of voices.

At least she could confirm that Nexon's clothes were clean.

She crept toward a set of propped-open wooden doors, where the sounds spilled from. She paused outside the doors, and then she realized she had no plan. What did she think she would accomplish by sneaking up on Nexon's followers while they saw to the washing? She could ambush them and slaughter the lot of them, but that would cause a commotion. She had already escaped Bradburn Castle twice with her life, and she didn't feel like testing fate a third time.

She took a step away from the door when a grouchy male voice spat, "Hurry up. There's plenty to be washed."

The sniveling, commanding tone grated on her ears.

And her former plan of ambushing them sounded so much better. She tiptoed back to the door and slunk behind the propped-open door. She peeked through the seam between the door and the wall.

The laundry room was large and square. Stacks of dirty linens and robes were stacked in wicker baskets, and a dozen servants scrubbed the dirties over washboards. Others pulled the wash through wringers, while others still hastily folded and separated them into piles of shirts, trousers, socks, underthings, and robes.

Juniper held her breath—they were castle servants, not Nexon's followers! Some still wore their simple servant clothes, albeit tattered and torn, with dirty or tangled hair.

Nexon had not killed them or made them into those beasts. He had turned them into his own servants. Slave labor, by the look of the mage sauntering about the room, a whip of stone curled around his left arm, nose pointed upward.

The mage paused by a servant folding clothes. The girl didn't notice; she continued to fold.

The stone whip slowly uncurled from the mage's arm, its motions smooth as a snake. The servant must have noticed, for she started to fold the clothes a little faster. As she moved faster, her folding turned sloppy.

"Garbage work," snapped the mage. His whip of stone shot forward and knocked all the folded clothes onto the floor. "Start over."

The girl didn't say anything. No one did. The girl's shoulders slumped forward, and she bent to pick up the strewn laundry. The mage sauntered away, proud grin on his face. As the mage turned, the servant shot him a vicious glare—it was Marcy, Juniper realized with a thudding of her chest.

Marcy was the servant who had tended to Juniper after Clara had gone missing. She and so many others were still here, locked away and treated like slaves.

Juniper slipped around the door, silent as a shadow, and tiptoed into the laundry. The mage's back was turned to her. Marcy's glare slid to Juniper. Her brows furrowed in confusion and panic, and then recognition widened her eyes and smoothed the hatred from her eyes. Marcy gently shook her head, warning in her gaze. Juniper put a finger to her lips and slunk behind a pillar, keeping it between her and the mage.

Whether Marcy knew who Juniper really was or not, Juniper didn't know. She would ask when she saved them all from this horrible situation.

Carol's bitter comment came back—*You just have to be the hero, don't you?* Juniper shoved the comment aside.

"What are you gawking at, rat?" snapped the mage. "Get back to work!"

A gasp, shuffling, and then a splash of water.

The mage marched around the room, his nose turned up, his face set in a scowl. Juniper kept in time with his steps, always keeping one of the many pillars of the room between them. The servants started to notice, though no one said anything. Their hesitation and confusion aggravated the mage, who lashed his stone whip through the air—not hitting anything or anyone—and barked, "What is wrong with all of you? Get back to work!"

The way several of the servants flinched, he had used that whip for more than just dramatic effect. Juniper felt an echo of searing pain across her shoulders and, with it, a burning rage.

Juniper slid out from behind the pillar, footsteps silent as a cat's, and stayed within the mage's shadow. Most of the servants had seen her, and most were watching—the mage tried to see what they saw and, thinking they gawked at him, grew angrier.

The mage growled in frustration, and as he raised his whip to smack the nearest servant, Juniper grabbed his wrist with a tendril of ice. He gasped, and before another word could escape his throat, she wrapped a second tendril of ice around his mouth. Another tendril wrapped his middle and snaked up his arm, securing his raised arm in place.

The stone under her feet started to move in a panicked and uncertain way, and she expanded her ice, encasing him almost entirely and blocking his magic.

"Guess who?" Juniper purred. "I'll give you three guesses."

The mage raged and panicked against the ice covering his mouth, his breath mumbled and hot. He struggled, but her grip was stronger.

"Oh, what's wrong?" Juniper purred as she started around him. His eyes flashed to his peripheral, and he watched her saunter to face him. "Not used to having someone push you back? Or, if my suspicions are correct, you are not used to being in charge. You've always been at the bottom. And now that you've got a little bit of control, a little bit of power, you're throwing it around because you can. Am I right?"

The mage's eyes burned with anger and fear.

"I'll take your silent rage to mean that I'm right," Juniper said. She looked him over. "And now the matter is what to do with you."

The servants abandoned their posts and circled the mage like vultures, their dislike obvious and vicious. Juniper stood stone still, afraid of turning that viciousness on herself.

"Drown him in the washing," growled one of the older servants.

"Smother him with dirty socks," barked another.

"Hang him by his ankles."

"Put his fingers through the wringer first!"

"I like the way they think," Juniper said to the mage. "I think I'll let them have you. Of course, my magic is the only thing keeping his magic at bay."

Two older servants approached the mage. They shared a silent glance. The other servants were looking at them—waiting for a decision.

"Snap his neck and be done with it," said one of the older servants to Juniper. "We will not stoop to his level of violence and cruelty."

224

An agreement went through the room, and Juniper obeyed—she encased him in ice and snapped his neck, muffling the sound of bones cracking.

"Who are you?" One of the older servants looked Juniper up and down. "Here to take his place?"

"No, I—"

"You're that girl," interrupted Marcy. Distrust shone in her eyes. Her water-wrinkled hands fisted in her dirty skirt. "The one the prince invited."

"Juniper Thimble." Juniper lifted the sides of an invisible skirt in curtsy. A flurry of surprise and whispers washed through the room. "But enough about me. I have wonderful news for you."

In as few words as possible, Juniper told them about the resistance in the Undercity. None of them argued—they all wanted out of the castle. Juniper directed them to the entrance to the catacombs that she had used. Luckily, the older servants knew the one she mentioned.

"We can be out of here before anyone notices," Juniper started. She took a step toward the door.

"We can't leave yet," said one of the servants.

Juniper raised her brows.

"The kitchens are worse than the laundry," the servant said, balling her fists.

"They *were* worse," corrected another.

"What's wrong in the kitchens?" Juniper asked quickly.

"Nexon and his fools eat more than twice what we're used to preparing, and call for food at all hours of the day," said Marcy. Likely to feed their magic appetites. "They're working the kitchen staff to the bone. They whip you if they don't like their meal."

"Which happens more often than not," added another, her tone lowly and bitter.

"Okay," Juniper said. "Go wait for me in the catacombs. Keep to the shadows. I'll see about the kitchens."

"But hurry," said Marcy. "Someone will come looking when the laundry isn't brought up."

Juniper led the servants to the portrait and then headed to the kitchens—the opposite way from the laundry.

The kitchens were easy to find—she followed the scents of roasting meat and herbs. She descended a wide set of stairs to the kitchens. Unlike the laundry, the kitchen had no doors. A wide archway led into the main kitchens, and the clatter of pots and pans echoed into the corridor. Juniper slunk down the stairs and crept up to the archway. Another haughty-looking mage sauntered about, scowling at the servants as they slaved away at the stoves and ovens. Steam and fire-heat filled the air, pressing against Juniper's ice.

With time not on her side, Juniper sent an ice arrow through the throat of the mage. The body hit the stone floor with a meaty thud.

The servants jumped and gasped; the commotion summoned another mage from behind the row of stoves. A beat passed—just enough time for a spark of panic to flash through the second mage—and an ice arrow tore through his throat.

The servants gawked.

"How many more?" Juniper asked, gathering ice arrows around her.

No one answered her. They looked at Juniper as if she had come to slaughter them all. Realization gradually spread around the kitchen, and the chopping, stirring, and kneading came to an end. Only the cracking of the ovens and boiling stewpots sounded.

"What are you doing?" came a sharp feminine voice from the far side of the kitchens. Footsteps marched across the room. "What's happened?"

"They're dead," someone answered.

"What?" A flaxen-haired woman marched around the ovens, flour splattered over her apron and up to her elbows. She stared at the two dead mages; then her panicked gaze bore into Juniper's.

Juniper's breath scattered in her throat—Glenda Sandpiper, Reid's aunt. "You're alive," Juniper gasped.

Glenda looked Juniper up and down. Her panic subsided. "You're taking back the castle?"

"No, unfortunately it's just me," Juniper said.

Glenda's lips pursed. A few servants whispered, too low and fast to be heard.

"But I'm in a rescuing mood, so let's go." Juniper waved the servants toward the corridor.

A few servants rushed into the corridor, but most hesitated. They looked at Glenda, who looked like she couldn't decide if being rescued by Juniper was worth being rescued.

"You can stay here, if you'd like," Juniper said, stepping backward. "I'm sure the death of two of his mages will be easy to explain."

"Oh, let that monster's dinner burn," Glenda barked. She undid her apron and threw it into the closest stove. The off-white fabric immediately caught fire.

Glenda marched into the corridor, and as smoke rose in the kitchens, the rest of the servants followed.

CHAPTER 48

Exhaustion tugged on Juniper's bones by the time she pushed aside the woven rug and led the procession of castle servants out of the ruins. Juniper didn't bother being quiet, and when she opened the front door to the abandoned house, the mage and knight were ready to defend—the mage held blades of air and the knight held his Mage's Bane.

"Stand down," Juniper commanded. "I've got a group of refugees."

The mage recognized her at once. His magic blades dissolved, and he dropped his arms to his sides. The knight hesitated, but as servants began to shuffle out of the house, he sheathed his blade. The servants marched into the Undercity, each carrying supplies stolen from the castle. Baskets of clothing, linens, soaps, dyes, grains, butter, bottles of oil, and bottles of ale—anything they could grab from the stores.

The knight and mage gawked.

Night had fully fallen over the Undercity, and most had gone to bed, but as Juniper walked with the servants through King Bradburn's sector, she felt a nervous energy underneath the silence.

They turned a corner onto one of the main streets, and a familiar masculine voice called her name, "Juniper?"

Juniper met Reid's eyes. Panic, worry, and anger seethed through his exhausted gaze. He wasn't wearing his armor. He started toward her, and she prepared herself for the rant, for the reprimand, for the shame and guilt for having caused him those emotions. She readied her defense too.

She paused as Reid came within arm's reach, but he didn't. He closed the space between them and wrapped his arms around her, pulling her into a tight embrace. His warmth seeped through her skin. She hadn't realized how cold she'd been.

"Where have you been?" he breathed into her hair. His embrace loosened, but he did not let go of her. He looked at the servants, the supplies they carried. His confusion grew. "What did you do?"

"Oh, nothing much," she said, shrugging. "Saving people, gathering supplies, you know."

Reid blinked at her, disbelief bright in his tired gaze.

"Yes, yes, I am aware I left without telling anyone, that I stole away into the night, on my own, without a chaperone to keep me safe from horrible decisions and the monsters in the dark," Juniper said, her tone lacking sincerity. "But as you can see, I am very capable of taking care of myself."

Reid started to speak when Glenda interrupted, "That she is." Glenda came to stand beside Juniper, herself carrying a jar of salt and a jar of honey. "We'd still be slaving away had she not decided to come find us."

The disbelief and worry in Reid's expression vanished. His eyes widened, and his lips parted—his breath hitched. Juniper wiggled out of his arms and took the salt and honey from Glenda. With her hands free, she embraced her nephew.

"We thought the worst," Reid whispered.

"As did I," Glenda said.

They stepped away from each other. Glenda motioned for the salt and honey, but Juniper refused. "No, you go on. I can handle the supplies. There's someone else you need to see first."

Glenda's entire expression shifted—first surprise, but then it softened into something Juniper had never seen. Juniper dared to call it warm. Before Glenda could change her mind about it, Juniper fell in line with the servants. A few knights had taken the lead of the procession, guiding the servants to the storehouse in the Commons.

The sudden appearance of so many servants and supplies caused a commotion to spread through the Undercity. Everyone wanted to know how it had happened and why and if anyone had been injured. A part of Juniper wanted to rush and embrace it, to be the hero, to soak in the praise and admiration, but another part wanted to vanish before anyone saw her.

You just have to be the hero, don't you?

Carol's spiteful words echoed in her mind, and before anyone could stop her, she ducked out of the warehouse line. She held onto the salt and honey and started toward the king's house.

Already, knights helped the newly rescued servants find places to sleep for the night. When given the choice, most asked to be in the king's sector. She felt their relief at hearing about their king and his resistance—almost palpable. She heard several promises of "It will be all right" and "You're safe now."

Juniper slipped through the front doors of the king's house. Both guards frowned at her—they had likely gotten scolded for not knowing where she was.

"There you are." Adrian stepped out of the washing room, hair still damp. "You caused quite the commotion."

She offered him a sympathetic smile and held out the salt and honey. "I brought gifts."

Adrian walked with her into the kitchens, and she set the salt and honey on the counter.

"Aren't supplies supposed to be divided equally?" Adrian asked, eyebrow raised. His voice held nothing of shame or judgment.

"Oh, you honestly think Maddox hasn't been skimming the best from what his thieves bring back?" Juniper scoffed. "Trust me, he isn't being completely honest. It's not in his nature."

Adrian nodded to the salt and honey. "And is it in yours?"

She shrugged. "I like honey in my tea and salt on my food. I can take them to the storehouse if my slight dishonesty bothers you..." She started to pick up the jars, but Adrian put a hand on her shoulder.

"No, no, your secret is safe with me," he said. "Between you and me, I like honey in my tea too."

Adrian placed the jars in the cabinets.

"Is your father angry?" Juniper whispered.

"Likely," Adrian said. "But he is a reasonable man. He will see the servants you rescued and the supplies you've secured. He will have a speech ready for you, something about reasonability and following rules. It's not so bad. I've heard it countless times."

Juniper hesitated, then asked, "I have another question for you."

Adrian stepped closer, brow cocked.

"What do you know about the ruins underneath Bradburn Castle being ancient dragon breeding grounds?"

Adrian blinked, and surprise brightened his entire face. "Is that true?"

"I found a mural that implied it." She quickly explained what she had found in the ruins.

Adrian's smile faded with each word, but his curiosity remained bright and strong. When she finished, he ran a hand through his damp hair. "I thought the dragon stories to be legend. My grandfather told me that, long ago, the ground the castle now sits on belonged to dragons. The Iluvin conquered the dragons and tamed them, and then Lendon Bradburn conquered them."

"What happened to the dragons?" Juniper asked.

Adrian shrugged. "No one knows. My ancestors hunted dragons for sport, as did knights, but few ever succeeded. Dragons are supposed to be clever and cunning, more than most men."

"Yet the Iluvin conquered them?"

"I can't say," Adrian said. "You are the only person I know who has met a dragon. You are more suited to answer than I."

She blinked—the stone dragons at the gate to the crown of the world. "I don't know if those were real dragons or enchanted stone."

Adrian leaned against the counter. "Juniper, do you think Nexon took the castle because of the ruins? Because of the ancient breeding grounds?"

"What could he possibly want with them? They're empty."

Adrian shrugged. "It's just a curious thought."

Footsteps thundered outside the house, then up the stairs. The king's voice rang above the others, ordering his men to secure housing for the newest refugees.

"We'll talk later," Adrian whispered, "when my father isn't so angry."

Juniper sighed and rubbed her temples. She'd had a long day. She and Adrian parted ways, and she headed into the bathing room before the reprimand.

Juniper lingered in the bathing room, cold water dripping from her face and into the emptying basin. The king had not called for her nor demanded her attention. He had returned to his room. She doubted she had evaded the reprimand entirely. She dried her face magically then tiptoed up to her room. The Undercity had calmed. From the windows, candles and lanterns glowed in houses previously dark. She paused in the hall; voices were coming from Captain Sandpiper's room—his and Glenda's.

"…I know how you feel, Carter, but maybe we were wrong," Glenda was saying. "She didn't have to save anyone, but she did."

"After the king had expressly told her *not* to leave the Undercity," Captain Sandpiper whispered back, his voice low and husky and angry.

Juniper bit her lip—they were talking about *her.*

"Carter, I know, but—"

"I stand by my decision. I don't care what good the girl has done. I know her list of crimes. She's done more bad than she could ever make up for. I refuse to stand by and let Reid marry a monster like her. He doesn't understand."

"Carter—"

"I will not let him become his father, Glenda. I will not let Reid marry a girl he barely knows because she spread her legs and made moony eyes at him."

She's done more bad than she could ever make up for.

Her heart had stopped somewhere within those words, and they resounded. With each repetition, the voice grew angrier and more hateful.

Before she could hear another word, Juniper slipped into her own room.

"You look upset."

Juniper jumped—she blinked, and the darkness yielded to her night sight. Blythe came into focus, her dark eyes and skin, her brown hair tied back into a bundle of braids. She sat cross-legged on her bed and wore no easy emotions. The fear that had once brightened her eyes had gone.

"I suppose you heard that," Juniper whispered.

Blythe nodded. "It's not the worst thing I've heard when someone didn't think I could hear. My father said worse about me. Far worse about my oldest sister."

Juniper swallowed her distraught emotions. "I hope you've brought good news."

"Maddox wants to talk to you," Blythe said. "Tonight."

"He knows the king is already mad at me, right?"

Blythe shrugged, and her eyes sparkled. She reminded Juniper of Amery—clever, sweet, and vicious. "I don't think he cares what the king thinks."

Juniper sighed and glanced at the curtain-door. The king would be furious if he found her gone again, as would Reid.

The captain's words resounded. Mean and hateful.

"I'll stay and tell them where you went," Blythe said. If it bothered her, she didn't show it. She remained still as stone. "Maddox said it was urgent."

Juniper didn't ask for more details. She climbed out the window and slipped into the shadows. In that moment, all she wanted was to be away from the hateful captain.

CHAPTER 49

Juniper loved the feeling of sneaking through the shadowed alleys and across empty rooftops, but this—being able to go where she wanted, when she wanted—was what she missed. She'd never had to ask permission to go anywhere or do anything; Maddox had never hovered. Juniper had never had to worry about other people before, and it was driving her mad.

She slid into Maddox's sector and through the window of her old room. Someone had claimed it as their own—a lump gently snored in her bed.

Her *old* bed, she reminded herself.

She pushed the emerging feeling of invasion down and let herself into the hall. She found Maddox in his office, bent over maps and lists. The office looked a bit more disarrayed than it had last time. Dust had settled, and no one had bothered to deal with it. Maddox lacked the sense of chaos—he looked as he always had in sleek black leathers and silks, daggers on his back, his middle, and in each boot. His dark eyes roamed over a map; the location didn't look familiar.

"I've got a job for you," Maddox said without looking up.

"What kind?"

"The king asked me to send someone to make contact with Captain Tinnly of the City Watch." Maddox straightened, folded his hands behind his back, and met her eye. "You're the best we've got."

Juniper bristled at the wording. She had disowned the guild. Someone else slept in her bed, and she had claimed a space in King Bradburn's house. Maddox's gaze bore into hers, daring her to challenge him. She might have, had Captain Sandpiper not been so nasty, had she not been eager to leave the king's house for a while. So, she lied to herself by thinking Maddox had said *we*, as in himself, King Bradburn, and Josephine.

"Xavier could also do it," Juniper said.

"He hasn't made contact with the captain before," Maddox said. "You have. Tinnly knows you. He might listen to you again. He will certainly listen to you over anyone else I could send."

"Why not send a watchman or a knight?"

"Both knights and watchmen lack the precision and stealth required to reach the captain," Maddox said plainly. "The knights and mages are currently learning mental resistance. Until they can defend themselves against a mental attack, they are susceptible to possession and enthrallment. I've been told you've a natural affinity for mental resistance, making you the perfect person for the job."

Juniper held Maddox's matter-of-fact gaze. "All right, what's the catch?"

Maddox smiled. "We don't know where he is. The king suggested he might be in Central Tower, but he might also be dead. He might have escaped the city entirely. If the captain is still alive and willing to assist us, then the king wants to get him."

"And if he isn't willing?"

"Then kill him, and we'll tell the king he was a thrall. The king gave me this for you to give to the captain." Maddox pulled a rolled note from his jacket. "If Captain Tinnly is the man the king believes him to be, he will not turn up his nose at the king's command."

"Is this going to be like the last time you sent me topside?"

Maddox raised a brow innocently.

"Uhls wanted nothing to do with us. You just wanted to show me what happened to the people who escaped the Undercity."

Maddox shrugged. "See it however you'd like. You made it back in one piece and learned the enemy is looking for you."

"If you knew the enemy was looking for me, why not just tell me?"

"If I had told you, you would have gone straight up there to find out for yourself," Maddox said. "You're stubborn like that. You could never be well enough with advice from others. No, you had to see it for yourself."

Juniper glared at him. He had known, and he had sent her topside anyway. And…he was right. She would have gone.

He wiggled the rolled note at her.

She huffed, grabbed the note, and tucked it into her pocket. "Fine. Consider it done."

"I've missed those words," he said, a sigh on his tongue. In the next moment, his masked smile faded. His exhaustion seeped through, pulling at his eyes and drawing lines on either side of his mouth and along his brow. His eyes returned to the map, and the expression vanished.

Juniper slipped out of the keep and into the night-colored Undercity. The chatter had softened, but the edge of chaos remained in Maddox's sector—a glimpse of the old Undercity.

She made her way toward the closest exit, one guarded by Maddox's people. They wouldn't be as inclined to tattle on her to the king as a knight would. The thugs glared but said nothing as she started up the stone stairs. Up and up they spiraled, and soon the magelight faded. The stairs led into the back of a tea shop that doubled as the best place in the city to fence silverware, china, and crystal.

NIGHTMARES IN THE ICE

Before, the tea shop had never closed, and ever since Juniper could remember, it had glowed with candlelight at night. Now, the tea shop was dark. The small kitchen was empty. Kettles had been overturned, and one rack had fallen off the wall—a spray of shattered teacups of every color decorated the floor. A cool breeze slithered in through the broken windows, and puddles of melted snow lingered on the floor. Gooseflesh erupted over her skin. Her magic danced in response.

She peeked through the curtain into the front. The windows overlooking the street had been shattered, dotting the shop with shards of glass. Dull moonlight filtered in, leaving the shop in shadows. Chairs and tables were overturned. Teapots and teacups had been dropped and shattered—the tea had spilled and stained the floor in dirty, dark splotches. A man hung over one window, dead.

"Damn," she whispered.

She tiptoed through the mess—avoiding as much glass as she could—and glanced out the broken window. The whole street was dark. Spring had arrived, yet the winter decorations remained. Garlands hung between lampposts, darkened and sagging from the weather. Wreaths of evergreens and holly hung around little carved figurines of Blugo, his wooden hands open to welcome weary and lost travelers. The scents of warm spices and chocolate drinks had decayed into something horrid, something forgotten and left to rot.

This time of night, Rusdasin would have been quiet anyway, but fear, despair, and uncertainty had tainted the quiet into something dreadful.

She slipped into the alley and climbed to the roof. A bleak overcast sky blanketed Rusdasin in low, bubbling clouds. She felt the brewing storm more than saw it—her magic called to it. An ocean churned in the sky, waiting, building. Her well of magic opened up as if to swallow that ocean. Her stomach dropped, and the world under her feet opened. She fell into a void of chilly shadows and ice—her knees hit the rough stone of the rooftop, followed shortly by her palms. She took a shuddering breath as the world righted itself.

She forced herself to exist beyond that void, and the sensation gradually faded. The feeling of an ocean above her head remained. It must have been the chilly night and the bubbling storm and the new moon—the Marca had taught about the moon, the sun, and the cycle of the seasons and how it affected magic. Juniper couldn't remember all of it, but for an ice mage, a new moon on a winter's night was the perfect combination of dark and cold.

Her magic felt fathomless.

Maddox was right—she was the best.

Juniper slid through the shadows of Rusdasin, through alleys, over rooftops, and across the empty side streets—toward Central Tower. She kept her eyes on the streets and the shadows between the few lampposts and magelights.

The City Watch had towers scattered throughout the city, with Central being the largest. It was home to the captain and closest to the castle.

Bradburn Castle loomed in the murky distance. Scorch marks arched from almost every window, and smoke still trailed from a few. Magelights hovered over a few of the open courtyards. To see the castle in such a nightmarish state plucked at a strange chord in her chest, as if these mages had struck a personal blow to her.

It was not the loss of the castle itself, but the meaning behind it. Nexon had yanked something from her, from the city—proving himself superior.

And she wanted to knock him off his perch.

The closer she came to the castle, the more thralls and mages she saw. Several had runes painted on their faces and arms. None were among the few she'd learned in the Marca.

Her chances of being caught this close to the castle were high, and they rose with every rooftop, every city block. She moved slowly, timing her jumps with patrols. The sneaking did not bother her. She had sneaked through the tightest security the city had to offer—manors with private guards, bank vaults with impossible locks, and gates topped with blade-sharp spires. The stakes didn't bother her either. The stakes had always been success or failure, and failure had almost always meant death.

Central Tower was surrounded by thralls and mages. There had been a fight. Thralls were gathering the bodies from the street and piling them into carts. Juniper scanned them quickly; she spotted iron armor of the Watch, gold of the Royal Guard, and the mismatched armor of empowered citizens. She spotted the silver of a few knights too.

Charging into the tower was out of the question, especially when she didn't know for certain if Tinnly was even inside.

So, she grabbed the first unassuming mage that stupidly wandered into an ally—to piss, of all things. She wrapped ribbons of ice around his mouth and hands and yanked him up the side of the building. She dangled him over the edge of the rooftop, facing away from her.

She loosened the ice around his face just enough that he could breathe.

Oh, her ice moved so smoothly!

"Let's play a game," Juniper said in a voice deeper than her own. "I'm going to ask you a few questions. For every answer you don't give me, you lose a finger to frostbite."

He mumbled against the ice.

"Scream, and you're going to know what Mage's Bane feels like," she hissed. She sharpened her ice into the shape of a blade and poked him in the back. "Understand?"

The mage pleaded against his gag, either a yes or a no—she took the chance and loosened her ice.

"I—I'll talk!" he gasped.

"Where is Captain Tinnly of the Watch?"

"I-in the tower," he said, his voice quivering with cold. "The master ordered him locked up. Said he might be useful. The boss says we have to keep him there until the master figures out what to do with him."

"The boss?" Juniper asked. "Who is the boss?"

"Lady Margret."

She fought hard not to laugh. She took a deep, calming breath, then said in her deeper voice, "You listen to that old hag? You could end her in a heartbeat."

"The master forbids it," said the mage.

Juniper took that information in. Nexon had forbidden his mages from harming Overseer Margret?

"Where is dear old Margret?"

"In the Marca. I—I don't know any more about her than that," gasped the mage. "I swear it, Espone as my witness, I swear it!"

"How many guard Tinnly?"

The mage hesitated, and she eased the ice blade a little closer.

"I—I'm not sure!" the mage said, his voice creaking. "At least one mage is there at all times, but I'm not a guard, I don't know. I've not been higher than the first floor."

"What floor is Tinnly being held on?"

"The top floor."

"What of his family?"

"They're there too."

Juniper didn't know if she liked that answer or not.

"What do you want?" gasped the mage.

"Information, obviously. Answer me this, mage, why follow Nexon? Is this Imperium the type of world you want to live in? Shattered glass on the street, bodies piled in wagons, people afraid to leave their homes? Mages bullying and tormenting because they can?"

"It will get better," said the mage, in a dreamy voice that edged on lunacy. "This is only the beginning. This is not the grand Imperium that it will become.

The master will usher in a new era where people don't fear magic, where mages don't have to hide because of their gifts."

"Is that honestly what you think Nexon is trying to do?"

"You don't know the master."

"*You* don't know your master," Juniper countered. "He will use you and toss you aside like a used rag." The mage started to argue, and she spat, "He's tossed aside everyone he's used. He used them like puppets, and once they outlived their usefulness, he threw them aside. He doesn't care for you. He wants power, he wants revenge, and he will trample anyone in his way to get it."

"And what are you going to do about it?" barked the mage.

"I'm going to stop him," Juniper said matter-of-factly. "And I am giving you one chance to turn your back on Nexon and—"

The mage scoffed. "Like hell if you think I'm going to—"

Juniper would never know what he would have said—her ice hands twisted his neck. The *crack* reverberated through her ice. She dropped the body on the roof.

She had given him a chance, she reasoned.

She crept to the edge of the roof. Three thralls stood guard outside Central Tower. Magelights brightened the street. More thralls heaved bodies onto carts. Mages watched them, lounging on the steps of the tower, drinking.

She would not be getting in through the front door, but that didn't surprise her.

Now that she knew Captain Tinnly was on the top floor, she had a route. She'd gotten into the top floor before, and she could do it again.

It would take precision and skill, but she had the dead of night and a storm on her side. And she was Juniper Thimble, the best the Undercity had to offer— the best it would ever offer. As the first raindrop hit the ground, Juniper rolled her shoulders and hoped this wouldn't be the day she finally slipped up and met her unceremonious end.

CHAPTER 50

Ison had never felt such exhaustion while simultaneously feeling restless. He had collapsed into his bed at Josephine's keep hours ago, thinking his exhaustion would help him sleep soundly. It had, for a few hours.

His mind refused to calm. Every moment since they'd returned from the quest had been hectic. So many things to do, to plan, to consider. Survivors continued to seek help from the resistance, and some had come to the Undercity—some sought to join the resistance, some sought shelter and safety, and others sought healers. An influx of infections, coughs, and burns had filled their healer's hut, so many that they'd had to expand.

Even a pocket of former Undercity residents had come back, though the change in order had stumped a few of them.

"Laws in the Undercity?" barked one crow-voiced woman as she dusted off her old stall's wooden counter. "Never thought I'd see the day. Won't be good for business."

Every potion he made left the workroom immediately. The healers were busy night and day, most working until they passed out from magic depletion. Even some of Abrielle's students had been forced to help.

During those first few days back in the Undercity, he didn't know if their dwindling stock of herbs would suffice. Thankfully, with the mages helping, their herb garden continued to bloom and grow. The Undercity had plenty of space, and Josephine had taken the neighboring house just for herbs. They also had Amery's garden for the delicate herbs that refused to grow underground, even with magic.

Maddox's people brought in a steady stream of supplies; King Bradburn's people kept them safe; and Josephine's people kept them healthy and fed. A semblance of life had returned to the Undercity. Ison should be able to relax. Yet he couldn't. The uncertainty remained. The fear of war turned the air dark and cold.

Having the Royal Guard and the City Watch in the Undercity helped morale. Ison had seen the change in people when King Bradburn walked down the street. They held themselves straighter, and their grimaces lightened. They dared believe in that shred of hope—Ison felt it too: that sliver of hope that refused to give up, that believed their pitiful resistance had a chance.

238

And he still couldn't sleep.

Ison pulled himself out of bed, pulled on his boots and a cloak, and left the keep. Once on the street, the tingle of uncertainty mixed with peace. A gentle hum resonated in the Undercity—the chatter of voices and life. They had achieved a relative calm, but he feared they stood in the eye of the storm. Or worse—he feared the storm had not yet begun.

Ison meandered through the Commons, where the commotion never ended. People chattered at counters, drinking and laughing. A few stews bubbled and boiled, wafting warmth and seasonings through the otherwise dank, mineral-laden air. Ison took it all in, heading for a counter that served tea alongside wine and ale.

A shadow fell in step beside him. He thought it was Xavier at first, but then Amery's voice chimed in his ears. "Strange, isn't it? To see the Undercity as a refuge?" she asked. "Nobles and commoners and criminals eating under the same stone roof. The scandal!"

Ison glanced at her. She wore sleek, snug blacks and three knives that he could see. Her Mage's Bane dagger hung off her hip. She held herself haughtily, like she knew something clever that Ison had overlooked.

"It's always been a refuge," Ison said. "People came here to escape the law and society topside, right?"

Amery hummed. "I suppose it has. Now it's a refuge for normal people."

As the words left her mouth, a bearded man with wide, bloodshot eyes wobbled out of an alley with a green bottle in his left hand and a brown bottle in the right. He mumbled incoherently, eyes flickering from side to side, yet he did not see them. He wobbled down the opposite alley.

"And then there are those," Amery said with disapproval. She snapped her fingers toward the alley. Two well-armed and black-clad individuals stepped around Ison and Amery and vanished into the alley after man.

Ison didn't jump. It didn't surprise him that Amery had her own private thugs.

"Will they kill him?" Ison whispered.

"Only if they have to," she said. "It's best to keep eyes on those types." They started walking again.

"Maddox says there are two reasons people get killed: they deserve it, or they're stupid." She held her elegant fingers before her. "Those types generally fall under the second category."

"What if he can't help it? What if his mind isn't all there?"

"All the more reason to get rid of him," Amery said matter-of-factly.

Ison's gut twisted. "Even if it's not his fault?"

"My situation isn't my fault, but here I am," Amery said. "Fault is relative and an excuse. People are too quick to assume that something is someone else's fault. It doesn't matter whose fault his situation is. The matter stands that it exists."

Ison gaped at her. "That's a cruel stance."

"It's a cruel world," Amery said softer. "That man is either very drunk or mentally incapable. If he cannot carry his own weight, then what use is he to society? He is a leech. Someone will have to work twice as hard to cover the cost of the leech. If no one cares enough for the man to do so, he will not survive."

"That's so…"

"Realistic?" Amery asked. "It's also pessimistic, but that's how the world works. Especially in a crisis. An animal that cannot hunt for itself will become the prey of another animal or die of starvation."

"But we're not animals," Ison defended.

"Is that so?"

"It is," Ison said firmly. "We have the ability to think and reason. We feel compassion and remorse. We shouldn't let a crisis get in the way of that."

"Ah, topside mentality." Amery sighed romantically. "It's always refreshing to hear. The Undercity doesn't run on those things, remember."

"It does now," Ison said firmly. "Or it will."

Amery didn't argue. She wore curiosity, not annoyance. "I assume you're wandering around because you can't sleep."

"Why's that?"

"You have that hounded look about you, the one men get when they're thinking too hard and not drinking."

"I'm not resorting to drinking."

"Not even one of those sleepy tonics?"

"I won't waste them on myself."

"Even if it would help you sleep, thus help you work faster when you are awake, thus benefit you *and* those who need potions?" Amery raised her brows, and her lips twitched. She knew she was right.

"I…" He didn't have anything to counter that with. "You're right, I guess."

"However, I am in a similar situation of restlessness. Shall we meander aimlessly together?"

He shrugged. He didn't trust Amery—she was too closely connected to Maddox—but he didn't mind her company. So they walked through the Undercity. Ison wasn't minding his feet or where they were going until he realized where they had gone—they were near the northern edge of the Undercity, a few houses down from the house with the hole that led into the ruins. According to Amery, a monster had crawled out of it during the City Watch's raid.

He could see the beasts in his mind, and he suppressed a shiver.

"Oh, did you hear about Juniper?" Amery asked, her tone gossip-hungry.

Ison sighed. "Gods, what did she do this time?"

Amery giggled. "She snuck out of the Undercity and into ruins and then into the castle."

Ison felt his heart skip a beat and gawked at Amery. "She what? She could have—"

"She not only returned unscathed, but with a horde of servants and supplies," Amery added, a bit giddy. "No need to get so worried about her. She's sneakier than a spider."

Ison rubbed his face. It did seem like something Juniper would do—reckless and heroic and without regard to others.

They approached the house. Silas and a younger knight guarded the entrance.

"Gentlemen," Amery said in greeting.

"Ma'am," said Silas.

"My lady," said the knight.

"Oh, the manners are refreshing," Amery said, sighing.

"Any news?" Ison asked, mostly to Silas. He felt the knight's eyes on him, running up and down to check for black magic.

Silas opened his mouth to respond—

A rumble came from under their feet, from the tunnels that led to the ruins. Ison sucked his next breath. Amery's olive skin paled, and her onyx eyes glared at the ground. The knight stepped away from the hovel and drew his blade immediately.

"What was that?" Silas whispered.

"I don't know and don't care," Amery spat. "Let's head it off."

Amery pushed through the door and into the house. Ison reluctantly followed. He couldn't let Amery face whatever it was alone, even though she likely had far more combat experience than him. She slipped through the house as easy as a shadow and pulled the woven rug aside. The hole vanished into darkness.

Amery pulled a mage stone from her pocket. With her touch, a soft blue glow illuminated the tunnel. Ison readied his magic for defense and followed. Silas and the knight came after, and Ison felt glad to have them with them.

The tunnel angled down and narrowed. Their footsteps echoed off the stone, and Ison thought he could hear the echo of his thudding heartbeat. He hated being underground. He had gotten used to the Undercity—the walls were far apart, and as long as he didn't look up, he could pretend it wasn't a cave. But this… If he reached, he could trail his fingers along the ceiling. His heart thumped, and his knees went weak.

Amery held up a hand, bringing the others to a halt. She nodded to the darkness ahead of them and whispered, "Hear that?"

Ison strained his ears. There, barely audible, was a faint scratching.

A short way into the Iluvin ruins, they discovered the source of the strange sound—a thrall was carving a rune into the stone. A magelight hovered above him, flickering in shades of yellow.

Ison tried to stretch his neck to see the rune. He couldn't. Amery started forward, but Ison threw his arm in front of her. She glared—he shook his head and pressed a finger to his lips. Amery frowned but didn't argue. Silas had stilled, and the knight looked as irritated as Amery.

Ison had done research on thralls—when he could spare a few minutes— and thralls were extensions of the mage who created them. The clarity of the extension varied. If this knight turned and saw them, Nexon would see them, and he would know exactly where the resistance was. It would draw Nexon's attention to them, and they did not need it.

He would see Ison too, and he didn't feel ready to face that particular beast.

Ison realized the others were looking to him, deferring to him, and his weak knees threatened to give. He swallowed. He tried to mouth the words *Don't let him see you* to Amery, but she rolled her eyes and pulled daggers from her side.

Ison summoned a wind to push or slice—whichever he needed. They would have a fraction of a second to act.

Silas put his hand on Ison's shoulder and stepped in front of him. Ison started to protest, but then the thrall turned around.

In that sliver of a moment, Ison's panic shot through his body like lightning.

Silas held his hand up—as the thrall turned, a film passed over his glassy eyes. He blinked, looking over the tunnel where they stood.

Ison's heart thudded hard against his ribs. The thrall wore the same look as the mages when Josephine taught them mental resistance. Silas had broken into the thrall's mind.

"He will not see us," said Silas, his voice deep in concentration.

What? Amery mouthed.

"He is seeing the tunnel without us in it," Silas said. "He cannot see or hear us. This way, his master cannot see us or hear us."

The knight growled. "How?"

"I've altered what his mind sees," Silas said.

"You…" started the young knight, aghast. "That is black magic!"

"Yes, it is." Silas slowly moved his fingers, puppeteering whatever fantasy he played out in the thrall's mind.

"Can you make him see anything?" Ison asked.

"Yes."

"Make him see the tunnel collapsing on him," Ison said.

The knight looked appalled.

"Nexon cannot know where we are," Ison explained, unable to hide the desperation in those words.

The knight scowled, but he did not object.

Silas inhaled slowly. The thrall looked at the ceiling, and his puppet-like movements went up to shield him from a nonexistent cave-in. As the thrall fell to the ground, Amery made her move—she drove her dagger through his neck. The thrall made no sound of surprise or fear or pain. He remained on the ground, face to the floor.

"That solves that problem," Amery said.

The knight, however, looked horrified. "That is black magic," he gasped, tightening his fist around the hilt of his Mage's Bane.

Amery laughed. "You realized this is the Undercity? The pit where criminals roll around in horrors like a dog in shit?"

"Yes, it is black magic and should be forbidden," Silas agreed. Guilt appeared over his face. "However, that black magic just saved us."

The knight hesitated, then sheathed his sword.

"You can do that?" Ison asked Silas. "Break into the mind?"

Guilt washed over Silas's features. "Many of the older Dual Fangs learned it years ago."

"You could have been helping Josephine teach the others mental resistance," Ison said, and it came out more like an accusation that he intended.

"I know," Silas said. "The other mages trust Josephine far more than they trust anyone who was a Dual Fang, and the mind is a sacred place."

"We can avoid bloodshed his way," Ison said. His heart skipped a beat. "If the thralls report the Undercity empty—"

"Nexon will have no reason to suspect it," Amery added.

The young knight growled. "I don't like it, but in this circumstance…I see no other way."

"I will see if the others are willing to use the skill," Silas said. "I also think it wise to have an earth mage seal this tunnel. We know it leads to the castle, as does Nexon. It is a hazard for us all."

"Before that…" Ison stepped over the dead thrall and motioned for Amery to shine her mage stone on the rune.

"What does that mean?" she asked.

"I've never seen this rune before," Ison said. "But if Nexon is commanding his thralls to draw them, it has a purpose, and I'm willing to bet it's not good."

He memorized the half-drawn rune; then they headed back into the Undercity to find an earth mage. He kept the curving lines of the rune in the front of his mind. It was more complex than any he had seen. Back in the Undercity, Ison headed immediately to the library in Amery's manor. The mages had left the books there—no one wanted to cart an entire library through the tunnel a second time. He lit a lantern with forever flame and got to work.

CHAPTER 51

Juniper snuck into Central Tower through a window on the second-to-top floor—Tinnly's study—just as the first crack of thunder sounded. It rolled against the clouds, low and heavy and threatening. Cold, fat raindrops struck the tower. The room had been ransacked. The heavy wooden table was overturned and smashed; the sideboard was ripped from the wall; shattered bottles littered the floor with colored shards. The door had been ripped from its hinges and lay against the wall, blocking half of the doorway. On the other side, forever flames burned in the place of torches, flickering in shades of blue-white.

She crept through the glass, careful of her footing, and peeked under the broken door. It opened onto a small landing. To one side, stairs curved up. To the other side, stairs curved down. A mage leaned in the doorway of the stairs going up, his gaze listless and bored. A piece of stone hovered above his palm, shaped like a bear. The little stone bear was walking around his palm.

Juniper did not send out a magic net in fear the mages might sense it. Instead, she listened. She heard no one else.

One mage—she could handle him.

Tendrils of ice slithered underneath the door. She gathered her ice, and then encased the mage.

His eyes remained on the bear, unfocused and bored. She almost felt bad, but he had made his choice by siding with Nexon. With a thought, her ice snapped his neck. She gently lowered him to the floor and arranged his body as if sleeping at his post. The forever flame continued to burn—another mage had placed it there.

It would buy some time, but not a lot.

She climbed under the door and tiptoed up the stairs. They led to a plain wooden door. Thunder rolled, shaking the city and the tower. Juniper readied a dagger of ice, inhaled, and knocked. No response came. She knocked again, a little louder.

Muffled voices came from within, then the shuffle of clothes, and then soft, controlled footsteps. The steps paused on the other side of the door. A lock unlatched, and the door cracked open. Tinnly appeared, his dust-blond hair dirty and uncombed. His beige skin had lost its summer tan. Bags hung under his wide eyes. He glowered at her, but a sliver of fear underlined his gaze. He held a candlestick, ready to defend.

"Good evening, Captain." Juniper gave him a friendly smile.

Recognition came over his face. "What do you want?"

"I am merely a messenger." She took the rolled note from her pocket. "From His Majesty."

Juniper sat in the sitting room while Captain Tinnly read the king's note. His wife sat opposite Juniper, her hands folded over her stomach. Her hair was loosely braided and dirty, her lips were pale and dry, and bangs hung under her eyes. Cold tea on the table stank of ginger. Juniper didn't ask, but she was clearly ill. By the look of her and the stench of vomit and bile that lingered in the room, she had been sick for a few days.

Thin streams of blue-white light slithered through the cracks in the door, illuminating the dust motes. The rain had strengthened to a dull roar. A few streams of rainwater trailed from the boarded window. It smelled musty and cold, like dirty clothes and canal water.

Juniper didn't like the waiting. Each moment they wasted here was a moment closer to when someone would come looking for the dead mage.

Tinnly finally sank onto the well-used couch beside his wife and ran a hand through his dirty hair.

"What is it?" asked his wife. Her voice was as hoarse and tired as she looked.

"They're hiding in the Undercity," Tinnly whispered. "I would join the king in a heartbeat—he knows that—but we're trapped here."

"To an extent," Juniper said.

"Lily is ill. She can't move very fast," Tinnly said, frowning. He looked at his wife with sad eyes. He still held the candlestick—because the mages had taken his weapons.

"Sneaking often happens slowly," Juniper said.

Tinnly rubbed his face. "There is a way out of here and into the sewers that lead into the Undercity," Tinnly admitted. "My men recently found it. It's under the cells, but...they're guarding every floor."

Juniper glanced at his wife, her pale lips, her slouched posture. Despite the exhaustion, determination heated her gaze.

"We can't hide in here until they kill us," Lily argued.

Thunder rolled, shaking the tower and the sofa.

"Leave the mages to me." Juniper stood. "I will clear the way. All you have to do is flee. Are you ready?"

"Give us a few moments," said Lily.

Juniper stood by the door, eyes on the stairs, ready to freeze anyone who dared appear. Tinnly and his wife gathered what they could from their quarters. More than once, Lily paused and placed her hand on her stomach, but she held her vomit in. They each wore a satchel, and Lily wore a bag on her shoulders.

"All right," said Tinnly. "We're ready. Are you sure about this?"

"I'm sure," Juniper said. "Are you?"

He nodded, as did his wife.

"Good. I am going to clear the way," Juniper said. "Get to the exit. Don't look back. I'm not following you."

Tinnly frowned, and a panic came over his face.

"Don't look so glum, Captain," she said. "I'm not dying tonight. I'm just taking the more dramatic exit."

Juniper started at the top—she stole rain from the storm and made it her own. Clear blue ice snaked in through the boarded window, across the floor, over the walls, and along the ceiling. It climbed down the stairs, through the study, and out the window. It spilled over the stone tower, gushing frozen tendrils, soaking in the rain as it hit. Her blue ice encased the top of the tower, creaking and sighing as it thickened. The ceiling groaned under the weight of it, but she wouldn't let it collapse.

Her ice flowed faster than it ever had. Power and magic poured out of her, as if the ocean in the sky was hers to command. Her well felt bottomless, almost oppressive in its desire. Magic churned within her, eager to be used, eager to use the unfathomable power all around her.

Thunder rolled above, an encouragement if she'd ever heard one. She started down the tower, leaving the stairs the only path. Her ice filled doorways, windows, and every nook and cranny. She blocked off every way but left an unobstructed path for Tinnly and his wife.

She met opposition on the third floor—mages panicking over the crawling ice—but they didn't stand a chance. Her magic rushed in through open windows, freezing the mages solid before they ever saw her.

Her ice closed over the entire Central Tower, from the spires of the roof to the sidewalk at its base. She sent ice spikes into anyone—mage or thrall—who dared get in her way. Many met their end within the walls of ice.

The magic kept coming—Juniper had never felt such a rush of ice, dark and cold and endless. She used and used, but the well never shrank.

She made it to the first floor. Her ice clogged every window and doorway and blasted the mages and thralls out of her way. She felt others outside the tower, pelting her ice with stone, fire, air, and water. They managed a few chips and dents, but her ice healed itself faster than they could harm it.

Unstoppable!

She clogged the first floor with ice and dropped into the cells underneath. In a few quick lashes of ice, she cleared the cells of the guarding thralls. The Watchmen in the cells panicked at the sight of her. Tendrils of ice broke through the locks, one at a time. The Watchmen didn't move at first—none wanted to join the thralls.

Juniper started to speak, but Tinnly's voice came from behind her, "Hold, men!" He made his way down the stairs, Lily behind him. "We flee with our lives!"

The men followed their captain to the hatch in the last cell, and one by one, they dropped out of sight. Several of them helped Lily safely down.

Tinnly lingered above. He looked at Juniper and said, "Bring it down when you're done. We need to make sure they cannot follow."

"With pleasure, Captain," Juniper said with a smile.

Then he dropped into the darkness.

Juniper started back up to finish the show she had started. She felt her ice weighing on the tower, pulling and pushing on the stones. She felt the commotion outside, the panic, rage, and chaos. She felt the storm pelting the city. With her blood pumping, her heart racing, and her magic itching to tear Central Tower apart, she sent a wave of ice into the front doors—with enough force to rip the doors from the hinges. Stone cracked and wood splintered—and Juniper rode the ice-wave into the street. It churned under her feet and crested high above.

Ice covered every bit of Central Tower, and the stone creaked and groaned. Below her, every mage and thrall gawked up at her with wide, frightening faces. She had never extended her magic so far. In that moment, all the power was hers. She commanded their attention, their fear—she could snuff out their lives in an instant.

And she loved it.

The rainstorm raged. It struck the street with vengeance, splattering the muddy slush, striking the mages and thralls as if it, too, hated them as much as Juniper did. In that short moment, the cold rain soaked her hair and clothes. It frosted over her skin, tingled on her lips, and leeched the warmth—leaving room only for cold.

The shock wore off—fireballs, stone fists, and bursts of air rushed through the night air toward her. Her magic swatted them away like flies. Voices rose, shouting and cursing. She barely heard it over the blood pounding in her ears.

After a dramatically appropriate time, she brought her wave of ice crashing down. As her ice crashed into the mages and thralls, Central Tower came down with her. Stone and ice and dust thundered through the night. The rumble shook the street and rattled buildings for a block in every direction.

And then, for a long heartbeat, only silence remained.

Every mage left standing sent a signal of red sparks into the air, exploding with light. A bell began to ring, loud and obvious. Mages came running from every direction, along with a small army of thralls.

Juniper released her grip on her magic as the tower fell, and her thoughts cleared—bringing down the tower would undoubtedly bring Nexon's attention.

Everyone in the city was looking for her, and now everyone knew exactly where she was.

And she had brought it onto herself.

Fire rained from above—Juniper encased herself in ice. Red exploded on the other side of her cloudy blue ice, flashing light over her shadows. She cast her ice forward and formed a tunnel—she started running. She closed the tunnel behind her and opened it up before her as she ran, and sent blunted ice spikes into thralls and mages who got too close.

As much as she wanted to, she couldn't stay and fight. She had very loudly and obviously exposed herself. She needed to get out of here while she could. A few mages and thralls, she could handle. A hundred? Two hundred?

At her command, the ice tunnel divided. One tunnel went one direction while the one she ran within another—the mages and thralls chased the first, while Juniper's tunnel appeared to end at an intersection of three dark alleys. The mages ran the opposite direction while Juniper vanished into the shadows. She zigzagged through the alleys and across rooftops, just like she had before her magic. The sound of chaos faded with each block.

These Marca mages didn't stand a chance to catch her. She had spent years perfecting her getaway.

Even as the chaos faded, she kept running. She didn't slow down despite the stitch in her side, the ache in her lungs, and the squeezing of her chest. She headed for the gushing of the Weslie River. She could use the canal entrance to the Undercity.

An alley away from the Weslie, she paused to catch her breath.

No one followed.

She allowed her heart to slow.

The rain had abated into a drizzle, though the storm clouds circled in vicious shades of charcoal and plum.

Emptiness pitted where her endless magic had been. She had used a lot of magic in a short amount of time, and the high from the power had eclipsed the emptiness. She felt it rejuvenating, pulsing against her bones. The rain and darkness and cold helped. It...comforted the emptiness.

She sighed and straightened—her magic well felt like any other overused muscle, only deeper and everywhere. It blurred at the edges, and with every heartbeat, her exhaustion thickened. Maybe she shouldn't have been so dramatic.

Juniper started toward the bridge. The lamps had gone dark, leaving much of the bridge in darkness. The drizzle pitter-pattered against the surface of the canal. The murky water lapped against the banks, against boats left at the narrow docks on either side, and something that looked suspiciously human floated downstream. Juniper didn't look any closer.

Gods, she felt awful.

Halfway across the bridge, she realized her mistake.

Mages emerged from the darkness on the far side of the bridge, along with several thralls. Juniper turned to run the other way, but another batch of mages and thralls already blocked it.

They'd trapped her.

Damn. She hadn't heard them approach.

"You're looking a bit tired," came a harsh, sneering voice that made Juniper's skin crawl. She found the speaker's face among the mages.

"Margret," Juniper said conversationally. "Fancy meeting you here."

Margret frowned. She looked as friendly as she ever had, only now she didn't have to pretend to like Juniper. She let her hatred seep into her wrinkled grimace. She wore a fine fur-lined cloak and what looked like velvet robes underneath.

"Your magic is dwindling," Margret said, her chin high.

"Oh, is it now?" Juniper half laughed.

"You would have frozen the river over the bridge and vanished by now, but you're still standing here, looking at me like a mouse that's been cornered," Margret said. "I can feel your panic, your fear."

"Or I could be waiting for the perfect moment," Juniper said, though her words came out a little more breathless than she would have liked.

"No, you have to show off," Margret barked. "Just like you did every day in the Marca, flaunting your skill, flaunting your friendship with the prince, flaunting your knight lover."

The mages around her scowled and sneered.

Juniper spotted a speck upriver, making its way down. A barge, likely. Odd. Most boats stayed off the canals during storms.

"I did not flaunt," Juniper said. "I excelled. It isn't my fault half the mages in the Marca had no talent."

Several mages spat unkind names for her, but they did not charge forward or attack—they were waiting for Margret.

"But why bother me?" Juniper asked. "I'm out of your hair, Margret."

Margret frowned. "Because the master demands it. He gave me one order: to find and get rid of you. I refuse to fail."

"And he handed you so many of his people too," Juniper said, looking around at the mages. "I'm surprised they listen so well to you and not to him."

"He has left me in charge," Margret said haughtily. "I will make sure he returns to your body flayed above his throne."

"Returns?" Juniper repeated.

Margret pursed her lips.

The words rolled around in her head—Nexon had left Rusdasin, but he would return.

"And you will not be here to see his glory," Margret commanded.

The mages readied themselves to attack, and Juniper readied herself—but not to fight. The barge was closer. If she timed it right, she could jump into the cargo and use the rest of her magic to propel the ship forward. She could lose them in the canal, like Margret said.

The barge came closer still, and Juniper formed ice swords on either side of her, as if preparing to fight. Her magic threatened to spasm. Whips of fire flashed through the night, scythes of air blurred, stone hammers readied to smash her, and water blades rose from the canal.

The barge came closer still. It carried flowers. *Flowers?* Juniper banished the oddity of it. She would worry about it later. She bent her knees to jump, and then—

The flowers in the barge exploded in a maddening dash of color. Grappling hooks flew over the side of the bridge, and with a rattle of harsh, guttural, vicious voices, men and women climbed over the side. They looked tough, tanned skin and evidence of sunburns, dirty trousers and weathered boots, tangled hair and dreadlocks.

The strangers rushed the mages, shouting and screaming—a terrifying mixture of wild magic and steel.

Hands grabbed Juniper and threw her over the side of the bridge—she screamed, but the sound ended abruptly when she landed in a pile of disarrayed flowers.

"Calm down, lass," barked a deep masculine voice. "We're on your side."

A tall, broad man stood on the barge. A sea of tattoos covered his bare arms and his neck, as well as scars. A scruffy black beard covered the lower half of his face. He had dark copper skin and molten brown eyes. He wore daggers and a compass on his waist. He looked every bit like a pirate.

Flower petals continued to flutter through the drizzle. Magic exploded against the night sky—fire, smoke, steam, and bits of stone.

The man looked down at her with a quizzical expression. "Maddox said you might need help." He leaned closer and narrowed his gaze. "You're younger than I anticipated."

Juniper pushed herself onto shaky feet. "Should I know you?"

"Nah," he said, shaking his head. "But you do now. The name's Captain Graves."

CHAPTER 52

The pirates made quick work of Margret and her mages. The magic flares faded, and the pirates dropped back onto the barge one by one—no more than shadows in the smoky darkness. Each thump jiggled the boat, not unlike Juniper's scrambled thoughts.

She had just been saved by *pirates*.

"They're either running or dead, Captain," barked one of the pirates.

"Ha!" Captain Graves let out a one-note laugh of victory. "No spines!"

"Should we chase 'em down and finish 'em off?" asked another.

"Nah, let 'em run scared," said Graves. "We'll square off before long."

The barge started upriver unnaturally fast, and the Weslie gave little resistance. It took Juniper a moment to realize that two water mages stood on either side of the barge, working in tandem to usher the barge smoothly along. Juniper sat on the bed of mangled flowers as the pirates navigated the maze of canals. They headed farther and farther south, away from the castle and Central Tower. The rain came down harder, blurring the distance in dreary grays and muffling all other sounds. Only the thunder rang louder.

Juniper relished the feeling of cool water speckling her face and neck, running along her scalp and down her spine. It refreshed her magic in ways nothing else could.

At last, they came to a floodgate underneath a wide bridge. A pirate standing at the bow summoned massive hands of pinkish-gold energy. The hands wrapped around the floodgate and lifted it from the stone with a horrible metal screech. Beyond, water sloshed against stone in inky darkness, echoing.

The pirate held the gate up as the barge passed through the opening. As the stern entered the darkness, the pirate fitted the gate perfectly back into the stone.

Captain Graves took a deep, loud inhale. "Smells just like just I remember."

Juniper didn't have the time to ask—the bow of the barge dipped with the water. A gasp left her lips as they started over the flood channel. Her stomach fell into her ankles, and her skin flashed clammy—but the downward jaunt she anticipated didn't come. Water cradled the barge and gently lowered it down the falls.

Captain Graves glanced over his shoulder at her and winked. They landed at the bottom of the flood channel, dark stone on either side of them covered in algae, and fungi, and slime.

She blinked; she hadn't realized she could see, but she could. Without her night sight. The flowers underneath her were glowing. The petals glowed in shades of pink, yellow, and blue. The stems glowed green and purple. She plucked one of the damaged flowers from beside her.

"What are these?" she asked the pirate sitting beside her.

"We call 'em glowers. They grow in the tropics. The weather's too harsh up here for 'em."

"Tropics?" Juniper repeated.

"Yeah, tropics. Glowers like the heat." The pirate didn't offer any further explanation, which Juniper didn't mind. His breath smelled like rotten meat and moldy fish.

The cold rain on her skin and in her clothes hung heavy, and she didn't have the energy to magic it away. The chill slowly sank to her bones. They sailed along the dark flood canal with nothing but the glowers as light. Juniper fingered the glower in her hand. It didn't stain her fingers or give off a strange odor. She imagined an island with meadows of glowers shining as bright as stars. How beautiful would that be?

"Ah, there it is," came Graves' voice.

Juniper looked up from the flower. A dot of light steadily grew before them. It was another metal grate, like the one they had passed through—and Juniper realized where they were. They had gone into the far eastern side of the Undercity. She knew of the grate. It led into the backyard of a competing guild.

And she would bet gold that guild had used it to slip in and out unnoticed. Maddox would have.

The pirate lifted the flood gate with pinkish-gold energy hands, and the barge passed under. They sailed into a little pond where the flood canal let out. Smaller canals took the excess water toward the fountain via underground pipes shaped by earth mages decades ago.

The barge could go no further, so they abandoned it in the little pond.

And not much to Juniper's surprise, Maddox stood in the backdoor to the guildhall, arms crossed, leaning against the doorframe.

"Ah, there he is," said Graves. He approached Maddox with a swaggering gait. The two men beheld one another for a moment, then embraced like old friends.

"I was starting to think you wouldn't be able to make it," Maddox said to Graves.

254

"And miss this party?" Graves laughed—a booming sound.

Maddox looked at Juniper. He had known Graves would be coming, but had he known she would run into him? She had questions regarding the chance encounter, but she kept them to herself. Maddox had that strange way of knowing things, and she didn't have the mind to pick through his brain for the answers. Not that he'd give them up.

Instead, she said, "I have news."

"As do I," Maddox said. "The king is not very happy with either of us at the moment."

Juniper groaned. She knew that would be coming. "It doesn't matter. Gather everyone. They need to hear what I've found."

Juniper paced the tavern floor while Maddox's scouts gathered the others for an emergency meeting. Several times the room blurred, but if she sat, she wouldn't have the strength to stand again. Maddox reclined in his chair at the table. Xavier leaned against the wall behind him, fingering a shadow blade. Maddox had given the guildhall by the floodgate to Graves and his crew, and they had declined the invitation to the meeting.

"Politics," Graves had growled. "I hate them more than leeches. I'm a man of action."

A round of agreement had gone through his crew. Maddox had simply shrugged, left the invitation open, and told Graves to send word with the scouts if he needed anything. Maddox and Juniper had gone straight to the tavern for the meeting, and she had been pacing since.

Josephine arrived first, flanked by an exhausted Ison and a curious Mabyl.

Ison's gray eyes fell on Juniper, and relief smoothed the wrinkles in his brow. "I heard—" Ison's words were cut short.

The door to the tavern burst open, and King Bradburn marched through. Captain Sandpiper, Reid, and Adrian marched on his heels—only Adrian didn't look as though he wanted to throttle her. Reid had been sleeping; his hair was slightly messed, and he wore his Mage's Bane but not his armor. By the bags under his eyes, he hadn't been sleeping well.

Guilt tugged on her heart.

"You best have a damned good reason for your behavior," King Bradburn snapped. He sat in his chair. "Sneaking out *twice*."

Reid took his post behind the king. His eyes burned—he had things he wanted to say, but he wouldn't say them in front of the others.

"I told you we should have locked her up," said Captain Sandpiper as he took his place. It would seem that saving his wife hadn't altered his thoughts of Juniper.

Juniper steadied herself and said, "You will want to hear what I have to say first."

All eyes in the tavern looked at her, some furious, others curious.

Juniper explained the events of the past few hours—King Bradburn sent scouts to find Captain Tinnly and his wife immediately—and then she came to the part where she encountered Graves and his crew.

"You were saved by pirates?" Reid asked, brows high. A bit of his anger had ebbed during her story. He knew how she would feel about being saved by pirates, given her collection of sea-themed books.

"That's not the best part," Juniper said. She held her tongue for a dramatic second, during which all eyes shifted back to her. "Margret let it slip that Nexon is out of town."

The news sank into the room.

"If Nexon is gone, now is the time to strike," Juniper said.

"Strike whom?" Ison asked. "If Nexon isn't even here—"

"Margret is held up in the Marca. She's using it as a command center." Juniper met Mabyl's eyes and added, "It needs to come down. The whole thing. I'm talking battle-in-the-streets, bring-the-Marca-to-rubble. We would end Margret and her little army of thralls. We—"

"We aren't ready for that kind of assault," King Bradburn interrupted. "We do not have the numbers, and the numbers we do have are not ready for combat."

"The knights have not mastered mental resistance, and neither have the mages," Josephine added.

"I refuse to risk the few knights and warriors we have to thralldom to feed your sense of revenge," said King Bradburn.

Juniper frowned at that. She didn't want to bring the Marca down in revenge, she…just hated the Marca. Was it revenge?

Ison appeared at Juniper's side. He said, "If you are so determined to bring the Marca to rubble, I might know a better way than storming the streets."

All eyes shifted to Ison. He pulled a folded piece of parchment from his robes and flattened it on the table. It showed several half-drawn runes.

"I've been looking into a rune a thrall was carving into the ruins close to the Undercity," Ison said. "This rune wasn't in any books Josephine had, so I had to seek help from the Dual Fang's library. I found it."

"I guess it's not good?" Juniper asked. For the Dual Fangs to have it and not Josephine, it could only be black magic.

"No," Ison said. "This rune is for destruction, particularly of stone. One of these runes isn't effective. But three or more of them would be. They connect to the others, creating a zone of destruction. If placed at structural points of a building, these runes would bring it down."

"Nexon was trying to bring down the Undercity?" Juniper whispered. "Or Margret?"

"A thrall works best when it is near its host," Josephine said darkly. "If Margret has truly been left in charge, then these thralls are likely hers, not Nexon's. Unless he has taught more of his followers to control thralls."

"Margret thought to bring the city down on top of us," Maddox added. He glanced at Juniper, dark eyes glittering with unreadable thoughts. "If we were to bring the Marca to rubble, it would put a dent in Nexon's plans. His followers would be reeling. It would prove the existence of the resistance to the rest of the city."

"I will send mages to scour the ruins for any more such runes," Josephine said. "And add runes for stability and protection."

Juniper stared at the half-drawn rune and the single completed rune. As Josephine relayed her orders to Mabyl, Juniper leaned toward Ison and said, "If we put these runes at the weak points in the Marca, we could bring it down."

"Without all the fighting and death an assault would bring," Adrian added from his side of the table.

"What about the people in the Marca?" Ison asked.

"The only people in the Marca right now are loyal to Nexon," Juniper spat.

"Are you sure of that?" Ison asked.

Juniper met his stare. No, she wasn't. The Marca was a big place, and there might be mages there against their will or without another option.

"We should spare innocents where we can," Adrian added.

Juniper looked between the two of them, outnumbered. Reid hadn't spoken, but by the look on his face, he agreed with them. Of course, she suspected he would agree with any decision Adrian made.

Juniper sighed and flattened her hands on the table. She liked plans where she didn't have to worry about other people. Other people made things difficult. "We send a team to plant the runes and another team to go through the Marca and find anyone to save," she amended.

"I like that plan better," Ison said.

"We use stealth," Maddox said. "Rather than burst through the front doors."

A heavy silence weighed in the air, and Juniper feared her plan would be rejected.

King Bradburn stood. "We begin planning first thing in the morning." His gaze bore into Juniper. "And I expect you—"

"To sleep soundly all night and wake up refreshed," Juniper said for him.

King Bradburn did not appreciate being interrupted, but he didn't correct her. With that, the meeting ended, and they filed onto the street. Reid fell into step beside her, but he didn't speak. The magelights reflected the misty rain above, glowing just enough to light the streets.

The king and the captain marched to the top floor, likely to continue their planning without Maddox and Josephine. Juniper, however, had no desire to plan or scheme; her exhaustion had caught up with her. She went straight for the bathing room, washed the stink of the sewers off her skin and out of her hair, and headed for her little room—only to find Reid sitting on her bed.

"You're not planning with your king and uncle?" Juniper asked, sitting on the bed beside him.

"They were furious," Reid whispered.

"Because you didn't want to plan?"

He frowned at her. "Because you vanished, again."

Sighing, she said, "Reid, I'm not made of glass. I can handle myself."

He leaned onto his knees and folded his fingers together. She remembered what she had overheard his uncle saying—he refused to allow them to marry. She looked at the moonstone ring on her finger. Reid had not received his uncle's blessing. Neither had she.

Another stone telling her not to get married.

"That was incredibly foolish." Reid stood and unbuckled his Mage's Bane. He set the sword against the wall.

"It worked out in our favor," Juniper said. "We have Captain Tinnly and a handful of his men, and we learned valuable information about the enemy."

"What if it hadn't?" Reid faced her, eyes burning. "What if you hadn't made it out of Central Tower? What if Margret had been one step ahead? What if Graves hadn't been there to save you?"

"Then we wouldn't be discussing this," Juniper said. Reid's disapproval pulled any lingering good feelings she had. "I'm not good with cages, even gilded ones. And if I had stayed here, your aunt would still be a slave in the castle kitchens."

"And your little excursion drew the attention of the thrall Ison and Amery caught trying to bring it down," Reid spat.

She opened her mouth to argue but realized she hadn't anything to counter. He was right—Ison and Amery had caught the thrall under the abandoned house. Nexon would have known about it since he'd sent his beasts through the same entrance.

"Damn," Juniper whispered, mostly to herself. She hadn't been thinking of the others. She had been thinking of herself. "I'm sorry. I didn't mean…"

Reid huffed a sigh and rubbed the shadow on the lower half of his face. He sat on the bed. "The tunnel has been sealed. I do thank you for saving my aunt and those servants, as reckless as it was. Uncle does as well."

"He's not very good at showing it," she said bitterly. "He's the one voting to lock me up."

"And you have continually given him evidence to support that idea," Reid said.

She huffed.

"Jun," Reid whispered.

"I don't understand why everyone is upset," she said. "King Bradburn does not own me. I am not a child. I can go where I want and do what I want. No one owns me. Not anymore."

Reid's hand graced her cheek, warm and calloused. The touch surprised her, though she didn't know why. It reminded her of the first time he'd touched her—the first time anyone had touched her with affection—and left her stunned and unsure.

"You are right about that," Reid said. He tilted her chin toward him. "But we worry about you. Your life is not solely your own anymore."

She started to argue at the mere thought, but before the words could leave, Reid lifted her hand. He held the moonstone ring between them and kissed her knuckles.

Ah. He meant marriage. As a wife, she would be tied to her husband. And her life wasn't…solely hers.

And she hated the idea of it.

But with Reid looking at her such sincerity and worry, she couldn't voice her thoughts. She didn't want to. Instead, she leaned into him. He placed a warm kiss on her temple.

"I would love to cross something else off the list," Juniper whispered. "But I might fall asleep halfway there."

Reid chuckled, and a light blush warmed his cheeks. "And these walls have little sound protection."

Despite everyone already knowing about their relationship, she'd rather not have them hear it. Later, she told herself, and climbed into the bed. She thought

Nightmares in the Ice

Reid would return to his room, but he stayed. He curled his body into hers and tucked an arm around her. His warmth comforted her exhaustion, and it wasn't until the heartbeat before sleep that she wondered if he had stayed to make sure she didn't leave again.

CHAPTER 53

Juniper woke after dawn. The magelights glowed soft bluish-gray, the color of morning fog. Reid stirred but didn't wake. She wouldn't mind lying in Reid's arms and warmth for a while longer, but her bodily needs demanded attention. She carefully climbed out of bed, dressed, and tiptoed to the bathing room.

She washed her hands and face in cold water. The house was quiet for the moment, and she tried to soak in that quiet. It didn't work. Her gut trembled, and anxious thoughts about Nexon, Isolde, Margret, Rusdasin, and a hundred more things refused her silence. She started toward her bedroom and to Reid, but her feet took her to the top floor. She wanted to watch the magelights brighten from dawn to day—just like she used to before the world turned on its head.

The meeting room had gone dark, save for the pale, misty light streaming in. Mauve drapes hung at the windows. They hadn't been there before, and they lacked the wear and tear and stains of Undercity drapes. Juniper made her way toward the southern window. The Commons glowed a little brighter than the rest of the city, not unlike the old market that never closed.

"Trouble sleeping?"

Juniper jumped, spun, and summoned a dagger of ice—King Bradburn sat on the far side of the room. His feet were propped up on an old barrel. He lifted an unlabeled green bottle, emptied the last drink into his mouth, and set it on the floor beside two others. She recognized those bottles—Undercity moonwater.

She dismissed her ice at once. "I didn't see you."

King Bradburn nodded. "I was being very still." He set his feet onto the floor and stretched his back. He made his way to where she stood. His first several steps wobbled, his back hunched, but by the time he arrived at the window, his kingly presence had returned. She caught the gentle scent of jasmine—the moonwater.

"Did you sleep up here?" Juniper asked.

"I might have gotten a few hours of rest." He looked like it too. His hair was in disarray and needed a wash, the lines on his face appeared deeper, and his eyes had aged by decades. "With a city on my shoulders, rest is a luxury. I ordered Captain Sandpiper to sleep well to make sure my decisions are wise."

Juniper half laughed.

A silence fell between them, and the magelight grew imperceptibly brighter.

"You should know that the mages' training is going well," King Bradburn said. "The knights' combat training is also coming along. Josephine tells me the mental resistance training is progressing also. Though we are far from capable of a full-scale assault. I have sent word through Maddox's scouts to gather my remaining forces. I haven't yet heard from my commanders."

As much as she didn't want to, she agreed. Sleep had restored clarity to her thoughts. They lacked soldiers, and though they had more mages, those mages did not know combat. Surviving a fight wasn't something to be learned in a few days' time.

"Your Majesty?" Juniper asked.

The king nodded his attention.

"When did you realize who I was?"

The king thought for a moment. "I suspected it the first time I saw you. You look remarkably like your mother. I thought it impossible that the gods would return you to me in such an uncouth fashion. Sebastian sent me his infant daughter in hopes that I would protect her, and when word reached us of Sebastian's death, I promised the gods I would. I thought the Royal Greenhouses would be the perfect place to hide, but you slipped away."

The coincidence stirred something in her chest. "Did Maddox know?"

King Bradburn did not answer immediately. "I can't say whether he did or not."

"Then you did," she started, feeling a pinch in her stomach. "You contacted him."

Guilt and shame mixed on his face, pulling on the lines around his mouth and darkening his eyes. "I tried to keep my identity secret. I sent word that I would pay dearly for the crown of the king, and that I would pay for his best. Had I known our ploy would bring Isolde back to me, I would have done it years sooner. I am sorry for all that's happened to you. I can't help but think it is partially my fault for not keeping you in the castle."

Juniper didn't know how to respond. The life she could have had flashed through her mind—growing up beside Adrian, learning how to dance and speak, being friends with Reid just as Adrian had been. Would Reid still have chosen her? He would have been the knight and she the princess—a far more romantic story than the one they'd written.

But—

"The Undercity part of my life might have been partially your fault," she started. "But all my poor choices were my own. You had no part in those."

King Bradburn offered her a small smile.

"And, if you had kept me in the castle, I wouldn't be able to defend myself like I can now." She summoned a dagger of clear blue ice and tossed it into the air. She caught it by the hilt. "And you might have had to send me to the Marca because of my magic."

"And Nexon would have found you sooner," added the king. "The temple teaches us that everything happens for a reason, and we are exactly where we are meant to be, and it is all leading us to where we are supposed to go."

"I've never been religious."

"It doesn't matter," the king said. "You are you because of your past. As am I, and my wife, and Reid. Unfortunate things happen, and it is up to us to decide if we will let those unfortunate things claim us or make us strong. You, dear, have become stronger."

Commotion sounded several floors below them, shuffling feet and muffled voices.

"Ah, the day has begun," said the king with a sigh. "Best eat something hearty for breakfast if we are to plan this sneak attack of yours."

Juniper followed the king down the stairs, turning his words over and over in her mind. She had become stronger because of all that she had gone through, all that she had done. The Undercity had taught her how to fight, how to be prepared for the worst, and how to be vigilant of others. And she liked that about herself. Maybe growing up in the Undercity hadn't been the worst thing that could have happened.

The planning began with little fanfare and several pots of tea. Mabyl, Abrielle, and a handful of mages proved invaluable to the planning—by mid-morning they had a detailed map of the Marca. By midday, they had something of a plan.

Excitement tittered through Juniper's bones, one she hadn't felt in a while. It tingled through her fingers and down her legs and made her feel like running. She wanted to send Margret and her goons into the rubble, and she would.

"Ison will place the runes at the designated weak spots," Josephine said, gracing her hand along the map of the Marca's lowest level. Five weak spots had been marked in red.

"I'm going with him," Xavier said.

Maddox glanced at him but did not argue.

"It is a stealth mission," Josephine reminded Xavier and Ison.

"All the more reason for me to go," Xavier said.

"I want Finn on the team too," Ison said.

Xavier frowned. Jealousy briefly flashed across his face before his cool mask returned. "I'm sure I can handle it."

"The moment we activate these runes, the stone will start to crack and crumble," Ison explained. "We will need an earth mage on our side to get us out."

Xavier glanced at the map. "Fine. You're right."

Josephine nodded. "I will inform Finn of the decision."

"And there is the matter of the survivors," said King Bradburn.

"I'm going," Juniper said before anyone else could volunteer.

Because the team looking for survivors would be scouring the Marca. She had thought about it all morning—if she were looking through every floor and every room of the Marca, her odds of finding the old hag were high. She wanted to bring down the Marca, but she also wanted to make sure Margret went down with it. Maybe Carol too.

The king nodded his permission. Captain Sandpiper scowled at her, like always. Reid looked like he wanted to argue, but he held his words. He knew he wouldn't be able to keep her safe in the Undercity. Most of the knights hadn't mastered mental resistance, and they would be staying behind to help the escapees into the Undercity. Reid and a few combat-ready mages would be standing back, just in case. They needed every skilled body they had, and the king likely knew she would go regardless.

"I'm going with you," said Mabyl. "I know my way around, and most in the Marca know my face."

"And you can shoot fire," Juniper added. She also trusted Mabyl. "Anyone else we could use on the team?"

Mabyl suggested Leon and Burke, two mages she had known from the Marca who had been among the few to escape. Both had been in the Undercity since, sharpening their magic skills. Leon, an air mage, could hurl invisible blades of air faster than nature. Burke was an earth mage, and he would be their way into and out of the Marca. Between the four of them, they would be a force.

By mid-afternoon, their plans were solidified. Juniper dressed in sleek blacks and lightweight leathers—not unlike her thieving clothes. She didn't need steel, but she tucked several daggers on her person and one in each boot. The weight offered familiarity and comfort. Mabyl and Leon dressed in similar dark clothes.

The teams gathered at the tavern. Juniper's team would move first, giving them a head start to look for survivors before Ison's team brought the Marca down.

"We will be waiting for any sign of trouble," said Reid. His hand tightened and loosened on the hilt of his Mage's Bane.

Juniper put her hand on his silver breastplate, over the heart. "We'll be fine."

He nodded. A war raged behind his eyes. He wanted to go with her, but he knew he shouldn't. A knight would only worry the possible survivors more. Reid had a natural talent for mental resistance—Nexon couldn't get in—but the idea of him becoming a thrall still terrified her.

They shared a quick kiss.

"Everyone ready?" came the commanding voice of King Bradburn.

Juniper glanced at each of her teammates for approval, then answered, "We're ready."

Ison did the same with his. "We're ready."

"Then we begin," ordered the king. He stood before the tavern, his crown a gleaming symbol in the magelight. "This will be a long evening as we trespass into the enemy's territory. May the gods watch over us all."

Juniper led her team to the Undercity's eastern wall, and Burke began his effortless and precise tunnel that would take them right into the Marca. Juniper had trouble controlling her anticipation; she bounced on the balls of her feet.

"Easy now," said Mabyl. "You'll get the chance to punch the hag in the face."

"Not soon enough," Juniper said.

They stepped into the narrow tunnel after Burke. Mabyl pulled a mage stone from her pocket. She could have summoned a flame, but Josephine had suggested they conserve all the magic they could.

The odds of them making it out of the Marca without a fight were slim—and Juniper wouldn't have it any other way.

CHAPTER 54

Burke's tunnel took them into a storeroom of the kitchens. The kitchens had the fewest runes for unwanted magic and were the easiest to break into. Mabyl's mage stone illuminated ceiling-high racks of goblets, teacups, and bowls. Mabyl led the way through the towering shelves, her light casting dangerous shadows in every direction. They entered one of the back kitchens, lined with woodstoves and coal-burning ovens. Heat lingered from dinner, as did the scents of buttery fresh bread and roasted meat. A magelight hovered near the ceiling, and Mabyl tucked her stone away.

On the far side, dirty dishes piled in the sinks. Voices drifted into the kitchen from the mess hall. Dinner was ending. Trays and dishes were being dropped into the vats for cleaning. Soon the unlucky mages would trudge into the kitchen for their turn at the dishes. It sounded as though life in the Marca hadn't changed at all.

Juniper and the others slunk into the shadows and waited for the evening march from the mess hall to end. Soon, the vats were rolled through the wide doors and into the kitchen, a task Juniper remembered with strange fondness—those moments on kitchen duty had been a break from the knights and the bullies.

Three mages trudged into the kitchen, none looking happy about kitchen duty. Two girls pushed the vat of dirty dishes, and a boy walked behind, scowling as the doors closed. Juniper recognized one of the girls as Seema. The other girl and the boy looked familiar, but she couldn't place either name. The girl looked several years younger than Juniper.

"Another night on kitchen duty," grumbled the boy.

"It would go faster if you actually helped," spat the other girl.

Juniper glanced at Mabyl. She knew the mages in the Marca better than Juniper did. After a hesitant moment, Mabyl signaled for possible friends.

The three mages started to unload the dishes and fill the large basins with water. Mabyl slunk out of the shadows first, and Juniper and Leon followed—daggers of ice and blades of air at the ready.

"Keeping busy?" Mabyl asked.

None of the mages looked surprised by the intrusion, until they took in who had spoken. Then their eyes widened, and the younger girl dropped a goblet into

266

the sink. The boy started to attack, but Juniper moved faster. A tendril of ice wrapped around him, covering his mouth and holding his hands behind his back. She lifted him off his feet.

"Mabyl?" gasped Seema. Her eyes quickly took in Juniper, Leon, and Burke. "What's going on?"

"It's nice to see you too," Mabyl said pleasantly. "How are things?"

Seema frowned.

"I'll be short," Mabyl said, pleasantness gone. "You want out of here? We're going to topple this place and end Margret. You in or out?"

"I'm with you," Seema said without hesitation. Her fists balled. The panic in her voice diminished, and determination replaced it. "I swear it!"

"I don't know," Juniper drawled. "You and Carol were awfully good friends, and she tried to kill me."

Seema hissed a curse. "She's the reason I'm stuck on kitchen duty. I don't want anything to do with that monster."

Mabyl glanced at Juniper, leaving the decision of what to do with Seema up to her. Juniper had already decided, but she pretended otherwise. Seema had never been outwardly snotty to Juniper, and she had gone out of her way to help her.

"All right," Juniper said. "I believe you."

Seema released a breath of relief.

"What about you?" Mabyl asked the other girl.

"She's all right," Seema said for her.

"You in?" Mabyl asked.

The girl nodded.

"And him?" Mabyl pointed to the boy.

He muffled against the ice, and Juniper released the tendril enough for him to speak. "I'm with you!" he gasped, his teeth chattering.

Seema half laughed. "He's a liar and a snitch. He'll run back to Margret the first chance he gets."

Mabyl let out a grievous sigh and looked at Juniper. She took that as the signal—she snapped his neck and dropped his body onto the ground.

Seema wanted to stay and fight, but the younger girl, Uma, vanished into the escape tunnel. Burke had opened a passage into the sewers. It didn't lead to the Undercity; it led to a safe house where others would be waiting. Just in case any snitches slipped through.

They searched the first floor with the same stealth tactic—Juniper and Leon ambushed unsuspecting mages, and Mabyl interviewed them. Thralls died immediately, as did some mages—they ambushed mages in the laundry who were being forced into labor as the servants in the castle had, and the mage lording himself over them died without trial.

Most forced into labor were grateful for the rescue. According to Seema, not all the mages had welcomed Margret's ascent to power.

"What is happening out there?" Seema whispered as the mages from the laundry walked through the holes in the walls Burke had made for them. "We've heard no news. Margret says the king is dead. She called this the beginning of the new Imperium and said mages will rule. All the knights are thralls, and Margret is recruiting mages for her Enforcers. Everyone else is locked away in here."

"Nexon and his apostate followers took the castle and think they've taken the city," Mabyl said. "The Order has fallen; the city is in a bit of panic."

Seema did not look happy at that answer. "Nexon? I thought those were just rumors. He's alive?"

"And thriving," Mabyl said darkly.

"But the city is holding," Juniper added. "The resistance to Nexon's rule is growing."

"We'll tell you more about it after we bring this place to dust," Mabyl said.

Burke closed the wall, and their hunt for survivors continued to the second floor. The Marca smelled strongly of natural magic—the floral stench was almost overpowering. Underneath it, Juniper caught the festering stench of black magic.

Footsteps sounded in the corridor.

Juniper motioned them into an alcove.

The footsteps halted. "Who is there?" said a flat, emotionless voice.

A thrall. Mabyl and Juniper released a collective sigh of relief. Mabyl and Leon jumped into the corridor, and as Juniper followed, stone hands were lifting a dead thrall into the wall. A heartbeat later, Burke had hidden all evidence within the stone.

"Maybe you should come to magic class when this is over," Mabyl said. "The earth mages could use that trick."

"Can we talk later?" Leon hissed. "We're on a time limit."

They went floor by floor, room by room, rescuing trapped mages and getting rid of Enforcers or thralls. With every mage they rescued, Juniper's guilt thickened. They had rescued more mages than Juniper thought they would, and she had wanted to bring the Marca down on their heads. She would have killed them to save herself the trouble of saving them had Ison not suggested otherwise.

When they approached Margret's office, Juniper's anticipation threaded through her limbs and through her magic.

But the overseer's office was empty.

Juniper stood in the doorway, glaring at the neatly arranged desk, the shelves of baubles. Margret wasn't in either of the adjoining rooms either.

"Of course, she's gone," Mabyl said. "She does enjoy making things difficult."

Juniper huffed and sent a wave of ice across the room, shattering baubles and instruments and sending the stacks of paper flying into the air.

"We don't have time," Mabyl said, yanking Juniper's arm. "Come on."

At last, they made it to the top floor. Her old dorm. Juniper felt a sliver of disgust. They didn't have much time left—Ison and his team would be entering the Marca once the sun set, and twilight already gleamed through the tall windows—so they split up to search the dorms. Juniper entered her old dorm magic-first. A scattering of gasps and screams greeted her. Four girls sat on the farthest bed. Juniper recognized them, but their names escaped her.

"You can stay here and die or escape with us," Juniper said. "You don't have a lot of time to decide. There's an escape tunnel in the kitchen. Go."

A group of boys ran past the door, from a dorm Mabyl had searched. The girls didn't hesitate any longer. They ran past Juniper and followed the boys down the corridor and down the stairs.

After the dorms, they headed to the library's door at the end of the hall. As they entered, the magelights brightened—signaling the end of daylight. The pale blue light of the fading evening barely glowed against the west. Ison and his team would be starting any time.

"We have to hurry," Juniper urged them.

Juniper made a lap of the library's top floor. A few fearful mages were lurking in an alcove, but at the sight of Seema and Mabyl, their fear transformed into hope.

"To the kitchens, the back storeroom," Mabyl commanded. "Hurry."

The mages ran as fast as they could toward the kitchens.

Juniper made a quick lap of the library's first floor, and started toward the stairs. The library connected the top three floors, and their plan had been to go up the eastern stairs and come back down through the library. As Juniper neared the staircase, an invisible blade sliced into the banister. Splinters shot in every direction. Juniper threw up an ice shield just in time; slivers of fresh wood peppered the ice. Within the same heartbeat, air slammed into her shield, shattering the splinters and cracking the ice. Juniper stumbled backward.

"Oh, look who came running back," came Carol's sneering voice from the floor below.

Carol and two of her cronies had taken over one of the larger sitting areas, and Carol was lounging in an armchair like a queen. Juniper's ice distorted her vision, but she felt Carol's hateful glare.

"Oh, look who's still here," Juniper mimicked. She formed her shield into three spears and hurtled them toward Carol.

She didn't move—one of her cronies magicked a gust of wind that blew the spears out of their trajectory. Juniper's ice narrowly missed.

Carol stood with lazy grace. "You were always the showoff."

"You're going to have to try harder to insult me." Juniper started down the stairs. She didn't have the time to rid the world of Carol's nuisance, but she would make the time.

Mabyl appeared beside Juniper and whispered, "Can I mention how horrible this location is?"

"Oh, what's wrong?" Carol asked. "Mommy won't let you play?"

Juniper didn't listen to Mabyl. She saw only Carol's sneer, and she felt only the burning itch of revenge.

Juniper made it to the bottom of the stairs. Carol's sneer stretched into a wicked grin. Two more of her cronies appeared from behind bookcases. Juniper's four friends joined her at the bottom of the stairs.

Somewhere, a crow called—rumor said they nested in the ancient turrets. A second caw followed, and two black shadows raced across the window. The crows had fled the Marca.

CHAPTER 55

Juniper hurled ice arrows at Carol. Carol summoned a shield of red energy that spread over herself and her cronies. The ice arrows deflected off the shield and struck bookshelves, furniture, and stone; splinters, bits of paper, dust, and couch stuffing flew in every direction.

Juniper turned the floor under their feet to ice—turning the tables in her favor. Carol slid forward and flung her arms backward. Juniper used the ice to move herself faster—she careened into Carol with enough force to knock the other girl off her feet and to the floor. Juniper's fist collided with Carol's face. As Juniper reeled her fist back for a second blow, a fist of red energy thrust into her chest, throwing her back.

She staggered to her feet. A flicker of light snagged Juniper's attention, and Carol stole the opportunity to knock her hard into a bookcase—the shelves hit her thighs, tailbone, and shoulder blades, and she felt the uneven spines dig into her shin. The bookcase swayed and then toppled, cracking against the stone wall and shattering the window. Glass and books clattered into the quickly fading vestiges of twilight.

Juniper fell to the carpeted floor, and the flash of light grew brighter and brighter—flames. They raced up the side of a bookcase, devouring books and jumping to the curtains. Smoke streamed to the high ceiling.

And Juniper understood what Mabyl had meant about the fight being a bad idea—Carol was a fire mage in a room full of dry paper and dust.

Mabyl tried to control the flames, but they raged far out of her control, jumping onto furniture, the rugs, the fallen books. In the short span of time it took for Juniper to stand, the smoke had thickened into a fog, and the fire raged toward the ceiling, licking soot along the walls. The room heated, and Juniper felt the heat push against her magic. A part of her felt a searing pain at the sight of burning books—but she reminded herself that these books were the safe books approved by the Marca.

Carol shouted, and then she and her cronies ran for the door. Juniper sent a spear of ice at Carol; Carol's crony thrust a wind at Juniper, whisking burning embers and smoke and ash into her face.

Juniper squeezed her eyes shut as the ash peppered her face and embers pinched against her skin. A fear of burning alive seared through her, and her magic acted in reflex—a thin layer of ice covered her skin from head to toe.

Time seemed to slow. Juniper was very aware of the ice and herself. The world on the other side seemed too far away to care about. Her magic snuffed the embers into nothingness, and the coolness of her magic eased the tiny burns. Her magic expelled most of the smoke she had inhaled.

Juniper's ice melted, and the reality of the world returned. The fire spread quickly, and as Carol and her cronies escaped through the door, fists of stone knocked two burning bookshelves over—they crashed against the door, blocking that exit.

"Go down!" shouted Seema.

Smoke billowed into the top floor, and they took the stairs to the first floor three at a time. The entire library had caught flame, and the heat pressed in from every direction.

Juniper smothered the fire closest to them with her ice, and Mabyl fought them with her own—but the fire spread too fast and too wild for either of them. It raced up the drapes and scorched against the ceiling. Half of the bookshelves on the first floor were already burning. Leon sent a wind ahead and thrust the library doors open with a vicious crack.

They rushed into the corridor. The flames did not spread to the stone, but the heat radiated off every surface. Relief spread over Juniper's skin and through her magic—the burning library at her back felt like a grand furnace.

Juniper paused to catch her breath—it felt as though she hadn't breathed since her ice had…done whatever it had done. She glanced back at the library. Leon had ripped the doors from the hinges. Fire consumed the entire library. The bright, angry flames licked at the stone corridor but found no purchase. The flames flicked embers and ash into the corridor.

"Let's get out of here!" Mabyl said breathlessly. She tugged on Juniper's arm.

Juniper tore her eyes from the fire and started down the corridor. Right—they didn't want to be here longer than they had to.

They ran for the stairs—as they started down, a flash of red surged toward them. The impact hit Juniper in the chest, knocked her off her feet, and threw her against the corridor wall.

"Going so soon?" came Margret drawling voice.

Juniper staggered to her feet.

The old woman sauntered up the stairs. Red magic ribboned around her fingers—energy magic. She wore robes of smoky silk. The light from the flames shimmered across the material. Margret glanced at the library. "Tsk, tsk. You've only just returned, and you're already destroying things. Typical."

Juniper half laughed and took a sauntering step toward Margret. Juniper had wanted this confrontation, and she had it. A pain wrenched in her side; she'd hurt herself somewhere along the way, either from the fight in the library or the impact. She didn't let it show.

Margret angled her path and left the stairs between them—a taunt.

"Jun—" Mabyl started.

Her words were cut short by a great rumble from under their feet. The stone trembled and shifted.

Juniper's heart dropped into her knees. They were out of time.

"Come on," Mabyl shouted.

Margret smiled, stretching the lines around her eyes and mouth. If the rumbling of the Marca surprised her, she held it in well.

Juniper knew what she wanted to do and what she should do—she had a tiny moment to pick one. Without taking her eyes off Margret's, Juniper cast a wall of ice between them, trapping Margret on the other side of the corridor and clearing the path to the stairs. Margret shouted on the other side and lashed at the ice with her energy—red splattered against the cloudy blue.

"Get out," Juniper commanded the others. "Get out before this place comes down."

"Are you serious?" Mabyl snapped. "I'm not leaving you here to—"

"I'm not sacrificing myself," Juniper snapped back. "I want to kick the old hag's ass myself."

Leon didn't like it either, but he grabbed Mabyl's arm and pulled. "Come on. We stay here any longer, and we're all dust."

Mabyl, Leon, Burke, and Seema ran for the stairs. When they were out of sight, Juniper shoved her ice wall toward Margret. The older woman lost her footing, and Juniper curved the wall around her, to encase her within it. Margret's energy flew around the edges of the curling ice, sharpened into points, and bent toward Juniper.

Juniper threw up an ice shield—the energy spears lodged deep into the ice. One broke through, stopping barely a finger's length away from Juniper's heart.

Behind her, the fire in the library raged and crackled. Bookshelves cracked and collapsed. The hot, smoky air clawed at her nose and throat. The heat and light dampened Juniper's magic. Between the burning library and the tremors, she didn't have a lot of time. As much as she wanted to drag this fight out and make the hag suffer, she couldn't.

Energy spears rushed at her left—Juniper feinted and blasted ice at Margret. The undignified attack burst into a thousand bits of sharp ice and half-frozen flakes; it splattered Margret in white. She staggered a step back, and her spears jerked—one lashed against Juniper's arm, and another struck her thigh.

Juniper cried out in surprise and pain. She gathered the wave of snow and ice and packed it against Margret—engulfing her in cloudy blue ice. Blood seeped into her sleeve and her pant leg, a shimmer against the black fabric, but Juniper sauntered to where Margret stood frozen. The stone under her feet trembled in anticipation. She fought against the ice, and it took all of Juniper's concentration to hold it.

Juniper melted the ice from Margret's head.

"Bitch," Margret spat.

Juniper rolled her eyes. "Why is everyone's first inclination to insult the people holding their life in their hands?"

"You deserve worse."

"I can't argue that," Juniper muttered. The ground shook. "I want answers. Why did Nexon leave you in charge?"

"Because he knew I would succeed."

"And yet you didn't."

Margret frowned.

"The Marca is coming down as we speak. Your thralls and Enforcers are dead, your prisoners have escaped, and we stopped you from bringing the Undercity down on our heads. From where I'm standing, you have lost," Juniper spat. "So, give me the juicy answer before this place takes us both down with it. Why?"

Margret hesitated, and Juniper sharpened the inside of the ice, jabbing her in non-vital areas.

"He loves me," Margret spat, her voice crumbling.

Juniper stared, waiting for the real answer. Margret didn't offer one. Her scowl had faded, and the hardness of her eyes had vanished into…vulnerability.

"But you're…" Juniper paused. "I was going to say old, but I suppose he's much older than you."

"We met when I was just a girl," Margret said. "He was the overseer as I am now, and he taught me so much more about magic than I knew existed. He promised I would live forever once he returned to his full power." Margret smiled—a mad woman's grin. "Once he finds the final two pieces, he will return at last, and we will rule the Imperium together."

Juniper groaned and pretended to gag. "That is a wonderful story, but I—" Margret's words snagged on her thoughts. "Once he finds the final two pieces of *what?*"

Margret's grin only widened.

The floor trembled once again, shaking dust from the ceiling. Stone groaned and creaked. This time, the tremor didn't stop. The floor viciously *cracked*, and the stones gave way.

And Juniper had run out of time for answers.

The stones collapsed, and Juniper lost her footing. The floor gave in faster than she could move, and she started to fall. She lost her grip on Margret, and her ice shattered in a burst of red energy.

Margret pushed off the crumbling stones and launched herself at Juniper. Their bodies collided and crashed to the floor as it fell to the floor below. Margret's nails tore through Juniper's sleeves, and one nail raked through the wound—a searing pain shot through her arm and into her fingers.

Juniper's back slammed into the floor. Already, the stones were crumbling and breaking apart. She yanked her legs up and shoved her feet hard against Margret's chest. Juniper felt bones break, and the old woman let go. Juniper struggled to her feet—a piece of stone slammed into her shoulder, and another hit her back. Another tossed her to the side. She fell on a semi-solid piece of the floor, and in the sliver of a moment—a pillar came down on Margret. The crumbling stone barely hid the sound of crushing bone.

Juniper staggered to her feet, but she had nowhere to run. The walls, the ceiling, the floors—stone crumbled and collapsed in every direction. The floor under her gave out, the ceiling came down, and the Marca crumbled in on itself.

CHAPTER 56

Reid watched the Marca collapse from the top floor of the safe house a block away. He and a handful of mages had greeted the survivors as they emerged from the tunnel in the cellar. Reid had left his silver armor behind and pieced together a ramshackle set of armor of hardened leather and plain steel. It wouldn't identify him as a knight or possible threat to the mages. When the tremors started, he'd rushed to the top floor, taking the stairs two at a time. He saw the flames first, rising to the sky from the library tower, staining the night in shades of violent orange and red.

Thralls on the street displayed no emotion at the destruction. They remained where they were stationed, the flames flickering off their silver armor. The mages panicked. He spotted figures fleeting back and forth, commanding water on the fire, shouting orders. It did little good.

The Marca went through several tremors before it began to collapse. He couldn't look away as the stones fell backward as if pulled, as the mortar dissolved, as the walls tumbled toward the center, shattering windows and shaking the very air.

He gripped the windowsill with white knuckles. Dust spat toward the sky, gray and angry. The sound tore through his chest. The sound shook the city, the ground, and likely shook the countryside for leagues.

And then the silence.

It pulsed against his ears as if tangible.

Footsteps came up the stairs. "Reid?"

"Have the teams returned yet?" Reid asked.

"A moment ago, yes."

Reid rushed down to the cellar. Ison, Xavier, and Finn sat on the floor, each covered in dust. A few healers checked them over. Mabyl, Leon, Burke, and a girl Reid didn't know sat on the other side. Abrielle and another healer saw to them.

He cast a quick glance around the cellar—no Juniper.

The door to the street opened, and one of the scouts bounced down the cellar steps. "It went as planned," breathed the scout. "No one on the street knows what happened. The mages are scrambling back to the castle."

Abrielle tended to a wound on Mabyl's arm. Mabyl glanced up, and her eyes met Reid's. Panic flared behind her eyes, and it stirred his own.

276

"Juniper," he whispered. His voice sounded too loud and not loud enough. He closed the space between him and Mabyl and knelt before her. "Where's Juniper?"

Mabyl didn't answer. Her panic turned bright and fearful—grief. Reid felt his heart stutter and stop.

"She told us to go," Leon whispered. "Margret ambushed us."

Reid spat a curse and stood. Juniper had told them to go, and she had stayed behind to fight Margret. She had bought the others time to escape.

And she had...

Reid rushed up the stairs and into the alley. He ran halfway to the Marca before he realized what he was doing, and that others had followed him. He didn't slow. He didn't look around to see who had followed or how many. He saw only the mountain of rubble that grew larger with every step.

The street was deserted. Reid raced through the strewn pieces of glass and stone and flaming bits of paper, and he began to climb the rubble. Books still burned among the stones, pockets of heat and light.

"Juniper!" he called, but no one answered.

He imagined her popping through the rubble, covered in dust and laughing about how worried he was, or her sauntering from an alley. She did neither.

"Juniper!" he called again, climbing deeper into the rubble.

Ison had joined him, as had Xavier, Abrielle, and Finn. They climbed over the stones with mirrored expressions of dread and fear. Reid scaled over broken walls, fractured pillars, and under—he called and called for Juniper. They searched and searched.

His hands began to shake. His knees weakened. The edges of his vision blackened. His heart thudded too hard, too fast.

He should have demanded she stay behind. He should have gone with her.

He started to dig through the rubble, grabbed stones too large to move, but he only weakened his footing. He stumbled.

A hand landed on his shoulder. He shrugged it off.

"Stop," came Finn's voice. "You'll only hurt yourself. Let me."

Finn's raw magic fluttered over the rubble, tendrils the color of sand. They slipped through impossible seams, under and over and around, deeper than any of them could go. Finn wandered over the rubble, searching with his magic. Reid followed a step behind. Shallow cuts on his hands stung—he didn't remember how or when he'd gotten them.

"There," Finn breathed—Reid's attention flashed to the mage. He stood atop a massive pile of rubble. Sweat shimmered on his brow. "Stand back."

Finn commanded the stones to move. Reid could barely breathe. He stood as the stones moved, digging deeper and deeper through the rubble, until they had reached what might have been the first floor.

There, between fallen pillars, was a chunk of cloudy blue ice. It was so thick, Reid couldn't see inside it.

"Juniper," he breathed.

Finn moved the stone from around the ice and formed a small nook. Reid slid into the nook and half fell against the ice. The ice was nicked and scratched and dented, and smaller stones were embedded into it.

"Juniper!" Reid called to the ice. He beat his fists against the outer layer. Cold seared into his hands, into his cuts, but he did not let up. The ice was not melting; Juniper was alive.

"Stop, stop," came a soft voice. Abrielle appeared beside him. "Let me."

Reid stumbled back a step.

Abrielle put her hands against the ice. Her magic caressed the outer edge and sank into the ice. A portion of the ice began to melt. Layer by layer, the thick ice melted. Reid held his eyes on the deepest point, as if he could hurry the process along.

A dark spot appeared within the ice. Reid crept closer. At last, Abrielle melted the final layer—Juniper lay curled around herself in the middle. She had barely left enough room for herself. As her protection melted, she lifted her head from her knees. Her sleepy eyes met Reid's—she tried to offer him a smile, but her eyes fluttered closed.

Reid pulled her into his arms, and the rest of the ice began to melt—as Juniper lost consciousness. She, like the ice, was covered in nicks and scratches. Her arm bled, as did her thigh. She breathed; Reid felt her breath against his cheek.

"I say we go under," Finn said. He carved a tunnel through the bottom of the rubble.

Reid carried Juniper through the tunnel, and the others followed behind. Finn led them to the sewers, and they took the same path the escaping mages had taken to the safe house. Reid set her gently onto the ground, and Abrielle at once checked her over.

"She's alive," Abrielle said. Sweat beaded on her brow, and her hands shook slightly. Her water magic leaned toward the healing arts, and it would have been difficult for her to melt through Juniper's ice. "Just a bit beaten up and exhausted."

Reid stood and said, "This is a victory."

No one looked like they were in a celebrating mood.

"I'll take the word," said one of the scouts. He vanished into the tunnel, heading for the hidden entrance to the Undercity.

A few others vanished into the tunnel. Reid did not follow. Not yet. He knelt beside Juniper as Abrielle healed the worst of her injuries.

After a while, Abrielle drew her magic back. "She'll be all right with a few healing sessions and bed rest."

"You could use the same," Reid said.

Abrielle offered in a kind, appreciative smile.

The remaining survivors followed Ison and Mabyl into the tunnel. Reid lifted Juniper into his arms and followed. The tunnel was dark and narrow, but it opened into an Undercity house filled with magelight and soft chatter. The rumble of music filtered through the shuttered windows—a celebration. As the survivors entered, the dread and panic withered from their faces. They dared glance at one another with hope.

"We'll get you settled," came Josephine's soft, authoritative voice. She stood in the main room, assisting the mages.

Reid saw no use for himself, so he skirted the crowd and headed into the Undercity. He felt no inclination for celebration, not with the girl in his arms in need of a healer.

CHAPTER 57

Reid leaned against the wall of Juniper's room as another healer tended her. Unlike Abrielle, this healer did not sugarcoat the extent of Juniper's injuries. Aside from the lacerations on her arm and thigh, she had two broken ribs, several fractured bones in her arms and legs, and several torn muscles. The healer saw to the worst breaks and fractures and instructed Reid to keep her on bed rest.

The healer left, and Reid pulled the threadbare blanket over Juniper. She remained asleep.

Reid lingered a moment more, then meandered into the corridor. Would she sleep long enough for him to find a drink in the Commons? Gods knew he needed one.

Adrian came down the stairs, eyes wide and hair disheveled. He must have been sleeping. "Reid? What's happening? Is the commotion from joy or dread?"

"Joy," Reid confirmed, and the subtle panic faded from Adrian's face. "Our mission tonight was a success."

"Thank the gods! I feared we were being invaded." Adrian put a hand over his heart and let out a sigh. He studied Reid, and his features twisted into worry. "Is something wrong?"

"Juniper is all right," Reid said.

Adrian's worry smoothed.

"She needs rest."

"And you need a drink?" Adrian said, sliding a step to the stairs. "Let's grab one before Father demands our presence in a meeting. You know how he is. He will skip over the celebration and jump into our next move."

Reid hesitated, glanced at the curtain of Juniper's room, then followed Adrian down the stairs. He said to the guards, "If Juniper wakes, tell her we've gone to the Commons and then tell her I highly recommend she stay here and rest."

The guards nodded in unison.

People flooded the Commons. Ale and wine flowed, several songs filled the air, and a dozen different instruments plucked at different melodies. The happy chaos reminded Reid of the days when he and Adrian would go into the finer

Rusdasin taverns, two unattached boys, and dance and flirt with strangers. The Royal Guard had never been far, even in those days.

Finding a drink was not hard—Adrian pushed a tankard into Reid's hand and clanked his own against it.

"Bottoms up," Adrian shouted over the chaos.

Reid and Adrian drank together—and choked on the cheap ale together. Reid's throat burned, yet he took another drink. Adrian did the same—until their tankards were both empty. Adrian laughed and joined a growing circle of dancing, and though he beckoned for Reid to join, he stayed behind.

Adrian danced with strangers, both mage and commoner and criminal. Reid spotted several familiar faces within the crowd, Royal Guard and knight— watching their prince. The ale hit his stomach like bricks, and Reid suspected that if he tried to dance, the ale would end up on the ground.

Yet, somehow, another tankard found its way into his hand. And he took a long drink of it.

"Are you really drinking that sludge?"

Reid's heart jumped into his throat—Juniper stood behind him, frowning at his tankard. She looked horrible. She hadn't changed out of her dusty, bloody clothes, and she had thrown her tangled hair into a messy, dusty braid. Her dark blue eyes shifted from the tankard to his. Her eyes were heavy and dark, and her skin was sickly pale.

"It's not that bad." He offered the tankard to her.

She took a sip. "Bleh. Yup, Undercity sludge."

"Did the guard tell you what I said?"

"He did, and I ignored it."

Reid half laughed. Despite making a suggestion instead of ordering, she'd still done what she wanted. "Feeling better?"

"I'm alive," she said. Her eyes followed Adrian's graceful dancing.

"Feeling up to a dance?" Reid asked.

She took a breath. That breath caught, and she winced. "Honestly? No. My everything still hurts."

"Why are you out of bed?" Reid asked.

"Because the king's house is creepy quiet when everyone is gone, and I could hear this madness all the way over there."

"Do you need some company?"

"What I need is about five drinks, a hot bath, and a pain tonic," Juniper said, frowning. Her eyes softened. "But I would like some company."

"Promise me a dance in the future." Reid held his hand out to her.

"Okay. I think I can manage that." She laced her fingers with his, her grip weak. "We will dance in the future."

She leaned against his shoulder, and they watched Adrian dance instead. Roslyn appeared, and the two of them danced as if no one watched, and naturally everyone watched. Neither were exceptionally talented, but they exuded joy. Everyone wanted to be around them, to soak in some of that joy for themselves. It was what made Adrian so popular with the people; even from a distance, the joy glowed.

That endless joy had lifted Reid when they were boys, after Reid had ridden across the kingdom with knights he didn't know to meet an uncle he had never met. Reid had lost everything, and Adrian's friendship and happiness had pulled Reid out of the darkness.

The celebration continued, filled with song and drink and laughter, and Reid allowed a small amount of peace inside. They had defeated Margret, put a stop to her Enforcers and thralls, and Juniper stood beside him.

For the moment, everything was all right.

Reid watched the dances until Juniper started to sway. He slipped his arm under hers, and when he guided her toward the king's house, she did not object. The king's house was quiet, and Juniper washed up in the bathing room. Reid intended to go straight to Juniper's room and rest, but voices drifted from the top floor. Juniper insisted they investigate.

King Bradburn, Captain Sandpiper, and Captain Tinnly stood over a map of the city.

"Ah, there they are," said King Bradburn when Reid and Juniper entered. "We have good news."

Reid felt beyond exhausted—he couldn't imagine how Juniper felt—but they both stood during the meeting. He kept his face masked. Captain Tinnly and several City Watch had joined their resistance, and the captain and his wife were given quarters in the house beside the king's.

No one topside knew how the Marca had collapsed. Nexon's mages were shaken. Without Margret, they didn't know who would be in charge until Nexon returned. The citizens suspected something, and a sliver of hope had returned to the city.

"With Margret gone, the mages have calmed," Captain Sandpiper said. "They have hidden themselves in the castle and armed themselves with runes and black magic."

"The castle remains impregnable," Captain Tinnly said. "They have added runes around the perimeter, blocking an assault. Above ground and underneath it."

"Our resistance grows stronger with each day," King Bradburn said. "I have received word from one of my commanders, in the Karna Province. He stands with us and has five hundred men marching south as we speak. We will continue to train our mages and our warriors. We will become a force strong enough to take back the castle and send Nexon to where he belongs."

"Until then," Juniper said, her voice dry and scratchy. "Our king remains king of the Undercity."

A small smile appeared on the king's face. "I believe it is time to move ahead with our previous plan." The king looked at Juniper and Reid. "I will send ambassadors to Delphine to speak with Queen Myrisha regarding these events."

Juniper straightened beside Reid, and his own heart thumped.

"I will also borrow a few scouts from Maddox to send to King Devlin de Caroel of Janti," the king added. "But there is much ale and wine to be drunk tonight, and we have earned rest. Tomorrow evening, we will begin planning our next step."

CHAPTER 58

Juniper slept through most of the celebrations. Songs came and went by her window. It sounded so joyful and friendly—so unlike the Undercity. It sounded like hope.

Her magic slowly rejuvenated. She barely remembered the fall. There had been debris knocking into her, and then there was ice. The impact that should have killed her merely knocked the breath from her throat and cracked a few ribs. She remembered holding up the ice in fear the debris would otherwise crush her, the agonizing effort it took, the urge to let go and let it take her. She had used every last bit of her magic to hold the ice, because she knew the moment she released her grip, the Marca could crush her as it had Margret.

And then her magic had responded to someone else—Juniper's grip had weakened enough for someone else to manipulate the ice—and she had panicked. The stranger's magic came closer, and upon feeling Abrielle's familiar magic, a warm relief rushed through her. She knew Abrielle had come to help her, and then Reid had pulled her from the ice.

Juniper blinked at the ceiling. How long had she been sleeping? A day? Two? Just a few hours?

The magelights dulled into evening gold, and when Juniper couldn't sleep any more, she got up. Her feet, her ankles, her legs, her arms—everything ached and throbbed. As Juniper made her wobbly way downstairs to the bathing room, she heard the rattle of pots and pans in the kitchen—the servants prepping dinner. Glenda's voice spoke over them, instructing.

Juniper filled the washing basin and used her flickering magic to heat the water. She needed a good bath, not the quick wash she'd had last night. Dust and grime and sweat turned the bath a disgusting gray. The wounds on her arm and leg were healed, and nary a scar remained. Her old scars lingered, but she didn't mind them.

As she soaked, she listened to the happy chatter in the kitchens.

Everyone in the Undercity seemed to be happy. Yet she felt... She didn't know what she felt. Exhaustion. Ending Margret hadn't been as satisfying as Juniper thought it would be. She'd nearly gotten herself killed.

While inside her ice, she had believed she would die. The stones had piled over her, crushing and cracking. Who would ever find her buried in the rubble?

And she had felt a hot panic—she didn't want to die.

She wanted to live. She wanted to marry Reid. She wanted to experience life.

Juniper took a deep breath of the warm, steamy air and let it out. She had never felt such a desire to live before—she had never had something to live for.

She got out and magically dried herself. Even that amount of magic tugged on her insides. She didn't have anything else to wear, so she pulled on her dusty clothes. She hadn't made it a step out of the bathing room when Glenda blocked her path.

"Where are you going?" Glenda asked. Flour dusted her apron.

"Back to bed," Juniper said listlessly.

Glenda looked her up and down, frowning. She clicked her tongue and said, "Come with me. I'll get you something clean to wear."

Juniper didn't put up a fight. Glenda led her to the closet beside the kitchen, and she searched through several crates until she found a simple day dress of sky blue. Glenda escorted Juniper up to her room, and though the dress did not require help, helped her dress anyway. Glenda then combed out Juniper's hair and twisted it into a braided crown.

"There," Glenda said. She stepped back to admire her handiwork and tucked a stray piece of hair behind Juniper's ear. A small smile turned her lips. She looked—dare Juniper think it—motherly. "You look more like a princess."

"He told you?"

"Of course he did," Glenda said. She sat on the bed beside Juniper. "It's hot gossip. It's not every day you realize someone you know is a lost princess capable of stopping whatever tide of darkness Nexon plans to bring."

Juniper slumped over. "I don't think it's me."

"Why not?"

"Because I'm *me*."

"Maybe it's you for the same reason you think it's not."

Juniper flattened her hands against her face. She didn't have the energy to talk in circles.

"Are you hungry?" Glenda asked.

"Yes."

"Then, come on, before the men get home and devour everything."

Glenda ushered Juniper back to the kitchens, where a handful of castle servants were cooking a fine dinner. Juniper sat at the empty dining table and Glenda fetched her a plate of roasted goose, vegetables, and spiced fruit. It smelled delicious—Juniper's mouth watered.

"A fine meal in the Undercity," Glenda said proudly. She returned to work as Juniper began to eat.

Juniper cleaned her plate and leaned back, listening to the kitchens. Glenda returned with a stack of dishes and a handful of silverware.

"Well?" Glenda asked.

"I feel remarkably better," Juniper said.

"A good meal will do that," Glenda said. "Why don't you help me set the table?"

Under Glenda's instruction, Juniper arranged the place settings. Compared to the last time the two shared a space, Glenda's attitude had greatly improved. The others marched into the house not long after, eager for a meal. Juniper sat between Reid and Roslyn. She ate a second helping of everything, and it tasted just as good. After the meal, they headed back to the tavern for a meeting.

On the way, Juniper whispered to Reid, "What have I missed?"

Reid filled her in—Maddox's scouts reported that the Marca's collapse had only hurt itself, and the buildings around it remained unscathed. Nexon's mages fled back to the castle, barricading themselves behind runes. Several of Nexon's mages had escaped too, and they claimed to have seen Juniper—and they blamed her for the Marca's downfall.

"Carol," Juniper spat.

"Who?"

"A bitch from the Marca. I saw her. Her and her little friends." She let out an aggravated sigh. "I would have killed her too, but the library caught fire."

"This might work out in our favor," Reid whispered. "Nexon will hear your name and think you were the sole person behind the attack."

Understanding dawned. "Just like I slipped into the castle," Juniper added. "And he won't have a reason to suspect anyone else, namely the king, involved."

Reid nodded. "He doesn't know the scale of the resistance."

A weight lifted from her shoulders she hadn't realized existed.

They came to the tavern, and their conversation ended. The king had arrived last; Maddox and Josephine were already seated.

"A bit of news," said Maddox. "One of my scouts retrieved a mage before he could flee to the safety of the castle. According to this mage, Nexon has heard of this disaster and is on his way back to Rusdasin, supposedly with more mages and thralls. We aren't sure because the mage didn't know where Nexon had gone—he suspected he had gone south."

Juniper knew what he meant by *retrieved*. That mage was either missing several fingers or dead. Very likely both.

"We need a stronger force if we are to retake the castle," said King Bradburn. "And our forces are growing. My soldiers will join us within the coming weeks."

Josephine magically unfurled maps over the table—hand-drawn maps of Duvane and Collatia. Juniper's eyes roamed over the south. Why would Nexon have gone south? How far south? What would he have been looking for—

A thought snapped through her entire body. She grabbed Reid's arm.

Her sudden intake of breath caught the attention of the entire tavern. All eyes shifted to her, and a strange silence took over.

"What is it?" Reid held onto her as if she might fall. "Are you all right?"

"I forgot." Her heart hammered. "Margret told me Nexon went to find something, the final two pieces of something, so he could return to full power. That's why he left."

"The final pieces of what?" asked King Bradburn.

"That's what I asked, but the Marca fell on us, and I didn't get the chance to beat it out of her," Juniper said.

"That might have been something Mason would have known," King Bradburn said lowly. "If we are lucky, the other archmage will know."

A pitting fell into her stomach, much the same as the silence that fell over the tavern—no word had come of the court magician's fate. None of the castle servants had heard or seen anything.

The king gestured toward Delphine, the Royal City of Collatia. It rested in the southern hills, drawn beside a waterfall and a great lake.

"We will move ahead with our plan to send ambassadors to Delphine to speak with Queen Myrisha about an alliance," said the king.

"And to see if their archmage knows anything about how we might find the other archmages," added Josephine. "Or how they defeated Nexon previously. We will continue our plan as well."

Josephine deferred to Ison, who seemed to shrink into himself at having the attention of the entire meeting.

"Which is about as vaguely planned as yours," Xavier said for him.

Mabyl added, "A small team of mages will attempt to infiltrate Nexon's camp in Baxion. Our goal is to disrupt Nexon's future plans." She gestured toward the vast emptiness of northern Collatia. Vast mountains, ageless trees, and jagged valleys had been drawn.

"And we will maintain the resistance in Rusdasin," said Josephine. "Nexon doesn't know where we are, and we will continue to keep the secrecy."

"And, together, we will stop Nexon's plan to take over the realm," Juniper said, eyes on the roads between them and Delphine, and those between them and where they believed Baxion to be. "And give him a swift kick in the balls while we're at it."

Ison nodded. "Our plan is still rough at the edges," he admitted. "But it's more than we had a few weeks ago."

Juniper smirked. "That leaves rooms for dramatic improvisation."

"I can't believe we're really doing this," Mabyl said, her voice eager. "You know how long I've dreamed of burning my way out of the Marca? And here we are, actually doing something. Changing something."

"We will stop him," Juniper said, meeting Ison's eyes across the table. "And whatever foul plans he has for this world."

A short silence of finality engulfed the tavern.

And then the planning started in earnest. The Undercity leaders talked strategy and timelines until the magelights had faded into the gilded gold of evening. Juniper didn't bother to hide her yawn.

"It's settled," said King Bradburn. "Reid, Juniper, and Sir Pinul will leave for Delphine tomorrow night."

"My scouts will secure passage through the city," Maddox said.

"And Ison, Xavier, and Mabyl will leave the following night," Josephine said.

Juniper hated the grim tone of the words, the warning within them. They had achieved a victory for Rusdasin. Nexon would have it out for her in earnest now, and he wouldn't be so easily deterred. He would counterattack. He had an army of mages and thralls and likely more of those beasts.

Not to mention the treacherous trek between them and Delphine. The roads through the southern mountains were filled with bandits, apostates, sheer cliffs, and wild animals. The dangers ahead were many, but as Juniper listened to the others plan, a sliver of hope started to grow once more.

CHAPTER 59

The next day passed in a strange blur. Supplies were gathered and packed. Horses were secured. A route through the city was planned, including several contingency plans should that route be blocked. Night came too soon. As the others saw to last minute preparations, Juniper went topside to Amery's manor. Their horses were waiting in the carriage house. Their horses were saddled, fed, and ready to go.

Juniper wished she felt as ready. Her body remained weak and restless. She tugged at her dark cloak and felt for the daggers along her arms and legs. With her magic still rejuvenating, she might need steel rather than her ice.

The night sky sparkled with stars, and her magic responded—not as much as it had during the storm. She took a deep breath of the city air, tinted with the florals and metallics of magic, the stink of the carriage house, and the blossoming stench of spring. Already, the tree beside the carriage house bore tiny unfurling leaves.

The backdoor opened, and light flooded the backyard. Footsteps approached.

"You haven't said goodbye," came Ison's voice. He came to stand beside her. "Were you planning on leaving without one?"

"I don't like goodbyes. They're so…final. If I don't say goodbye, I don't punctuate our friendship with that finality, and I leave it open-ended. It leaves room to meet again. I want to remember our friendship as it was, not how we said goodbye."

Ison nodded. "I understand that, but I refuse to leave without one."

"Fine." Juniper heaved a dramatic sigh and turned to meet his steel-colored eyes. He wore a serious and genuine expression, and she knew that face would be stamped in her mind forever.

"First, I want to thank you," Ison started. "For everything. I don't know where I'd be if I hadn't met you. Either brainwashed like Nexon's mages or dead by Mage's Bane."

"I don't like either of those options," Juniper said. She hated goodbyes and all they stood for. Ison's words struck something in her chest, and it turned her resolve into bits of hot air and splinters.

"Neither do I," Ison said. "I am glad I met you, Juniper."

"And I feel the same," she said, though the words felt like poison on her lips. They embraced, and it added the final blow to the finality of it all.

"Oh, and before I forget, a girl named Helena told me to tell you not to get yourself killed, and that she loves you and wishes you the best," Ison said, the words recited.

Juniper half laughed.

"Is this girl…special?"

"My sister," Juniper explained. "Helena Thimble."

"Ah," Ison said, understanding widened his eyes. "That explains why she told me to say the same to Xavier."

The backdoor opened again, and voices spilled into the courtyard—Juniper thought she had been saved from any more awkward goodbyes, but then her name drifted over the yard.

"Juniper." It was Captain Sandpiper.

Ison gave her a worrisome look, but she shook her head. She could handle the captain, as fussy and ill-tempered as he was. Ison returned to the house, and Captain Sandpiper marched across the yard to Juniper.

"Come to deliver your ill-wishes to me in person, Captain?"

The captain exhaled sharply. His lips parted, but doubt crept into his features. He closed his lips again. In this rare moment of uncertainty, he looked more like Reid.

"No." The captain tightened his hand on the hilt of his sword. "I came to speak with you."

Juniper motioned for him to continue.

"I have spoken at length with Glenda and Reid," said the captain. "And I have come to a decision."

A beat passed, then another. Somewhere close, a crow cawed.

"Based on those discussions…" He paused, and Juniper had the feeling he was stalling. "I have decided to grant you and Reid my blessing."

Something tight unraveled in her chest. "Those words sounded like they were hard for you to say," Juniper said, smiling. "But thank you, Captain."

Captain Sandpiper groaned. The stoic mask that had always covered his face slipped, and a thousand thoughts churned behind his green eyes. Juniper had seen the expression before, on Reid—the captain had things he wanted to say, but he didn't know how to say them. Instead, he reached for his pocket and handed her a sheathed dagger.

Juniper blinked, confused, then realized what dagger it was. "Is that…"

"Yours," he said. "It was among your things when the guard arrested you. Reid suggested that I retrieve the dagger if nothing else."

She took the dagger in both hands. Reid had given her the dagger during her stay at the castle, when they were hunting demons in the undercroft. She unsheathed it—the blade shined.

"It's been sharpened," the captain assured her.

"Thank you." Juniper pushed against the tears swelling behind her eyes. She returned the dagger to its sheath and slid it into her belt. "I fully expected to never see it again. I…I promise to keep Reid safe."

"I will sleep better, knowing you are with him," said the captain. "And we expect the both of you to return before you wed. No eloping. Glenda's command."

"On your orders, Captain," Juniper said.

"Good." Captain Sandpiper started back toward the house. "Now, get in here. The others have been looking for you."

Juniper groaned and followed. She pushed herself through a series of goodbyes and embraces. Adrian wished her the best, and Roslyn told her how wonderful the shopping was supposed to be in Delphine.

"My cousin went there a few years ago, and she said she saw colors of silk she had never even dreamed of," Roslyn said.

"I don't know if we'll have time to shop," Juniper muttered to Roslyn.

Reid scowled, and added, "That is not why we're going."

Roslyn and Juniper giggled.

"I wish you were going," Juniper whispered to Roslyn as Reid fell into conversation with his uncle.

Roslyn shrugged. "Someone has to keep these fools in line, and the queen can't do it all by herself. And without Reid here, someone has to keep an eye on Adrian." Her brown eyes softened. "Keep yourself safe, Jun. I expect a wedding invitation."

"As do I," Juniper said.

After a round of goodbyes, Juniper's heart felt near to bursting. As she followed Reid and Isaac into the cool yard, relief washed over her. The dark and the night caressed her magic and soothed her. Like her, Reid and Isaac both wore dark traveling leathers and hooded cloaks.

"Are we ready?" asked Isaac.

"As ready as I will be," muttered Juniper.

"Safe travels, friends," said King Bradburn. He stood tall and proud outside the house, flanked by Captain Sandpiper and Adrian.

Isaac, Reid, and Juniper started their long journey in silence. They passed through the back gate one at a time. An illusion-ward had been erected there as well. Juniper could see the others on the street, but once she passed through the illusion-ward, the courtyard and carriage house behind her appeared empty and dark. The powerful scent of magic faded, as did the din of voices.

They started through the darkened streets of Rusdasin. Juniper had plenty of experience traveling through the shadows and hiding from people who wanted to kill her, but she had never been on a horse or in a group. The hooves echoed off the cobblestones. They rode far enough south of the city center that the streets were mostly quiet. Maddox's scouts had mapped out the best route south, and Juniper spotted the dark-clad figures perched on balconies and roofs, watching for threats or disruptions.

They crisscrossed alleys and through the slums. Though they had delivered Nexon a blow by destroying the Marca, his mages and thralls still patrolled. At each street intersection, a scout gave them a signal either to halt or to continue—at the signal to halt, Juniper readied her magic, and Reid tightened his grip on his Mage's Bane.

Thanks to Maddox's scouts, they remained hidden and didn't have to defend. She spotted one small, lithe figure with bushy black hair—Blythe. She signaled for them to continue.

Street by street, they slowly made their way out of Rusdasin. Once in the outskirts, they started to trot. They did not travel along the South White Road—it was too obvious. Instead, they wound their way through small, lesser traveled roads, gradually heading southeast.

Anxiety coiled in Juniper's stomach. Their escape had gone too smooth. She never trusted a route that came without trouble, and as they rode into the night, she kept glancing behind her to make sure they hadn't been followed.

They rode south until dawn. The eastern glow warmed the low rolling hills and the scattered ranches and farms. The hills would become plains, and those plains stretched to the coast. The ocean felt ages away, but Galamond had once seemed as far. They paused beside a stream to rest the horses and eat from their rations.

"We need to get as far as we can," Isaac said when Juniper offered to catch fresh fish instead.

They traveled through the day. They did not ride fast, lest they spark interest or concern in the small villages they passed.

As the sun touched the western horizon, they stopped to camp. They divided the work, and Juniper volunteered to fetch clean water for their canteens. When she returned, bedrolls had been laid out, and the campfire burned bright.

She sat beside Reid, whose eyes lingered on the southern horizon.

"Something on your mind?" Juniper asked.

"We aren't that far from my home," Reid said, his tone quiet. "From where my parents...lived."

Where they were murdered.

"We might be able to bully Isaac into adding a small detour," Juniper suggested.

"No," Reid said at once. His fists curled then relaxed. He sighed and shifted his gaze into the fire. "There wouldn't be anything to see. It's been years. Someone else has likely moved into their home, and I doubt anyone remembers them beyond their deaths. I knew few people, and there wouldn't be anything but ghosts and memories waiting for me."

Juniper didn't argue. She understood. It was the same reason she didn't want to go back to the greenhouses. Although, in her case, the greenhouses weren't home. They had never been, not really.

They struck out at dawn, traveling southeast through the thick forests of blooming oak, maple, and cottonwood. Isaac estimated it would be summer before they arrived in Delphine, and Juniper's heart squeezed. How long before Nexon made a move against them?

They traveled eastward for several long days. Juniper lost track of how many. They spoke little and stopped only when necessary to rest the horses and themselves. Dawn to dusk, dawn to dusk. They pushed onward. Juniper had little time to speak with Reid, mostly greetings in the morning and a few words at night. Their grueling pace ran them all into exhaustion, and no one had the mind for conversation once the bedrolls hit the ground.

One clear morning, the mountains that separated southern Duvane and Collatia rose on the horizon. They were not as tall or as unforgiving as the Dolomon Mountains, and their peaks were not covered in ice and snow. Isaac had plotted their route through a treacherous mountain pass that saw few travelers. That pass would take them over the border and into the Kingdom of Collatia and meet with what remained of Juniper's birth family.

If they were indeed her real family.

Juniper's stomach tied itself in knots at the thought, but she held herself straight in the saddle. This wasn't about her—she had a kingdom to save, and a monster disguised as a man to stop.

COMING SUMMER 2024

STARS AND BONES BOOK V

Witch in the Wilds

BOOKS2READ.COM/WITCHINTHEWILDS

ACKNOWLEDGMENTS

This is where other authors paint vivid pictures of where they were when they wrote the book, but I can't tell you anything about when or where I wrote *Nightmares*. I don't remember if I worked on it during the pandemic, but I likely did. (I was still working, so those months are a blur.) I can tell you that this was the first book in the series that I didn't have mapped out beforehand. In the early drafts, I realized that the second half didn't match the first, and I completely rewrote the second half of this book. At the time, it was one of the biggest writing obstacles I had encountered. And I made it. I love the way this book turned out, and I love the way the rest of the series fell into place.

First, of course, I must thank the teams at A4A for the support and their belief in Juniper that brought this series to life. I don't know where I'd be if we hadn't taken a chance on each other way back in...2019? Wow. Look at us now!

And to the girls in the basement who were more excited to learn I wrote books than anyone else I've met, and who sat through my rants and whining about publishing without knowing a thing about the industry. Thank you for letting me be me.

My wonderful parents, who I know will never actually get this far in any of my books, for letting me stay up too late finishing a chapter or letting my TBR get a little too high, and for letting me get another bookcase to house them all. Love you guys!

And the thirteen people on my newsletter list, and the five of you who signed up for the book boxes before anyone else.

And of course to the dear reader, who has enjoyed and reviewed and shared this series. And the reader who, like me, searches endlessly for the next book we can't put down, that will make us stay up far later than we need to.

ABOUT THE AUTHOR

Beatrice B. Morgan lives in southern Illinois. When she isn't reading or writing, she is most likely playing a video game. She is a night owl, caffeine addict, yoga enthusiast, dog person, hopeless romantic, optimistic, and a shameless Ravenclaw.

Follow her online:

www.bbmorgan.com
TikTok: **@beatrice_author**
Twitter: **@BBMorgan_W**
Instagram and Threads: **@BBMorgan_W**
Facebook: **@BBMorganBooks**

Also by Beatrice B. Morgan

Hard as Stone

Hard as Stone Book 1

Hard as Stone

Beatrice B. Morgan

Seventeen-year-old Raven Thane wants an adventure...and she's going to get one. Just not the way that she expected. Bored and disinterested with a routine life in her remote underground community, she fails to notice a thief during her turn at guard duty. Zander, a charming sharpshooter, tasks her with helping him retrieve the mysterious stolen item. Posing as a couple on the road, they'll face deadly automatons and Gray Elite soldiers, entangle themselves in a complicated world of spies and freedom fighters, and hide secrets of their own. Can Raven fix her mistake and prove herself more than a simple country girl? Or will she create even more chaos?

books2read.com/hardstone

AUTHORS 4 AUTHORS PUBLISHING

www.ingramcontent.com/pod-product-compliance
Lightning Source LLC
Chambersburg PA
CBHW010514100726
47903CB00009B/2745